FROM A REVIEWER...

I AM NOT A FAN OF HISTORICAL FICTION, particularly that which is written about the antebellum South by white authors. As an African-American, I find the genre predictable, trite, and, to be frank, boring. However, sometimes God intervenes in such an extraordinary way in presenting a book to you, that you have no other choice but to read it.

The Dark Sun Rises, the first of a trilogy written by Denise Williamson, is an unusual book in that it, for me, breaks all the "formulaic rules" of historical fiction.

Set in the 1800s on a South Carolina plantation, this multifaceted story chronicles the struggles of a young slave and manservant named Joseph. The care and attention given to his story is unprecedented, the historical research superb and rich in detail. We see black people that use *every means* at their disposal to secure their physical, psychological, and, most important, spiritual freedom. Joseph's quest for this freedom is the foundation of his growth into manhood, and we grow with him.

We are reminded that Harriet Tubman did not and could not lead *every* slave to freedom by way of the Underground Railroad. Here we see that the sea was used just as skillfully by those who shall forever remain nameless. We also see and begin to understand that which our ancestors learned: to be free in Christ Jesus is to be free indeed.

One finishes this book feeling uplifted, joyful, and so proud of the blood of our ancestors that continues to flow in our veins. Oh, that we knew God as our ancestors knew Him!

One word of caution: read this book with a friend or, even better, a group of friends, because you will want to discuss it.

Finally, we anxiously anticipate Ms. Williamson's second installment of this wonderful work.

—Billie Montgomery-Cook writes a book review column
for *Excellence*, an African-American women's magazine.

THE DARK SUN RISES

DENISE WILLIAMSON

BETHANY HOUSE PUBLISHERS
MINNEAPOLIS, MINNESOTA 55438

Published by Bethany House Publishers
A Ministry of Bethany Fellowship International
11400 Hampshire Avenue South
Minneapolis, Minnesota 55438
www.bethanyhouse.com

Printed in the United States of America by
Bethany Press International, Minneapolis, Minnesota 55438

ISBN 1–55661–882–4

To the memory of

Daniel Alexander Payne
(1811–1893)

who by word and deed
opened my eyes to the reality that
"history is philosophy teaching by examples."

DENISE WILLIAMSON has published six books and is a full-time writer. Coming from a family of writers, she has written for many magazines and worked as an Environmental Education Specialist for the Pennsylvania Bureau of State Parks. She and her family live in Pennsylvania.

When I fall

on my knees

an' I face

that risin' sun,

Oh, Lord,

have mercy

on me.

— RICE PLANTATION
SLAVE SPIRITUAL

ACKNOWLEDGMENTS

SOME SAY THIS PART OF HISTORY should be forgotten, but I have found it better to look at it hand in hand with friends. I thank my husband, Gary, and our family, who have walked beside me. We thank our extraordinary friends: Frank and Marsha McKenzie; Curt and Judy Ashburn and Camp Oak Hill companions from Pennsylvania and Anacostia; African Methodist Episcopal pastors Reverend Lawrence Henryhand and Reverend Gregory Nelson; and several groups of believers who continue to pray for us.

Without the insight and dedication of dramatist and fellow writer Billie Montgomery Cook, ROOTS OF FAITH would still be a dream. Not knowing me at the start, Billie nevertheless committed herself to serve as story consultant and to labor and pray through every rewrite and revision. Deborah Grazette, a close friend from Barbados, came to our house in the "eleventh hour" to help me meet deadlines.

Dr. Dennis C. Dickerson and Dr. Bernard E. Powers Jr. took time as historians to comment on my research. Avery Research Institute in Charleston opened its archives to me. Living History Tours in Charleston helped me retrace Payne's steps.

Sharon Asmus and others at Bethany House Publishers were infinitely patient in allowing a team of us to grow together, enlarging our understanding and appreciation of the project, which enabled me to write a fuller, more honest work.

In writing this story I found that there is one place where the past can be changed—where it meets the present. I hope you will see the truth of this and the challenge it presents for our time as a small sample of history's cloth, inextricably woven in black, brown, and white, is unfolded here.

PART ONE

The

Fall

From

Grace

APRIL 1834

CHAPTER 1

JOSEPH, MASTER ABRAM CALLCOTT'S twenty-year-old man-servant, lifted the second-story bedchamber window and locked it into place, his fingers clouding with the mansion's dry whitewash. Out across the misty low country, the sun rising from the rippled sheets of the Ashley River seemed for a stunning moment to highlight Joseph in its glory, as though he were just as worthy as the graying rice planter seated near him at his writing desk.

Instantly Joseph's mind filled with words that no one in all of South Carolina, slave or free, would have ever spoken: *All human flesh is equal, and therefore, every soul the flesh contains.* If found out, such an idea might cost him his life, yet now it felt as natural and as God-breathed as the salt-scented air streaming in. While white gulls twisted and screamed over-head, he prayed, using the formal religious language Master and Mistress Callcott had taught him. *Oh, thou has seen fit to tell me who I am!*

He raised his hand, his heart beating wildly like an African drum.

Almighty God! I do worship thee! His black flesh shone against the pearly vault of sky. Surely he was seeing and knowing himself now as the Creator had always seen and known him since that morning when his fourteen-year-old mama had screamed with the pains of his birth.

Behind him footsteps rumbled as someone took the hallway's open stairs two or three at a time. Joseph turned in time to see Master Abram's son, Master Brant, come in. Brant, only two weeks younger than Joseph, spoke contemptuously.

"Whatever is he doing at that window?"

The sun on Joseph's back became heat as his gaze slipped right and he watched his lean, middle-aged owner answer without looking up from his work.

"Airing the room."

"You shouldn't let him do that! It lets in miasmic air! Besides, didn't you see him raise his hand just now?"

"I saw it."

"It could be some kind of primitive hoodooism."

"Brant! That's uncalled for!"

"I'm serious. You have no idea what these darkies know! Our scientific knowledge is just now revealing the connection between swamp air and fevers. But Africans have known it all the while."

Joseph tried his best not to be unnerved. He knew nothing about swamp fever except that it had claimed the lives of Master Abram's wife and two oldest sons three planting seasons ago. Once more Joseph looked at Master, and this time he saw the man's sky-blue quiet eyes. Training had taught him never to gaze upon any adult white face but this one, yet he could still feel the younger master's angry glower. Joseph shifted his vision to the neatly made-up bed with its chevron-patterned curtains and white mosquito netting hanging down along each slender post.

He stared hard at those draperies while Brant took his seat in one of the two green upholstered chairs flanking a brass-trimmed but otherwise dark hearth. Joseph's one glimpse of the master's eldest surviving child had shown Brant, blond and strong of build, in his favorite clothes: a short, snuff-colored jacket, spotless white breeches, and knee-high riding boots. Now Joseph heard him unbuckling the saddlebag he had carried in. The son had been told to come, Joseph knew, to give an account of Delora Plantation's first-quarter expenses and progress before the rest of the family gathered for devotions.

Master Abram was training Brant to do the work his older brothers had done. While Brant organized his ledgers, Joseph pulled at the wintertime livery Master still had him wearing despite the humidity of April. He smoothed the stiff red trousers and shifted the dark satin vest buttoned over a pure white shirt.

Joseph counseled himself to be patient with the heat, for in another hour he and Master would leave for the seaside town of Beaufort, a forty-mile boat ride south out of Charleston.

As he had done for the last five Aprils, Joseph would attend Abram at the annual convention of the Society for the Propagation of the Gospel to Children and Africans, an organization that the gentleman and his wife, Oribel, had founded six years ago. In preparation for this trip, Joseph had a second shirt and one extra pair of socks folded on the floor beside him. He had Master's portmanteau packed and in the hallway so that Unc' Ezra, the coachman, could come up and claim it once he had the brougham brought to the door. Joseph was eager to be away, for Brant seemed more antagonistic toward him by the week.

"Show me the seed rice figures," Abram said.

Having served the older planter for more than a decade, Joseph knew Abram's two passions: maintaining peace and prosperity on Delora Plantation, which his daddy had raised out of swampland after the revolution, and bringing the Gospel to slaves who now, by the thousands, worked the nation's soil.

Cautiously Joseph watched Brant come and stand by his father. "The Madagascar rice crop should be in by week's end if the weather holds." Brant visibly flinched when new wind filled the curtains. "Doesn't it worry you at all that *he* opened windows for Mama, Curtis, and James till fever laid them all in their graves?"

"No." Master was just as calm as before. "What concerns me is how you do not trust him anymore. Why is that?"

"Because *you* are so incautious!"

Joseph was startled that Brant dared to speak so disrespectfully. Perhaps he was emboldened by his newly confirmed partnership in the family business.

"You've spoilt him at every turn—teaching him English, dressing him in such fine clothes. Since Mama's passing you've chosen to completely ignore that he is African."

"He serves me perfectly."

"But what's under that perfection? Day and night he is as near to you as the breath you breathe. He could do anything to any one of us, for he has the run of this whole house."

"You have no cause for concern."

"I believe I do! Take the window, for example. Did you tell him to open it, or did he do so on his own?"

Abram hesitated.

"See there! That's my point exactly!"

"Why should I tell him when he already knows what I want?"

"Because you allow him a great measure of freedom in that."

"In what? Expecting him to do what is needed and good?"

"Yes! Because you allow it to be by *his* will and timing!"

"But that is exactly what makes a trained servant valuable."

"The more he convinces you to trust him, the more neglectful you grow in watching him. Some day or night he can take advantage and strike with disastrous *dis*-obedience."

"Where do you hear such things? From the Young Planters' Club you've joined? Or maybe from Theodore Rensler alone!"

Brant did not answer.

Master Abram raised his right thumb, the wordless sign used to tell Joseph that he wanted the desk chair turned so that he would be facing the room when his two other children came through the doorway for prayer. Joseph aptly moved the piece of furniture while his master stood. The planter left the slim ledger books and his son behind him when he sat down again. "This is the kind of relationship you want. Managing a plantation is not just about facts and figures but about setting your workers into quiet, efficient routines."

Brant sighed audibly.

"My practices may conflict with the advice of your many new friends, but experience and example are on my side, son. And over all that, I am your daddy and the one responsible for training you to be a wise and compassionate slavemaster."

"It is different today than when you started!" Brant countered as he never would have just months ago. "The Negroes we have are not right off the boats as yours once were. Almost without exception ours have been birthed on free soil, which infects them with an unrest not known even thirty years ago!"

"Your responsibility is to learn how to deal with *our* people, not the slave population at large. The world can give only worldly advice. As a Christian, Brant, be slow in taking it."

"This isn't about religion but about science! Go back to the issue of this swamp air. Possibly Joseph and Maum Bette and others know about the natural poisons drifting in the mists."

"You want to accuse our houseservants of murder?"

"I want you to be wary! It is possible that you do not know Africans as they really are."

"It *is* Teddy Rensler who plants these worries in you!"

"Whether you like it or not, Daddy, he's come back from Harvard a very learned and competent doctor—"

"That may be, but he's also come home filled with the 'free-thinking' philosophy of the Unitarians up there."

"Again, that's your assessment—"

"*Again* based on facts!" Abram turned to his son. "Teddy cares nothing for the Gospel, even as it relates to his own salvation; therefore, he does not understand or accept the transformation of soundly converted Negroes—like Joseph or Maum Bette or any of our others."

"I'm not speaking against your faith—"

"My faith? What about your faith? And *his*?"

Joseph felt Abram's pointing.

"You are speaking against him. Theodore wants you to find fault with black converts. He wants to stir up your whole generation because he wants planters in their twenties and thirties to think that the Gospel is unproductive in reforming heathens. That way he might justify cruel force as the only means for controlling Africans. His uncle, the colonel, also believes that way. Don't you see it?"

"Teddy's not cautioning us about miasma just to control slaves. I can prove that. Here's a printed report he purchased at Harvard, which he has been handing out to all the planters."

Joseph glimpsed the papers changing hands.

Abram looked at them for only a moment. "This is just one doctor's opinion, and he's from New York. What can a *northern* man possibly know about health conditions here?" The master made Brant take the pages back. Then other papers fell to the desk while Brant impatiently tried to stuff the first away.

"And what are those?" Abram said, his ill humor aroused.

Brant grew more defensive. "Just some of my own sheets for figuring—"

Abram took them before Brant could reach them.

"I wanted you to see those, too, but not now," Brant said. "I was thinking of giving them to you to read in Beaufort so that maybe you could discuss them with your friends."

"I have so little time there!"

"I know, but I thought you might not like these suggestions—at least at first—so I had the idea of asking you to present them to the counsel of men you do trust."

"What are these figures anyway?"

Brant avoided the question. "Two attorneys from Columbia came down to speak at the club. Because of the growing conflicts we face with the North, they gave us advice on wise investments that can endure even the possibility of war—"

"I will hear none of this!"

Joseph's head turned sharply when Abram shouted, for then the master tore Brant's work.

"Wait! I spent hours on that! The advice is sound! If the Federals plan to defeat slavery, then we'll need gold instead of servants! Gold that can be stored or taken with us!"

"I—will—never—sell—one—Negro!"

"But I marked out only our surplus chattels, those who negatively reduce our resources now. And a few likely troublemakers—"

"No! No! A thousand times, no!" Abram tore the papers again as he met Joseph with a fierce glare. "Boy, go to your place!"

Joseph tried to move toward the dressing room where he slept, which was built behind the hearth, but Brant surprised him by coming at him, meeting him shoulder to shoulder, for they were equal in height.

"Why do you always send him out when we talk about slaves? You *don't* really trust him, do you?"

"Moments ago you criticized me for not controlling him. It's my decision to keep him from the indelicacies of his race."

There was anger in Brant that Joseph could feel as the man stayed near him. Straining his neck, Joseph looked back at the window while the son raged.

"If I must learn the difficulties of being a planter, then your *black pet* here should be made to understand his condition as a prime, matured, full-hand *buck!*"

"You will not use that term for him! You call him 'boy' or 'Joseph.' Nothing else!"

"It doesn't matter what we *call* him! It matters what he is!"

"Joseph! Go to your place!" Abram roared, rising to separate son and slave.

Joseph bowed, then headed to the side room, quivering from head to toe. He had never heard anything about war or about anybody coming to end slavery. He had never heard that young planters wanted to trade slaves for gold. And once the door was dutifully closed behind him, he could hear nothing more.

The small, tight place to which he had been sentenced held Master's wardrobe, a chest of drawers, a full-length dressing mirror, and the hard, narrow bed Joseph slept on. He sank down to the unpadded stool beneath the room's only window. It was the one seat allowed him in the house. Joseph prayed the best he could for some comforting new sign that would tell him God still was willing to meet him and love him *as a black man.*

Yet by now the dawn had bled into morning, making his earlier dreams seem like irreverent foolishness as he peered through his own opened window. He wondered bitterly, *Has Brant listed me as one to be sold?*

CHAPTER 2

ANGRY BEYOND WORDS, Brant sat down on the hearthside chair. His daddy loomed above him.

"I cannot believe you so quickly take the counsel of others over mine."

"It was a plan I wished to discuss with you man to man, not a predetermination—"

"Your granddaddy started this plantation under God, and I will continue it that way."

At the risk of being banished from the room, Brant dared once more to try to make himself understood. "If it's religion you're counting on to civilize and pacify the Negro, then I beg you, look at history. The most terrible revolt of all time was led just months ago by a Bible-spouting buck who thought himself *called by God* to kill Virginians! Women and children died before he was hanged. And what of Charleston's own Denmark Vesey? In all your justification about Negro conversions you neglect to say anything about that crazed black 'Christian' fool and his associates."

"You're reciting the standard, irrelevant arguments used by unbelievers. We promote *supervised* instruction, given by masters. Tell me—do your card-house historians ever mention that insurrections have been cut off by *Christian* servants? Do your young counselors name those blacks who have *saved* their owners trouble? I'd guess not, for Theodore and the rest of them want nothing to do with evidence that reminds them of their real responsibilities. Yet, Brant, in the Final Day, God will settle accounts not only for our own souls but for those of the inferior race, which Providence has entrusted to our care."

His father breathed through clasped hands, a sure sign of tension.

"*Control does not have to be the adversary of compassion.* Open your eyes. See what we have here. This is what must be continued, for God will hold us *both* accountable in judgment."

"Behind our backs neighbors speak against us. They say our overseer is a lamb and our black slave driver is as full of himself as a calf in spring grass," Brant countered.

"What does it matter what people say? *Righteousness has no respect for rumor.* Remember that too, Brant. If you need proverbs to help you learn this business, then start with these two."

"More than half of our boundary is up against Rensler property, and Teddy is the captain of this year's St. Andrew's Parish Patrol. The talk about us is not just going to stay talk. The patrollers are just *waiting* for our Negroes to fail—"

"Well, don't you join them! With God's help, they will not fail!" His daddy looked at him. "Dear Brant, if Annie Rensler's birthday party wasn't so important to you, I'd insist that you come to Beaufort with me. It occurs to me that I may be winning over more planters to the idea of slave evangelism, while losing the support of my own son. I do not want that. You must continue our grand mission *here!*"

Brant wanted to explain his feelings, but his daddy pressed on.

"Come Sunday, Colonel Rensler and Teddy will both be at our chapel's dedication. It's been my prayer that they might see the light of our calling. Perhaps during the service they will start to view converted darkies with favor."

Ten months ago Abram had Delora bondsmen build the small clapboard church he called Our Savior's Chapel on the northwest corner of their property as a memorial to their departed loved ones. He hoped the slave church would serve as a model for other evangelism-minded planters.

Brant tried to make him see the truth. "Teddy and his uncle will come only to be gentlemanly and neighborly, which are the only two reasons you are allowing me to go to Ann's party."

"God can and should have His way in everything," his father replied, not speaking directly about either the chapel or Ann. "The Lord can work in the hearts of men mysteriously, but of late, Brant, you seem not to believe this."

He knew it would hurt his father to comment, but he decided to be honest, since the rift was already started between them. "How is one to trust Providence after all we've been through?"

The man winked away tears, which Brant had not seen since those dark hours when death had given them three family funerals in one week. The renewed sorrow made him look old—even frail—and that terrified Brant, for his daddy was his shield against having to manage the entire plantation on his own.

"God helps us daily! Have you stopped respecting even the Almighty?"

Brant was anguished by the burning questions in his soul. "What good will your philosophy of Christian love do if this nation does go to war, or if the Negroes rise against us? I don't see God's hand of protection anywhere!"

His father's woundedness changed to sad compassion. "Son, you must learn to trust again. God does not bring evil to us; He is the one who guides us through it."

"Every planter but you sees our political predicaments!"

"Dear Brant! God *is* our advocate to protect and preserve us. What He requires in return is our full allegiance to Him, so that we might know and do His will. This is at the heart of our Gospel Society: that God be honored by our efforts to convert as many Negroes as we can. This is a holy cause, since God has seen fit to bring them across the waters to us for salvation."

"You believe you can save the South by saving the slave!"

"I do! God sides with righteousness, so He will continue to side with us as long as we stay faithful to His call."

Brant knew now that his father would be the laughingstock of anyone who might hear his pathetic, distorted reasoning. With Joseph out of the room for once, Brant got up and started to gather the torn pieces of his own special dream. He wanted the security of gold; the security to abandon this property if war should ever overcome this land.

"Leave that for my boy," his father said. "This evening he will burn it all in the fire, for I am serious about never adopting any plan that includes the sale of Negro chattel."

Brant straightened but stayed beside the desk. "You're not taking him to Beaufort?"

"No." The answer sounded hard, as though his daddy were on guard now against any further verbal wrangling. "Just this morning I decided against it." He came to the desk and handed Brant a letter from it. "This was brought over late last night from Pine Woods. You know my friend Nathan Gilman, the shipwright from Boston. He's staying with the Renslers right now—"

"Yes, I know." Brant unfolded the long, handwritten note. "I met him yesterday. He's brought his daughter Felicia down to visit Annie for her birthday, since they were friends during the two years when Ann was up in Boston at Pemberton Female Academy."

"For all six years Mr. Gilman has been our society's *only* northern supporter," his father explained. "He learned about our mission through Ann's friendship with Felicia."

Brant was unaware of society business. He paid little attention to the organization that occupied so much of his father's time.

"Nathan's son William is here too," his daddy said.

"Yes, he rode with Teddy and me to Summerville yesterday." Brant skimmed more of the letter. "He's a dreadful horseman."

"Because he's a shipbuilder like his daddy."

Brant's eyes flowed to the letter's end. "So Mr. Gilman's own purpose for being here is to attend the society meetings? I thought he had come down only for Ann's sake."

"This is Nathan's first extended stay in the South. Though we are well acquainted with each other through the mail, I am just now learning more about him as a person. You see, he confides in that letter about being uncomfortable with having colored servants in his room. In Boston, his family relies on paid Irish help."

"Then he's a cursed abolitionist!" Brant guessed. "What business does he have even being down here?"

"Brant! The gentleman's motives are exactly like mine. He wants souls saved—regardless of their color."

"If he likes black folk well enough to see them in heaven, what's his complaint? Unless, of course, he knows how very easily they can be swayed back to heathen ways."

"Don't you go to condemning Joseph again! In the North the different races keep their distance."

"Then have Joseph sleep in the hall."

"I considered it, but since Mr. Gilman is traveling without a valet, so will I."

"To accommodate one blamed Yankee!"

"No. To accommodate a dear supporter and friend. In my time of grieving this man wrote me letters weekly. And that's not all. Nathan has a third reason for being here. After the convention he'll stay on till he can reach a decision about whether or not to build a shipyard on land already owned by Colonel Rensler. Need I say how important that would be—to have a sound fleet of *southern-made* and *southern-run* packets and steamers?"

Brant felt unpleasantly subdued. "No, sir. But I never would have put it all together. Annie told me there would be another party in two weeks, at which time her daddy would make some important business announcements. I certainly never expected it to have anything to do with Gilman Shipping."

"Well, it does. If Nathan decides in favor of the shipyard, then Linford Rensler is ready to agree that young William Gilman can be put in charge of it. That's a big step for a northern man to leave his son alone in the South. And a big step for a southern planter to adopt northern leadership when times are so tense."

"You trust the Gilmans not to be spies or lures for the federal regulators already patrolling our shores?"

"Oh, absolutely! Nathan's sacrificed so much for us already. Even now there are Unionists who will not send a dollar's business his way because he supports our society. Slave emancipation is the only mission most churches up north want to entertain."

"What can they know about us and the way we live?"

"That is a very good question."

For the first time that morning they had found something to agree on, and that felt good to Brant. Then his daddy's eyes slipped to the mantel clock.

"Ring the bell to call Joseph back. I really must not be delayed much longer."

With reluctance Brant went to a small cluster of satin bell ropes hanging over the washstand beside the bed. *Clearly Daddy has made Joseph into more than just plain Negro help, since he always wants the African to be beside him, nearly like a trusted companion,* Brant thought. *Why, we cannot even have family devotions without him.* Brant resented having a "dark shadow" whenever he and his father were together. Forgetting which rope was threaded through the ceiling to the dressing room, Brant pulled them all.

"After I leave, I want him to change into his ash clothes," Brant's father said of his slave while he was emerging. "He'll help with the cleaning. I want everything in good condition by Sunday, when many of the Gospel Society delegates will come for the dedication. At night, let him sleep in the dressing-room bed."

Joseph stood near them, a study in perfect servant submission with his shoulders square and face held down. Brant's daddy spoke to him directly.

"You heard what I said just now. I've decided to leave you home so you can help with the work."

"Yes, sir." Joseph had an emotionless voice, but one that sounded like a planter's, since Brant's daddy had chosen to tutor him in language. Early on he had been required to abandon the rough Gullah mixture of African and English words spoken by Negroes and poor whites.

"Have your best livery on by Saturday noon, for some of our weekend guests will arrive for supper."

"Yes, sir."

The boy's easy assertion to do exactly as he was told felt galling to Brant.

Their coach driver, Ezra, appeared in the hallway to take Abram's luggage. His daddy seemed too intent on Joseph to notice. Otherwise, this older slave would have been brought in, too, to stand at attention during morning prayers. A few moments later Brant found his daddy looking at him.

"Joseph is uneasy around you," he said within the boy's hearing. "I want you to consider him as you would a valuable horse being boarded for a friend. You would not be heavy handed with another man's steed, would you?"

"No, sir." Brant hated how he sounded like Joseph's echo.

"Then you perform the same kind of service for me. I don't want to come back to find any marks on him."

Brant had never been left in charge before and had never faced the task of controlling this houseboy. He considered the counsel that Teddy and his club friends might have given him. Surely it would be absurd to pledge no repercussions in front of a slave who might later need physical governing, so he said nothing.

"You let Maum use him as she will. You keep to your focus on the fields and rely on Overseer Gund's good counsel."

"All right." Brant was glad the boy had no permission to see his face, for he felt distraught. His father handed him the planting ledgers, which seemed to indicate that they were through with speaking about business. Two other houseservants, Maum Bette and Jewell, came in, perhaps because Brant had wrongly rung the call bells.

"I want to talk about Ann," his father ventured even with this wider audience. "Yesterday I sent my letter to the colonel explaining why I am not supporting any proposal of marriage this year."

Brant loathed being discussed in front of the family's servants, who only pretended, he was sure, to have ears as deaf as doors. "Must we speak about this now?"

"Yes, because it relates to your behavior this evening. You have my permission to attend Annie's party, but you will guard yourself from any actions that would indicate you are special friends."

Brant closed his eyes. "Did you write what *I* said too?"

"I did. I explained that you are still certain of your love for her, and that the reluctance toward matrimony is mine and mine alone. I addressed the matter of merging our properties, since that has always been related to the subject of your futures."

"Did you say that I don't care about the property? Did you say it's *Ann* I love, not Rensler land?"

"What I wrote is that I continue to have little interest in merger because of our certain philosophical differences."

Brant sighed. By *philosophical*, his father meant *religious*. In short, he was not interested in working with anyone who did not see slaves, first and foremost, as pitiful souls to be cared for and saved. Miserably, Brant considered how unfair it was that he and Ann had been reared to think of marriage even before they knew the flowering of romance. But now that they knew they truly loved each other, their families continued to make arrangements for them, even though they were adults.

"I felt the need to summarize those things in writing, since I will not see the colonel tonight. Don't look so bleak. You're young," his daddy said to console him. "You should be thankful you have time to consider well what spouse God wants for you."

Brant frowned his intense disagreement. He wanted the conversation brought to an end, but his daddy continued it.

"Marriage is often about sacrifice, and I'm not sure Ann could ever understand that with the kind of faith she holds."

Again Brant made himself stay silent while inwardly his arguments raged. *Has death so robbed Daddy of life that he now sees even love as nothing more than postponed pain? Does everything—even romance—have to have its morbid center in a bleeding, dying God? Where is all the joy of faith he learned from Mama—before Omnipotence allowed her to be buried?* No wonder only Negroes found pleasure in his daddy's teaching: they were not made for love and reason, so they could be content to wait for joy in a life to come.

"What are you thinking, son?"

Brant found it hard to engage him with a glance. "That you still mourn too much," he said warily.

His father grimaced. "You are right. And that is difficult for you, I know."

Brant again saw tears well up like dew on the lower edges of his father's pale blue eyes. He looked away, scared to be raised to leadership by one so saturated with disaster. The weight of his family's sorrows felt smothering, like a house polluted when the chimney clogs. For that reason he made one more desperate attempt to keep the way open to the one he loved: Ann Rensler. He tried to reason like his father so that his thoughts would not be dismissed. "I don't condemn you, for I, too, benefited greatly from Mama's love. But what if this is Providence intervening by putting Annie here for me? Her laughter! Her beauty! Even the music she could bring to this house! Perhaps God knows she is what we all need."

His father looked at the clock, his face shedding much of its emotion. "We will talk about this more when I come home. Now it's absolutely necessary to get to prayer." He nodded for the servants to gather at their regular standing places right inside the door. Brant's fourteen-year-old sister, Mayleda, and his ten-year-old brother, Eric, came in also. Unlike the expressionless servants, Mayleda beamed from ear to ear.

"We were up in the attic looking through Mama's box of ribbons to find just the right one for Annie's present," the young mistress announced brightly while crossing the bedroom on slippered feet. Her dark curls bouncing around the fringes of her linen cap, she took the chair beside Brant. Eric, his brown hair uncombed, flopped down on the floor near the hem of the flowered wrapper Mayleda wore over her narrow petticoats. Her straight posture portrayed her strong opinion that their daddy had been gracious in allowing Brant to offer Ann the same string of pearls he had given their mother the year she turned nineteen. Brant dismissed her opinion as that belonging to a child.

"Oh, I wish I were allowed to go with you tonight," Mayleda said to Brant, eyes pleading toward their father. However, that matter had been settled too. She would go to no parties until the Graftons' rice ball next summer, at which time she would be introduced to Charleston society as a lady.

"I'm glad I don't have to go!" Eric pouted, tossing his head. "I hope I never get old enough to be *commanded* to parties." Had their mother still been living, Eric would have been ushered to a proper seat. As it was he rarely received discipline from anyone, and frequently he gave impish grins to all, be they parent, sibling, or slave. Brant's father, however, did call for silence before instructing Joseph to get his Bible and prayer book from the shelf built behind the hallway door.

The clock struck half-past seven, and Brant dreaded the next five days alone as manager and substitute master of this house.

Nobody was surprised when Master Abram announced he would read the twenty-first chapter of the book of Proverbs, since he daily read a chapter of ancient wisdom coinciding with the date in his almanac.

As he commenced, Joseph was again drawn to the window. While Master read the words aloud, Joseph's own thoughts and prayers exploded once more like celebration fireworks. *Heavenly Father, please show me anew what that sunrise meant. Even if I have sinned against thee with my understanding, show me. For you and you alone are worthy to have your way.* He bit his lip, for having somehow slipped into addressing God with common words. *Oh, forgive me! I only desire to know thee as thou art. Has it been good—or selfish—in thy sight for me to see myself as more than a slave? Speak to thy servant, I beseech thee, that I may understand and not sin. Amen!*

While he searched the horizon he found nothing. Moving his eyes the other way he saw Delora's head servant and cook, Maum Bette, round and stocky, and his own Mama Jewell, the Callcotts' housemaid, looking like a tiny brown sparrow beside her. Both women were dressed in indigo-dyed homespun with aprons and headkerchiefs sewn from the same cloth Jewell had used to make his shirts. The women's eyes were closed as they recited supplications memorized from Master's prayer book. But young Miss Mayleda was watching him.

When his gaze connected with hers, she demurely showed him a soft, pink-lipped smile. This she had done almost daily since those times when as a child himself he had been assigned to rock her cradle and wave the eyed peacock feather above her porcelain face to keep the flies away. Her skin was still dinner-plate smooth and as colorless as cotton. Her eyes had always intrigued him, for they were as dark as any Negro's.

He thought with sadness that presently their times for quiet smiles would end, since Master must soon declare her too much a woman to let Joseph ever look again upon her countenance of innocence. Already she was a dark-haired beauty, so much like her mother. Still he could not keep himself from hoping that her kind notice of him would go on forever. Though it was unreasonable, he nourished the idea that they might always be like friends, despite race and class and opposite genders.

Instead of smiling back as he would have done had they been with Master Abram only, he dropped his eyes, fearing Brant's possible condemnation. Few things in a male slave's life equaled the danger of being accused of having impure looks for any lady. With his head low he considered anew the dreadful days that could come once Brant claimed full ownership of them all. By law every slave was classified as chattel, no different than livestock, furniture, or grain. Wherever they were shifted or housed and whatever they were put to doing, slaves were expected to endure, having no more say about life than individual kernels of the master's cash crop—rice.

Abram's benediction pulled Joseph from his thoughts.

"Children, get dressed so you can come down to say good-bye at the carriage."

Maum Bette led the younger two away. Then Abram invited Brant to walk downstairs with him, leaving Joseph behind like an unneeded cloak. From the hallway Master Abram did look back.

"You help Maum now any way you can."

Joseph nodded through his tangle of unhappy thoughts. "Yes. Godspeed, sir." It was one blessing he could utter with full truthfulness, for he had begun to think in earnest of life under Brant's ownership—perhaps even starting now if something should happen to Master on his journey down the coast. His discomfort caused him to repeat himself quite loudly. "Godspeed, sir!"

The master, as far as the stairs then, laughed approvingly. "Yes! My good, reverent boy."

When the two gentlemen were gone, Joseph started to pick up the pieces of Brant's papers thrown to the floor. On hands and knees he reached for the tiniest scraps that had floated under the desk. Carefully he kept his eyes away from the pieces he handled. To do otherwise would be to engage the deepest and only secret he carried about himself, which no one—black or white—knew. With a decade of practice on moonlit nights, using only scraps of discarded print like these, Joseph had taught himself to read—a practice strictly prohibited by society.

Though he never had used his secret skill to pry into Master's business, he knew the papers in his hands had to do with slavery. Still disciplining himself completely, he put the stack on the desk, knowing that if he were going to dare to read these papers, he had to be certain that both masters were gone. Going to the opened window, he gazed at the sandy loop of driveway as he waited for Master's carriage to be driven out. The whole place was quiet while the coach stayed at the front of the house.

It occurred to him in this odd time of idleness that he had never stayed in these rooms alone. He reflected on his childhood. Birthed in the kitchenhouse shanty behind the mansion, he had shadowed his Mama Jewell everywhere until the day he turned six. That morning he had been given a new set of clothes—combed cotton not flax—and sent here to learn to wait on the master of the house. From that day until now he had slept in the dressing room instead of on a mat beside his mother in the cellar.

At first his training was with Mistress Oribel, but soon he was put under the softly spoken but always exacting directions of Master himself. Had he been reared as a field hand instead of a houseservant, he would be living across the driveway in one of the log shanties behind the row of evergreen camellias on a section of the plantation known as the "quarters" or the "street."

Overseer Hampton Gund, a short, uncomely white man, and Bette's huge black husband, Billy Days, were the only two individuals Joseph knew from there, since only the overseer and the big slave driver had permission to cross the driveway. Joseph leaned against the sill considering his early, almost carefree, days. He had never been punished for simple childish failings in this house. On the contrary, he had often been rewarded for work done well, since this was part of Master's benevolent, Christian plan, at which other slaveowners often scoffed.

Many times Joseph had earned hours of play by his youthful diligence. During hot summer afternoons when the elder Callcotts napped or read on the second-floor piazza, Brant and Joseph would skip off together. Those had been days of true guilelessness, when they shared equally the wide swampy wilderness for adventure and sport. Joseph had ridden horses with Brant, fished, trapped, and rowed the awkward, heavy punt Unc' Ezra used to take the family into town whenever the roads were impassable because of rain.

Odd as it seemed now, Brant had welcomed the companionship then as much as Joseph had. As a boy, the planter's son quenched his thirst from the same drinking gourd Joseph used. They never squabbled when one sweet peach was shared between them. But then Teddy had come to Pine Woods, a scrawny orphan just a few years older than they, to be reared like a son by his uncle, Colonel Linford Rensler. Having no playmates of his own, Teddy began showing up on lazy afternoons. Often Teddy brought along an innocent-eyed, copper-colored houseboy called Cecil to follow him as Joseph did Brant. Even now Joseph had to bat his eyes to ward off incredible feelings of helplessness as he thought about this other slave, for he knew Cecil had been mercilessly whipped for some small crime and sold away soon after the spring when Joseph turned twelve. After that Joseph was permanently kept in the house and forbidden to play.

Joseph looked at the palms of his hands, as light as cream compared with the rest of his coffee-colored self. He had spent days and nights in his youth praying that his end would not be like Cecil's, that God might even make him white. He had so feared being sold and separated from his mama and Delora that he used to sleep with his hands wrapped around the low post of his bed so that no one could carry him off in the night.

He also remembered his first great day of terror, which came within months after Cecil had been sold. Skinny, pinch-faced Teddy had found him alone at the well house. The white boy cornered him as a shrew does its prey. In those awful moments Teddy told him a "special" Bible story while trapping Joseph's hands within his. In Theodore's tale there was a third intelligent being living in the Garden of Eden with Adam and Eve. According to Teddy this living form had the looks of a man, but not his wits or soul.

After the fall of real man, Teddy said, God allowed Satan to have this third subhuman being for himself. Then, squeezing Joseph's hands ever tighter, Teddy had dropped him over the well house stairs to show how Satan dangled his poor unnamed being over the pit of hell until all but the palms of his hands was toasted brown. Teddy said that Joseph's color was the sure sign of his being the descendent of this cursed fool, and therefore, he was marked until damnation to do the white man's labor.

As a child Joseph had been too afraid to ask Master Abram if the story was true, for it might be and then his every hope for salvation would be lost. That caustic experience birthed in him the desire to read the Bible for himself so that he could know the truth. Though he could now read well, he had never read the Bible because reading needed to be done in secret.

He looked to the front again, where the family was still taking its leave. Though his curiosity to see Brant's notes bubbled hot as a cauldron, Joseph held himself at the window, not wanting to risk being discovered. Far away across the river he heard the field slaves singing. As a youth Joseph occasionally had visited Bette and Billy's shanty down at the top of the street.

He remembered the paper square framed over their featherbed, a gift from the master almost too fine for belief. Maum had pointed out that their printed Certificate of Marriage was just as great a treasure as the bed, for few white men believed in slave matrimony. Peering at that ink, Joseph had wondered how such tiny marks could contain the "voices" of memory, as Bette said they did, recording the day and year when she and Billy had come together, sanctified by God, to share this marvelous sleeping place. When he had asked Billy that question, he had been sadly disappointed that the best black "uncle" in his life did not know anything about the mysteries of reading.

Yet the kind man helped him in so many other ways. Full of faith and full of life, Billy was allowed to come across from the quarters on Sunday. Along with Bette, Jewell, Joseph, Ezra, and Ezra's wife, Nancee, they'd sit until nightfall talking, laughing, and relishing permissible leftovers from the master's table.

Unc' Billy—called Billy Days by their owners—had a rich voice like the humming of a flax wheel that could readily lull a weary, work-worn servant to drowsy sleep. Yet Joseph would always stay alert, for Bette's man could sing and joke and tell such tales that you had only to close your eyes to be someplace you'd never been before. There were plenty of times when Joseph wished this man were his daddy, though the uncle gave him grand portions of attention anyway. Those precious weekly meetings were Joseph's only link to Gullah and to the stories and history of his race.

Though Bette and Billy had one child three years older than he, Joseph had never met him, since their son was not allowed to cross the driveway. Joseph did know that Master called him Parris, after Miss Oribel's favorite city, which supplied glassware and fabrics to the house. Maum and Billy talked about their son being good-hearted, strong, and steady. Even now at the window it was Parris's voice Joseph heard leading all the others. Driver Gund relied on Parris to set the pace, be it for hoeing, planting, or harvesting. Joseph had learned to distinguish his voice while working beside Maum Bette in this chamber.

Finally the coach rattled below him as it started out toward Kings Road, which led down into Charleston. A minute after that Joseph spied Brant going off toward the stables. Unable to make himself wait any longer, he rushed to the desk and put together the largest fragments. In a moment he had awful news: Parris was one Brant wanted auctioned! A neatly printed sidenote told why: *Bucks related by blood will fight to the death in uprisings.*

Like an insect with its life sucked out, Joseph staggered to the bell rope. Fiercely he pulled the cord leading down to the porch, where it tossed a bell that could be heard from the kitchenhouse across the yard. The moment Bette appeared, he shared the terrible secret without confiding how he knew it. As he finished and she was reduced to tears, Master Brant strode in, shocking them both. Shutting their mouths, turning their faces down, they thought they had been saved, for the man went straight to the saddlebag he had inadvertently left there. Then he saw the papers pieced together on the desk.

Instantly Brant drove Maum down the stairs with threats that she had better not say a word to anybody about what she had just seen and heard. Then he grabbed Joseph by the collar and pulled him to the desk. "You can read! That's how this report got put back in perfect order! Why did my daddy hide this from me?"

Joseph tried to breathe, but Brant was shaking the life from him. His windpipe opened slightly. "He doesn't know!"

"You're lying!"

"No! It's truth."

Brant twisted Joseph's arms behind him. He pulled him to his heaving chest. "Either you had his permission to learn, or you stole the privilege from him and all the privacy that goes with it. You tell me which it is, or I'll break you in half."

Outside a gull cried loudly, causing Joseph to think of the sunrise and his prayers. *Lord of all!* he prayed inwardly, his sight blurring because of the pressure on his shoulders. Was this the time to prove himself equal, regardless of the cost? *Oh, God!* He had wanted something wonderful. Not this.

Brant freed one hand so that he could point. "What's that say? You read every word you can in my hearing!"

Joseph blinked at the lines waving beneath him. " 'Slave man-age-ment be-gins with un-der-standing . . .' " he struggled.

"I can't believe it!" Brant shoved Joseph's head, bobbing his eyesight to another piece of paper. "What's that say?"

" 'There have been or-gan-ized up-rising' . . . ah!"

Brant pulled his collar once more. For a moment Joseph could see only the ceiling because of Brant's hold.

"You dog! You dog!"

Joseph heard, then saw, Mayleda scream as she came at them like a bat from the attic. She caught Brant as he pulled Joseph toward the dressing room. Small beside them, she still proved to be all fight and fury. Her scuffle gave Joseph lifesaving breath.

"Get away, girl!" her brother threatened. With one hand he pressed Joseph to the wall beside the fireplace, with the other he pushed her. She fell to the floor. "This pet you all love is nothing but a cheat, a liar, and a betrayer!"

"I'll not believe that—ever!" She wailed as she struggled to her feet and ran off.

Brant dragged him to the dressing room, kicking the door closed behind them. Squeezing Joseph against the wardrobe he managed to lock the door. Soon Bette and his mama were on the outside, crying and hammering on the wood like terrified children in a thunderstorm. Maum dared to speak for him.

"Oh, Mass', you know you' daddy don't want him harmed!"

Joseph felt his alertness leave him as the son's fingers tightened around his neck like snakes. Brant kept him on his feet, marching him straight to the long oval mirror. Covered with rolling sweat, Joseph stared at his own heaving reflection. Brant's face, directly behind his, was red and wet too. His yellow hair fell against Joseph's well-groomed head like pieces of a broken halo. He smashed Joseph's nose and chin against the silvered glass.

Joseph feared it would shatter into a thousand pieces, but it held him while the image of his face disappeared in breathy mist.

"You son of perdition! Do you have any idea what the patrol would do if they found out what you've done?"

Joseph managed, "Yes." He had thought about punishment. Often. Though he had never heard of any other pure-blooded African reading, he knew terrible stories from Unc' Billy about brown men who had lost their lives or had their fingers cut off for trying to learn to write and read.

"You spoilt creature!" Brant pressed him harder so that Joseph felt the mirror would explode in his face.

"Please," he begged with lips pinched. "I meant no harm." Rolling his eyes upward he could see Brant's worry reflected in a small shiny patch of the mirror above his head. The pressure lessened just a little.

"Till my daddy comes home you will not speak at all—"

"Agreed!" Joseph cried his relief, catching precious breath as Brant pulled back.

"You expect me to simply *trust* you?" Brant fumed. With a tight hold still on him, Brant made Joseph bow down with him as he reached into the rim of his right boot. Another moment and Joseph saw the glint of a thin-bladed hunting knife coming up toward his throat. It gleamed in the looking glass, moving within inches of his chin.

"Nooo!"

"Stand still! Open your mouth, fool, so that I can prick the tip of your tongue. It will not hurt forever, but if you speak again this week, I shall dip it in salt."

Joseph's eyes flooded just to think of it. He clenched his jaws tight, not wanting pain.

"You stupid boy! Don't defy me, or I will make it deeper." Brant pried his lips until Joseph tasted metal. Then blood. Terrified, he tried to pull away. The knife slipped high and deep within his mouth. His temples spiked with pain. His eyes closed. His head pounded. When he cried, red poured out like a waterfall.

———

An explosion revived him. With ragged vision, Joseph saw the door off its hinges. A new white face was over him—Overseer Gund's. It looked on him with pity.

Then Joseph dreamt he was a piece of lumber, lifted by slave hands that had no connection with faces. He dreamt he was a dead leaf, swirling stem down the servants' winding staircase.

But in the bright outside air he knew he was a man again—or at least a dying slave—for the salty breeze was razor sharp in his mouth as he struggled to keep on breathing. He tried to scream his anguish, but there was no sound. And no movement in his blazing tongue.

After that he remembered being set down on a gritty floor. On his knees he vomited blood, enough to fill a washerwoman's piggin. When he had been pumped dry by retching, he lay down, happy to die. His faith in God washed back and forth like shorebirds chased between incoming waves. He remembered heaven and closed his eyes to look for the light of it. But darkness came instead.

CHAPTER 3

IT WAS SEVERAL HOURS before Brant faced the toolshed again, and this time Teddy Rensler was at his side. Delora's worried overseer, Hampton Gund, trailed them both because Mayleda had run down to the fields to call him up while Brant was locking Joseph in the dressing room. Brant had never expected his inexperienced attempt to quiet Joseph to end like this. Against better wisdom, Brant thought, Gund had brought their black driver, Billy. He had used the big worker to clean out the tools and then to carry Joseph's lifeless body down to this secluded place. To keep all the other slaves away, Gund had assigned Billy to guard the yard.

Maum Bette and Jewell had packed Joseph's mouth with rags soaked in wine and clove water. Other strips had been wrapped around his chin and head to keep full pressure on the tongue. But still the blood dripped out. Brant had finally sent a stable groom, astride his own horse, to Pine Woods to call his doctor friend. As much as he dreaded getting Teddy involved, Brant feared Joseph would die without a doctor's care.

Upon Teddy's arrival, with hands as stiff as the wooden bar he raised, Brant removed the slim outside beam that locked the toolshed door. He swung the door wide and found Joseph lying face down, looking like a corpse. Mayleda sobbed as she watched from the distant mansion porch. Brant stopped Teddy from going in and yelled back to her. "You want to help him, May? Then go inside and stay there!" Mayleda rushed through the back door.

Teddy spoke to Gund. "You make sure your nigger driver keeps all the darkies and the Callcott children away from here."

Gund looked only at the unconscious boy. "Help him, sah! It sure don't look like you have much time." Fretting, Gund pushed back the brim of his woven palmetto hat. He had a poor-cracker's flushed, freckled face. Despite being outclassed by two planters, he had dared to speak. His pleading had an edge of authority to it, though it was as thick as a Negro's Gullah.

Teddy brushed Gund off. His attitude stayed harsh as he went in and cautiously stooped beside the lifeless form. "Sometimes these buggers will feign unconsciousness just to lure you close."

"My daddy's going to kill me if he dies," Brant worried. Reluctantly he entered the shed, which was hot as an oven. Crouching down by Joseph and across from Teddy, Brant focused on Teddy's familiar profile—the beakish nose like half a Cherokee's arrowhead and the weak, deep eyes, which ever since college had had a respectable pair of oval glasses over them. "What do you think? How bad is he?"

"I can't say yet, man. Help me pull him into full light."

Unhappily Brant grabbed the clammy-skinned slave under one of his bare arms while Teddy took the other. Brant had stripped Joseph to his linen underwear right after the accident so that the livery would not be ruined. At Teddy's command they rolled the boy from stomach to spine. It caused Joseph's eyes to flutter open. His cheeks bulged horribly with Maum's packing. The slave looked desperate to swallow, which he could not do. His naked chest heaved. Brant looked away. Teddy might be content to think of him only as an animal needing care, but Brant could not dismiss the thought that he had seen Joseph's chest before, smooth and glistening just as it was now, when they used to swim together in the river as youths. Why had he so quickly decided to use one of the club's techniques for punishing a Negro's wagging tongue? He could have merely confined him. The dangerous consequences of his poor judgment were clear. Joseph's suffering was real, and Teddy, captain of the patrol, had been alerted to the incident by Brant's having called him here.

Alone, Brant bore the riddle of how this pitch-black African had come to read. It was a question he could never confide in his friends, for Joseph's unwanted literacy would bring retributions even to Brant's family. For months Teddy had been leading a movement to draft new state legislation making it unlawful for any colored individual—slave or free—to ever learn to write or read.

Teddy cut the cloths binding Joseph's jaw. Using a piece of kindling to prop the mouth wide, he brought Joseph to his senses. The boy writhed like a flag in a gale. "Grab his wrists!" Teddy ordered. "He's got more strength than I thought."

His slave looked at him wildly, making Brant feel like Teddy's unlucky servant when he rushed to hold him. The other planter tied Joseph's arms to his waist with the bloodied cloth strips. Joseph's eyes, glazed liked marbles, stayed fixed on Brant, begging for help in silent terror.

"It's not the tongue that's causing the loss of blood," Teddy said as though it were a textbook problem. "You nicked a crucial buccal vessel. See?"

Brant's whole body tingled. "No. I don't want to." He fled outside.

Theodore laughed. "So anatomy doesn't interest you."

Bracing himself against the doorframe, Brant tried to be brave. He looked in just far enough to see Teddy's steady hands threading a long curved needle. "It's as easy as darning socks, once the professors give you practice."

"Please—"

"You are the one who cut him," Teddy said coolly. "You would have done better to beat the rebellion from him."

Brant gave no explanation of why he had done this, even though Teddy kept prompting him to do so.

"The whip and the paddle do not devalue them, but some traders do mind when you take the speech from them."

Brant came around. "You mean he will not speak again?"

"Does it matter? If so, then I should suture the tongue."

Brant leaned against wood. "Yes! Help him—any way you can."

"Knowing you as I do, Brant, it's hard to believe the damage done here," Teddy said. "This nigger must have done something extraordinary to make you take your knife to him."

"I didn't plan for it to be this way," Brant limply confessed. "I only wanted to prick his tongue, as we talked about doing for chronic tattlers. But he moved—"

"He resisted you!"

"It was an accident." Brant quickly covered for both Joseph and himself because he wanted no trouble with the law. "I was unsure. I was too indecisive. And he was fearful."

"He struggled! That's the plain truth of it!"

Brant bit his lip. To admit even that might send Joseph to his grave, for Theodore was very good at seeing slaves receive death penalties for any amount of resistance against their owners. Anew, he feared for Joseph's safety. Perhaps his friend was even heartless enough to make Joseph die now. For that reason he forced himself back inside to keep watching.

Teddy did not speak another word until his medicines were put away. Then he met Brant at the door. "You see what's happening?"

Reluctantly Brant surveyed Joseph, who was awake and gurgling coarsely with the stick still in his mouth. "That's not just physical pain you see. It's anger! He's still too much of a mule, it seems, to accept what disobedience will cost him. You can't be finished with him yet. Not when he's displaying looks like those!"

"What are you saying? He could die in this state!"

"Or he could live. And if he does, then he will live to fight again. See! He's not ashamed even now to look you in the eye."

"He's begging for help and an end to his suffering."

"I would gladly put an end to him."

"He's my daddy's favorite."

"Brant, this boy needs to be *broken* of his will and spirit. I certainly do hope you see that. If you don't, it will soon enough become a matter for my patrol."

"I don't want any more violence."

"As captain of the company, I've taken an oath to come against any sort of insurrection. And as a club member, you've taken vows, too, not to maintain slaves in ways that will jeopardize others."

"But I don't see how he can be of danger—weak as he is."

"I am a good doctor. In as little as a day you might expect him to be on his feet, unless the lockjaw or fever claims him. What do you plan to do with him?"

Brant tried to maintain a measure of confidence so his friend would not take him for a fool. "I'll keep him confined."

Teddy walked outside, then called Brant around the corner to the shed's shady side. "You cannot ignore this. You have a rebel on your hands. It would be helpful if you just opened up and explained what got him into this much trouble."

"I'm sorry, I can't." Brant looked into the yard where the houseservants did their chores.

"Either you break him of his willfulness, or he will turn on you, endangering you and others. If you're not ready to handle that kind of responsibility yourself, I can help you. I have legal right through the parish patrol to come to your aid."

"I must wait and speak to my father."

"You think that's going to make it easier to do the right thing with him? I strongly advise you do the breaking now and have it over with. They go down easier when they are physically weak."

"I can't risk failing again," Brant said bitterly.

Teddy raised his eyebrows. "Then, friend, you need to hear my plan— and right away."

Brant walked away toward the fence beyond the woodpile, but Teddy followed him. "I hate them all," Brant confessed. "If I had *my* way, I would never see a black body again. I envy you with your northern education. Believe me, Teddy, if I had been you, I would never have come back here."

"Oh yes, you would have. There's so little open space in New England. And no understanding of our quiet luxuries."

"I don't consider it a luxury to be dependent on Negroes. More and more I hate seeing their black prying faces everywhere!"

Teddy chuckled. "I dare say you're more jealous of that one than hate-filled for them all."

"What! Me? Jealous of our slave?"

"Yes indeed, and I'll say why. It's quite a common phenomenon associated with those who are reared right in our houses. You remember our boy Cecil?"

"Of course. I can't forget him. He's the one your uncle made you whip and take down to the slave market yourself."

"That's right, and, Brant, you could have benefited from such instruction as that. See, old Colonel knew Cecil was the one for me to learn on, for he was the one that came nearest to ever seeming like a friend."

Brant was sickened. "I couldn't have done it. I was there when you tied him to the fence just for breaking a platter."

"It was planned. My uncle was waiting for just such an occasion. At the time, of course, it was humiliating for me to have to learn the use of the lash in front of all those gentlemen who were at his dinner."

Inwardly Brant cringed, thinking of Joseph, immobilized and scarcely breathing. "I'd rather not talk about it."

"Do you yet know how to use the whip?"

He would not answer.

"See, that's a problem too. By now you should have the skills for this business. You can't be a planter without the right restraining tools any more than you can be a horse trainer without a bit and bridle."

"There's no cruelty in the latter."

"There's no cruelty in the former, either, once you get each African to know his place. The cruelty comes in letting the door open for moments of rebellion, as you must have done this morning. The cruelty comes from shoddy management, which opens the way for some to dream of revolt or revenge. Be honest. You saw something like that in him."

Out of their view, Joseph suddenly sounded as though he were choking. Brant started to rush to him, but Teddy held him back. "He's all right. He's still conscious enough to roll to his side to help himself. He'll not drown in saliva. Let him have this time to grow fearful of what his strife has won for him."

"They are not beasts. I'm sure of that."

"They are your hands, your back, your feet, Brant. They are either your obedient workers, or they will become your murderers and thieves—"

"I don't want to hear it. I've made up my mind. As soon as Daddy's home, I'm leaving Delora, and he can do with Joseph as he pleases. Let him wait till Eric comes of age to train his heir."

"Ha, Brant! If you're not a planter, what will you do?"

"I don't know. Right now I hardly care."

"And what about Annie? She was in tears today because of your daddy's letter to the colonel. The only thing that comforts her is the fact that she believes you still love her."

"I do love her!" Brant turned away with distress and lifted his face to the sky. "But I doubt that I deserve her, being so unhappy with plantation life."

Teddy actually touched him. "You need not be like this. Didn't I already say that I have a plan?"

"I won't see him hurt more. I can hate him but still not want him destroyed. I'm not like you. I don't find pleasure in beating them down so low. I was angry—no, furious—with him. But now I'm only tired of it all."

"That just shows what kind of burden your daddy has you under,"

Teddy quietly explained. "You know what's right to do, but your father's expectations keep you from doing it. You can bring this all to a rapid end by having Joseph kiss your boots."

Brant looked at Teddy, unbelieving.

"It's true. When they're hurting enough, you can get them to do almost anything. And when you have him broken enough to embrace your feet, then you know you can begin to trust him for service."

"I could never do it."

"Then your attitude needs to be broken too. Deep down you still be-lieve they have some right to personal pride!"

"His mouth is too sore to command him to do anything."

"You're resisting because sometimes you don't believe they should be shamed. But either a slave will have only *your* will, or he will have his own. If you had the spine for it, you'd admit that is just what you found true this morning."

Brant did not respond.

"It's easiest to whip the uppitiness out of them. Or you can send them down to the Charleston workhouse to paid floggers if you feel reluctant to do the job yourself. Your daddy thinks himself a tender-hearted master because he won't dole out physical pain. But now you see the outcome of his philosophy. A buck that can't be trusted. A buck that may someday have to be put out of his misery if no one takes the initiative to train him rightly now."

"There must be a better way!"

"You brought me here to save him, and I believe I've done that. Now I can help you keep him out of the clutches of the law, for you know that breaking slaves is not an unfamiliar task to me. I wasn't joking when I said you should make him kiss your boots. Daily, for a while."

"What if he wouldn't do it?"

"That's not a question. You make him do it, man."

Brant was trapped. If he admitted that his father had forbidden him to use force, then Teddy might exercise his power as patrol captain to put Joseph under his own authority. But if he agreed to make Joseph bow, and Joseph resisted again, then Teddy would know firsthand that he had no power over him.

"You can have him soft as butter in three days," Teddy promised into his indecisive silence.

"Without whipping him? I don't want to have him marked."

Teddy smiled glumly. "You're the master. You do as you must. I'll guide you any way I can. While I finish up with his mouth, you find clothes for him. Anytime they go through physical trials like this, you must take precautions against congestion in the lungs."

From where he was standing Brant could see field-slave shirts hung out to dry on the yard's picket fence. Going over, he claimed the largest one, then came back to Teddy, who was already at the toolshed door. Together they went inside and put the shirt on Joseph, who was unconscious again. Teddy painted Joseph's gaping mouth with ill-smelling liquid that made the boy groan and cry in his nightmarish sleep.

After that Teddy went out to get a pair of lightweight shackles so they could move Joseph to the yard where the air was cooler. While Teddy was off, a three-quarters-grown slave hollered over the fence to Brant. "Massa, sah! Somebody done stole my shirt, so's I don't have nothin' to wear 'cept skin."

Not knowing what do to for a moment, Brant finally asked, "What's your name?"

"Colt, sah." The boy clung to the pickets.

"All right, Colt," Brant said, hoping the Negro would prove as dumb as he sounded and looked with his overly large hands and ears. "You go knock on the back door. Tell Maum to dress you so you can go inside and work for her."

Colt's face split with a grin. "You picked me for the house! Oh, thank-yee, sah!" He ran off, as though forgetting completely his first reason for being at the fence.

Teddy walked up to Brant by way of the driveway gate. "Your daddy's sure not going to be pleased with that one in the house!" He smiled good-naturedly.

Brant snapped back. "I'm done with having smart comely ones!"

"I'll say you are."

From an upstairs window, Mayleda's face appeared, her eyes glued on the chains in Teddy's hands. Brant felt like a criminal under her gaze. "Don't you judge me!" he yelled up at her. "Either I take care of him as I see fit, or he'll come under the law."

He was glad she withdrew. They went back inside the stifling shed to lock the iron bands on Joseph's wrists and ankles while he lay senseless. The boy started to shiver, despite the day's heat. Inwardly Brant vowed anew never to be a master while he worried out loud, "What's happening?"

"I think it's just a reaction to the drug I gave him to keep his heart beating strongly," Teddy said, lifting Joseph's eyelids as he examined him. "Let's put him out in the shade as planned, then I'll stay to check on him."

––––––––––

There was fire in Joseph's mouth and the feeling that great boulders had been rolled upon his hands and feet. He smelled the stench of death upon himself. His eyes, though wide open, took in only darkness. He felt drowned by thirst, the pain driving him mad. He remembered being in the yard hours earlier, but now he was inside that dark furnace again.

His vision at sunrise came back to mock him. Had it been a cruel trick of his own imagination to make him think of manhood only hours before the masters destroyed him? Or was this God's retribution, swiftly meted out for his wrong, sin-filled desires? He heard the scrape of the toolshed bar. It panicked him. As best he could with his weighted hands and feet, he drew himself into a ball. He would not have spent so much energy on movement had he known the voice and the touch were going to be kind.

"Joseph? It me, Billy Days."

He wept silent tears.

"Hey, man, it's a'right." The uncle gently stroked his cheek. "The massas done just set down to supper, so's I thought this wa' a safe time to sneak in."

Joseph moaned, mourning his mute condition.

"I couldn't see my way clear to bring you no dipper or bucket. But here . . ."

Billy carried water to his lips by holding a soaked rag against the heat of his mouth. Joseph fought for every drop the man squeezed to his tongue, for his thirst far exceeded his meager skill to swallow.

"I cain't risk stayin' long, 'specially with Mass' Rensler still near. But I gwine come again. I promise."

Joseph tried to reach Billy, too pained to feel ashamed that he was as lonely and as scared as a child. When his hand did move, he saw in the dusk that he was lying chained. He groaned his bitterness, and Billy raised his head to cradle it in his strong rough hands.

"I sure do wish you could tell me why Mass' Brant did all this to you."

In response, Joseph again began to cry.

"Sh-sh-sh!" The man said like a daddy. "Bette was there, you remember? You just let me find out from her what I can t'night."

"Aaa-Aaa!" Joseph wailed, feeling shut in and frantic because he could not speak. He longed to say that he could read.

"Hush now. You rest. The Good Lord, He done a'ready knowed all 'bout it. Don't you worry 'bout nothin', 'cept gettin' you'self well." He put his hand lightly right atop Joseph's mouth and prayed in Gullah. "Dear Papa-God, hear this, you' most unworthy servant's prayer. Have mercy on this here young'un! They done a'ready got most everythin' from him. Please, dear Lord in heaven, don't let 'em have his life. Or even his words. Heal him by that same Holy Ghost power what did lift Jesus from the grave."

There was something so soothing about those words that Joseph felt himself almost instantly moving toward sleep. Every few moments he awakened and found Unc' Billy still there, praying without ceasing. By and by Joseph felt himself sensible enough to join those prayers for life, not death, and for speech instead of silence.

Brant sat at his own supper table, uninterested in food.

"You're worrying about Annie waiting for you at the party," Teddy said easily, raising a glass toward him in the long-stemmed candlelight of evening. Mayleda was the only one with them, for Brant had sent Eric off to eat in the kitchen and then go to bed.

"I am worried!" Brant responded with impatience. "The last place I want to be right now is here."

"She'll understand, and so will the colonel. In fact, they all will be pleased once they hear what actions you are taking."

"It might have been bearable had I sent her a message."

"My uncle will be grateful that you did not. Your daddy's boy is well known on both our properties. If any of our servants heard about his fate, it might cause an unwanted stir." He spooned red spicy rice from his plate. "I'll be sure to take your letter and gift directly to her, once I get home."

In truth, Brant worried about Joseph also. Every few hours Teddy was putting some kind of pill under his tongue to keep him alive. Out in the air that afternoon he had seemed to do all right, but back in the shed, which was still as hot as day, he languished dangerously. Despite Teddy's counsel, Brant had given Joseph water, but the boy had no power to drink from a cup. Of course they discussed none of this, not with Mayleda across from him, ignoring her supper too. Brant wished he had sent her off with Eric.

"I'd like to be excused," she said as a bold announcement.

Brant unhappily waved his permission, but Teddy chose to suspect her motives. "Don't you go near that toolshed. Your daddy's boy's not the docile slave you all once thought he was."

Mayleda did not even show the respect of a curtsey. She headed out to the hallway stairs, angry and silent, with her mouth sour and her head dropped down.

"She's quite a little weasel!" Teddy teased, as though admiring her because of that.

Without heart Brant took a sip of the coffee Bette had just served, while Teddy appeared to relish it.

"Cheer up! With Felicia Gilman at Ann's side, you would not have gotten even one word to her all evening had you been there. Those two girls have not stopped chattering since Felicia first walked through our door. I do pity William having to escort them both."

Brant pushed himself from the table. He had not considered until now that the northerner was there to accompany Annie to the dance and dinner. Jealousy seeped into his thinking, and he began to suspect Teddy's jollity all the more. Was he pleased that his cousin was with William instead of with Brant tonight? He thought about how Ann and he had recently pledged their ongoing faithfulness to each other, regardless of what others in their families thought. He hated his predicament all the more. He might lose Ann this night just because of Joseph's imbecilic desire to read.

"It's past time that we go look after Joseph," Theodore said. "After all, that's why we stayed here, isn't it, to make sure you don't lose him through the night?" He shook his head, misreading Brant's reluctance to move. "Don't worry. We won't start making him face your boots tonight."

Without Joseph there to help them with their coats, they put them on unaided. Teddy took one last sip of rich dark coffee, then led the way outside.

————

Through the darkness Hampton Gund saw the masters coming. He slipped to the toolshed and on a hunch knocked against the wall very lightly. Having not seen Billy Days for the last hour, he suspected the driver had risked going inside to be with Joseph, though the command had been for all to stay away.

Inside he heard the scrap and shuffle of movement, telling him his guess was right. The tender-hearted Delora driver would risk much to see that the boy did not suffer alone. Now Hampton put himself in jeopardy, too, by warning him.

Walking quickly out toward the gentlemen's swinging lamp, Hampton greeted them. Right behind him, cloaked in darkness, he caught a glimpse of Billy's rugged form scuttle by. Hampton pretended he saw nothing. Instead he made himself sound eager and casual. "I was gettin' worried an' just 'bout to have a look at him myself." That much was true.

The men carrying the light let Hampton turn around to lead the way. Hampton prayed that Billy would have enough time to make himself scarce. The lantern pushed back the stuffy shadows when Hampton entered the shed. He breathed a great but silent sigh of relief, for Billy Days was one smart Negro who had left no telltale signs of his having been there.

Joseph was awake. The light seemed to terrorize him, and rightly so, for it announced Teddy's presence. Rensler roughly poked and prodded Joseph's terrible-looking mouth. He painted it with the same kind of salve the grooms used on horses. The biting medicinal smell rose and mingled with the odors of linseed oil and iron left behind by the tools.

Soon Teddy was back out into the night, but Brant stayed now with Hampton, who looked as nervous as a boy stealing candy.

"I'm going to bring out my own brace of pistols, Mr. Gund. You put them on and guard my house and yard tonight. I don't want any bad incidences occurring because of Joseph."

"Yes, sir. I understand." In this kind of situation Hampton felt he had no more choice than a slave did. Thus he prepared himself for what might turn out to be a long, sleepless night.

———

Because of Mr. Gund, Billy had been able to escape his own brand of disaster. Silent as a fox, he climbed over the backyard fence behind the kitchen shanty. He stayed in the shadows along the driveway for a while, picking up as much as he could of what the three white men said. Finally he sneaked down to his cabin after seeing Hampton take up his post near the dark well house. From there the white man could have a clear view of the driveway, the mansion, and the path down into the street.

Bette was already in their featherbed when Billy came in. Undressing, he climbed in beside her and slipped his left arm under her head.

"How's he?" she asked, rightly guessing that he had been with the houseboy.

He kissed her gently to make her silent. "Honey, the Lord got him in

His hands." He felt her tears as they found strength and comfort in each other.

"Can he live?" she stammered after just a little while.

Billy lay back, feeling guilty for his own sweet comforts. "God knows," he said numbly, coming to accept how he loved Joseph almost like a second son. "It be shameful what the massa's done. I think I done got him to drink a little, but his poor mouth ain't much use right now. I'll try to find a way to take him more—"

"I took in a soaked dishrag when none wa' lookin'."

He lightly smiled a kiss upon her forehead. "Why, that just 'bout what I done. But you take care now, for Mass' Brant has made Mista Gund into his own personal arm'd guard. That lad's scaired on account of what he done to Joseph. So don't you go roamin' 'bout now. Or Mista Gund's likely to shoot somebody by mistake."

"You don't think the overseer sides with the massas? You don't think he's out there thinkin' ill of us all in our sleep?"

"I dunno. At some point Gund's whiteness is gwine come to him, I guess, an' mebbe he'll turn out like all the rest. Howsumever, recent as t'night he helped me slip away clear."

"This ain't the last of our troubles, but the first only," Bette cried. "You need to know. Joseph's sufferin' as he is 'cause of somethin' he were tryin' to tell me this mornin'."

Lightly but anxiously he turned her face to his.

"Somehow Joseph got word 'bout Mass' Brant wantin' to sell some of we—"

"Lord of mercy!"

"Yeah. Mostly babies hardly growed an' some old gray-heads—but also our Parris, since he don't want no daddy an' son to stay t'gether." Her weeping turned to quiet wailing.

"Bette! Gal! Hush! Ain't gwine do none of us no good if the massas come here a-runnin' on account of you' tears." Giving no account to his own splitting, aching heart, he said the same thing to her that he had said to comfort Joseph. "The Lord done knows all 'bout it a'ready."

However, this time the saying seemed to stick in his throat, almost like the blade that had been used on Joseph.

CHAPTER 4

ANN RENSLER ORDERED HER MAIDSERVANT Corinth to leave
the candles burning after she and Felicia came home from the disastrous
evening. Having no patience and on the verge of tears, she stood for the
tedious process of being undressed by the slave who had not been there
to witness her humiliation. Corinth was thick with child; it was uncomely
for an enceinte servant to wait in public. But in Ann's room Corinth unpinned her dress and petticoats and unlaced her corset—all of which took
longer than usual because of the forty-year-old slave's cumbrous condition. When Corinth reached for her nightgown, Ann stopped her. "After
all I've endured I will not sleep a wink. Give me my dressing robe. I cannot
go to bed."

Though well past two in the morning, Ann and Felicia still had received
no word on why both Brant and Teddy had failed to come to the party at
Retreat, the Renslers' hunting lodge. Flopping down on her bed, Ann took
up one of her pencil sketches of a new spring gown.

Felicia came into Ann's room wearing a simple, loose-fitting shift and a bed cap tied over her long auburn hair. Ann collected some of her favorite dress styles from their afternoon session and invited Felicia to sit beside her, at the same time setting the small china-head fashion doll from Felicia on her lap. The lifeless little form modeled permanent elegance, for Felicia had painstakingly dressed the doll in small samples of the gray-blue muslin and silk she had brought to Ann as birthday gifts.

Since Corinth could sew any dress, Ann had only to pick the design she wanted. Felicia's daddy had obtained some fashion magazines from Philadelphia, New York, and London—three ports regularly served by Gilman vessels. Anxious to forget the party, Ann opened her pencil box, saying, "I have a new idea."

Felicia shook her head in motherly fashion. "After the evening you've had, everything will come out looking like a *habit de deuil*."

"I don't know what that means!" Ann said, in no mood for going back to the French they had suffered through at Pemberton.

"It means 'mourning suit,' silly," Felicia told her bluntly but kindly. "Definitely you should talk about what's on your mind and heart. Then, perhaps, we both can rest."

"What is there to say?" Ann asked sharply. "At least my cousin could have come. As for the *other* gentleman? I do not even want to speak about *him*."

Felicia smiled her concern. "Poor Brant Callcott."

"How could they *both* let me down? Did you hear what was being whispered at the tables?"

"Yes, some of it, but I think you should be most concerned for those two men. They may still be missing—maybe due to some illness or accident."

Ann felt convicted by Felicia's worry but protested anyway. "No, if it were something awful, Daddy would have heard by now. He would've left his overnight guests at Retreat to come tell us."

"I suppose you're right." Felicia sighed.

"I fear that Theodore and Brant came up with some plan—"

"For what purpose?"

"I don't think ill of Brant, but Teddy can be harsh. I fear he may have persuaded Brant to do something foolish. Brant admires Teddy more than he should."

"What kind of plan could you fear?"

Fighting back tears, Ann said, "This was to be a very special party. Since

I was a young girl there's been talk in Brant's family and mine that he would propose to me on my nineteenth birthday."

Felicia's mouth opened slightly. "You were expecting this?"

"No, I wasn't," Ann said uncomfortably. "There have been changes since Brant's mother's death. I'm not sure why, but Brant's daddy doesn't favor a wedding anymore."

"But Brant still loves you, doesn't he?"

Ann fingered the fashion doll's tiny hand. "He says he does, and just this week I avowed my love to him. But how am I to know if his love is sincere? I mean, until Mrs. Callcott died, our future marriage was as sure as next year's planting because it was never about just the two of us. Since our properties lie side by side, our daddies long ago decided that merging plantations would make us some of the richest planters in all the eastern shore."

"Oh, Ann, that's sad." Felicia's words struck a nerve. "I mean, to feel that you would marry to strengthen business."

"Yes, there was a time when I resented it very much. But then . . . well, I fell in love. After that, the idea of marriage and bringing the lands together became simply wonderful. A fairy tale come true as soon as I was old enough to be the princess bride."

Felicia sat down with her. "But now you can't marry him because of his father's feelings? That must be terrible."

"What if Brant inwardly dislikes me? What if he was secretly glad to have a reason to excuse himself tonight because he knew some guests there would be waiting for the proposal?"

"Oh, Ann, I'm sure he likes you. I've read some of his precious letters to you while you were just a girl in school."

"That was years ago. It's possible that he's glad for his daddy's decision and eager to comply."

"Do you really not know his deepest, most private feelings toward you?"

"No."

"Then you need to ask him. It's that simple."

"It's not. It's an awful situation. Even in his latest letter, Mr. Callcott assured my daddy that marriage might *someday* be possible. What if, by then, I knew Brant did not love me? I would have to live with him anyway. Oh! I would rather not know."

"Surely your daddy would not make you marry just for land."

"He would if he could find a way around Brant's daddy's opposition, for my daddy has a close widower friend who keeps asking for my hand. This man has spent his life abroad. He's wealthy and influential but not a planter. My marriage to him would displace Teddy, since Pine Woods must go either to my cousin or to my future husband."

"You don't really think you would have to marry that man!"

"I will have to marry someone. But I would rather that it be Brant, for, truly, I do think I love him."

Felicia leaned back. "It's all so complicated! I still don't see how this relates to your fears about Teddy and Brant."

"Well . . ." Ann sniffed, trying to describe it as easily as possible. "I think Teddy realizes that he could never work with the Callcotts because of the way Brant's father insists that slave evangelism be considered just as important as slave production. And if Teddy believes he could not abide a merger, then he might try another plan."

"Such as . . ."

"Oh, it embarrasses me to say it. I'm afraid he will tell Daddy I should marry William, since it seems that our daddies will be partners."

Felicia seemed breathless. "Ann! You must pray to God to help you!"

"You believe God has interest even in matrimony?"

"Of course He does! There's nothing that affects a woman more than marriage. It has tremendous bearing on men, too, and on our offspring!"

Ann got up and walked to the window, peering through it to the wonderland of silver shadows outside. "In the South we are taught to love family *and* land. As women, we are taught that our menfolk are always right—husbands, daddies, brothers, or cousins—whether we privately esteem them or not. Our men are our protectors—whether or not we want it that way." She turned to Felicia. "My daddy will decide who I marry. And I must honor his choice, for he will say that he is doing it for my good. That's how the world works here."

"What makes a woman any different from a man in choosing the things that will change life most? If you aren't free to make your own decisions, then you're just like the slaves."

Ann nodded glumly. "So others have said."

"Oh, Ann, it would be so unjust to have you marry against your will, especially when there's already someone who loves you."

"I'm not in the mood for joking."

"I am not joking. If Teddy was trying to work his plan, then maybe it actually will work in your favor."

"I don't understand!"

Felicia touched her robe. "William thinks he loves you."

"William is as much a brother to me as he is to you because of all the time we spent together in Boston."

"That doesn't mean he can't think the sun rises and sets because of you. When our father suggested starting a business down here, William was reluctant over every aspect save one, and that was being brought near you again."

Ann spoke into her folded hands. "I can't believe it, but it is thrilling to think somebody likes me—just because of who I am."

Her friend seemed cautious. "Oh, please, Ann, don't say a word to him about this. He'd be so angry with me that I'd probably have to swim back home. I've betrayed his secret, but only because I love the two of you so much. He's convinced your father would not think him a worthy suitor because he's from New England."

"But he'll be part owner and manager in my daddy's business."

"Yes."

Ann's mind was racing. "Oh, if only Theodore were not such a rogue, I believe he could be interested in you. Oh my! Wouldn't that be something! Best friends! And then nearly sisters-in-law."

Instantly she realized how much she had hurt Felicia. She opened her mouth to give apology, but the girl shrugged it off.

"It's all right, Annie. I'm at ease with the idea of not being in love. In fact, I think God may be directing me to teach. Even in the North, *married* women need not apply for that profession."

"So you think God is more than just romantic? That He can also whisper into your ear about some vocational calling?"

"Why shouldn't He do that? Scripture affirms that He created us to do good works, which He's already planned. The Proverbs say, 'In all thy ways acknowledge him, and he shall direct thy paths.'"

"You'd get along famously with Brant's daddy," Ann mused, feeling almost sad because of Felicia's deeply religious convictions. She had always held them, Ann knew, but never had she so blatantly discussed them as she was doing now.

"I think God will hold us accountable for right living in accordance with His Word. So in order for us to be accountable, He must give us clear direction, or how will we know what to obey? Doesn't that make perfect sense?"

Ann didn't need to answer, for just then Corinth, who had been dozing on her stool in the corner, awakened. The slave stretched her swollen ankles exposed beneath the hem of her striped skirt.

"Is she all right?" Felicia fretted, peering at her.

"If she's not, it's her own doing. My daddy never expected her to get herself in this way. When he first detected it, he locked her in the attic for two days, hoping the heat would rid her of it. Then he even sent her down along the river with a dollar gold-piece to meet the gypsies, for they have potions that can be used, you know—"

Horrified, Felicia stopped her. "She's carrying a *child*."

"No. An *issue* Daddy never wanted. Her job is to work in this house. Look what it's cost us already. Everywhere I go now is without Negro help. Daddy would have her sold, but we can't replace her readily. She sews like a dream and can iron the frailest lace. While I was at Pemberton she redid this whole room, down to the crocheted rosebuds up there on the canopy."

Corinth's hands went around her big belly. With force she leaned forward. "Oh, Missy. I think . . . my time . . . has come."

Felicia shrieked. "You mean to be delivered? Ann! We're here alone. All the men are still at the lodge. What are we to do?"

Ann grabbed Corinth's apron, rudely coaxing her to her feet. "You get yourself out of here!"

"You can't mean that! Look at her! She can't move!"

"From the start she's known this has been wrong. Now she'll not disgrace the house. . . ."

Corinth breathed through her teeth, then she rose and started walking. Ann followed nervously, wishing the wench could be pushed faster or carried outside. She had no idea how long the process of birthing might take. Perhaps a tiny new Negro would drop out onto the floor any moment. She had to hurry Corinth along! Getting her as far as the stairs, Ann was foiled when Corinth doubled over. The servant stood there stooping and panting like an old man who'd just raced a mile.

"We have to help her," Felicia cried, stepping down in front of her to guard Corinth on the stairs. When the attack in her belly was over, the slave moved again, rapidly this time, as though she, too, wanted to be out of the house. Felicia followed her, not hesitating to use the slaves' door.

Ann sighed with relief and came after them. At least the house was cleared. Then she had an incredible thought. Since Maum Jane and the other servants had not stirred, and since their daddies were away, she said to Felicia, "Let's go watch how she's delivered."

Felicia turned as red as an apple in the back porch's light. "We're virgins! That's no business of ours!"

"Oh, I've always wanted to see something being born, but Daddy has always kept me away, even from his broodmares and ewes."

"Where will she go? Where is her husband?" Felicia said, bursting with odd questions.

"Slaves have no husbands, Felicia. They do not marry."

"Then the child's illegitimate."

"It's not a child. Slaves are bred. To watch a birthing would be no different than watching your cat bring forth kittens."

"No! It's wrong. I know it! She's not an animal."

"Oh, come on! Please! I don't have the nerve to go down alone, but Corinth will never have this happen again, so this is my only chance to see. . . ." Ann took Felicia's hand and, not letting go, raced down the porch steps. Her friend stumbled after her.

Corinth's outcries drew them to one of the slavequarter's shabby cottages. Some of her daddy's field hands had awakened and were coming out of their shanties in their ragged clothes, scratching their lousy heads. Spindly females also emerged, wrapped in drab cloth the color of their skin. But close to the cottage door was a short, mixed-race male, his small face trimmed by graying curls that grew both from his head and his chin. In stature and slimness of body, he was like a child.

"Oh, don't let him look in on her!" Felicia pleaded the moment someone's torchlight danced onto his curious countenance.

But they saw that the females gave him a place of prominence. Ann was totally unused to being among the workers in this dirty place that smelled of scorched rice and charcoal. Her daddy's slaves were wary of her also, so much so that they left half the doorway empty just to keep their distance from her. Ann took the space and looked inside where Corinth was lying, twisted in pain, on the bare dirt floor. Gray-headed females gathered around her, soothing her with their strange language and gestures that Ann judged to be superstitious and primeval.

"She's acting as though she's in pure agony," Ann said, pushing Felicia to stand with her. "It's the easiest thing on earth for them to breed and reproduce."

"She is not pretending!" Felicia groaned. "Whatever you've been told is wrong! She's a *woman* giving birth. My mother's gone so far as to tell me it's difficult. But I never imagined—oh!"

Ann folded her arm around her anxious friend. "A white woman certainly doesn't do it like this," she said to comfort her, pulling her to the smoky outside wall.

The drama continued and soon it was Felicia, not Ann, who wanted to see it through to its end. She seemed to be captured by the scene playing out before them.

Ann was bored and chilled. "Let's go," she urged after the first touch of red dawn reached the sky. But Felicia would not move. Suddenly they were discovered by Maum Jane, who came rushing down with torn rags and a bucket of water. The maum's scowl toward them was darker than her penny-colored skin. "What you two missies doin' down here? If you' daddy knew, he'd use the cowhide on you both."

She rushed inside the shanty, and soon those who kept vigil at the door started jumping and shouting, "Glory! Yes now! The chile's a-comin'!"

It amazed Ann how quickly Felicia found the courage to stand on tip-toe and look through the dark slit that served as the shanty's only window.

"Oh yes!" Her friend marveled. "One of the old women has her hands under the babe's head. Oh yes! See for yourself!"

Instead of using the window, Ann looked through the door. That one male slave was still standing there, uncomely with his grimy wool cap off his head and drooped between his dirty hands. "That be Corinth in there!" he dared to say, as though Ann did not know it. He was breathless and he spoke the rough Gullah, which Ann barely understood. "Poor, poor gal!" His small face crumpled, though his eyes and mouth showed remnants of smiling. "She' a'most done, ainty?"

"Don't be standin' out there, Ebo!" It was Maum Jane who appeared from the dark to call him in. "You got you'self a boy!"

"Oh, the gods be praised!" His voice was so loud it squeezed tears from his face. Other bucks came out from the shanties that had protected them in the night. With blazing pine-splint torches they met the one called Ebo to slap his shoulders, clap his hand, or throw an unwashed arm around his neck.

"Don't you be scaired to come on in here now, brother!" Maum Jane urged again with even more joy, for now the offspring was crying almost in rhythm with its daddy's happy dancing. All seemed to forget that Ann and Felicia were still there. The pine torches, hot and bright, seemed to hasten the dawn.

When Ebo emerged into their false daylight, he had the small wailing issue wrapped in a piece of African quilting, alive with all the colors and patterns Ann's daddy forbade them to have, as they were sure signs of heathen spirits. "Corinth fine. Just fine!" the slave boasted. "An' lookee here—a boy-child! Ooooo, if they be gods up in the heavens they be good to me, for see this done happen 'tween two old persons what ain't got a day of spring left inside they bones."

"It's too bad they don't know the real Lord," Felicia whispered. "You can see how reverent and in awe they are." Suddenly Ann's mild friend walked right in among the Africans. To Ann's amazement the primitive crowd accepted her.

"Your child is beautiful!" Felicia exclaimed with much sincerity. "Oh, I never watched a baby being born, but it's God you must praise. He's the Lord of heaven and the Father of Jesus Christ, our Savior."

The slaves hardly knew what to make of her. Some drew back, and some looked so threatening that Ann tried to reach in to pull her from the dangers. But Ebo, whom Ann now recognized as one who worked around their horses, must have recognized Felicia as one of their northern visitors. Showing a great command of the situation, he actually grinned right into Felicia's pale face. Then he laid his bundle in her arms. "May my boy-child find favor with you' God! An' may somebody like you, young missy, some-day bless him with just a little bit o' happiness 'n peace."

"I can't believe you'll let me hold him!" Felicia said.

"I can't believe you're here!" The thunderous voice that pulled all eyes to itself belonged to Ann's white-haired father. Ann spun away from the Africans, terrified of her daddy who quickly commanded her to march up to the house. He was flanked by two Negroes carrying dead raccoons by their tails, evidence that at least some of the gentlemen from her party had spent the night gunning.

She squealed a quick apology as her daddy grabbed her elbows. "We just came down 'cause Corinth had her baby!" Ann covered her mouth, aware that she had unconsciously been swayed to use Felicia's word.

"This is no diversion for young ladies!"

"Yes, Papa! I know!"

"Get yourselves to the house!"

"Yes! Yes! We will!"

Then Ann caught sight of William, who had been out on the hunt. Embarrassed by her slovenly appearance, she pulled her hands to her bosom and hastened up the path, fully expecting Felicia to come right after her. When she didn't, Ann turned around. Her father had the slaves' issue in his hands. It had been stripped of its native bunting. Torchfire showed off its tiny flailing limbs. Her daddy held it high by its head and buttocks like a butchered, suckling pig. Ebo, the little Negro sire, still had his cap in his hands, but he was right beside his master.

Ann couldn't see the darkie's face, but she heard his voice, higher and with a fool's edge to it that had not been evident before. "Yesindeedy! He be strong an' lively as they come!"

"Don't try to persuade me to change my mind! He's going on the auction table the moment he can survive the trip to town."

"Sah! I not askin' for my own sake, but yours!" Ebo reasoned. "He grow up an' take my place, a hund'edfold an' more!"

Ann's daddy laughed mockingly. "And be the next fine talker like the piteous buck that planted him in Corinth's womb!"

Felicia covered her ears but stayed beside the Negroes like their personal crusader. "Oh, Colonel Rensler, please have mercy! The mother and father of this baby love their child."

"For the traders I will call him Zeus," Ann's father announced, ignoring Felicia's pleas but speaking to her face.

"Zeus?" the natural daddy murmured. His head went down.

"Don't trouble yourself, Ebo! The issue's destiny is the auction house, and it need not concern you anymore."

"No! Please!" Felicia joined the cries of the little slave man who fell to his knees.

The man begged. "I not gwine be useful to you fo'ever, sah! Sell me now, but let the child with he mama."

"I should sell you all—and separately!" Ann's daddy fumed.

"Oh, Massa! I gwine do whatsumever I can to bring him up obeyin' you if'n you just let us have some seasons with him, since the missy here's Lord God Jesus' done been so good to us all."

Instantly Ann's father tossed the Negro baby into the arms of waiting slaves. Taking his leather riding crop he struck Ebo again and again. "You won't disgrace God Almighty by uttering His name."

Ebo's swollen, half-eyed glance went right beyond Felicia's terrified face. "Don't blame the young mistress, sah. Just somethin' I remembered t'day from way back in my boyhood. Somethin' from my first marse in Virginny."

"I declare, nigger tongues aren't fit to speak God's name!"

Ann came down and pulled hard at Felicia's hand. "Come on," she wailed as her friend had tears streaming down her face. "We need to obey my daddy and be back inside the house."

Felicia would not sleep. After a bright dawn the day turned gray, and all Ann wanted was to be back in bed. While the wind whistled eerily around the edges of the windows and thunder rumbled the foundations of the house, her friend continued to pace the floor.

"Get some rest," Ann begged wearily. "Nothing's going to change because of your fretting."

"I just can't stand it! How could your father do such a thing?"

"Daddy wants strong ones. Not more like Ebo."

"But your Negroes must be people even as our Irish are back home!" Felicia agonized aloud. "They speak. They cry. They praise. They mourn. *They have children!* What more proof is needed? But you buy them, breed them, and sell them!"

"Our system of labor is every bit as humane as yours," Ann said defensively, explaining things exactly as they had been explained to her. "We take care of the sick and the elderly, while in Boston and New York poor white children and seniors starve or are abandoned if they can't make their own way. That's why darkies are not unhappy living as they do."

"How can you think them happy after what we saw?"

"Don't blame me, Felicia. I have nothing to do with it. As I told you before. That was *my* first time in the street."

"Oh, it's so cruel. That man Ebo wants his child, and your father beat him even for speaking Jesus' name."

Ann moved under her covers. "My daddy doesn't think they are worthy of prayers. And you could never trust Negroes not to pray against us. If Daddy let Ebo have his way even once, that would set many others clamoring for the same kind of freedom."

"Then maybe that's a sure sign they should be free!"

"Felicia, you don't know what you're saying. Think what you have seen down here. Darkies outnumber us three or four to one. And they're as strong as mules. If our guards were ever lifted, they'd all go on a rampage till not one of us was living. Something like that happened in Virginia. Rioting Negroes! Killing, raping . . . murdering even innocent children." She felt her body begin to tremble. "Oh! Didn't Ebo say *he* was from Virginia?"

Felicia's eyes were compassion-filled. "You dwell in fear!"

Ann felt herself speaking in hushed tones. "Even in Charleston there have been attempted uprisings. And sometimes you'll hear of something awful, though my Daddy makes it a rule never to speak about it in my hearing. But I know that field workers have murdered their overseers and run off. And maids have tried to poison their mistresses. And that does make me think of Corinth. After what happened today, I can honestly say I don't want her back."

Her friend sat on the bed. "How can you live this way?"

"I take courage and comfort in the fact that Teddy and Daddy have strong overseers. I don't normally fear because I know these men are in charge. Besides, there's a group called the parish patrol that travels around day and night."

The door latch rattled, sending Felicia to hug Ann in her bed. "Who's trying to get in?"

"*Ohhhhhhhh, daughters of gossip . . .*"

Felicia's eyes swelled, but Ann started laughing. "It's just Teddy!" She crawled out of bed and let him in while Felicia covered herself with the quilt. "Where have you been!" she demanded, seeing that he was dressed to ride on this dreary day.

"I just came back from Delora about an hour ago. And I'm going back again." He handed her a letter and a slim box tied up with ribbons. "Brant's having trouble with one of his slaves, and he needs me, as he did yesterday and last night."

"That's why you both missed my party?"

"It is. I've had a chance to explain it all to Uncle. But I thought you'd want to know that Brant's taking a strong stand with one of the Callcotts' most loathsome darkies. It's something that needs to be done while his daddy's away."

Ann's eyes went to the present and to the letter sealed with wax. She wanted to complain, but Teddy spoke first.

"I assured Brant a thousand times that you would be understanding. He has to take care of his business. There was no choice about last night."

She nodding, remembering that Felicia had already counseled her to be concerned for Brant's sake and not just her own. "Is Brant's family all right?"

Teddy showed her one of his tight-jawed smiles. "It's all in the letter—love!"

She felt herself blush, and he teased her. "You're turning red, and you haven't even laid eyes on what he's said."

She pretended to be furious. "Did you break the seal?"

"I don't need to read your mail to know Brant's heart, for I've just returned from spending hours with him."

She held Brant's small package to her heart. "Thank you, Teddy, for coming here to see me. And for explaining."

"The slave needs medical attention, so I'm going back. But I did ride over here before the storm sets in to change my clothes and give you that. Brant's almost out of his mind, fearing what you think of him."

She dared to speak her heart. "Tell him that I love him."

"If it stops raining later, why don't you come by and tell him yourself? William could escort you and Felicia."

"Yes! We can do that if the weather clears."

After she had closed the door, she went back to the bed. Felicia let her be alone while she poured over Brant's note for a long time. It was filled with sweet flowery allusions to springtime and love. Ann then opened the box and showed Felicia the beautiful set of pearls. "These were his mother's," she explained. "Mr. Callcott gave them to the future Mrs. Callcott the day she turned nineteen."

Felicia squeezed her hand and helped her to put them on over her robe. "There!" she said. "They're lovely. I'm happy for you, Annie, but sad for my brother."

Ann fingered the necklace. "You said your God has His plans."

"I know He does."

"Then please pray for me that the senior Mr. Callcott will find it in his heart to accept me as Brant's wife."

CHAPTER 5

THE SOUND OF THE SLAVE DRIVER'S horn often teased Rosa in gentle ways. While she lay on her bare sleeping board, pegged between the shanty's chimney and its corner of chinked logs, those quavering notes sometimes came through the window laths like the easy laughter of a husband she loved but never had. More often they caressed her in sleepy moments of defenselessness like giggling kisses from Kulo, her little girl-child with the angel cheeks. No matter what the deception, those distant blasts from Billy's conch shell made her last breath of night ecstasy, but her first breath of morning raw despair.

Today it was more haunting memories of her precious three-year-old child—conceived in terror, clung to in love, and lost to disease—that pushed her out of bed toward the reality of day.

On calloused feet Rosa took the half step needed to reach her one piece of clothing, a coarse, walnut-shucks-dyed dress. It hung from a peg on the slabwood wall that separated her tiny corner from the rest of the one-room cabin where old Negozi and Abiel—her "husband-in-the-sight-of-God-Al-mighty"—as well as their numerous children and grandchildren slept on the floor like coons holed up in a stump.

As Rosa pulled the sweat-and-dust-laden garment down around her lean, light brown body, she glimpsed the aging Negozi in the doorless en-tryway of her tight corner of privacy. The only light was that of the low fire in the hearth, but it was enough to show Rosa the worry sealed up behind the slave woman's lips. They traded silent glances while the aunty twisted her thin arms like courting snakes to tie up her sparse gray hair under a dull red cloth.

At the same moment, Rosa started braiding her own thick black tresses.

"Missy, this ain't the time to be dreamin' or preenin'," Negozi told her, the tension finally spilling into talk. "Somethin' happen at the big house yesterday 'tween the massa's son an' his daddy's manservant. The poor young waitin' boy might be a-dyin'. That be all we know. Still 'n yet, it be causin' a stir to come our way big as the storm what's blowin' in over we heads t'day. Now you hurry an' you watch you'self with all that mopin' you sometimes like to do, for Abiel's been up an' back from the driver's house a'ready. They says even Mista Gund has pistols, like they was 'xpec-tin' trouble to pop like rabbits."

Rosa responded only by widening her eyes. The old field hand was known to be a worrier and a meddler, though there was not one Delora slave Rosa loved or trusted more.

"I mean it, gal!" Negozi said while nodding. "Look alive t'day an' don't give them no cause to be suspectin' you of trouble."

Rosa did hurry then to cover her hair in a turban just the color of Ne-gozi's. At the same time, she watched the old African, thin and gnarled as a little willow tree, move haglike toward the outer door, which stood open to the rain. Surprisingly, the house was already emptied of everyone else, another sign of the woman's tension. Rosa followed her but then stopped to look at the low fire being left unattended in the great black hearth.

More than words, these cooling embers spoke volumes of the aunty's deep distraction, for Negozi was from that remnant of workers who could remember being plucked out of Africa and heeled in again on Carolinian shores. Like those other *Saltwaters*—the name given to these unwilling transplants—Negozi lived as much as possible by her former ways. And that included believing it was safer to shed blood than to let the fire in one's hearth go out.

Though spiritual mysteries from Africa meant nothing to Rosa, she took time to pay tribute to Negozi's fire because she loved the woman. Kneeling down under the monstrous chimney's gaping throat she put in new lengths of hardwood from the stack piled on the hard sand floor. She waited until yellow flames caught and grinned against the bark. Then she picked up her rough shirt and raced outside, down the three rickety porch steps into cold rain without having any protection at all.

To her shock Hampton Gund, Delora's overseer, was there to meet her. As an instant precaution she curtsied, dipping one knee toward the short, slouch-hatted man with a belly that hung over his indigo blue pants like a sack of cornmeal. Usually the white overseer and the black driver Billy Days, who worked directly under him, were content to wait for the people to come up to the gatherin' place—that worn-out patch of ground at the top of the street near to both their houses. But Negozi had been right. Today was different.

"You best get those black feet movin'!" Mr. Gund said, speaking harsh words that for once matched his looks. Unless his character was known, anybody, slave or free, could easily judge him to be one of those molesting tyrants. He had a perpetually sunburnt neck and a pinkish bulbous nose, common to that kind of poor white stock that was often raised just one step above slavery in order to work with bondsmen and command them. When she hurried past him, she noticed that Negozi had been right about another thing too. Under his undone vest she saw the matching handguns.

"Get!" He shooed her, and she went flying up the street.

Billy Days suffered mightily from his sad and sleepless night. Close to dawn he had tried to sneak in to see Joseph in the toolshed, but Gund, still awake and watching, had quietly turned him away after admitting that he had already been in to give the boy water on a cloth, since his mouth was still too unhealthy to use a dipper or cup.

Though his own body was in the right place to begin a new day, Billy's mind stayed on all that he had seen and heard and felt. He had been sworn to secrecy by the massa's son concerning how Joseph looked when he carried him downstairs. But in the street those sealed lips of his hardly meant a thing, for three to six half-grown, half-hand yard boys had seen Joseph draped limply over his arms. Lingering at the fence they had watched every move, and then having their eyes and their imaginations filled, they all scattered like chickens before the foxes, Massas Brant and Teddy, could catch them.

In truth Billy had talked to no one except Bette, who told him every-thing she knew while they lay in each other's arms. What stuck in his mind the sharpest was that his own Parris was marked as one to be sent away. Whenever he thought on that, his heart broiled. After serving two Callcott generations, after all his sweat and the work he had done so well, was this third one about to rise up to betray him? It was hard not to think that what had happened to Joseph was a sign of things to come. The boy had been whole and hearty yesterday; now he was mute and half out of his mind with pain.

Billy picked up a short stick at his feet and moved off a little ways from the workers standing bedraggled in the rain. Gund was still down the street checking for stragglers because they expected that members of the parish patrol might descend on them today to judge their competence in handling the slaves. Mista Gund was not used to being anybody's adversary. In fact, before this morning Billy had never seen him with a whip or a firearm. Now he had both close by.

Whether against beatings or sale, South Carolina slaves were defense-less. They might try running off only to come to other plantations or to snakes and alligators that would just as soon eat them as look at them. They might try to defend themselves, or even their wife or child, and then they could be shot or lynched for striking out at white men.

Mired by such thoughts, Billy tossed the stick so that one of the quart-er's mange-scarred hounds could chase it down. The thin, lolling-tongued animal pulled up short when the piece of wood accidentally went too far and clattered against the white picket fence guarding Gund's garden and blue-painted cottage. Gund's wife, Dell, and their two young daughters looked out at him through the only window on the street that had glass panes. The white woman pushed up the window sash.

"You watch what you doin'!" she commanded in Gullah. "Don't you send no fice dogs in y'ere to wreck my peas!"

The Gunds were folk used to living side by side with colored neighbors, so the hatefulness in the white woman's voice took him by surprise. De-spite the rain, Billy pulled off his woven wide-brimmed hat and dragged his toe backward through the sticky sand. "Missus Gund, Miss Sarah, Miss Lillian, I didn't mean no harm."

"Well, from y'ere on out, you try harder to keep away from us all. An' tell you' Bette she can start gettin' the massas' eggs someplace else besides our hens."

Billy looked through the rain. Before yesterday there had been no problem with him going up into Gund's porch or even taking either one of his daughters up onto his lap.

"Yes, ma'am," Billy said, trying to restore some of the peace that had been lost because of how Brant had cut the boy. Everywhere there was fear of the slaves striking back because of it. *Suspicion surely is a strong miasma*, Billy concluded as he turned away from the only painted house in the double row of shanties. *And the most terrible disease it spreads is hate*.

From the corner of his eye he could see Gund coming. The man was half defensive and half apologetic. "Dell's nervous over all that's happened, so for the time bein', Billy, you just keep you' distance from my family."

"Yessah." *So*, Billy thought with sadness, *this is the start of a brand-new tribulation. As with the Israelite slaves of old, it is going from bad to worse. First was just the bondage, but now those over us are concocting reasons to hate us as well.*

Gund knew him well and probably nearly read his mind. "Hey, don't take it personal. I have to tell my own to be careful after what the yard boys called to them. It's just all foolishness, but some dared say there would be those who are ready to strike back."

Don't take it personal, Billy thought. Joseph was cut. His only boy might be sold. *But just don't take it personal*. "Sure, boss," he mumbled. There were so many things even the most well-meaning white man like Hampton Gund could not know.

"We best get down there." Gund pointed the way to the gathered group of people. "Have Parris start with prayer."

Hampton Gund watched Billy join the dark, restless cluster numbering more than eighty who stood under the clouds pouring water on their woolly heads. Even in his thick cape Hampton felt miserable, so he was sorry for the workers. Despite the day he saw wisdom in sending them out. The thunder was over, and the winds might soon be dying. If the parish patrol wanted to do any unannounced inspections because of Joseph, Hampton decided he would rather have the officers find the people working.

With somebody as powerful and domineering as Theodore Rensler steering at the helm, it would take only one incident, no matter how small, to open the door for parish control. Knowing how things worked in St. Andrew's Parish, there was probably enough testimony circulating among those with power to have Joseph strung up in the nearest hanging tree. It all made him start to hate his life again, which he had pretty much stopped doing during Delora's last peaceful years.

He wiped his face of distress as well as rainwater and put his attention on Parris. The boy had come up through the crowd and was standing on the old weathered block that had been used as the base for a whipping post only by Delora's first master, Abram's father. Billy Days' offspring, twenty-four or twenty-five years of age, was like a tree towering in the berry patch. No prime slave Hampton had ever laid eyes on was physically finer.

Stocky like Billy but much taller, Parris had thick arms that bulged from the sleeveless, undyed shirt he wore. Having an arrow-straight spine and well-formed head and shoulders, he rose above every other buck his age. For decoration Parris always wore a flat, fan-shaped shell on a leather thong around his neck. It reminded Hampton of some of the metal charms he had seen on Ashanti warriors who had been transported on the slave-traders' vessels that he had seen as a boy.

Of all the master's field-slave converts, no one was a better example than Parris. Today, however, Hampton was nervous even when this faithful boy claimed his usual spot for leading worship. Tension seemed to continue to buoy all the slaves.

Of the few masters who were dedicated to evangelizing their Negroes, Mr. Abram Callcott was pretty much alone in his idea of grooming one African—like Parris—to teach the Gospel to others. Having had his unique status of being called Delora's "slave-preacher" for almost three years, Parris performed his duty with great dignity and with a cadence in his speech that sounded nearly like hymn singing. It was almost as though he carried the breath and life of some ancient ruling clan within his bones.

Parris raised both his hands and his voice in the rain. "Let us pray!"

Because of his responsibilities and his worries about this particular morning, Hampton did not drop his head while others bowed. In the next few moments he saw something he had never noticed before. Rosa, Delora's only brown woman, was being eyed by Parris even as he prayed. Having never made any profession of faith, Rosa had her eyes open. Hampton took in that their connected gazing lasted only a second. Then the woman put her head low. Parris continued, never falling out of rhythm as he spoke words that sounded as compelling as a song. "The Lord be in His holy place! Let all the earth keep silent 'fore Him."

Hampton wondered what the gal was feeling, for he knew her past. She was terrified of men.

"Blessed are you, Jesus!"

All of Parris's words had been taught to him as a young child by Master and Mistress Callcott. From what Hampton knew, Parris could speak at least an hour's worth of English common prayers by rote. This is what he drew from every morning, as the Spirit led. " '. . . we commend to thy fatherly good all those who are anyways afflicted, that it may please thee to comfort an' relieve them, giving them patience in they trials an' a happy issue out of all they afflictions. An' this we beg for Jesus' sake.' "

"AMEN!" the people said.

Now Hampton wondered what Parris had heard about Joseph through the yard boys or even through his daddy, though the driver had been warned not to talk. Any ordinary morning, Parris would not have recited a prayer for the sick.

These devotions, which were required by Master Abram, finished in great haste as the wind whipped up again. Billy came over.

"Boss, we really gwine send them over to the fields?"

Hampton looked at the unstable sky, feeling inside that this was going to be a most miserable day, and not just because of awful weather. "Let's load the flatboats," he decided. "If it don't clear in an hour, we'll take another look at what to do."

He was last on the second boat that was pushed across the foggy, coffee-colored water by young black lads wearing only white billowing shirts. As much as any bondsman could today, Hampton dreaded the hours still to come.

———————

As usual Rosa stayed close to Negozi and to Abiel, who was a field-worn, bowed-legged miniature of all the other male workers, most of whom were only half his age. The old man had quiet stamina, but Rosa never feared him, for over the months and years he had never spoken a crude word to her or gazed at her in any way that was not sympathetic and fatherly. She could not say the same for the rest of the males in Negozi's clan. On normal workdays there were old men and young who looked and sounded too much like those slaves who had caused her months of living damnation four years ago when she was only sixteen.

Because Negozi and Abiel had been with her from the moment of her rescue, Rosa perceived the elderly couple to be almost like adopted family. Though she did not feel sisterly toward any of their daughters, Rosa tried to be patient with their family, for they had truly helped her. As with so many other slaves, Rosa saw in them a pathetic dullness of mind, body, and spirit that certainly came from knowing only the life of toiling for somebody else's satisfaction and gain. When Rosa worked with women she stayed with Negozi. If she found herself in that terrible position of having to be assigned to work with men, she hid in Abiel's small shadow and spoke only through her aged "uncle," who accepted her silence and defended it before others who often came up to urge her to say something herself.

On this terrible morning Rosa stayed pressed between both of them while they raked nearly shoulder to shoulder on the bank, clearing one of the flooded rice fields of floating debris. When they had worked about an hour, Parris sauntered up. Often he had more freedom than the rest, since part of his duty was to raise a song or word that could keep them all doing their best.

"You know I gwine be a-preachin' to *white folk* this comin' Sunday," he whispered close behind her. "I be standin' right there in the pulpit of the new Our Savior's Chapel. An' for onc't, gal, you won't have no choice but to hear me."

She had no choice about hearing him now, but she just went on with her raking. The mud sucked her feet as she moved slowly.

"I gwine keep them all wide awake an' mebbe even make a few of them tremble," he boasted, following her step for step.

Then Rosa did look at him but only to show her disgust for his willingness to put on a show for anyone, including the masters who controlled their every hour. Though her own apparent haughtiness might have wounded him, he chuckled as though undaunted. He enlarged his audience to include Negozi, Abiel, and some of their married daughters. "You all be my witnesses now. If it takes till the day I die an' half the angels in heaven to help me, I gwine find some way to make this gal talk—an' smile."

The other women were approving, but Negozi stayed protective. "Save you' voice an' use it to break somebody else's heart."

"Aw, Aunty!" he boldly teased. "At least let her speak my rejection for herself." Even with his words there seemed to be no break in his grinning. "Rosa. I think I hear them angels now!"

"I says don't push her!" Negozi was only as small as an insect beside him, but her warning had the sting of a bee. "She don't think of herself as one of us. An' every man she ever knowed done brought her only harm. So just let her go!"

Parris kicked a muddy clod away. "Some days I don't think of myself as just another nothin' nigger! Someday she might be real glad I kept on with my head high an' my heart to her!"

Rosa could not wait for him to move away. Negozi, who still was with her, hobbled close, speaking to her now. "He don't mean no harm, honey. You know there ain't a man here what wants to see you hurt. And that's for true."

Looking out to the rice-field pool prickled by rain, Rosa wanted to believe that was true. Yet the scars of her past seemed as tight and as close as her own flesh, and for as long as it felt that way, she knew it would be impossible to find either trust or love. She had grown up a privileged, only child of free brown Haitian parents. They owned a large rice plantation on the Waccamaw River, which had been started by her daddy's daddy after he had escaped slave revolts on his island to come to America, bringing his own black male workers with him. Never in her most horrific dreams could she have imagined living out the same existence her family had once imposed on their chattels.

But four years ago her parents had been brutally murdered, maybe by white neighbors, though Rosa never knew for sure. Their lovely house had been razed, and in the chaos her daddy's slaves had captured her and penned her with them so that she would be sold as a "pretty copper wench" to the traders. The black Haitians, of course, got no monetary rewards for their action, only revenge toward her family for abusing them. Revenge that had turned every night of her next five months into living hell as she continued to be driven with twenty men on their way to be sold in Charleston's auction houses.

A gush of wind almost sent her into the rice-field water. At the same moment Billy Days blew his horn, calling them from their work. Shivering, Rosa joined Negozi's family for breakfast. One of Negozi's daughters had carried out the family's iron kettle, filled with rice and boiled over the shanty's fire in the predawn hours. Under the greasy wooden lid, the rice was hot and soft and steaming at its center, crisp and brown around its edges.

Everyone reached in and ate with their hands, all keeping watch on Overseer Gund. He alone could decide whether they would stay out in the rain or be sent inside the barns to do work, such as shucking last year's corn. Rosa took it as an indication of the white man's changing mood that he would let his employer's valued workers be exposed to the elements. Perhaps he was trying to punish them all in some way for the one house-servant's actions. Or perhaps the overseer feared what so many individuals of color might do if they were given idle time.

Their hopefulness at being released did not go unnoticed by him. Gund spoke directly to Negozi's little group. "It's gwine clear, I think, soon as this blows over." He seemed nearly apologetic and even went so far as to do some explaining, which was uncharacteristic of white bosses. "Any of the patrollers come t'day, I'd rather they found you all out hard at work."

Had Master Abram not been away, they might have been warm and dry right now. She took what little heat she could from the rice in her hand before it, too, grew soggy and cold. Before she could dip her fingers into the kettle again, a reckless horseman on an ink-black mount burst from the distant forest. He rode at a gallop along the sandy path that headed for the river. Billy Days saw the rider, too, and pulled close to Mr. Gund. Because the overseer was standing near the family, Rosa clearly heard the two men's conversation.

"Ain't that Mass' Theodore Rensler a-comin' this way?" Billy said.

Rosa stayed in her crouched position by the cooking pot. She kept her head low as she heard the horse draw near.

Overseer Gund called out. "Mornin', sah! What has you comin' to Delora this way?"

"There's a tree down on the road," the stranger answered. "I'd like to cross over on one of your flatboats."

"Yesindeedy, Mista Rensler," Overseer Gund said in a carefree manner. "There's boys down there. Just tell 'em what you want."

But the visiting planter stayed. Even with her grounded vision Rosa could see his wet boots trampling the weeds after he had chosen to dismount. She began to shiver, though at first there was no earthly explanation for it other than the rain. Then this white man walked to her. After a few strides he touched her head, which she now bent completely to her chest in agony.

"Say, Hampton!"

Rosa could feel the water dripping from the stranger's cloak.

"I didn't know you had a brass-ankled gal in your gang."

Gund sounded tense. "She just a field hand, Mista Rensler."

The man changed his position, and now Rosa felt his horrific touch at the base of her neck. "What do you call her?"

In the overseer's silence, Billy moved closer.

"Man, I asked you her name!"

Gund shifted his feet. "Rosa, sah."

She felt the man's hand being lifted. "Stand up, Rosa."

It was imperative to follow a white man's order, yet she hesitated. Billy reached and took her hand. "You need stand up, gal. He won't harm you, for Mista Gund's obliged to watch over all Mass' Abram's sheep an' give them safety."

The stranger chuckled and accepted Billy's language. "This is one incredible brown lamb in an all-black flock." He laughed at Billy. "And I suppose you are the big-toothed sheep dog. Well, you needn't be so tense, Uncle. I was just thinking of the wonderful possibility of bringing her in out of this rain."

Without warning the man slipped his hand down inside Rosa's dress to feel her bare shoulders and spine. Rosa quaked. The overseer bristled.

"You don't touch Delora property without no massas' permission, sah!"

The man pulled away. Rosa doubled over as Negozi and Abiel came around her.

"Then be sure I will seek the owners' permission. What is she? Half Cherokee?"

"No," Gund volunteered coldly. "French and Haitian. Now I was just 'bout to send them all back to work."

"*Mais oui!*"

The man came to Rosa as she was trying to hide among the others. Despite Gund's warning he reached into the cluster of slaves and pulled her headcloth so that her hair fell to her shoulders uncovered. She heard his low, ugly whistle of admiration.

"She's an angel or an Ethiopian queen in disguise."

"You hear'd the bossman!" Billy seethed, putting himself between the master and Rosa. "This here's Delora property."

Rosa pulled herself into the tightest ball possible while crouching in the grass.

"All right, you old bulldog!" Teddy laughed. "But there's nothing to say she won't someday be Pine Woods property. She's got a good, clear back, which I appreciate. The pretty-faced ones can sometimes be the most disobedient—and marked up underneath."

Gund actually set a hand on one of the weapons showing under his vest. "If you have business at the massa's house, sah, then that's where you should be a-goin'."

"You're a rude, simple cracker! And a nigger in every way but color. Don't think I'll forget that, *Mister Gund.*"

The overseer held his ground despite the offense. When the planter finally took his horse down along the river, Mr. Gund unfroze his movements just as Billy did.

"He' sure 'nough is a snake with a memory, sah!" Billy warned. "I'd watch my back an' my front for days to come."

Gund settled the pistol out of sight. "Rosa, you all right?"

Rosa couldn't speak with every inch of her flesh burning and vomit rising in her mouth. His awful touch had brought back every moment of abuse she had ever endured. The only difference was that he was white. She closed her eyes and rubbed her fists to her skull. In the days when she was being marched down toward Charleston, she had begged white planters along the way and the white traders who held their shackles' keys to save her. But they only mocked her because of the Negro blood polluting her veins.

Once again she mourned her innocence, stolen and shattered. Whimpering, she fell to the ground and pressed her face into the weeds. Negozi spoke as the woman's family made a dry circle around her.

"Rosa, you done knowed the Callcotts won't sell they people. Nor do they let white buckra set foot in the street."

Rosa sobbed. She had already been destroyed. Nothing could change that. Over all the people, she heard Parris.

"He got no right to do this to her!" He said it over and over.

Negozi went on like Parris's mama. "Now don't you come near her, son! The demons of her past are pouncin' on her again."

"It's not demons but a *buckra*!" Parris seethed.

Rosa glanced up to see him pacing like a tiger. Billy caught him.

"Don't you let on 'bout you' feelin's. That can aggravate a white man. Make him think he must have her 'stead of you."

"*White demon!*" Parris raged, looking out toward the river. It was the true translation of the Africans' word *buckra*. Negozi was wise enough to keep Parris from her. It mattered nothing that he cared for her in ways that might be right. At this moment his touch—like any other man's—would have driven her to insanity.

Parris vented his distress by shaking a fist toward the riverboats. "I don't care what kind of judgment come down on me—in this life or the next! If that buckra comes near her again, I gwine break his neck!"

CHAPTER 6

WHEN THE COLD MORNING DOWNPOUR finally slowed to a drizzle, Brant pushed himself out of the lime green wicker chair on the lower piazza. Since dawn he had been there with only one thing on his mind—finding a way to leave Delora the moment his daddy returned. Joseph, it seemed, still lay at the brink of death. Just once since daybreak had Brant opened the door and looked in on him. The boy was breathing but wholly unresponsive. He knew the overseer and driver had taken the slaves out into the fields, for he had seen the flatboats tied up on the river's far shore. Now when he looked, one was returning with a horse and rider. Teddy.

Reluctantly leaving the porch, he went down to meet him. One of Delora's yard boys ran up alongside them to lead the horse off to the stables.

"There was a tree blown down across the Church Creek bridge," Teddy told him before Brant could question his route. When they were up on the piazza he took his cloak off to dry on the railing. "How's your Negro?"

Brant let his sigh be known. "Unconscious."

Teddy gave a reassuring smile. "Well, now, that's why I'm here." He shifted his saddlebag of supplies from hand to hand. "Let's go and see what can be done."

––––––––––

Joseph had managed just moments earlier to push himself to sit against the wall. When the door scraped open once more, the sound prickled his arms and back. White light blinded him. He could do little to hide his wakefulness, as he had done earlier in Brant's presence. Under the masters' gazes, his hands and feet were weak as grass pressed by the weight of his chains. He thought of what Maum had said on her last visit to him. "*The Lord didn't fight his own enemies, neither, an' this ain't no time for you to be fightin' your'n.*"

If the two slaves and Mr. Gund hadn't slipped water to him, Joseph knew he would not have survived through the night. But now the masters talked about how much stronger he looked. It alerted him to the possibility of more punishment and danger. His mouth hung dumbly open while he listened.

"Just stay as you are," Brant told him.

The men walked to him slowly. "I'm going to let you go out in the shade again to rest," Brant promised cautiously. "All you have to do is prove to me that you will no longer exercise your will over mine. To do that, I want you to lean down now and kiss . . . my . . . feet."

Joseph looked at the floor. Without a doubt this was Teddy's doing. He was certain he could feel Brant's reluctance as the young Callcott slowly slipped his dark, dusty boot into view.

"Do it, Joseph." It was almost pleading. "There's nothing painful or harmful about it. Just do it. Then you can have your reward."

Joseph had a spurring thought. What would a *man* do, not just a slave who wanted to be released into the air and light?

"Don't hesitate, for then there will be consequences," Brant said with earnest warning in his speaking. "Be smart!"

"You don't beg them. Command them." Teddy intervened. "Boy! Move! Put your ugly mouth to the leather."

Would a man do that? Joseph numbly decided he would not bow.

Instantly he paid for his decision. The planters pulled him to his feet and marched him out the door, though he could barely stagger. They kept him going, through the gate, across the driveway to the barnyard. Teddy's voice was low, like the devil's.

"Today you'll learn to kiss your master's boots, you uppity crazed fool!

Today you will learn never to counter your master again."

————————

Brant had agreed to be prepared for this even before they went to the toolshed, but now that it was happening, he berated himself for trusting Teddy's judgment. The boy would stoop without a fight—Teddy had promised it. But since Joseph had not, he felt like the one enduring the sad consequences. For a brief moment, Brant reflected that he might have done the same had he been Joseph.

However, the luxury of speculation was over. To prepare for the worst in Teddy's idea, Brant had sent four or five boys down earlier to heap up fresh manure from the pigpens and cattle stalls. The morning of rain made the barnyard a stinking mud field, yet they pushed Joseph into it and shut the gate behind him. The slave in chains sank into mire deeper than his ankles. Seeing Joseph trembling and dazed, Brant decided that he must not follow through with their plan. He reached for the gate, about to let Joseph out, but Teddy took over.

"That pile of dung over there is your task today, boy. You move it out the back gate over yonder and spread it onto the stubbled hayfield."

Joseph raised drooping eyes, showing disbelief.

Brant moved behind Teddy. "Let's not have him do it."

"You never go back on what you tell them to do," Teddy murmured before insulting Joseph again. "Use your black hands and arms! That's what they're colored for."

Bitter acid rose in Brant's stomach. He opened the gate and rushed in, not according to their plans. "Save yourself, boy! Get down. Kiss my boot now, and then you can have rest."

"Naaaaaaa!" the stunned slave cried.

"Then till dark you'll carry dung!" Teddy threatened.

Joseph tried to shake his head, but even that small amount of movement threatened his precarious balance. Wading in the mud, Brant went over and steadied him. "Come on. You're not strong enough for this. But now be warned. This is what is to come if you will not obey me."

The slave started to walk with him, but Teddy blocked the gate. "I'm not serving as his doctor anymore! From here on out I'm on your property as an authorized representative of the patrol. Now get me a whip, or I'll go to the barn and free my own from my saddle."

"You're not going to touch him!" Brant dared. "Look at him! You'll kill him with force."

"You're right. It would kill him to whip him now. So send one of your half-hands out to fetch your overseer and your bullish slave driver. Gund will whip Billy till the boy does his work."

Joseph turned around, his chains clogged in mud. "Naaa!" Like a lamed bird he hobbled slowly back toward the pile.

"He's doing it now to save the driver!" Brant judged with emotion.

"It's too late. And for the wrong reason. He'll do what he's told to do because he's *told*, not because he thinks he has the power to save some-body. Or even himself. He'll do what he's told for obedience only. Now, if you don't call Gund and Billy, I'll go get them myself. I'll not leave De-lora till I'm satisfied that full control has been gained here."

———

Hampton was horrified to see that young Mass' Callcott had let himself be talked into such a plan. When he and Billy came up side by side from the fields, they found Joseph on his hands and knees, covered with manure and working against the weight of his chains to lift dung by the armfuls. The hateful young Rensler told Billy to take off his shirt.

"Put five on him now, Overseer, and then five more the moment that boy takes his rest."

"It's unfair, sah!" Hampton dared, his heart beating nearly out of his chest. "I'm here to work them to full capacity. And that's what I see Joseph doing now—and more. By rights I should not be ordered to jeopardize anybody's health."

"You whip the driver to prove yourself responsible enough to be in charge of this street. The boy didn't do what he was told to do when he was told to do it. That is his offense."

Hampton could scarcely hold the leather pressed into his hands. For the sake of satisfying the parish patrol he had cut down cornshucks and stacked hay to practice the strokes required of overseers who ruled by the whip. But in all his years at Delora, he had whipped only a few—drunkards all—under Master Abram's supervision, and then mostly to put the re-forming fear of God in them rather than to break their skin. But something very different was being demanded of him now.

Billy was told to take hold of the second lowest fence rail. The man's spine rippled into view as his back was bowed.

"What are you waiting for?" Rensler chided him. "Do I have to ad-minister the lashing for you?"

Billy never once looked back at Hampton. As though it were as heavy as iron, Hampton raised the unfurled braided strap. Just then, from the corner of his vision, he saw three horses coming up the driveway. Two of the riders were female, and an unaccomplished horseman rode between them. It was just cause for laying the whip aside.

When the riders got close, Hampton recognized them all. It was Ann Rensler and her two friends from Boston.

Joseph saw the wonder of how Billy had been saved. Taking the moment to rest as the heat of the now clearing day poured down on his hatless, throbbing head, he lifted his face from the stench that rose around him. He was covered with filth, and he heard the one young white woman speak with alarm.

"What are you doing to him? And to the other one waiting for the man to strike him! Oh! I cannot believe you all live like this!" Her words broke.

Joseph guessed that she was Nathan Gilman's daughter.

"Take her up to the house," Teddy ordered to his cousin Ann or to the northern girl's brother who was with them.

Joseph saw none of the movement going on, for he was very careful to keep his eyes toward the barn all the while.

The same young woman screamed, "No, if our being here will stop you from using that whip, then I will stay forever if I have to."

"We will not!" It was Ann Rensler who spoke. "They are getting only what they deserve. You would not interfere with a daddy spanking his son. This is really no different, though it's more important, for slaves must be kept in line. You should understand by now."

"I don't understand, and I won't understand! Whatever they've done, you could forgive them."

"I'm afraid, miss, that forgiveness is for contrite hearts, not contrary ones," Teddy put in, his voice as hard as rock. "Now, you girls go on up to the house. Miss Gilman, understand! You will only make matters worse for both these boys by trying to defend them. They're being taught rightness, and once they have that down by rote, be assured all will be peace."

Joseph could hear Miss Gilman cry as her voice faded toward the house. He waited for another miracle, but soon he heard the first of five whip strikes on Billy's back instead. His mouth dropped to the dung as he scrambled to start moving more. Billy Days, the uncle he most admired, was taking punishment because of him.

———

The first thing Bette noticed was that Miss Ann's pretty little northern friend was sobbing like a broken-hearted child into her dainty handkerchief. The man at her side tried to comfort her with reason as they took chairs on the porch.

"Sometimes, just like horses, they need to be broken."

Bette's hands tingled. They were talking about Joseph, she was sure. She listened intently, but their talk told her nothing, and soon it turned to other things.

"I'd like to show you the house and grounds," Miss Ann said, obviously working hard to make things sound bright.

Steeling herself against all the hateful feelings that wanted to rise like wasps within her, Bette put on her blandest of expressions and presented herself for service. The Pine Woods mistress was not timid about taking command.

"Get us lemonade and bring two extra glasses for Master Brant and Master Rensler when they come up."

"Yes, ma'am," Bette said, glad for once that eye contact was not expected of her. Otherwise, she might not have been able to conceal her burning soul. What were the two masters doing with Joseph?

Moving through the hot, humidified shade of the now bright day, she filled the glasses. Miss Ann continued to be cheery.

"I wouldn't be surprised if it was one of your daddy's steamers that carried this ice down here to us."

The other girl only sniffled and did not speak.

"Listen to the workers singing out in the fields," the girl's brother told her. "Doesn't that make you feel better? Doesn't it prove that bondage is not always irksome to them?"

Bette curtseyed to get away, as though having pressing kitchen duties. She did so because she felt her ears were playing tricks on her. Or else somebody was truly rattling the air by snapping a whip in the distance. Her heart was in her mouth, for it had been years since she'd last heard that evil licking sound in the quiet countryside. She feared for Joseph mightily, for seeing a whipping would have made a northern girl cry. Bette fled through the yard to the one place where she could get a view of the barnyard. She found Miss Mayleda already there, gripping the picket fence with thin, white knuckles.

"Oh, Maum!" Mayleda cried. "I heard the awful sound at least ten times, but I can't see a thing. It can't be Joseph. Look for yourself! He's there, crawling through the barnyard just the way Teddy and my brother have been forcing him to do the whole last hour."

Blocking the sun from her eyes, Bette began to mourn with the girl. Joseph was in the dung, his one arm cradling manure as he slowly moved on his knees and with his one freed hand.

"Lord of mercy! Oh, Lord! Help you' chile!"

The bell suspended on the porch rang harshly, calling her back to service. Miss Mayleda looked at her, questioning who was there.

"It Miss Ann an' two of her friends," Bette explained.

Mayleda's eyes narrowed. "I'm going into the house to write a letter," she said with determination. "I'm going to have Unc' Ezra row down to town to mail it to my daddy today. I'm going to tell him that he must come home at once."

The girl's vow was hardly comforting. A letter might take days, and Bette doubted that the girl could even know her daddy's temporary address. "That's real nice of you to think that way, missy," she said before heading back toward her duties. The girl stayed behind to continue watching Joseph and share his pain.

Bette walked and prayed to the rhythm of her fast-moving feet. "Oh, Papa-God, have mercy on us all!"

She skirted the wide shanty that held both the kitchen and the laundry, and there she glimpsed Colt loitering in the shade. "I done told you onc't a'ready what needs doin'! The washer girls need those kettles filled an' two fires built." She pointed to brass containers as wide and high as barrels.

The boy slouched off in such a sorry state that she went after him. "No food for you, not till the work be done. That's right from the Good Book, so don't you give me any of you' evil eye."

Bette got back to the porch and saw the two young masters relaxing on chairs, apparently conscienceless about Joseph's fate. The dung of their cruelty still clung to their boots, a vile testimony to their participation.

"You know, I saw a very pretty sight this morning when that fallen tree changed my riding course," Theodore Rensler said after he took one of the misty glasses from Bette's tray. "I didn't know until then that you had any 'high yellow' wenches on your property."

Bette almost spilled the other glass intended for Brant. She dared not look anywhere near her young owner.

"I don't know our field hands very well," the young Callcott said feebly.

"Oh, you would remember this one!" Brant took his glass, and Bette fled behind Miss Ann's chair to stand with the tray. "A lovelier specimen of Negress beauty I have never seen."

The northern man—William, they called him—cleared his throat. "I don't think things like this should be talked about in the presence of ladies!"

"Indeed!" Brant sided with him at once.

Their protests made the other master laugh. "It's precisely for Ann's benefit that I did say it. Last night her Corinth was delivered of the 'blister' she's been carrying. Now, I know what my cousin needs—a comely maid to replace her in the house."

Miss Ann drew breath. "You're not thinking of suggesting the one you saw in the field."

"You haven't seen her yet," Teddy pushed unashamedly. "The driver told me she's part French. She has the look of a savage princess, even though she's been subjected to the weather. You can tell she wasn't birthed in any shanty."

"My father won't think of parting with any slave," Brant said as Bette's stomach tightened. "So don't even ask."

"I have no intention of offering to buy her," Teddy said. "But it would be most neighborly to loan her to us for a time, while Ann needs help."

"I . . . I couldn't do that, either. I'm sorry," Brant stammered, the ice rattling in his glass. "And I seriously doubt that Daddy would agree to it."

From what Bette could see, Miss Ann looked glum. "I can't imagine ever wanting a field slave anyway."

Her cousin said lightly, "The day's turned out to be gorgeous. Let's ride out so you can see her. You may think differently then."

"No," Brant said. "We don't let visitors in our fields."

"Then we'll view her from the riverbank," Teddy concluded.

"I've seen enough of slavery," Felicia protested.

"I don't think you have, miss," Teddy said to her. "It's a marvelous thing to see darkies work together. And I'll give credit to Master Brant here. Delora slaves are some of the most consistently productive in this parish."

"I'm all for seeing your workers, Mr. Callcott," William said as one gentleman to another. "Production's just the thing I'd be working toward should my father and the colonel come to full agreement concerning a business partnership. To this point I've seen very little management that I would truly call Christian."

Ann took Brant's arm as they all stood together. "It would be fun to all take a ride together."

"Then let's ride by the girl," Teddy pushed again. "After that we can show them the far side of the river."

A moment later Bette was left with empty glasses.

CHAPTER 7

AS THE SUN SNUCK OFF past the hickory grove, taking the strong light with it, Bette mourned for Joseph, who still had not been brought up to the yard. All day long her mind had been with him. She had gone about her twilight chores distracted and resentful that she would serve another supper to those—Theodore Rensler included—who made him suffer. All of them in the house would expect her to work in that dining room as though she had not a care in this world.

Back in the kitchenhouse she ladled sauce over the joint of venison, then pulled the pot of rice and peas out from the coals. With duty as her harsh master, Bette stood near the window warming the serving platters by wrapping them in cloths heated by the fire. Outside in the darkness she thought she saw her own man, Billy, come through the gate, though he was not to be on this side of the property during the week. His presence brought her out of the kitchen at a run. "Where's the boy at?" she demanded as soon as she was close enough to question him.

A slim field gal had followed him. The worker stood far short of them in the deep shadows of the yard's ancient live oak.

"Mass' Brant done told me to bring you some more help for the housecleanin'," Billy said, sounding tuckered.

"Help's the last of my worries! Where's Joseph?"

Her husband shrugged, showing that he knew a whole lot more than he was about to say. "They gwine bring him on up soon 'nough. I saw both massas still in the field near where he wa' t'day."

"They gwine find cause to kill him yet," she worried.

He seemed almost shy. "It be they goal to keep him wide awake an' *livin'* 'cause they want him *broke*, not dead."

She bit her lip, for Billy himself sounded so pressed down.

"They gwine keep him in chains outside in the yard for t'night. That I do know. Now, no matter what he look like, you don't go to him no more! I gwine try to keep on helpin' him in secret as I am able, but don't you—"

She moaned to break his words. "What he look like! I know what he look like! From this here yard I can see 'xactly what they done to him all the day long."

"Yes," Billy said with mourning, "but you not gwine make it no better for him by meddlin'. The boy's got to do what he's got to do. He ain't gwine down so easy."

"You mean he fightin' them! In he sorry state?"

"Yeah!" There was pain in his eyes but pride in his voice.

"Well, shooo, old Negro! You need tell him there ain't no use! Even Jesus' sufferin' wa' unto death! An' his will be, too, 'less he give in on the *outside* to make them think he won't go up again' them no more."

"Now, woman, don't you unda' estimate him just 'cause he been the houseboy. He got courage what makes him keep his head up. An' God hisself seems to give him strength from the very depths of his soul."

"They'll sell him, an' don't you think they won't! Or they'll lynch him! The chile's gotta know that now, an' from you! He ain't got control of nothin' in this life 'cept maybe he shadow."

"No, Bette, I not gwine discourage him. Whatsumever he fightin' for is waaay dooown deep inside of him. You can see it, though I for sure don't know 'xactly what be drivin' him."

Bette considered the matter, then revealed another of the terrible weights that had been hung around her heart all day. "Well, I might know," she said nearly lost in thought. "Miss Mayleda been so worked up 'bout this all. We talked, an' she says she wa' right outside her daddy's bedroom door, hearin' an' seein' everythin' what went on 'tween the massa's son an' Joseph. An' *she* say that all this ruckus come from Mass' Brant discoverin' how Joseph can read!"

Billy moaned.

"I know it be impossible! Howsumever, *she* says, honest as a preacher, that Joseph can read just like a schoolhouse scholar."

"Oh, Lord of glory!" Billy shouted so loud that the report of his voice seemed to stir everything in the night, including the girl standing silently under the tree.

"That not for nobody else ears!" Bette silenced him. "How can you even believe it true? You know there ain't no full Africans what have a mind for learnin'!"

"An' just *who* been sayin' that?" he challenged. "*White folk*, of course! Great day in the mornin'! What glorious news!"

Her hands, empty of work for once, went to her waist. "I sure ain't seen nothin' worth celebratin'! The boy's half dead for whatsumever he done."

"Oh, honey, there's so much hope in this. Think! A *black* man readin' afta every planter an' poli-tisian done told us 'No, it cain't happen!' Joseph! Able to open up even the Bible—"

"We don't know that for a fact!" she reminded him. "An' even if he can, he cain't come close to *no* book without gettin' hisself beat to a pulp. I know they done whupped him a'ready. I hear'd it, an' later I seen his blood spottin' Mass' Brant shirt."

"No, they didn't! That I guarantee. The Lord keeps him. He'll do a'right long as no other whites find out what he can do!"

"I know Miss Mayleda won't say nothin', but what 'bout the young massa. He fool 'nough."

"I think he done know what it gwine take to keep the law from comin' down 'pon his daddy. Fact is, I think that's why he ain't tellin' the parish cap'n nothin' specific 'bout what happen." He lifted what appeared to be tense and weary shoulders. "The way I guess it now, they gwine put Joseph back in the dung pile t'morrow, but they won't break his flesh, an' they won't kill him neither."

He sounded so matter-of-fact it puzzled her, for she knew he loved him like a son. Maybe he was saving a larger kind of mourning for their own Parris. Or maybe her man was just resigned to know that Christian *death* was often preferable to Christian *life* with suffering.

The girl under the tree dared to step closer.

"Come on out," Billy coaxed her lightly. He spoke pretty loudly, for she still was quite far removed from them. "You done know my Bette, an' she sure do know you."

Bette was surprised and angered after a ray of houselight caught the woman. "Why, it be Rosa! What she doin' here?"

Billy sighed and took off his hat. "She the one Mass' Brant done chose to have up here."

" 'Cause he in league with the devil!" Bette minced no words but spoke them very low while she ruminated concerning the conversation on the porch that afternoon. "That Rensler buckra got he eyes on her."

"Don't I know."

Bette hung her head, for there was nothing they could do. "They all done went rode out an' got a look at her afta' Rensler told everybody she wa' such a comely beauty."

"He done more than look," Billy reported with sad disgust. "He touched her like a buyin' trader with money in he pocket."

"Lord have mercy! Miss Ann wants a maid to replace her Corinth what just been delivered of a child."

"Hush!" Billy scolded while Rosa was still coming to them at a snail's pace. "You don't have to let on how much you know. Just watch her an' keep her close. Mebbe Mass' Brant set it up in just this way, 'cause he know the last Delora Negro anybody gwine dare to cross is you. Mebbe he mean it for her protection."

"You think Brant got heart, after what he done to Joseph?"

"He be young an' inexperienced. The real firebrand of cruelty be his best friend, Theodore. I keep on hopin' that boy will come 'round an' be more like his daddy."

"Rosa be nothin' but trouble up here," Bette confided in whispers. "Not 'less she changed a whole lot since the last I knowed her. She never done accepted herself as no slave."

"Just try an' understand her," Billy pleaded as Rosa came fully out of the shadows. "She ain't a bad girl an' not lazy. You just gotta take some consideration of where she been an' what she been." His uncertain smile was nearly childlike. "You all will do just fine t'gether."

Bette blinked at his tenderness. For being such a strong man he sure could let his feelings rule him—but in a noble way. She saw anxiety clawing at the corners of his mouth.

Bette showed more of her own opinion by crossing her arms. "You just wait till Mass' Abram get home. If Mista Gund don't tell him, then sure 'nough I will, 'cause Mass' Rensler don't have no business sniffin' 'round here like somebody else's dog!"

"You ain't gwine say nothin', an' this be why!" he warned her, even with Rosa standing near. "Mass' Rensler be cap'n of this year's patrol, an' he just watchin' an' waitin' for any old reason to put us all unda' his thumb. If that man find out it wa' the Maum what tattled on him, he got the power to loose his hate even on you. Mebbe you don't know how much disrespect goes 'round these parts, simply 'cause Mass' Abram grants us the dignity to pray. It makes everybody suspectin' of us all."

Bette caught Rosa looking at them warily. Now that she was in the light of the kitchen shanty Bette understood why the bloom of her womanhood was something impossible for men to ignore. And that, she knew from her late-night talks with Billy, included their Parris, whom she rarely saw, since he was assigned to the shanty that held many young men without partners or families.

"Mass' Brant wants Rosa out of these field clothes so's she can look the part of a houseservant while she here."

"That sure ain't surprisin'!" Though she did not feel any natural affection toward Rosa, Bette could still be defensive of her just because she was a woman. She thought back over all the hours and days she had spent with Mistress Oribel and Negozi right after Mass' Abram had bought Rosa from the traders. It had taken weeks to nurse Rosa through to even partial sanity, for the gal had found her family murdered, and then she had been raped by more than a dozen slaves who hated her for what her daddy had been and done to them.

"I guess I done said all I came to say," Billy told Bette after they all had stood in silence. He turned to Rosa. "You see Maum's weariness? Now you help her all you can."

Either downright scared or bewildered, Rosa looked around the whole yard. She didn't say a word but went over to the woodpile outside the kitchen and filled her arms.

"See, she showin' you she can help. An' since her baby girl done died, she been talkin' some. Just give her time."

Bette did feel compassion toward the girl who went inside the kitchen. "Even now she's on the lookout for attackers, ainty? Negozi has it 'bout right, though I don't agree with her hoodoo ways of thinkin'. Poor Rosa's like a woman stalked by demons."

"She need come an' know the Lord," Billy said, looking sadly toward the double shanty that held the laundry and kitchen. "I been a-prayin' that somehow she see hope an' justice in the Lord—if not for this life, at least for the next one." He reset his hat. "It gwine be good for her to get away from menfolk an' hear the Gospel from you. Even Parris ain't been the best evangelizer of late. His human heart's got itself just too entangled."

"That not surprisin' the way she do carry herself."

"That not pride you see, but just her upbringin'. Unda' them squared shoulders you can find a gal bowed dangerously low with all her hurts an' troubles. All I ever seen her live for wa' her little Kulo."

"I was there when you preached that baby's homecomin'," Bette said softly. "It be sad but good, I think, when slave babies is laid in their graves 'fore they know a day of sorrow."

"Parris don't think much on Rosa's pain. I try an' tell him to be gentle, 'cause human love ain't never gwine be strong 'nough to free her from fear. Only God's glorious work! Somehow. Someday."

Bette joined him in reflecting on all of the young woman's sorrows. "She been hurt from all sides."

His smile was warmer than hearth fire, and Bette found herself longing to stay with him. When he started toward the gate she stepped along with him. "When Mass' Abram finds Rosa here it will set him a-wonderin'," she said, thinking aloud to comfort them both. "Then he sure will investigate the gwines-on for hisself, with none of us havin' to say nothin'."

"Yep, I think so too." Billy downed his vision. "I just hope the massa come home 'fore it too late."

"Miss' Mayleda pledged to write him a letter."

Billy raised his eyes.

"She give it to Ezra. That I know."

Bette felt the burden Billy shouldered as Delora's head slave. He was always the one being rubbed and chaffed like a bumper cushion between the slaveholders' desires and the hopes and concerns of the plantation's colored folk. Right along the fence he stopped to look at her evenly. "Baby, I think we both better start lookin' beyond that day when Mass' Abram gwine be here to rescue us. You know there gwine come a time, soon or late, when Mass' Brant gwine take control. We need to get prayed up, an' stay prayed up, 'cause there ain't no way of knowin' 'xactly when that day gwine come." Suddenly he seemed to speak as a prophet. "Soon an' very soon, this ain't gwine be the Delora we onc't know'd—" He turned.

"Oh! Billy!" Bette cried, seeing for the first time ragged stripes of blood crisscrossing the back of his shirt. "What in heaven's name? You wa' wincin' all this while, but I thought it wa' on account of Joseph an' Rosa's pains—"

"It were—"

"No, sah!" She put a hand on his familiar rock-hard arm. "Who done this?" She would not wait for his answer. "Brant!"

"No." He moved only his head to look at her. "It wa' Mista Gund, if you must know."

"Lord, the stars be a-fallin'! So they wa' whuppin' *you* to keep Joseph movin'! Oh, how could Mista Gund get wrapped up in this when you'all've not done nothin' to nobody?"

"Guess he decided he had no choice." Billy sounded bitter, and he closed one eye wryly. "But Mista Gund just weren't apprenticin' out there. He put them on deep."

"Oh, Billy! This ain't the way of the Callcotts an' Delora."

"This *weren't* the way."

"You come inside! I gwine get Rosa to heat some water an' we'll soak off that shirt."

"No. I can't stay an' get accused of bein' idle. My work ain't over yet, an' neither is your'n. Mista Gund been stationed here yet another time to watch for restlessness 'mong the slaves—or mebbe for restlessness 'mong the patrolmen what want to put us all down hard."

He walked away directly, then stopped. Instead of leaving, he smiled. Surely he knew the nature of her heart, how hurt she was, how angry, frustrated, and confused.

In their more than thirty years of knowing each other, they'd probably never said more than a half dozen words concerning love. But from the time she had been bought from a neighboring plantation, they had known love and practiced it as husband and wife. Bone of one bone and flesh of one flesh, as the Scriptures say. She felt his suffering as he did hers.

He came back a little ways. "When you' work is done, gal, you come down to the house an' care for me any ol' way you please."

Bette thought about her new obligation to watch over Rosa. It was something she must not take lightly. At the same time she wanted those few precious hours of intimacy with her husband. Old, leftover feelings of her former youngness stirred in her. She grinned, feeling good in spite of their trials. "You ol' fool."

He nodded. "You know I love you."

Bette clung to her apron while watching him walk out wearily to face again his own set of troubles. Then she turned to face hers. When she did, she glimpsed Parris darting up across the driveway, which was both the natural and the enforced boundary between field slaves and the servants of the house and yard. She didn't even have time to cry in alarm, for Billy saw him, too, and went wild because of his coming. "I told you! Never set foot over here!" he shouted and grabbed their son by the arm.

"Pa! You can't let this happen! You know what they up to—"

"Get back out there!" Billy ordered, tackling him again. "There ain't nothin' in here for you to do." Still as strong as his son, Billy pulled him back across the drive, releasing him at the line of camellias.

Puffing her distress, Bette ran as far as the fence. Billy came back to her after it was over. "What am I s'pose to say to him?" he mourned, his face wet and his hands raised. "What am I s'pose to do? I have no more right than he does to protect any of our women. How am I s'pose to rear a son in this world when nobody will even allow me the rights of a moral Christian man?"

His dejection went beyond the depths of her womanly understanding. It had always been her private notion that slave women suffered more grievously at the hands of their oppressors than did their bondsmen brothers. Now she was rethinking her opinions. For every atrocity a colored woman endured, there was a daddy, a husband, a lover someplace suffering humiliation and pain because of her ungodly trials. Maybe it was even worse for the men, though she had not thought of this before. She knew what it felt like to be powerless and held down against her own will in somebody else's ugly hold. But more often than not, colored *menfolk* had the sorrowful task of keeping themselves from striking out, of pretending that nothing ever violated or wounded them as they watched their sisters, wives, and daughters being taken and used as some man's property.

Bette kept her tears hidden so she would not hurt him more. "God knows. God sees. Go an' remind Parris of that. It be foolhardy for him to risk hisself for somethin' that ain't ever gwine change."

Billy took her counsel like a bitter pill. "Sometimes I wonder—is this all God's callin' us black men to do?"

Conscious of his torn-up back, she reached across the fence and embraced him very lightly. But he caught her around her arms and held her smotheringly close. Bending his head he kissed her lips, not with youthful passion but with sober compassion born of long-suffering sacrifice and maturity. It created a feeling of wholeness in her, despite the world's reeling like a rich child's top out of control. They pulled apart without a word of farewell.

She went back to the kitchen to find that Rosa had been watching from the shanty door. "You ever cooked?" Bette said, making herself all business now that she knew Rosa had witnessed their show of affection.

The girl looked at her with incredible and seemingly all-seeing green eyes. "No, ma'am. Aunty Negozi always leaves that to her daughters."

Bette was encouraged. In her first days at Delora, Rosa would never have talked to nobody, nor would she ever have considered any bonds-woman worthy of a respectful "ma'am." In fact, Bette had never heard her speak prior to this evening. The girl then amazed her more by extending the conversation of her own free will.

"I think I can learn to do any kind of work, for I have seen all the work of a house being done. Just keep me busy, please!" she begged. "I know what's happening! Mr. Theodore Rensler wants to take me to Pine Woods, and I must not be allowed to go there—ever!"

"Oh, honey, Mass' Abram won't allow it."

Her brown face darkened. "Master Abram isn't here." She turned to the wall where skillets, ladles, and trivets hung like a gentleman's display of works of art. Even from this angle Bette saw her tears.

The brass call bell rang as those in the house finally protested the delay in supper. Fishing for strength, Bette hurried double-quick, picking up her tasks where they had been left off. Bette found things for Rosa to do to help her, but then Bette was obliged to leave the girl behind because no-body had said she should enter the house. "You stay right here," Bette told her. The girl smiled gratefully, and Bette knew why. Teddy Rensler and Ann Rensler were both in the dining room.

————————

Brant could hardly believe that his gentlemanly duty of hospitality was being stretched again by Teddy's presence. And tonight Annie and the Gil-mans were there also, having spent the whole day on his property. Nothing was said through the whole meal about Joseph.

After the tense dinner he dismissed his siblings and guided his guests to take their coffee in the study while he carved out time to speak with Ann alone on the porch. When he had her out in the nighttime air, it was she who spoke first.

"I'm sorry for all that is happening to you." Her sympathy comforted him more than he could have imagined.

"I hate this, Ann!" he confessed to her openly. "I'm no good at it. I'm sure I don't have to say that in words."

"I can't think it would be easy." She brushed her fingers against his lips. "But you should just trust Teddy. Many planters in this district pay him to discipline their slaves. I know he can bring success to you."

"I wish it would be soon," Brant said with a sigh. "If Joseph weren't such a fool! If he'd just give in! Oh! I must have this worked out before my daddy comes home!"

"You will." She lifted his hand and smiled against the back of it. "I have faith in you."

"You shouldn't! For I don't have any faith in myself! I don't even know if I have faith in this business."

"Someone has to grow rice for this nation."

"But does it have to be me?"

She shrugged. "Oh, Brant, it's just one slave that has you bothered. Being out in your fields today, I'd say that overall you're doing all things well. Our slaves are always complaining, breaking tools, and lagging. But here, your Mr. Gund doesn't even have to say a word to them. You should be happy. Proud."

He considered the truth in that. "I don't want to see Negroes abused. If I could always have them singing and working, then maybe I would be a planter, after all."

"Silly! Why do you say that? You are a planter now!"

"I may not be for long."

She kissed his hand. "Don't punish yourself. See the matter through with Joseph. Then let me hear what you have to say."

He smiled at her, for her wisdom—like her beauty—was balmy salve for his soul. "Teddy promised the breaking would take no more than three days."

"Then be content to wait three days."

"But I hate what's happening."

"I know you do. But think about what you have overall. Focus on the fact that you and your daddy have the best-run plantation in all this parish. Even my cousin cannot escape the fact of that. Can you rightfully think of yourself as a cruel ogre when your house is in nearly perfect order? I think not."

He replaced her fingers on his lips, even kissing them, wanting to believe her words were true. At that moment he would have been slow to do anything that might cause him to lose her, and that included making a decision to leave Delora and the South he once had loved.

CHAPTER 8

HAMPTON ENTERED his two-room cottage after ten, wanting only supper and time alone. Yet he hadn't even hung his hat inside the door before Dell got up from their bare table and raised the lamplight.

"Some yard boys done called over our fence sayin' you flogged Billy Days. That for true?"

He attended to his cold supper set aside on a pewter plate without a word.

She asked him again. "You done whupped Billy?" Now she was fishing like a bead-eyed heron.

"Yeah." He sat down on the bench, skipping grace because he felt so unworthy of it. Dell put herself across from him, watching as he ate without tasting. Being home and having victuals did nothing to fill his hollowness. Sorrily, he decided his wife should know. "Mista Abram's manservant been in trouble," he said, his throat so tight that the last bite of bacon scraped going down. "And since Mista Brant ain't s'pose to lay a hand on that houseboy, the patrol cap'n decided I would put ten stripes on Days instead to keep the boy movin'." He winced at his hands, still struggling to believe he had done such a thing.

"That broke the young'un?" She looked for vindication.

Hampton detested her attitude but said nothing about it. "The boy's too sick for anybody to judge his mood."

"Well, Billy didn't give *you* no fight, I hope."

"No."

"You can't fault the young massas for handlin' things that way, not with so many tales of nigger uprisin's."

Hampton ran his hands over his hair. "It wa' Rensler's idea. I don't think Mista Brant woulda done it on his own."

"It's the patrol's duty to keep things in order."

"You don't need to tell me, Dell."

"But you so down in the mouth. You regrettin' what you done to Billy when there ain't cause for regret."

"The boy won't be broke," he said quietly.

"Then you gots to keep the pressure on him. Negroes gots to know their place. But you mournin' over him instead! Ah! You spend way too much time with them nigras. The Callcotts need hire somebody 'sides you, so's you ain't down there every minute like you wa' nothin' but black flesh you'self."

"Dell, if they put Joseph back to movin' dung t'morrow, an' if they call me to whip Billy more, well, I just don't think I can do it. I'm not for havin' no Negro riots! But neither I am out to slice somebody up just on account of his color. Joseph's been a good boy. An' Billy ain't no trouble."

"Sounds to me like you almost friends with them two! What kind of *man* has niggers for companions?"

"You listen!" Hampton pounded the table, unable to have patience after so much worry and fatigue. "I want you to start believin' there's some kind of future for us someplace other than here."

"Twenty-two years this has been our home. In lots of ways we're as dependent on Callcotts as them slaves."

"Not true!" Hampton said, cautious as to how he should explain his plan. "I have them small investments I've been makin' in the Canal an' Rail Road Company. The line's doin' real good. Someday, most of upland cotton gwine come in to Charleston just that way. Soon as Mista Abram's home, I'm gwine ask for some leave time. Then I'm gwine go lookin' for a job with the South Carolina railroad."

"What in heaven's name would you do that for? You got you a good job here."

"You have not been listenin'! I can't work under the son! An' that's what I see a-comin'. 'Specially if Mista Brant do marry in with them Renslers."

"The massas are you' bosses! You duty bound."

"Slavery's wrong, Dell. I've knowed that since my youth. The whole country would be better off without it."

"You not gwine change it."

"I didn't say I could. I'm just sayin' what's been eatin' my soul. I feel too close to these people to just start beatin' up on them. If Joseph don't settle t'night—"

"You *gots* to make him settle! I won't have our girls growin' up no place but on some good plantation. An' I sure don't want to live beside no free nigger neighbors."

Hampton blew out an exhausted, angry sigh. "Go back thirty-some years to that day I saw those two Delora slaves capsize their canoe when they couldn't swim. I didn't dive into snake-infested water lookin' for no job. I went in 'cause I have always believed in practicin' compassion on *everybody*." He rubbed around the fringes of his sideburns. "An' that's why Mista Abram offered me this here position. 'Cause he wanted it instilled on somebody what weren't out lookin' to lord over his people."

"There's always gwine be bad apples to sour a barrel, an' nobody should be ashamed to pluck 'em out."

"Woman, this ain't 'bout apples!"

"Oh! Bein' 'round them day an' night has warped you' judgment! If you could only see you'self from you' own outside in, you'd know! Whatever it takes, you gots to keep us livin' here."

"Whatever it takes!" He stood, knowing his house could no longer be his refuge. "I whupped a man I done knowed twenty years! I took part in treatin' a boy like he wa' swine, with his tongue cut up an' dried up. That's what it took, just for t'day! Whether you want to hear it or not, we'll not be here forever!"

"Where are you gwine?"

"To work!" Reaching the rack beside the door, he took his sweat-soaked hat and planted it on his head. "I gots tools to sort, an' I need to count heads. Then I'm gwine up to check on Joseph, for nobody's even had the decency to wash him off or give him shelter for the night. Don't wait up for me, 'cause I don't know when I'm gettin' back."

"Don't you go out angry," Dell said. "I wa' speakin' what's right an' best for us!"

"What is right?" he questioned hotly. "I don't think I know *right* anymore, leastways not as it's talked about here." He grabbed the latch, then slammed the door behind him.

Outside, the air was fresh, the street quiet. After dark every Delora slave had his or her assigned place, and only hearth fires were allowed to burn at night. Hampton did not count heads like he said he would, nor did he usually do so. He liked giving the poor tired souls, especially the married ones, some time to themselves. There were enough of them either born outside Delora or having worked other places to know that this was sort of his own special gift to them in reward for their hard labor, given without stubbornness or complaint. Once in a great while he'd call on the shanty that housed most of the unpaired bucks just to show that he was responsible about keeping his eye on them. Having grown up motherless himself and dragged from plantation to plantation by a drinking daddy who earned cash by tin tinkering to buy his whiskey, Hampton had seen enough heavy-handed dealings with Negroes to last him a lifetime. By the time he was ten, he was making it on his own, working his own odd jobs wherever his daddy led them to bunk.

In those days of lice and misery, his stomach often went empty, even when slaves were being fed. Yet he never learned to hate the dark race. His eyes and ears were constantly filled by the sights and sounds of cruelty imposed on blacks by whites, and he never relished the idea of gaining power just to join a class of highborn abusers. In most places, slaves had no privacy at all. Some places, masters even chose what males and females lived together for the sake of breeding the next generation, which they also held title to.

During all of Hampton's life, slavery had been like a whirlwind to him. Not until coming to Delora had he ever experienced one season of mental rest. But here he had been able to slip into a satisfied state of believing that chattel slavery and Christian management could work together. He had held to that belief until he had seen Joseph lying in his own blood on the master's floor. As he walked toward the mansion, the workings of slavery grated on him anew. And it wasn't just because of what slavery did to the black man, but also what it did to folk like himself. Landless and insignificant was the way the highborn judged them. Without slavery, poor whites might have chances to earn wages for the work the slaves did now.

Swatting mosquitoes, he went through the mansion gate. The day had been plenty hot for April, but now the night was chilly. He worried about the boy chained outside with only a horse blanket for protection. Hampton wasn't sure how he could help him without directly countering the massas. He had the last of Dell's biscuits under his shirt, thinking Joseph might eat them if he tore them up fine.

At the oyster-shell path connecting the kitchen to the house, he walked faster, avoiding the lighted places. When he crossed in front of the kitchenhouse, a girl shrieked and ran out, almost colliding with him as her skirts fluttered like a low-flying phantom. He thought it was Rosa and dared to stop her fleeing. She screamed again.

"Gal! It's you' overseer. You got nothin' to fear."

"Oh, Mr. Gund!"

Hampton dropped his hold, for it was the master's daughter. "Miss Mayleda! I never expected you—"

"I came out to look for Joseph," the girl sobbed. "Instead I found Teddy Rensler touching Rosa in the laundry!" She pointed to the roofed house over the well. "He went off that way!"

"You go back inside and stay with Rosa!"

Hampton began to chase after the Pine Woods master, never expecting to catch him except that at the last moment Rensler turned around, even though he had climbed the fence and had his mare's reins in hand.

"You're coming after me, *Mista* Gund?" He laughed.

Hampton halted yards inside the fence. "You get off my employer's land. I told you this mornin' I am at liberty to do what's necessary to protect his property."

Rensler's clucked his tongue. "What have I done? Who's to bring a word against my character? A girl? A Negress? Overseer, don't you trouble me, for I have the power to remove you from this parish at any time."

Angry, Hampton stepped back. It was true. According to the standards of their culture, the gentleman had done nothing wrong except, perhaps, in trespassing, since Rosa was not his property. Overseers and drivers were taught to turn a blind eye and use a dumb mouth whenever planters were inadvertently discovered with slave women. But Hampton's eyes stayed wide, and his tongue felt sharp with truth. Delora's darkies needed an advocate, and he could think of no one but himself.

Rensler raised himself in his saddle. "Tell my cousin and friends that I will meet them at home. Have a good evening, *Mista* Gund."

While Rensler slipped away like chaff in the breeze, Hampton thought it odd that the Bible came to his mind. There was instruction in it that a believer should love his enemies, but also that he should show justice to those under persecution. Wrapping his hands around his folded arms he spoke aloud. "Lord, how's any man s'pose to do both those things at onc't?"

"Hey there, sah!" It was Billy Days who hollered as he emerged on the driveway, just about where Teddy Rensler had been. "I seen that Pine Woods massa sneakin' into the kitchenhouse, but I could do nothin' but pray. Then here you come—the answer to my prayers!" The slave bowed. "You didn't have to stand up to him, sah, but you done it anyhow."

Hampton felt a chill like one experiences after having a close call with disaster or death. "It wa' Miss Mayleda what really saved Rosa. Her comin' scaired Rensler off." He walked down so as to be face-to-face with the Negro as thoughts of the morning whipping badgered him like the wind. "The young mistress is still with Rosa in the kitchen, but Bette should come up to be with her instead. In fact, why don't you just take the girl on down with you, where she can stay the night with you an' Bette."

He saw the driver's worry even in the dim light. "I gots Parris with me, sah. He been sleepless on account of Rosa bein' delivered up here."

Hampton nodded, knowing Billy had done the wise thing to keep his son where he could watch him. "Then Bette will have to come up here. I'll leave it to her to send Miss Callcott to bed."

Billy seemed chagrined. "Mass' Rensler must have just been a-waitin', sah, for Bette weren't down at our place more than a quarter-hour till he done sneaked in."

"I guess," Hampton sympathized, feeling another stab of guilt about whipping Billy and knowing that by now Bette and Parris would be aware of his actions too. He changed the subject, hoping to put himself in better favor with those he had harmed. "I was on my way to seein' Joseph. Mebbe give him somethin' to eat."

The driver responded only by looking down.

Inwardly Hampton could not hold back his longing to make amends. He ventured to talk about the day, since Billy Days was the closest he had ever come to having a friend. "Look, I know I'm puttin' myself way 'cross the line, but I want to say I'm sorry 'bout this mornin'. I hope you know I really had no choice."

"Ahhun," Billy said, seeming very cautious.

"I mean it! If I hadn't done what I done, *they* would have done it to you."

The dark man's cheeks expanded, but no words came out.

"What are you thinkin'?" There was almost amusement in Billy's eyes, which put Hampton on guard.

"What! You want a darkie to speak his mind for onc't?"

"Didn't I just say that?"

"Mebbe. Are you askin' to hear what you want to hear, or what I want to say?"

"How can you be so smart-mouthed afta' all I tried to do for you an' you' race just now an' t'day? Why are you choosin' to act the fool now? I just wanted to make sure you understand when I whupped you, it wa' for you' best." Hampton deliberately made his speech like Billy's.

Billy nodded dispiritedly. "A'right, sah, so now I know what it is *you* want to hear. 'Thankyee, sah, for breakin' my flesh an' bein' so very helpful.'" He even bowed and dragged his toe in the dirt.

"That's not how you really feel!"

"I didn't say it wa'. But it be what you want me to say, so I says it. Now, can I be dismissed?"

"Billy, why you actin' like this t'night?"

The African paused before answering. He was still looking down, maybe with real contrition now. "Well, sah, I s'pose I wa' just testin' the small amount of hope I had that you *might* be interested in what I has to say for true."

Hampton felt his muscles tighten. "What! You think I like what happened t'day!"

"I didn't say that neither. In fact, I didn't say nothin' out of my own mind yet. But mebbe that's just the way it gots to be 'tween you an' me."

"What are you tryin' to say? Spit it out. I wanna know. I done asked."

"A'right." Billy turned slowly to show the welts on his bare back. "In the future, sah, please don't feel obliged to do me no more favors." The slave started to walk away.

"Days! You come back here!"

Billy turned, full of silent subordination so that every move between them pierced Hampton like a sword. "Yessah, Mista Bossman." He dragged his toe again.

"Don't you do this to me! Don't you treat me like you never knew me!"

"Do I know you, sah? An' do *you* know *me*?"

Hampton felt a great heaviness of heart. "I had no choice!"

"Beggin' you' pardon, but it seems that it's the very nature of *free* men to have choices. It only be *slave* men what don't."

"You think I have it easy! I can lose everythin'!"

"Leastways you *do* have somethin' to lose. Slave men don't have nothin'.'"

"Just now, Rensler threatened my life!"

"Yessah. I gwine give you that. But you can walk away without gettin' shot in the back, Mista Gund, whereas me an' my kind, we can't even *run*."

Hampton took off his hat while the slave went on.

"You think you suffer from the same despicable institution what's keepin' me. Well, I daresay you don't, sah! When was the last time *you'* wife was taken or *you'* child was listed on a bill of sales?"

"You are right, Billy," Hampton breathed, rubbing his eyes. "You are right. I am sorry. Sorry for it all. Howsumever, I just can't abide the notion that you think I have it easy, for I don't!"

They locked eyes, hard at first, but by and by they softened. "That is for true, Mista Gund. An' for that, I am sorry. This whole world in a sorry state, sah. I s'pose way down everybody might have reason to be sorry."

Hampton confessed candidly, "I'm not sure what to do. I'm tellin' you that . . .'cause, well, you are really the closest I've ever come to havin' a friend." In the silence that followed this confession Hampton grew uneasy. However, he couldn't dismiss the conviction that he had been right to bare his heart to the Negro. Inwardly he felt he was understanding even the black man's silence. Maybe they had crossed some kind of bridge where Billy now knew he didn't have to say just what was expected of him.

He could see Billy as his friend, but if the driver didn't feel that way in return, well, then the Negro had a right to his own opinion. Hampton had learned something through this painful evening. And for that reason he accepted Billy's honest silence as a gift, though one that hurt him. It came clear to his mind that the best way to prove he was a friend was just to be one. While they stood there longer, Hampton felt some of that hollowness filling in.

The whole way back to his shanty Billy chastised himself for having dropped his guard to a white man, even one so seemingly different and sincere as Hampton Gund. Talk cost a white man nothing, but one careless word out of a black man's mouth could cost him everything. Wasn't his back burning already? Why would he want to trust the very one who had wounded him?

Down near the chicken coops the roosters were already crowing, though it was still hours to first light. Billy went up onto his porch and past the pan of now cold water Bette had been using to bathe his back when he had seen Teddy Rensler going into the massa's yard. He pulled at his door, aware of how very quiet everything was now. He found Bette standing right inside in the dark.

"The boss needs you back up with Rosa at onc't," he said, whispering so as not to be heard by Parris. "To his credit, Mista Gund done had the nerve to drive the planter off."

Bette grabbed him by both arms. "The moment Mass' Rensler rode out, Parris done run outta this house, not to come home since."

———————

Hampton stayed at Joseph's side for more than an hour, accomplishing little in the moonlight. The boy was too sick to eat, and though he had a wet cloth to soothe Joseph's mouth, the slave could not even hold it because his hands were caked with dung. The whole time Hampton sat there, he was thinking of Billy. *What must be in that black man's mind and heart to see Joseph tortured in this way?*

Beside him Joseph shivered, leaning against the fence where he was chained but not sleeping. Hampton realized clearer now that the boy had thoughts and feelings also. He wondered what Joseph would say if he had his tongue back and could speak with honesty. Moving slightly, Hampton pulled the thick blanket up around Joseph's shoulders to protect him from the mosquitoes and the dew.

"This should not be happenin' to you." He dared to speak his mind with tenderness, though he had no business to counter what the massas did.

He kept himself from saying he was sorry, for as Billy had pointed out to him, what good did it do to say that if his words changed nothing? Joseph turned his head, looking directly at him for the first time ever. His facial features appeared midnight blue in the moonlight and chiseled with pain. Hampton saw his great weariness.

"Mebbe you should try again to eat?"

For a moment Joseph eagerly eyed the biscuit, but then shook his head. Hampton went back to comforting him with water, his heart expanding toward him all the while. "Don't give up," he found himself pleading. "There got to be some way through all of this."

The boy's head dropped back against the fence, and he shut his eyes. Hampton thought he heard someone coming toward them, though no one but the massas were to know where Joseph was. He got to his feet, sure now that he heard hard breathing in the dark. "Who goes there?" he asked defensively.

"Sah! I . . . I need you' help!" It was Billy running with a light. "I done looked everywhere I can think of! Parris's skipped off. Mebbe to find Rensler."

"We'll take horses!" Hampton decided, leaving Joseph behind.

Side by side they ran to the stable, but as Hampton put his hand to the latch, Billy stopped him.

"Listen! Out in the forest beyond Hermon Creek."

It was a series of whistles, too odd and stiff to be anything but human. Billy led the way down into the pasture, keeping low and crouching along the fencerow. Hampton stayed at his heels, his hand atop one of Brant's pistols still strapped at his waist. Billy seemed ready to give up when nothing moved in the field. Hampton could understand his motives. His mind was set on finding his son. For the good of Delora, however, any illegal bootleggers or intruders lurking in the woods near slave quarters must be stopped. So he told Billy to go on with this searching, certainly against the slave driver's wishes.

Walking into the pasture with great caution, they faced the nerve-wracking unknown together.

In his head Billy knew it was right to be chasing down the poor-white intruders that sometimes came to prey on the street, eager to trade home-made liquor for rice or bacon stolen from the massas' larders. Yet in his heart he wanted only one thing—to find his son safe and alive.

Since he and the overseer had successfully chased down moonshiners before, there was no need for them to talk about a plan. After jumping the creek and coming silently to the edge of the forest, they separated in an attempt to sandwich the troublemaking trespassers between them. Billy thought of the pistols Gund could use by law to defend Delora slaves. He closed his own fists, since that same law said he could strike, in this case only, to save his white boss from violence.

Gund was probably moving under the trees by now, since Billy could not see him. He slipped through the tangles of vines growing where field met forest, then went deep among the well-spaced trunks. There was nothing to disturb the night. No frog. No cricket, which was a pretty clear sign that the swampy ground had recently been disturbed by men. Billy's eyes adjusted. He could see among the trees and he crouched, knowing that if his vision was this good, then so might be the vision of those who would not hesitate to do them harm.

Time passed, and with it Billy's belief that they would catch the intruders. Whatever trespassers had been there, they must have been wise enough to sneak off by some safe route. Then ahead, near a cluster of smaller, denser trees, he thought he saw Overseer Gund's short, stretch-bellied shape. With the stealth of a deer Billy moved closer. When he was sure it was Gund, he stood.

The overseer called to him, "I found Parris!"

Then Billy saw him, too, sprawled in the leaves.

Even working together Billy and Gund had a hard time getting Parris on his feet. The reason for his being in the woods was perfectly clear—by the smell on his heavy, belching breath. Billy had never seen Parris drink, let alone drunk. It was shameful how his boy laughed and cried and burped without reserve as they moved him along with one of Parris's heavy arms over each of their shoulders. The weight on Billy's whipped back tortured him, but not as much as seeing his grown child in this condition.

Parris's sorry explanations came out in spurts like water being pumped. "Ohhh! Paaaa! 'Tis sweet to know nothin'! Ask me! Ask me! Cain't even tell you her name!"

"What you steal to buy this poison?" Billy demanded.

Parris pulled himself up boastfully. "Why nothin'! They all know I's the preacher, so they let me drink free! A whoole bottle myself."

"That's how much you had?" Billy groaned.

He showed his stinking smile even to Gund. "Every nigger should drink, ya know, sah! Makes a body feel fine!"

"Shut you' ugly mouth!" Billy nearly wept his words. When Parris would not listen, he plastered a hand over his mouth. His son vomited into his palm, then dropped back.

"You so mean! So mean to drag me back!"

Gund stopped in his tracks. "We got to get him quiet! We cain't take him into the quarters like this."

To make matters worse, Parris bellowed out a slave hymn with his rich magnificent voice *"Ohhh wayyy, fa' awayyyy! Jesus wants his chilluns' sar-rowwws fa' awayyy!"* Gund clamped his hand over Parris's face while Billy wiped his clean on the grass.

"Yeah, you gwine sing, boy!" Billy raged against him. "You gwine sing while Mista Gund strings you up in the street an' makes a sorry example outta you."

The overseer heard him. "Billy, I'm not gwine make no spectacle outta your son!"

Billy looked back in disbelief. "That's Mass' Abram's rules. Somebody caught drinkin' or carousin' they get put on display an' punished."

"I don't care what the rules say. I'm not gwine do it. How could you think I would afta' the talk we just done had t'night?"

"What I said then has nothin' to do now with punishment an' justice!" Billy said, unable to fathom why he had to explain. "Parris need know that wrongdoing brings its own unhappy consequences! Lord, have mercy! I don't want my child gwine down to hell on that wide slippery trough of sin!"

Hampton's face twisted like a man in pain. "If I use him as an example, then that's just what Mista Rensler wants. A chance to scoff at Mista Abram's converted Africans—"

"But what 'bout my boy! If he get off with nothin', he likely to come on down here again! He's my son, Mista Gund, though in this life I don't even have the right to claim him. But in the glory to come, sah, I want him there! I cain't just turn my back an' forget him, not when he's a-totterin' on some brink of hell."

Gund seemed broken by his words. "Then you stay out here an' I'll never say a word 'bout it. You do what you think is right—as his Christian daddy."

Then, seeming true to his word, Hampton turned and walked away.

CHAPTER 9

BEFORE DAWN BETTE LEFT the laundryhouse where she had spent the night with Rosa. In the damp, unhealthy air she pulled up a pail of water from the well and took one of the hollow calabash shells to be her dipper. Going out the seldom used back gate, she went to look for Joseph. Following the fence, she found him moaning softly, trapped by his chains and the smell of manure.

Billy had warned her not to look for him, but she could not keep herself away. It was on her heart to give him a drink before the massas would come for him again. She knew that Billy and even Mista Gund had been wetting his mouth whenever possible. But after a day in the sun and a night in the chill the boy needed sustenance. That's why she had a little jar of molasses hidden inside her apron. Standing near him she stirred some of the sticky sweetness into the bowl of the gourd.

"Joseph? Honey? It's Maum." He did not move or show his face. "I done brought you some molasses an' water to strengthen you."

He shook his head, not lifting it at all while he stayed against the fence like a heap of stinking rags to be burned.

"Come on, chile. Come on, honey. You gwine have to give in on somethin's to those men t'day in order to save you'self."

He groaned and pulled his face even lower. "Naaa!"

She touched the horse blanket on his shoulder. "Just till Mass' Abram get home."

He was a rock, not listening. And dawn was breaking.

"Here! Try some of this here sweet water."

His whimper reminded her of a plover trying to lure intruders from its nest. She studied him. He was slovenly covered with the hairy wool, his manacled hands and feet clotted with the dung the massas were using to tell him he wasn't more than an animal himself. As a girl she had seen others punished this way, but never on Delora soil. "Please, honey, if only for the sake of you' mama an' me."

There was a delicate voice behind her. "Maum, could I try?"

Scared to death, Bette turned to find Rosa silently standing near them. "What you doin' out here, girl?"

"Is this Joseph? The one Billy and you spoke of?"

"Yes! Now you get you'self straight back to the kitchen."

"I'd like to try to help him."

Bette frowned at her hard, for nobody would think of Rosa as being a body with compassion. "What could you do? What got you out here?"

It puzzled her to see how the young woman, so afraid of all male flesh, got down right beside Joseph. She seemed ready and able to ignore the ugly sights and smells that hemmed him in. "Why, he's pure African!"

"Of course he is!" Bette snapped, suddenly distrusting Rosa even more. "What that to you?"

By now Joseph had raised his eyes to Rosa.

"I . . . I thought he would be mulatto," she stammered, obviously shaken and embarrassed. "I mean . . . because of what you said to Billy Days about his knowing how to read."

Suddenly Joseph was like a man with coals on his head.

"AAAA! AAAA!" His chained hands swung out to the girl. She pulled back, emitting a terrible cry of her own.

"You want the massas to come an' whup us all?" Bette silenced them both with fury.

"No," Rosa said, regaining some of her composure but now holding her hands tightly against her small, shapely bosom. "I'm sorry. I just never heard of a black man reading. They say it's the white blood coursing in our veins that lets us do it."

"Aaaa!" Joseph cried out at her again, this time with tears pouring down his face. His swollen mouth trembled as he tried hard to form some kind of words.

Rosa became intent on his struggle. "You didn't know that any of us knew?" she guessed with awe, speaking just to him. "Of course! After your tongue was cut, you were despairing that anyone beside the masters would ever know!"

"Yaaa!" he cried, communicating his thoughts, but with a voice that reminded Bette of a simple-minded fool. It closed her throat to hear what Brant Callcott's cruelty had done.

Joseph kept nodding to show his relieved gratefulness until finally the action closed his weary eyes. Rosa crouched closer.

"I understand, for I know how to write and read."

His eyes sparked open. He started to reach again, then seemed to re-member her earlier reaction. He stared at her, his eyes melting with thoughts he could not speak.

"Missy! Them is dangerous thin's to be sayin'!" Bette chided. "Affa' what done happen to him, what you think they'd do with you?"

"I know, but see how our knowing gives him hope? They want to break him of thinking that he can and should read."

"Mass' Abram not taught him, that I know!"

"Then he learned it in secret! It can be done!"

Joseph nodded, wide-eyed and sighing.

"I know you'd never give it up," Rosa whispered boldly. "I know, though for me now, it's been four years since I had any kind of book. Four years of terrible isolation."

Joseph was like somebody waking up in a strange place. He breathed hard, seeming to be agitated by all Rosa said.

"This ain't gwine help him none," Bette decided. "Book learnin' ain't gwine do nothin' now to save his life."

But suddenly Joseph showed interest in the gourd still filled to the brim. Rosa squinted sorrowfully as she crept in closer to look at Joseph's mouth, now haplessly hanging open with anxiety. "There's a muscle on the right side that has not been cut."

Bette looked at her blankly.

"The tongue's a muscle! He needs it to swallow—" She took the dipper with haste, and using a dampened corner of the apron she had just started wearing that morning, she washed a clean spot on Joseph's right cheek. "If you can just tilt your head, the water can come in here." Even as she spoke, Joseph was moving, following what she was trying to do.

A moment later he swallowed the first steady stream of nourishment he had since the struggle began. All their eyes—Rosa's included—flooded with tears of joy. Through the next dangerous moments, Joseph consumed the whole jar of molasses. Afterward his deep brown eyes rose to the sky. Frowning he twisted his head to look back toward the house.

"He worried for us!" Bette guessed. "An' he got every right to be." But regardless of the haste needed, Bette took time to pray. Rosa stood by woodenly while Bette quickly laid her hand on Joseph's uncovered head. "God, give him strength for t'day an' you' blessin'. Oh, if it can be you' will, Papa-God, let this old cup of sufferin' pass Kwash by this day. In Jesus's name."

"Why do you call him Kwash?" Rosa asked, causing more delay.

"That be my name for him from the day he was birthed!" she said remembering that event for an instant with pleasure. "Hurry on back now!"

"But what's it mean?"

"Come along! It just mean 'Sunday's Child.' There, now that sure ain't worth the price of bein' discovered!"

But Rosa stayed planted, still studying the boy who kept his gaze on her.

"Come on! Just like Negozi done calls you Dara. Now will you hurry!"

Then Bette noticed Joseph's eyes had moved to her. There was tremendous brightness in them, making Bette wonder if he remembered enough of what he had been taught on Sabbath afternoons to know the second African word meant "beautiful." He released her from his view, as though protective of her too. Like a hen, she ushered Rosa through the gate to safety.

Joseph kept his mortification under control until the two women fled. Then he turned his face to the fence and wept, knowing he had once prided himself in fine clothes and his dignified position as Abram's favorite servant. He then saw the foolishness of such grieving and begged God for the strength Bette had already called down upon him. He had asked for God's will to be done. Certainly the suffering and torment did not seem like God's will. But maybe there was divine purpose and strength in the enduring.

He thought of Rosa, whom he had never seen before, visiting him like an encouraging angel. She had spoken the very words he needed to hear, for now if he died, the other slaves would know the secret of his knowing how to read. Like the hope he gained from seeing her, the sweet taste of the water lingered too. Perhaps he would not starve or shrivel up with thirst now that he had proved to himself he still could swallow. If Mr. Gund would dare to bring him food again, he might try to eat. His flat, clawing stomach ranted for nourishment.

He touched his dirty hand to the place where Rosa had wiped away the filth, smearing it again so no one could see he'd had visitors. It was done just in time, for the gate squeaked, letting in Teddy and Brant. With hesitation, the young Callcott presented his boot once more under Joseph's downcast eyes. But refreshed and hopeful now because of the women's coming, Joseph felt new determination not to be forced to grovel at any white man's feet. Holding firm to his knowledge, his vision, and his hope that he was equal to these other two in every way but cruel intention, he dared to raise his eyes and shake his head.

Instantly the blanket was pulled from him, and he was yanked to his feet.

"You are going to be sorry, boy!" The threat was Rensler's.

Brant broke in, quite pleadingly. "Can't you understand it's no use? You can be bathed, fed, and rested today if only you will submit. Then it will not be hard for you."

Joseph lifted his eyes past Brant to gulls spinning merrily overhead. The leg-irons that had held him to the fence were unlocked for a moment, then put on again. Able only to shuffle, he was driven back to the barnyard. Dizzy and weak, aching and hungry, he still had a kernel of hope inside him. The other Africans would know why this was happening, as they heard from Bette and Rosa. He could wallow like a pig and feel no humiliation. Instead, his punishment would be a broad proclamation of what a black man could do with the help of God.

"You know what to do," Rensler growled.

It did not bother him to have them see him again sinking into the mire, drier than yesterday because of the sun. The heat poked his flesh, which had been burnt to tenderness the day before. He hardly cared. Perhaps God had him on a mission. He kept his ears atuned to the wild gulls in flight. In his heart he also had a new gift to treasure: *Dara*—beauty in the midst of ugliness.

"You'll be a boot-sucking dog by the end of this day—or a dead one!" Rensler called as the gate closed behind him.

Joseph shut his eyes and prayed. His mind filled with thoughts of another Servant who had not been broken by humiliation. Though naked, scorned, flogged, and crucified before all, Jesus never lost sight of who He was.

Maybe this was also his call from heaven—to suffer with grace so that others might have the courage to know themselves and do likewise. Even now he was aware of black faces looking in on him, as they had done yesterday, with both compassion and horror. Stableboys. Yard boys. The smithy Samson. He found himself praying for them as he prayed for himself. *God, may we all come to find ourselves in you.*

Bette found Rosa ready to busy herself with every job given her. She worked in total silence, with eyes that roved and would not focus.

By late afternoon they had finished doing up the laundry so that the pressing irons, which had been heated on the hearth plate, could be cooled. Bette decided, prayerfully, that it might be time to reach a little further into the girl's knot of sorrows and fears.

"Come on outside to the well while I rest my weary self." Bette sat down on the bench in the shade, but Rosa walked farther, using their first moments of idleness to go to the fence where Joseph could be seen in the barnyard across the driveway.

Bette got up and joined her. "He do show courage, ainty?" she said, feeling soft compassion for both youngsters. "To just keep on gwine so's that nobody but him is made to suffer."

Rosa nodded, her gaze never leaving the sorry, distant scene.

"He a'ways been special," Bette mused, her own hands coming to the fence. Gently, after they had stayed for a time, Bette called her back to the cool well-side bench. She sat down and Rosa sat beside her. "You done absolutely the right thin' for him this mornin'. No doubt in my mind, girl, but you saved his life."

"You were the one who dared to find him." Rosa returned no smile, but her eyes did warm, and her next words proved her interest in knowing more about him. "Why did you call him Kwash?"

"Ah," Bette said, for some reminiscing was sweet. "He were born on Whitsunday, twenty years ago."

"What's Whitsunday, ma'am?" Rosa looked blankly.

"Why that be the birthday Sunday of the church what's celebrated each an' every year. Ain't you never hear'd of it?"

Rosa shook her head.

"Well!" Bette swung her bare feet, since the bench was high. "That be the day when the Holy Ghost of God first come down onto ordinary folk, settin' flames of fire 'pon their heads!" Inwardly she enjoyed the girl's surprise. It was the kind of story that could make even the most uninterested sit up and take notice. That's what happened with Rosa, so Bette went on. "From that day till now God keeps on bringin' his Holy-Ghost fire to every believer's heart whenever somebody done make the choice to call Him Savior an' Lord. We all just be little movin', breathin' dwellin' places for the Holy Ghost."

Bette spoke this way because she knew the girl had been raised to believe in spirits, first by her free Haitian mama and then, sadly, also through Negozi, who to this day leaned toward practicing her hoodooing whenever life seemed unbearable.

Unfortunately Rosa didn't seem interested in any more talk about faith. Still Bette took her story one step further. "Joseph. He done know God's Holy Ghost be dwellin' in him."

Rosa frowned. "I can't believe in a God of mercy or love." She nodded toward the barn. "And Christianity is the *last* religion I would ever trust in when so many slaveholders gather piously under the church steeples and then do things like this!"

"I know 'xactly what you sayin', gal, but there's another side to it too. Take Mass' Abram. He don't lack for no holy love of God. No! Mebbe earthly wisdom to know how to carry it out, sometimes." The thought seemed confusing to her. "I mean it, chile. With all that's in me, I say it be the day to pray for the full enlightenment of folk like Mista Abram! You think back, an' you know it wa' compassion from the Lord what done led that man to rescue you. An' it wa' just the same for Joseph's mama too. She be the gal Jewell what works as the head maid. Mass' Abram done brung her here when she weren't more than fourteen an' a'ready big with chile."

"And that was Joseph?" Rosa's eyes were wide.

"Yes, it were." Bette grinned, for now the girl was ready to listen to her witness again. Inwardly she said a prayer that God would heal the child's heart, maybe even because of what she now would say. "I'm gwine tell you some hard thin's, but that's only 'cause you had hard times too. Mass' Abram an' his coachman Ezra seen Jewell lyin' unconscious one afta'noon on the riverbank when they was on their way home from Colonel Rensler's place—Pine Woods, you know—what lies just upriver."

The girl sighed, her tension showing. "Yes!"

"Well, the two of them stopped, an' then Massa took her to Renslers' 'cause they guessed—an' right—that she was Pine Woods property. Howsumever, afta takin' one look at her, the mean old colonel done declared she weren't worth savin'. So right then an' there Mass' Abram said he'd trade two ewes with lambs for Jewell, an' that's what he done to bring her here."

"And then she birthed Joseph."

"Yeah, but there be some thin's in 'tween what I think you ought to know. Jewell's natural daddy done been tradin' her to men overnight who would pay him for the favor in wine or rum." Rosa looked away, for she understood directly what treachery Joseph's mama suffered. "I was first to care for her right over there in the kitchen. She was skinny as a fence rail 'cept for the baby in her belly. Remind you of somebody else, ainty."

"Yes, Maum!" Rosa's voice quavered.

"At first it seemed she could not live, though Massa an' Missus done all they could for her. Miss Oribel wa' the one to stay with her most, prayin' an' readin' the Scriptures over her."

"Yes." Rosa gulped another word of understanding, for that was exactly what the kind mistress had done for her too.

"I know it's hard for you to hear all, honey, but I think it shows the goodness of God's people, even if they not be perfect. From all that care, chile, Jewell got strong 'nough to brin' forth her healthy boy-child. An' then to have him come at dawn on such a special Christian holiday, well, you just had to say God's hand wa' 'pon it. 'Sides that, Miss Oribel wa' delivered of a son just two weeks later. Often young Jewell set out here, just where we settin' now, sucklin' them two new babies t'gether—one black an' one white, just like they was twins."

"The other baby was Brant Callcott." That did not please her.

Bette spoke against Rosa's earnest frown. "Yes, it were." She brought the telling back to Joseph. "Mass' Abram wa' so pleased, he done give Jewell the blessing to name her chile herself, which is somethin' rare you know, for most whites will name the slave babies they done own."

Rosa appeared too filled up with feelings to say anything, but she was shaking her head. And then Bette remembered that the Callcotts had also let her name her baby too. "Dear chile. You thinkin' on you' own Kulo! Well, cry, but don't be so sorrowful, for I says by the Word of God, you' little girl's safe in heaven now."

Rubbing her eyes, Rosa gathered herself. "You were speaking about

Joseph. Why did Jewell name him such an English name?"

"She wa' thinkin' of the Joseph of the Bible, 'cause of what Miss Oribel done taught her in her time of confinement." Bette smiled then.

"I don't know the stories of the Bible, Maum."

"Oh, chile! The Joseph of the Scriptures wa' a free man but sold to slavery by his jealous brothers." Rosa's gaze came up, for she, too, had been free and then betrayed. "Joseph wa' forced to serve 'gainst his will for years. But he never done give up his trust in God. An' by 'n by, his courage an' wisdom saved not only him, but his whole family. There's one verse in the story what goes somethin' like this: 'What man meant for evil, God meant for good.' An' that's 'xactly what Jewell would say from the time she brought forth her chile." Bette paused, her own voice tripping on her emotion. "Sorta hard to say that now, but God can still make it true!"

The girl bit her lip. "He's been out there so many hours. I wish they would bring him up."

"I know. It be my constant prayer."

Rosa dropped her head, not ready, it appeared, to believe that God was a hearer and an answerer of prayer.

"Mebbe his mama's special Scripture is encouragin' him now. I don't believe a man could have endured like he done without help from above."

Rosa wrapped herself in her arms and began to weep.

"Now, now. One of the reasons I done told you this story wa' so you might start believin' the Holy Ghost power can help you too."

"I'm not crying for myself, but for him."

"You sweet chile!" Bette did not embrace her, for she knew Rosa hated being touched, but she stood like her guardian because just then Mass' Brant and Mass' Rensler came up through the gate. Both men marched straight up to them.

"Where is Joseph?" Mass' Brant demanded of them.

Rosa's terrified eyes met Bette's. "For true!" Bette said. "Neither of us knows! We just done saw him in the barnyard!"

Rensler threw up his hand and swore into the air. In a moment he was on his horse, going to round up his patrolmen.

The search kept up till suppertime. Then all the patrolmen descended on Delora expecting to eat. Bette hustled about preparing a larger meal. The men had gone as far east as the river, as far west as the main road, as far south as the city, and as far north as the trees beyond the slave graveyard and Hermon Creek. They had checked the house, too, just in case Jewell was somehow managing to hide her grown son. The men were especially suspicious of Mayleda, but Rosa was sure the young mistress knew nothing because of how she had sat and cried at the news of his disappearance.

Rosa kept herself numb instead of sorrowful. It was the only way to push herself to help Bette with the food while the hound dogs, eager for Negro blood, barked and bayed just outside the kitchen walls where they were tied to the fence. As she was spooning butter into a bowl, one of the riders strode in to demand some freshly brewed peppermint tea for his stomach. Rosa fought to keep her angry eyes away from him. What was a stomachache compared to what they had put Joseph through?

As soon as the man was gone, Maum sent her out into the weedy marsh behind the kitchen fence to cut fresh mint, since the mint jar was empty.

"Don't dawdle!" Bette warned.

Outside, the dusk was red like a stained-glass dome above her. She left by the same gate they had used to find Joseph. She waded into high, dry weeds in search of tender, spring-growth mint. With dogs still yapping along the driveway, horrible memories began flashing back at her like bolts of lightning. Fear locked her bare feet to the soggy ground, for the weeds whispering that night sounded just as they did the night she had stumbled upon her parents' slaughtered corpses, brazenly tossed into the fields behind her burned-down house.

The closing darkness was also as it had been then, when slave men had grabbed her while she screamed. Then they had locked her into the barn with them so that she would later be counted among her deceased family's chattels. Her time of terror had begun on an evening just like this. Now it was back to haunt her. She could not make herself go in deeper just for some bold buckra's tea. Her eyes slipped down before she turned to run. Just inches from her she saw the legs and feet of a still, dark body in chains. A nightmare returning—but this time Joseph was the corpse! She pushed herself to flight, but by the time she was almost to the gate, her senses returned. *What if he is still alive?* After supper the dogs would be released again to find him and would tear the flesh from his bones.

She went back through the weeds again. After seeing death in her parents' bodies, the death of her beloved child had left her trembling. She didn't believe she had the courage to look on death again. Yet she kept walking to Joseph.

When she came to him, she parted the weeds and knelt down. The devils of the dark world seemed to crawl through her stomach and spine.

Her mother had been petrified by the thought of dying and had taught Rosa as a child to say Latin and English words from a poem, that they might act like a spell. *Timor mortis conturbat me:* The fear of death distresses me!

She found herself crying this aloud in both languages as she gathered herself like someone holding feathers in a storm. Fearfully she reached and touched Joseph's shoulder. He moved. He breathed. She screamed in relief that he was still alive, muffling the sound in her hand.

Using her bare hands and some water from the ditch, she took his head to her lap and washed his swollen blistered lips. "It's Rosa," she whispered, not knowing if he was alert enough to hear and understand. She pulled off her headcloth and wet it in the ugly water trickling beside her. As she washed his face he revived and looked at her, wildly scared at first and then completely pacified.

She was afraid to leave and afraid to stay, not knowing if any breath might be his last. Surely he must have wandered here in search of water. Perhaps it was one of Bette's God's miracles that they had looked for him every place but here.

Even in suffering Joseph had an incredibly handsome face, like a piece of artwork carved from the rarest and darkest of woods. She drew in her breath, feeling unnerved that she had chosen to touch him. She found comfort in his name. "Joseph," she whispered, but this time his eyes closed and his breathing became shallow and tentative. She didn't know what to do. She felt certain they would find him here, and she had not the strength to hide him in a better place.

Quaking, she knew she had no choice. Laying Joseph's head gently to the ground, she ran back to find Maum.

Joseph remembered Rosa leaving him.

The world stayed dark for a time, and then it was lighted with a beam that shone directly into his vision. He wanted the light to be heaven, but he heard the rumble of Rensler's voice. Then a boot once more was thrust toward his face, which was pressed to cold, wet ground.

He did not know where he was. Or why. But all the details of the ugly challenge set before him were as clear as his pain.

"He'll do it now or never." Joseph heard Rensler say.

Joseph would not put his lips on it. He waited for the violence to follow. But instead, the boot was pulled away.

"I'm done with this, Teddy!"

Joseph clung to the vague awareness that Brant had saved him. The sores in his mouth roared. Every muscle began to twitch and tremble. He had not succumbed to them, but now every fiber in his being seemed to be breaking and dying. He thought of Rosa. He wondered if he had really seen her and felt her touch, or just dreamt it. If he could regret leaving earth for heaven, the only regret was because of her.

A strange benediction grew from deep inside. It was the prayer for the sick that he had memorized long ago in Master Abram's clean, confining quarters. *Defend me from the danger of my enemies. Keep me in perpetual peace through Jesus Christ.* "AAAA-MEEEN!"

The slave's scream unnerved them all—Mayleda, the houseslaves, and even Teddy.

"Lord of mercy, he was praying even to his last!" Bette sobbed and Billy drew near her. They all looked down upon the boy, at peace now beside the black, sluggish waters that looked like ink in Brant's lantern light. Brant's own hope for forgiveness would die with the boy. What had he done! How would he ever explain it all to his father?

Teddy reached down and touched Joseph's neck. "There's still life in him."

Brant was sick with worry and shame. He had taken Teddy's advice for two days, and everything had worsened. He felt the eyes of all his daddy's people on him now, for all had gathered because of the terrifying experience of having patrollers everywhere.

"I want the shackle keys," Brant declared feebly.

Teddy handed them over. "You'll be sorry if you give in now. Show him your boot once more."

But Brant didn't care about the future. Ignoring Teddy and calling Gund to help him, Brant dug through the dung and used the keys. Gund would have done it for him, but something inside Brant drove him to touch Joseph's misery. The boy was too weak to know he had been loosed.

Over them both Teddy spoke. "You had better hope he dies, or your problems will be back."

Brant stood and pressed the soiled keys into Teddy's hand. "Do you ever think you could be wrong? I wanted your help. I trusted you. But it's led to this!"

"Your slave did this to himself, and don't you forget that. I certainly will not be forgetting it."

Brant's skin tingled. "Get off my property," he seethed, not knowing what else to say. "Billy! Gund! Wash Joseph up and have Bette do whatever she can to save him."

"You're fearing only your daddy," Teddy surmised, "when what you should be fearing is harboring nuisance chattel like him."

Mayleda came out of nowhere to hug him as Gund and Billy quickly and carefully raised Joseph in their grasp. "Oh, Brant! Thank heavens! You've changed your mind!"

Brant watched Teddy walk through the frenzied dogs to meet the other patrolmen, all looking hungry for the use of force. Some of them were friends from the Young Planters' Club—or former friends. Likely they'd all be adversaries now.

"Don't thank me yet," he said unhappily to his sister. "I have a feeling this fight because of Joseph has just begun."

CHAPTER 10

THE CONVENTION SEALED a lasting friendship between Abram Callcott and Nathan Gilman. Together they had faced a crucible of trials. In the very first session there had been a sustained vote to make South Carolina residency a new criterion for membership in the Society for the Propagation of the Gospel to Children and Africans. It felt devastating to Abram to watch Nathan quietly come forward to present his resignation.

In the privacy of their sleeping quarter, Abram expressed his regret. Nathan decided to see the convention through, since the new bylaws would not take effect until the coming year. Despite the rejection, Nathan seemed determined to continue making a prayerful decision as to whether or not to build ships for southern ports. For the next two days he became the quiet but ubiquitous observer at every session.

Then today, Thursday, Abram received an unexpected letter, which was delivered to his room prior to breakfast. Nathan was with him when he read Mayleda's brief remarks: *You are needed at home*. Out of kindness

Nathan offered to catch the next steamer home with him. Climbing into a coach, Abram worried both about Delora and about what would transpire at the final plenary session.

The day was hot, and the prospect of rushing home made it seem long. He rubbed his forehead, for he had not been feeling well.

"Are you all right?" Nathan asked as the rented coach jolted them on their way toward the wharves.

"Yes. It's only that I have a terrible headache."

"No wonder! In those meetings you are the lone voice crying in the wilderness. I appreciate all you tried to do to hold to the society's standard of 'Christ first, and Christ only.'"

Abram sighed. "It was not enough."

When they got to the wharf, Abram needed to take Nathan's arm for support. The movements of the seaport worsened his condition. Weakness washed over him while Nathan helped him to the gentlemen's on-board lounge. "It's good to have a friend on the *Goodfellow*," Abram said, trying to make light of his disconcerting health.

Nathan reached into the pocket of his coattails before he sat down. "I'd like you to have this," he said, showing Abram one of the small leatherbound Bibles he had imprinted with the Gospel Society's name. "I know my idea of handing these out to trusted Negroes was voted down. Still, I thought you might understand my giving this to you as a token of my thanks for all you've done to bring the Gospel to Africans."

"I'm honored." Abram sighed, putting the book inside his coat. Nathan had brought five hundred more such Bibles, which the society had rejected despite a terrible shortage of books. They feared that the gift would embroil them in conflicts over Africans and literacy. Because of that his friend had been forced to ship his crates back to Boston aboard one of his own vessels. For the duration of their travel, the well-dressed, reserved Gilman read newspapers borrowed from the steamer's small library while Abram tried to rest. Ever so often his heartbeat quickened. He hoped it was only because of his worries about home. As he had done with the society, Abram committed his household to God through prayer. "Christ first; Christ only." Even for his home.

When they reached Charleston, Abram feared he might not even have the strength to travel farther. While he stood on the wharf, his head swimming in the smells of Negro sweat and tar, Nathan said, "I'll secure a coach and go home with you." Yet just as he was sprinting to the hackneys and drivers across the way, a small open chaise pulled up in front of them.

Beside the Negro driver, Abram saw an old friend, the Reverend John Bachman, pastor of St. John's German Lutheran Church in the city.

"Well, hallo!" Bachman called out. The blond, energetic man emerged to the street for a moment. "If I'm guessing right you've just come back from your annual gospel meeting."

Abram smiled tentatively. "Yes, and I've come home early because of an anxious letter from Mayleda."

"I'm sorry to hear that. Indeed, I'll let you go straightway. Do you need a vehicle?"

Abram looked and saw that Nathan had already engaged one. "No, thank you. My friend is right over there with a driver now." Despite his eagerness to leave, Abram kept his manners. "Before we go, John, let me introduce you to Mr. Nathan Gilman."

"From Boston?"

"Yes, sir!"

"Why, then you're John Audubon's *coleopteran* collector."

Nathan seemed shy as he walked into that greeting. "Yes, I am. And very surprised that you should know!"

The information surprised Abram too. He wasn't sure what the word *coleopteran* meant, but the life-loving pastor was quick to explain. "I commend you, Abram, for keeping such fine company. You do know how valuable this gentleman is to us? How greatly and how thankfully both Old Jostle and I depend on his support?"

By Old Jostle Abram knew Bachman meant Audubon, the artist who was traveling through the nation to draw wildlife before it might be lost to a tamed land.

"Besides that, Mr. Gilman has created a marvelous collection of beetles for our study."

"The coleopterans do fascinate me," Nathan admitted. "And they are much easier to trap and save than birds and quadrupeds."

"I concur!" Bachman nodded to barrels and crates strapped to the back of his vehicle. "Audubon is a demanding master," he said with joking. "Continually he begs me through his letters to go into the swamps to collect for him. That's what takes up so much of my time during spring and fall migrations. But speaking of time, I won't take up any more of yours." He thrust his hand out first to Nathan. "It was a pleasure to meet you, indeed. And to see you, too, Abram. You know I'm not an idle promiser concerning my prayers for you."

"I know and appreciate that," Abram said. They started to part ways when a slender pale youth walked up to them all. "Say, you're the preacher and scientist, Dr. Bachman, aren't you?" The questioner looked nearly like a boy.

"I am," Bachman answered with a little coolness in his voice.

Abram and Nathan exchanged glances, for the lad definitely had northern-sounding speech.

"Well, then, I'm interested in hearing how you delineate one species from another," the youth said without the courtesy of any introduction or query as to whether this was a convenient time.

"A commendable question, young sir," Bachman said diplomatically. "But not one by which to take up my friends' time." Reaching for a small leather pouch he pulled out a printed card. "Here's my home address. Come, make an appointment."

"I'd like to hear you explain it now," the bold speaker proclaimed.

Bachman showed more surprise but also patience. "I don't understand the urgency, but since the answer's simple, I will. Animals of one species share a common life-style. They have similar physical characteristics, and they can interbreed, producing viable, fertile offspring. There! Now go on your way."

"Then men *and* women are one species?" the youngster persisted.

The gentlemen shared fatherly smiles, for perhaps the young man had just survived a fray with the opposite sex. Bachman calmly tolerated him. "This is not exactly talk for the street, but yes, for the sake of the propagation of our species, I am certainly glad God made it that way!"

"And all are called *Homo sapiens*, meaning 'wise ones'?"

"Yes. Since you know that already, what is your real business, lad?"

"What about *him?*" The boy boldly pointed to Bachman's driver. "Is that one *Homo sapiens* too?"

"Ahhh!" Bachman cast another look at Abram and Nathan. "If you wish to discuss the races, I will. But in my office."

"Sir!" the boy challenged doggedly as they all tried to go their separate ways. "Are you *afraid* to speak your mind in front of these, your fellow slavemasters!"

"I am not!" Bachman retorted, still composed. "But it will take some time to explain it all to *you* rightly, since I believe you already have your mind set for disagreement."

"I know you believe God created only one human species. I've read that about you, so the Negro must be able to trace his lineage back to Adam—just as we do."

"That is my position, based on science and faith."

"Then how do you justify enslaving *biblical relatives*?"

Bachman stepped away, bowing graciously. "I knew you were driving at this. You have the right to your opinions, and still my offer stands. Come, and we will discuss this in private, for these other men must be getting home."

"You distorter of the goodness of the Gospel!" the boyish man raged, his face turning red quite suddenly.

"I warn you in fairness," Bachman countered, "you can be arrested and put out of this city for accosting us as you have."

The man did not desist from pointing at them all. "God's judgment against each one of you!"

"Wait, young man!" Nathan stepped to the accusing finger, speaking his clear Bostonian dialect. "You have no idea what you're saying. These gentlemen are fine Christians!"

By then a crowd of men and ladies had gathered. At the sound of Nathan's voice the boy turned and fled, with planters and two port guards racing after him down one of the side streets that made up part of a smoky fish market.

Bachman shook his head. "I'm sorry, friends. That was a rather unpleasant end to a very unexpected but pleasant meeting."

Nathan seemed shocked by the incident. Though he had just defended them, he now sounded quite defensive on behalf of the one getting away. "I am *ashamed* by his approach, but his passion *shames* me," he confessed to Abram when Bachman was gone and they were alone. "That young man believes slaves are human beings, and he's out to defend them in whatever ways he can. My own fervency, even for the Gospel, is timid compared to that!"

Abram felt another wave of sickness as one of the puffing guards came back to them. "Gentlemen, do you know his name? Or did you recognize him?"

"No," Abram said, speaking for them both.

"We think it could be Thomas Diller," an officer said. "He's the one that's come down from Lane Seminary in Ohio to start the next full-scale nigger uprising, some folk say."

"You know that much about him, yet you cannot catch him?" Nathan asked.

Abram was sorry his northern friend had opened his mouth, for now the guard looked at him with suspicion.

"Yes! That's right! Would you happen to know *anything* about him?"

Abram answered for them both again. "No, we don't."

The guard wiped the palms of his hands together. "The darkies hide him like he's one of their own."

More eager than ever to be away, Abram and Nathan stepped into the hackney that had taken their fare. The extra excitement, combined with his concerns for Delora, left him exhausted. Happy for rest, Abram slumped in the seat, assuring himself that this was only a temporary round of some fever-producing cold or influenza.

———

Joseph lay on the floor in the dusky light of the quiet laundryhouse. With fever-blurred vision, he kept watch on the door and the brighter day outside. He was glad for shelter and shadows, since his two days of misery in the sun had left him burned and dried like a raisin. As best he could tell, it was afternoon of the day following the night he had been discovered near the ditch. He knew he had staggered across the driveway without permission in search of water, which had continually been denied him by the masters. That had been part of Rensler's plan to "break" him—the terrible term used to describe those morbid plots to end every form of a self-respecting African's resistance.

Between that moment and this one he remembered little except being awakened at least once by Rosa's voice. He knew it had been Brant's decision that finally stopped the punishment. And he knew he now had clean—if sore—skin because Billy Days had stripped him and laid him out in the yard to scrub him down like a reclaimed board. When he breathed in hard he could still smell wonderful soap. With a dreamlike sense of rest he looked down across himself. He was dressed in washed field-hand clothes, and his scabbed-over wrists and ankles were finally free of chains.

Weariness continually pulled him toward sleep, yet he remained watchful. The next moment or the next might bring him danger again. Theodore Rensler could use his authority in the parish to arrest him. It was not beyond a planter's reasoning to drag him to a hanging tree or to the slave court in Charleston because of resistance and certainly because of his reading, if Brant had told anyone. His only comfort was that Brant should not tell, for then Master Abram would also be in trouble with his neighbors and with the law for allowing such a thing to happen.

Joseph closed his bruised mouth and tried to prepare himself—with God's help—for whatever would come. Having been so close to death, he found himself without fear of dying. All men might be against him, yet his quiet confidence in God seemed stronger than ever. That he had survived continued to give him a sense of God's presence.

He had no idea what events were taking place in the mansion. As far as he could remember, Brant had come only once to check on him here. When he had stood over him, Joseph had kept his eyes shut to avoid revealing his consciousness. Bette was the one in charge of his care, and she came often.

He wanted her to come again, for he was still thirsty and hungry. He tried to swallow, but the smallest motion of his tongue felt like tearing flesh. On his back, his head slightly to the left, he heard and then felt footsteps as they came toward him from the adjacent kitchen. He could not see the connecting doorway because it was near the chimney behind his head. But these steps were not Bette's. They were lighter, faster. Then Rosa appeared, dressed in blue and beautiful as the sky.

Yet he shut his eyes, as he had done with Brant, for earlier that morning Bette had given him a detailed account of why this troubled girl was so frightened of anyone from his gender. He mourned what she had suffered, for in learning her story, he felt he had gained terrible insight into what his own mother had endured in the days when she conceived him. It made him ashamed to think how animal-like men of any race could be.

"The master's home," Rosa said in a weak nervous voice. "Maum's been called inside, so she sent me."

At the surprising news Joseph tried to raise himself from the mat. *Master Abram home—already! Praise be!* Suddenly he realized that his unexpected movement had Rosa pressed to the wall with terror. She must have thought he was going to try to touch her. The only thing he could think of doing to tell her differently was to point toward the mansion he could scarcely see through the outside door. "Aaaa!" His tongue was dead in his mouth. "Aaaammm!!" He tried again to say the simple word *home*.

It took several moments for her to stop her trembling. He lay still and prayed, keeping his eyes either to the door or the walls.

Finally she came near and said, "Forgive me." She touched him enough to help him sit against the flour sack Bette had used to support him when she gave him drink. Rosa administered the cup from the side where there were no cuts on his tongue.

Seeing how unnerving it was for her to be so close to him, Joseph fought his dizziness and took the pewter into his own hands. Still not looking at her, he struggled to swallow the small watery meal. That much of the sugary liquid went down his chin was embarrassing, for he knew the girl watched him. Their fingers brushed momentarily when Rosa gave him a ragged piece of cloth so he could wipe his face.

His condition seemed too much to bear, for it gave him a clue of what life might be like if his tongue never healed. In his mind he formed words that could have encouraged her to trust him, but he could not speak them out. His desires were pure, but how was she to know that? Her presence cheered him so much, but how was she to know that either? He grimaced and closed his eyes, and strangely, that prompted her to speak.

"You will get better now that Master Abram is here to protect us."

Immediately he began to mull her words. Protect *us*, she had said. Then she, too, had things to fear and dread. In the silence while she was still beside him, Joseph contemplated the reasons why he had never seen her before and concluded that she must have just been moved from the street. Joseph's considerations drew him to think on her troubles, not his own. For that reason he dared to show his gratitude. Working his mouth very slowly and putting a finger on his sore tongue to hold it behind his teeth, he fought to speak. "Thaaa—yuuu faaah yuuu heeelp."

She said nothing, and he could not resist taking a quick, searching glance of her face. More soothing than drink was the incredible discovery that she was smiling. He grinned back, almost to the point of tears.

"You will be able to speak again!" she said.

Then he realized Abram Callcott was silently watching them both from the outer doorway. The Delora master came in wearing the same travel suit Joseph had dressed him in on the morning of his departure. Instinct prickled as Joseph realized he had never reclined or even sat in the man's presence before. At once he tried to stand, but just as quickly the planter rushed to him, touching his head to keep him down.

"No, Joseph! I've heard everything that's happened from Brant. You must rest."

Joseph lay back against the flour sack, dizzy and weak, but not at all restful now that Master Abram was home. It seemed that the world had changed forever in this man's absence, and Joseph felt wary, even though Abram's presence represented security as no one else's did. What would the man say about his secret reading? Would the older master have his own ways of punishing him now? Would he break his resilience or simply haul him to auction? And if he did that, how would Joseph ever endure being sold?

Maum Bette came in, and the gentleman pulled up the shanty's one unpainted, backless chair so that he could sit down beside the mat where Joseph lay. Rosa again backed herself to the wall and stood silent as a picture. It worried Joseph as he discerned that Master Abram was suffering his own private battle, whether physical or mental he could not tell. The first question Abram directed was to Maum about Rosa.

"Why is she here and dressed in something my Oribel once wore?"

Maum curtseyed. "Mass' Brant done send her up from the fields, sah, the day afta you left."

Abram's frown held tension that Joseph could feel because he knew the master so well.

The gentleman turned to Rosa, who had her slender arms tight against her apron. "Are you content to be here, Rosa, or do you want to go back to Negozi?"

As Maum had done, she curtseyed, but when she spoke, she had the voice of a highborn lady. "As long as I might be of help to Joseph, Mr. Callcott, I would like to stay."

Her response chilled Joseph's spine. Indeed, she must be the daughter of planters, just as Maum had said. What gave him any right to hope she saw him as her equal? He was black and slave-born; she was brown and should be free. Yet she had asked to stay with him!

"I'll consider that," Abram told her gently. "Now I want to be with Joseph alone."

As soon as the women were gone, Abram slipped from the chair. All strength and calmness disappeared from his face. "Oh, my boy! I cannot believe that Brant did this to you!" He commanded Joseph to open his mouth as wide as possible. Joseph could smell the stench of infection while Abram steadily peered inside. "There are no stitches in your tongue."

Joseph nodded, grieving, for regardless of what Rensler had told Brant, he had done nothing to repair his mouth for speech.

"Yet I saw you speak to Rosa," the man said. "Speak to me."

Not knowing what to say, not even knowing how to go about it well, Joseph put his finger back into his mouth. "Saaa."

Abram intervened. "Are you in pain now?"

Joseph closed his eyes and concentrated fully. "Yeaaa-saa."

As a father would his child, Abram felt Joseph's forehead with the back of his hand. "You have a fever, boy."

Joseph teared. "I knaaa."

The master saw the clay bowl and damp cloth Bette kept near him. Taking it into his own hands he quietly soothed Joseph's face. "If you can get well, I've already decided that I will take you to Charleston."

"Aaaa! Naaa!" Joseph cried, daring to grip the man. Going to Charleston meant being sold!

"No. Not for sale!" the owner said, understanding him precisely. "To be hired out. Away from Brant. And away from Theodore Rensler's St. Andrew's Parish Patrol."

That was awful, too, to be sent away from everything he had known since childhood!

The man frowned at him as Joseph wanted to bury himself from view. "How long have you secretly been reading?"

Joseph considered the question, having no compulsion to hide the truth. He held up all the fingers of both hands, and then added a few more.

"I'm talking about years."

Joseph made his nodding firm.

"That is impossible."

"Naaa," Joseph said, his eyes finally falling.

When Joseph looked again, Master Abram had a small new Bible in his hands. He gave it to Joseph. "If you have the strength and ability, find the Proverbs for me in here."

Joseph accepted timidly, quite conscious that his hands were ungloved, which was seldom true during his service in the house. Weakness and fear made his fingers tremble, but in a few moments he found the first page of the Old Testament book. Abram's mouth opened slightly as he crouched beside Joseph's shoulder to survey it. Joseph was unable to detect his mood then. "Look at that page! Point out any word you know!"

Puzzled by the request Joseph complied to the best of his ability by taking a shaking finger down across the entire onion-skin sheet.

"What! Are you saying you know most all the words?"

"Yeaaa." Joseph breathed out uncomfortably.

The master grabbed the Bible back, opening it again and again to different places. Each time, however, Joseph could say he knew each word, or else he could have sounded it out using his knowledge of simpler words that often made up the larger ones. The master climbed back on the chair, looking piqued. Joseph waited nervously, unable to guess his fate.

"Who put you up to this? Who instructed you? Who convinced you even to try?"

Joseph batted his eyes against each question. Each one seemed to have the same answer. Though he knew it could ignite the slavemaster against him, he still pointed upward. "Gaaad."

"Do you know that even brown, free men have lost their lives over writing and reading!"

Joseph nodded, deeply sorry for them.

The master sighed. "I wish you could tell me why you dared to go against everything I stand for to do this behind my back."

It was something Joseph decided he could communicate without words. Reaching for the small Bible again, he hugged it in his master's presence, then pressed it to his forehead. "Taa knaw."

When he looked up, Abram Callcott was as sober as a mourner.

After heavy moments of silence the man asked, "And can you write as well?"

Joseph had heard the most terrible consequences for slaves learning how to read, so since his youth he had disciplined himself with a pledge never to try. He shook his head.

Pressing his temples Abram seemed satisfied that this, too, was truth. The man stood, leaning on the table used for folding clothes. "At the convention I had the opportunity to speak with a Mr. Horace Wahl," Abram said. "He owns a small plantation along Kidding Creek, but most of his time and energy is invested in helping his wife's family run Grafton Mills. He works there as the master-foreman over a small force of literate slaves who take and fill the millers' orders. They're all mulattos, I am certain."

Joseph eyed him.

"I spent a few agonizing hours with him and some of the others discussing the relationship between converting slaves and entrusting them with moderate measures of education."

Joseph felt his cheek twitch as his shoulders came free from the flour sack. The master evaluated his interest with suspicion.

"You think you could be educated, just like a brown boy?"

Joseph was cautious about appearing to have an ungodly sort of pride, yet he nodded while looking at his hands.

"You think you could learn to cipher? To write? To think? To reason as free children do?"

It hurt to know that these skills were questioned by this man who had in so many ways been like a loving daddy to him. He wanted to say he could do every kind of skill known to man if only he had the freedom and opportunity! Yet now his tongue was held from him, so his response could only be, "Yeaa-saa."

At that, Abram stood and walked as far as the outside door. For moments he stood there with his face pressed against the slave-house wall. Then, without hearing another word from him, Joseph watched the man walk away, with no hint of what would be done with him next.

Abram was tempted to blame the agony within his heart on the illness brewing in him that day. He got only as far as his porch and then stopped to consider anew what must be done. Jewell, Joseph's mother, was weeping inside the house even now. It was a real possibility, he knew, that Joseph might die. There was an odd and ugly sensation within him of the wrongness of Joseph's dying in despair. Perhaps that is what pushed him to walk back to the laundry. Or perhaps he was really sensing the courage to express his incredible idea.

With every uncertain step Abram reevaluated the facts. Even though he had raged against Brant for an hour because of what had been done, and then closed him out of his chambers, his son had dared to come back to say what he thought was true.

After meeting with Joseph now, Abram saw that Brant's description of the boy may have been correct, for indeed, Joseph had taught himself to read. That forced Abram to have to agree with Brant's conclusion that it was foolish to trust a *reading* slave in the house. So it naturally followed that he must plan to put Joseph elsewhere. But only to some place safe, away from Brant and the patrol. The banishment, however, galled Abram sorely. It moved him nearly to tears to think again of Joseph, *dear good Joseph*, embracing the Scriptures, hungering to read them at any cost. This was exactly what he had worked for all these years—to have Africans fall in love with God's words and commands.

He was nearly at the laundry door now. What if the Lord himself had entrusted him with this African who had the God-given talent to read just to test him—or to teach him? Joseph's tongue had been nearly severed. The boy had endured two days of violence. And for what reason? What if God was the one giving Joseph the intellect to do what he had done? And what if Joseph was not the only African God had so endowed? Then one must conclude that current public opinion had esteemed the Negro wrongly. Oh! And what then! What then!

Never escaping this mad flurry of confusion, Abram stepped back in-

side the laundry with one goal in his mind. Despite both law and convention, he must somehow expose Joseph to a full classical education. Then
he would have proof of what a pure African was capable of knowing.

Joseph believed he was dreaming when the master was back so quickly,
pulling him from his first smooth moments of sleep. The face he saw was
Abram Callcott's, but none of the words flowing from his lips could have
been his master's, for they were saying, "Joseph, you must get well. God
will hold me responsible if I have acted all these years in ignorance!"

Jolted by the pain of being shaken, Joseph knew then that he was not
dreaming. The master, without hesitation, crouched down and put his
hand to Joseph's mouth. "You must learn to speak and quickly. Then I will
take you to Charleston and perhaps to a Negro teacher who can tolerate
my urgency to put you in school."

Waking or dreaming, Joseph sat up, his mouth burning . . . his emotions also. *School?*

"Come on, boy. You can move your tongue!"

Joseph fought more anger than he had felt in the barnyard mire. No
one could order him to speak, for his mouth had been ruined! It was not
like telling him to light a candle or fetch water. He wanted to speak and
to eat—but physically he could not. Was the white man so blind as to not
know there were things about Negroes that could not be ordered, even as
there were things in the weakness and the failings of every man? Yet Master Abram was doggedly and mercilessly pressing him to do the impossible.
The only thing that kept Joseph focused, that kept him from fighting to
be free of his master's hold, was that the man had talked about Negro
teachers!

"Say *I*, boy!" Crudely Abram pressed his tongue.

"Aaaa!" Joseph fought the pain.

"No! A clear *I*!" The master changed the pressure in Joseph's mouth.
There was more excruciating agony.

"Aaaa!" Joseph cried, wanting only to get beyond the anguish.

"Joseph!" The slaveowner pinched his tongue behind his teeth.

"Hhhh-aaa-eee-*I*!" Joseph screamed.

"There!" Abram let go. He dried Joseph's saliva from his fingers on the
rough field shirt. "I didn't mean to hurt you, but you must practice every
moment so there can be hope of finding a school for you. No one, I think,
will educate a mute."

Waiting for the other man to be gone, Joseph lay back, his mouth and his emotions shattered. He had never felt so low as he did now. Yet two words kept him floating like wooden planks for a man in danger of drowning: *Negro school.*

CHAPTER 11

SATURDAY NIGHT ROSA CAME IN with a candle and found Joseph sleeping. Since Mr. Abram's return two days ago, the young man had done little but sleep. Rosa set the tin candle holder on the laundry-room table and knelt beside him. Having done this often as he slumbered, she believed she now knew every inch of his face, so taut with discomfort and determination.

Joseph's mouth was still swelled open, which created great thirst in him whenever he was conscious. By now Rosa was skilled at giving him both water and soft foods like warm grits and mashed yams sweetened with molasses and butter. She looked at him with indecision. Mr. Abram had asked her stay with Joseph tomorrow while the rest of Delora's slaves and family attended the dedication for Our Savior's Chapel. Maum had predicted that she would not stay because of her fear of men. But in truth, she found Joseph's company both comforting and encouraging, even in his weakness and his inability to say one clear word.

A second reality troubled her. He could die in her care if the fever held on much longer. Yet it was more troubling to think he might die in the care of another. Her decision was made.

When she rose and claimed the candle, it shook in her hand. Consciously she knew her fear of death had just been conquered by an even stronger enemy—*grief*. Grief, in thinking that death might steal him from her as it had done her precious daughter. She slipped out while he was still asleep.

———

From Ann's perspective, the whole dedication was nothing more than a promotion for Mr. Callcott's society. Scrubbed-clean pickaninnies filed up front in the white-paneled chapel to sing and grin, recite and grin, then take their bows and grin.

Ann found herself in the minority by color, a situation that also was occurring in respectable city churches. Bold Negro converts were popping up everywhere as a result of efforts like Mr. Callcott's. Fortunately, today her daddy, Teddy, and Brant's siblings maintained the whiteness of the pew in which she sat. At the last moment Felicia and her father had stayed home, since Mr. Gilman did not want the Gospel Society's work to be condemned by local planters for having a northerner present.

Ann was disappointed in Felicia's decision, but it hardly surprised her. Felicia had a great sense of loyalty, and from the moment she perceived her daddy's heart, she was determined not to leave him. William, however, had been eager to come, and now he was beside Ann, since Brant was obligated to be with his daddy in the front pew. The older Callcott was making slow recovery from an illness that Teddy had not identified, even after careful examination. Ann had heard him tell her daddy privately that the man might just be suffering from the tension of going against majority opinion on so many issues.

Raising her finely woven bonnet slightly, Ann surveyed the crowd of darkies packed into the upstairs gallery and along the benches that stood against the walls. Morbidly she considered what a slave uprising now would mean. Surely no one in Brant's family, or hers, could survive such an ordeal. The blackening population of Charleston's churches was something Teddy also hated, even more so since his return from Boston. In part Ann knew why, because of her own experience of living outside the South for two years. In New England, colored folks were hardly visible. Never would they have taken up church space as they did here. That's one reason her family had stopped going to St. John's, even though it had been her maternal granddaddy's congregation. Everybody at Pine Woods agreed they saw enough darkies through the week. They didn't need to drive to church to see more.

Today her daddy and cousin were here for two reasons only: to honor Abram Callcott's departed loved ones and to please Nathan Gilman, now that her daddy and William were ready to get the new shipbuilding operation underway. Ann knew that Felicia's daddy believed they all needed to come here to be "saved." Even Felicia had pressed her on the subject more than ever before. Jesus Christ was really God, she had said more than once. He died for human sin and conquered death by coming back to life in a tomb.

The darkies seemed enthralled by such a message of glorious, everlasting life with God. It was the theme of their exuberant singing. Yet most planters didn't want their darkies thinking on anything—including an eternal future. With caustic joking before the service, her daddy had said, "The only good to come from Negro chapels is that then we can clear them out of our real churches."

The slaves' enthusiasm for worship put a troubling pulse in the air. Ann tried to make herself stop thinking about rebellion. She turned her focus on Brant, who looked so somber beside his graying father. Mr. Abram Callcott finally stood up and went behind the podium. At the same time Teddy spoke in her ear. "He's still not well. The man should not have pushed himself to come just for this."

"I'm happy to say that my own Parris will speak a few words to you all now." A huge buck came forward dressed in a sleeveless slave shirt and wearing a shell around his neck. He had no reservations, it seemed, about planting his black feet right behind the altar rail. Ann crossed her arms, uneasy to see a Negro stand at the front of a church.

Then she heard Teddy turn to another gentleman sitting near them. He whispered with a nod, "Ready to take offense if offense is given." Ann realized then that members of the parish patrol were inconspicuously interspersed within the congregation. Feeling more secure but not more happy, she endured the travesty of hearing a prime black tongue repeat memorized Scripture.

The room was airless. They were all pestered by flies. Halfway down the pew, Eric fidgeted and sighed. Even so, William, beside her, was now intent on the show. "That Negro speaks with the grace of some untamed, agrarian poet," he said, enraptured.

To Ann, this Parris was talking the way all Negroes talked, his voice rising and trailing and getting tangled up in Creole sounds. *How absurd to think the boy an artist!* Then she remembered that William had paid a dollar to one of their Pine Woods' bucks just so he could possess a slave's handwoven basket.

Ann's daddy and brother were much less impressed. As the black boy stood stringing Scriptures together, they only squinted their tolerance. The more the speaker went on, the more spirited he became. Then the buck looked away from Abram, who had been guiding him along, and looked daringly upon the crowd. His Gullah became stronger so that Ann completely lost her understanding.

"De good nyews be dat Jedus wern't nothin' but a lub-slabe to he Papa-God! He done make de whole world, but then he owned nothin' ob it— not eben 'nough ground to bury he own body. He be like God slabe to us in he lub fa' us. Nothin' like no high-falutin' massa we done see in des y'ere las' day. . . ."

"He's preaching against whites!" fumed one of Teddy's friends behind them. Then standing, he shouted, "That's enough, nigger!"

Brant's daddy, looking gaunt, scrambled up beside his Negro. "He's just talking about the person of our Lord," he said in defense of his slave. Some darkie dared to cheer, but he was overcome by the booings of many whites. "This is the house of God!" Brant's daddy pleaded.

"Then treat it as such, man!" the gentlemen behind Ann roared. "Get these chattels off sacred ground!"

Some others, who must have been from the Gospel Society, rallied around Mr. Callcott and his darkie property. Brant appeared in the crowd to help his daddy step to the nearest pew. It was hard to see after that, for so many, both black and white, were standing.

Happily the protest was cut off without real violence, and they all were able to go outside into the fresh air. The big Negro who had dared to speak was led through the milling crowd looking bleak, as though someone was about to whip him. His head was low, but his eyes were roving, making Ann's skin crawl as he passed her by in the company of Delora's overseer. What she had witnessed in the church felt like sparks struck above dry leaves. Now she knew more than ever that the world she loved could be suddenly destroyed by the conflagration of revolt.

Tempers cooled. The Negroes still were allowed to cluster on the sandy soil under the pines, but with many supervisors watching. The whites took seats at long tables set up in the shade. Baskets of prepared foods were set down in front of colored folk and white alike. "It's one day in the year, besides Christmas, when Christians are encouraged to serve their darkies," one society man explained as he sat down near Ann with his own young family. She could not let go of the worry in her. Even being near this planter's brood of young children unnerved her. In slave rebellions, white women and babies were slaughtered.

Suddenly she felt William's hand cover her own. "Are you all right? You were absolutely white with fear inside the church."

"I do hate this," she whispered. "I hope this is the last time I am ever told to come."

William's soft brown eyes went wide as he looked around the breezy churchyard. "I think this may be the last time for many things. I can't see your neighbors tolerating more Negro preaching, though I don't think there was any harm intended in what the colored man said. Still, Mr. Callcott made a serious error in letting the slave speak."

"Indeed he did!" Ann's daddy instantly joined their private conversation. Then he smiled, a little puzzled, perhaps, because William still had Ann's fingers wrapped in his. Ann pulled away demurely, not ready to be seen as a traitor to Brant simply because of Mr. Callcott's disgraceful choices.

Looking up the rows of tables, she saw him helping Mayleda into a chair beside their father and brother. Silence prevailed and reverence was restored when several speakers briefly eulogized Brant's mother and older brothers. The Callcotts sat sad-eyed, listening through it all. Then the meal was blessed, and guests partook of the ample menu.

"Well, see here—this meeting has finally been redeemed," Teddy teased, cutting into a full slice of ham, stabbing it with his fork, and showing it off to everyone. "I have finally found something to relish about a church for darkies."

William engaged him seriously. "I do think it's right to teach blacks that God watches over them. And I think you would be wise to see such instruction as beneficial. Christian Negroes should be obedient Negroes, for the Bible tells servants to obey their masters—"

"Hah! Religion will do nothing to make them docile, William. Of that you can be certain."

But the northerner did not completely back away. "I'm just stating *my* opinion, Teddy, which, as I remember, did amount for something when we were pals in school."

"Negroes are a kind of flesh all their own," Teddy said, chewing. "Any black boy who tries to put on human airs should be destroyed—and quickly—for uppity niggers are the devil's pawns. There! I've stated my religion, when you judge me to have none!"

William said nothing after that. Dessert was passed around, and still Ann had not had a moment with Brant. Even with the meal over, the Call-cotts remained obliged to stay together, since well-wishers were coming by to talk with them.

After a while Teddy tapped the table, getting William's attention. "You want to go down and look for alligators in the creek?"

"Seems like worthy afternoon entertainment." William smiled placidly, likely forgiving any tension between them. "Certainly that's something we never hunted together outside Boston."

Though Ann was in her best summer gown, she tagged along, staying at the edge of the chapel's yard. Giving up their search, the men began performing silly, boyish dares, leaping from root to root and balancing on cypress logs in the green water. It reminded Ann of some of the prankish fun they enjoyed in the Gilmans' home during their breaks from Harvard and Pemberton.

Now, as then, she played the role of angry mother, scolding them for jeopardizing their fine Sabbath clothes. But they came back to firm ground only on their own terms, sweating and exhausted. When they all sat down on the benches near the water, Ann looked back to see Brant alone at the head table. It troubled her that he seemed free now but uninterested in coming to meet them. Watching as long as her patience allowed, she finally excused herself and went up to see him, even though a small interior voice counseled her to let Brant have his privacy on this particular day.

Brant saw Ann coming and judged his actions carefully. With every grace expected of a gentleman he stood, greeted her, and set a chair beside his. He felt the eyes of others drawn to them. Now that Ann was beside him, they would both be objects of attention.

"Why didn't you come down?" Ann said.

He answered, not sure what he wanted to say to her in public. "It looked like you were having fun without me."

"I was waiting for you, and now I've proved it by coming up here to rescue you."

He was uncomfortable with his own reluctance. "I'm sure it would be better if I didn't join you."

Her simple pout made him realize that she might not know the complexity of the situation now affecting them. "Your daddy and cousin were both furious because of our Parris's unruly conduct," he said, self-consciously whispering his explanation. "I know it, and frankly I am, too, though that counts for nothing now. This is not the time for me to align myself with you—not with your family and Teddy's friends here."

"That's ridiculous. They've known we've been paired for years, and they can't blame you for your daddy's choices."

"Yes, they can. With something as soft as only a word or with something as deadly as a dueling pistol, your daddy has every right in this community to confront me and defend your honor if he openly declares that I am unworthy of you."

"Oh, Brant, I can't imagine that."

"I can." Halfheartedly he surveyed the pines above them. "It's become clear to me today that it will not be easy to separate myself from Daddy's reputation. In fact, I've decided that if I can escape at all, it will be at the price of leaving Delora and maybe even South Carolina."

"You would not do that!"

"There's no other way. My struggles with just one slave have shown me how unfit I'd be to supervise them all. And while I don't agree with my father and all this—" he motioned to the chapel—"I don't believe in your family's way, either, of housing them and treating them as unfeeling, unthinking beings. That leaves me with exactly nothing, for I can see nothing in between." Then he grinned glumly, feeling sarcastic. "But I'm sure you can make the best of this bad news. I doubt you will miss me for long."

"Oh, Brant, you know I would!"

His eyes slipped to Teddy and William, who were now walking back to the tables. "You wouldn't mourn me forever. It's time to grow up and face the fact that things are not the way we dreamed they could be when we were children."

"You're not serious about this!"

"You don't have to pretend to care so much. This very difficult week has proved that I can take care of myself and accept the fact that you can too. I saw William take your hand."

"As a friend!"

"Then what are we to be?"

"You're jealous!" She smiled as though that could please her. It hurt him more.

"I'm being realistic, Ann . . . maybe for the first time in my life. The

Gilmans and the Renslers are infinitely closer to being merged by business than your family and mine."

"Oh, Brant." She touched the necklace that had been his mother's. "I don't want this to be about business. I want to hope that there is something good up ahead for the both of us."

He could not escape her enthralling beauty, yet he bit back his feelings and said only what he felt was true. "Maybe that 'something good' is William." A side glance told him how many guests were looking and turning in their direction. "This isn't the time or the place, but I owe you that much explanation."

"Then promise me you will come to me when we can speak alone."

There were tears in her eyes, and he wanted to believe they were signs of her real emotions.

Suddenly his sister and little brother were beside them. "Oh, Brant! Daddy's collapsed on the grass!"

Brant squeezed Ann's hand for just an instant, then ran to call Teddy and find his father. Muscling back the dazed crowd, Brant made a way for Teddy. Members of both the patrol and the society pushed the onlookers farther away so the sufferer could have air.

Brant did not breathe again until his father did.

———

Despite changing hourly between shivering chills and sickening fever, Joseph had never known a happier day. Soon after Delora had been deserted by everyone but Rosa, he pushed himself to go outside and get the secret scrapbook of discarded print he had hidden deep within the pile of broken bricks behind his master's privy.

To their delight, he and Rosa spent the day reveling in words: poems, funny half pieces of newspaper advertisements, and even long passages of Scriptures, which Rosa read out loud from the society Bible whenever Joseph had to rest.

Because of the hope of school and his eagerness to have this friendship, he practiced speaking, though he hardly had the strength to do so. Rosa gave him gentle encouragement, and he responded to it. By afternoon he could say, "ah," "aa," "I," "e," and "oo," but not any hard sounds like "d" or "t," which he prayed would not be beyond his reach forever.

From their one-sided conversation he learned many things about them both. Rosa told him things about her family and their plantation called Aspidae; however, she said nothing about her terrible experiences, which

Joseph already knew because of Maum Bette's tales. It surprised him and gave him cause to think that even her free years had been unappealing to her. She hated her father for his cruel actions and assumed that Joseph hated Brant the same way. Yet Joseph was puzzled at himself. He did not feel hatred, for in his fevered dreams he often saw Brant's face as it had looked in childhood, before the days when maturity and manhood made them adversaries.

Had Joseph had voice he would have gladly bared his soul to her. As it was, they spent the day immersed in the ideas of others through reading. Then, while the sun was still high, they agreed they must hide Joseph's makeshift book again so that it would not be discovered. Rosa offered to do so, and Joseph reluctantly accepted in order to save his strength. Yet he did not want her to go, even for a moment. When she walked to the door he delayed her by calling, "Waai—!"

For the first time that day she seemed edgy, and instantly he lamented his decision. His incredibly unpleasant voice made him sound demanding. He saw how it devastated her when she felt trapped by his command. He dropped his eyes, his only sure way of communicating respect without using any words.

"What do you want from me?"

Even then he did not look into her face. Cautiously he held out one special scrap of paper from his book that he had removed before he had opened it to her the first time. His hand trembled. He laid the paper at her feet. "Faa you."

Swallowing in pain, he watched her read it while she stood. It was a tattered fragment of poetry he had saved from one of Miss Oribel's ruined books that had fallen into the river on a picnic afternoon. Late at night Joseph had gone back and rescued it. The piece he gave her was from the writer Byron.

> She walks in beauty, like the night,
> Of cloudless climes and starry skies.
> And all that's best of dark and bright
> Meet in her aspect and her eyes.

Joseph closed his lips when Rosa fled from him because of his gift. In trying to tell her of his admiration, he had stirred up agonies from her past instead. He turned to the wall, angry with himself for risking himself and for hurting her.

Fighting wild emotions, Rosa ran to the brick pile. Perhaps Joseph had entertained her like a friend just to take advantage of lusting after her. She buried the book quickly and then pulled the flesh on her cheeks, telling herself this could not be true. At first she had wanted to see Joseph only because she had heard that he could read. She was the one who should be disdained for judging everyone on appearances only.

Being brutally honest with herself, she admitted she had despised his blackness and his terrible appearance that first moment she laid eyes upon him chained to the fence. But her despising had lasted only moments because she had seen the nobleness of his character, even in suffering. It was as clear as a sunrise on a cloudless day. What she had been taught to judge as *disgraceful* turned out to be her closest glimpse of a life filled with *grace*. Through his expressions and actions she saw his nonavenging spirit, though she did not understand it.

Looking at the few lines of poetry he had chosen for her, she hated herself for fleeing and giving in once more to her haunting fears of men. She pressed the paper to her lips, mourning that she had deserted him without a word. Though wrinkled and mildewed, the poem was tangible proof that he was reaching not for her physical body, but deeper . . . to see if she, too, might have character. *Purity*. That's what she saw and felt in him. And that's what she wanted to have and to give in return.

Immediately she started back to the shanty, but as she moved she caught sight of dust rising in the driveway. At first she assumed it was the family and slaves coming home, but then she saw it was three white moonshiners, riding mules and moving to the foundation of the new stables under construction.

Hiding herself near the laundryhouse, she put terror behind her so she could see what they would do. The men dropped what looked like tin lanterns into the stacks of shingles, igniting them into a yellow blaze. The strangers held iron rods. No, branding irons! They heated them red, then went everywhere, hollering, and marking every building along the driveway with circular smoking burns. She delayed no more and ran inside to Joseph.

He was resting with his face to the wall. "There are strangers outside! Bad men with brands! Destroying property!"

Joseph looked around at her with rheumy eyes, then sat up instantly. Looking toward the door, he saw the men come into the yard. Though he had not been on his feet since morning, Joseph was standing in a moment. He grabbed her. He almost carried her through the inner door to the kitchen side. With one hand he pulled down the rope ladder that hung from the loft. Her skirt made her climbing slow. He stayed on the floor to steady her way. When she was in the attic, he tossed the rope to her and motioned for her to hide. She froze, knowing he was cut off from escape. The men were already in the laundry. She moved into the attic's recesses. Terrible rumbling voices came from below. She coiled against the wall unable to see anything.

"Well, boy, why aren't you with you' massa's other holy-ghost niggers? You speak when you're spoke to, y'hear! Look smart, you!" The air was charged with the sound of Joseph's flesh being repeatedly struck. "You answer us!"

Rosa covered her ears, helpless to stop the strikes and oaths. "Lookee here, inside that mouth of his! Why, he's the very one, ainty! Won't be broke, eh, not even by Mista Rensler!"

"What better messenger than you!" they gloated. "So you're the dumb house nigger! Well! We gwine leave a message with you for your fool massa what neither he—nor you—will soon forget. This is for him and his whole nigger-lovin' society."

"Aaaahhhh!"

Rosa wept as Joseph screamed.

"There! Let him read this on you, cuffee! Let him know folk all over St. Andrew's Parish feel this way! *Christ is for whites!* Now you won't forget that, will ya! Live long 'nough to get that message to him. Then the devil take you to hell."

Rosa sucked her knuckles. There was a crashing of dishes and furniture, then utter silence. "Oh, Joseph, Joseph, Joseph," she moaned, rocking silently, her face against the floorboards.

Through the attic walls she heard sounds of the men riding away. Yet she had no strength to move. She was ashamed, for she had left Joseph alone. Finally she crawled to the rope and threw down the ladder. She descended to a place in shambles. Benches smashed. The table overturned. She could not find Joseph until he groaned. Digging frantically through splintered wood and pottery, she caught a glimpse of his smooth bare chest. She dug, weeping aloud, for she had seen her father do the same thing to his slaves. To immobilize Joseph they had lifted his shirt and knotted it over his face and arms.

On her knees she struggled to free him, a new sob coming forth each time his ribs expanded to draw in air. "Oh, friend!" Finally she uncovered his face and drew it up into her arms until it nearly touched her own. He moaned and shut his eyes. She smelled the terrible stench of burned flesh. When he struggled to sit up, she released him. A raw wound as large as her hand had been seared into the small of his back just inches from his right elbow. It was in the shape of a cross within a circle. She helped him lean his head and shoulder against the nearest wall, glad for him that he was rapidly losing consciousness.

Though she felt helpless and terrified, she made herself leave him to run for cold water. In doing so she knew she risked meeting these human demons herself. While drawing water, she saw the Callcott carriage roll in and she ran out, crying, "Men attacked Joseph! Oh, help him! Help him! He saved my life!"

Brant Callcott descended from the carriage. "Hush, girl! The master's ill. I'll check on Joseph once my daddy's put to bed."

"No!" Rosa raged, grabbing and holding the young master's coat. "He's been branded! He needs you now!"

CHAPTER 12

ABRAM AWOKE to the pounding of African drums. These were forbidden everywhere in South Carolina, though he sometimes went against the law and allowed them to be sounded at slave funerals. *Joseph!* Shattered by the thought that Joseph had died, he struggled to sit up. "Joseph's dead!" he cried.

Mayleda was seated by his bed. "No, Papa! This morning one of our hands was delivered of a stillborn baby."

Abram looked around. It was probably near dusk, since slave burials were conducted at night after the work was done. "Have I slept all day?" He felt amazed and still weary.

Mayleda seemed puzzled. "Why, yes. . . ."

"Where is Joseph?" He panicked again.

Mayleda pointed to the dressing room. "He's resting in there, just as you requested."

Abram drew his hands across his face. He could recall Joseph, branded, and Rosa saved by him, but he could not remember giving any instructions. "Why didn't you wake me for this funeral?"

"You don't know! You've been here three nights and two days with fever."

"Oh, my darling." He grabbed her hand and saw remarkable strength in her caring face. Yet now a tear trickled down her solid countenance.

"I feared I would lose you," she confessed. "Teddy has been here often. He says it might be the first stage of yellow fever!" Biting her lip, she turned away. "He brought medicine. Perhaps he saved your life."

"No, sweet child. God did."

She brushed his forehead. "How are you feeling now?"

"Tired." He did not want her to know more.

She hugged him around his shoulders as though she were still his little girl. "Oh, I'm grateful! God knows I am!"

The world and all its problems came clear to him once more. "Is Brant at the funeral?"

Mayleda nodded. "Yes, and with his prayer book."

Abram smiled, pleased with the idea that Brant might represent him well. Truly the boy seemed to have a contrite heart after all that had happened concerning Joseph. Perhaps steadfast faith would become him yet. "I want to be at the service."

"You've only been awake for moments!"

"I must add my condolences. Get Colt to bring me my razor!"

"You cannot think of going out! Mr. Gund reports how very worried our people are down there on your account."

Abram, in that moment, knew he had no strength to put his will into action. He lay back and considered that the prayers of slaves may have preserved his life. Still, he was unwell.

"I'll ring Bette for supper. You must be ravenous."

In truth he had no appetite. "No. I want to see Joseph. Is he well enough to come here to my bed?"

Mayleda showed her first smile. "Oh yes! His fever broke on Monday, but I thought it best to keep that secret so that no one would question his need to continue being up here."

"My good girl!"

"I didn't think you'd mind. And I let him have the Gospel Society Bible Bette found when she cleaned the laundryhouse."

"Does Brant know he's reading?"

"I don't think so, Papa. Joseph keeps it well hidden."

Abram felt as though a great weight had suddenly been set down on his heart. How was he ever going to reconcile what law and custom allowed with what Joseph could do?

"Shall I ring for him now?"

"No. Please call for him in person."

She looked at him oddly but with a certain amount of girlish excitement. "He'll be so glad to see you, for sometimes at night I know he comes to your bedside in secret to pray."

Joseph was not used to having anyone knock at the door, and when it happened, he slipped the Bible under his thin mattress and waited. In the evening shadows Miss Mayleda came in. For the last few days no one could have been more respectful of his anguished struggles than she. The candle in her hand beamed onto her face.

"Daddy's awake! He wants to see you!"

Dwelling in so much isolation he nearly forgot he had no voice. "Yess!" His mouth and breath worked together better than he expected. He dared to try more words. "I'll come!"

She looked at his success as though it were written all over his face. He smiled, though every movement of his mouth cost him effort and pain. Mayleda led the way, then left them alone. It was distressing to Joseph to see the chamber in such disarray. At once he reached for socks on the floor, but the master, sitting up against his pillows, scolded him.

"No, indeed! I did not bring you in here for that."

Joseph stepped close to the bed. Master Abram was as pale as his sheets. The man told him to turn around and lifted Joseph's shirt with an unsteady hand.

"It must be very painful."

Cautiously Joseph nodded. The burn—and the nightmares that came with it—had kept him sleepless for whole days and nights. But more awful than what had been done to him was his constant awareness of what those men might have done to Rosa had they found her. As though reading his thoughts, Abram said, "Do you know who attacked you?"

What could he say? They were poor white men, of that he was certain. But he did not know their names, so he shook his head.

The master sighed. "Rosa spoke to me at length."

Joseph's hand cooled simply at the mention of her name.

"It's quite possible they never expected to find any slaves here. It may have been just a cruel inspiration that made them burn you." The planter stopped and closed his eyes. It was obvious that the conversation taxed him. "However, they did seem to know you. Rosa heard their crude talk."

Joseph felt terrible for her.

"I've seen the symbol before." Abram let the shirt fall. "In fact, we discussed it at the convention. Some have had their cattle scarred this way just after they started holding evangelistic meetings for their slaves. I suppose the same kind of heathens came here because of the chapel dedication."

Joseph knew what the scar he would carry for life looked like, for he had stood in front of Master's mirror to view it.

"I am so sorry! First your mouth, and now this! Can you ever forgive me for allowing you to be so vulnerable to danger?"

Amazed, Joseph looked at him. Was Abram too ill to know he was asking forgiveness from his slave?

"I don't want to meet God without full repentance for this!"

"You wiiill beee weeell, saaah!" Joseph proclaimed, unnerved by this cloaked reference to his dying.

"You are working on your speaking! Good for you!"

Joseph felt selfish and insensitive, yet he seized the moment to remind the master why. "Yeess! Faa schoool!"

Abram sucked in air. "You want that so desperately?"

"Yeess!"

"Then you are not afraid to go to Charleston?"

Indeed he was, but he answered, "I'll go!"

"You are willing to leave your mama—and now Rosa?"

The question startled him. How did this man know his feelings toward Rosa? When Joseph glanced at him, Abram looked at him hard.

"You have been a fine servant. But now I fear heaven because of how I have dealt with you and all your kind. What does God desire for the Negro? And what does He expect from Christian masters? My time may be short! I must be at peace before I face my Maker."

Joseph could not believe what he was hearing.

"You think you can cope in school?"

Joseph dared to face his master's eyes. "I hooope!" When he considered the gravity of his admission, he lowered his head.

Abram spoke kindly. "It would be better to have you out of this house. I will take you to Charleston—and maybe to school."

It was too fantastic to be true!

"Understand, your education will not be for your benefit so much as for mine. Let me see what you can learn so that I may be removed from any ignorant, sinful misunderstandings concerning Negro minds. I may not have time to straighten out the whole matter! Oh! Please . . ." His entire being began to tremble. "Forgive me if I have judged you wrongly! Beg others to do the same if I have been wrong! Oh, and do not harm my family in revenge! If slavery be sin, Joseph, remember that my children are young and innocent of their daddy's ways!".

Abram twisted his fingers into his sheets. He was copiously sweating. Joseph waited no longer and rang for help from Maum. Then dipping a cloth, he washed the man's face to cool him.

"You are the only one I will tell—" the man gasped. "Nor do I want any in this house to know it—slave or child. I do fear that I have yellow fever. Ah, Joseph!"

Joseph looked around, believing that he must not be asked to carry such a weight alone.

"Pray! You know the fever! It can consume its victim in an hour or let him dangle month after month."

"I dooo knaaaw!" Joseph had seen Miss Oribel and two Callcott sons slip from one world to the next in agony.

Abram's eyes suddenly cleared. "You will help me take you to the city. I must not die, leaving you here. Pack my clothes—"

"Ohh naa!"

"Do this! I will take you to Mr. Horace Wahl."

"Saaah, please rest!"

"Yes, while you are packing! Take two of my shirts for yourself and three changes of my linen. Dress right now as you would have done for the chapel dedication. Wear your livery shoes. Oh yes, take my old cloak to wrap the Bible in. These are my gifts to you so that you may *know* the Word of God and know that I did everything I could at the end not to harm you."

Too emotional to struggle for words, Joseph only stared.

"Pack all those things in the trunk Eric uses for travel! Pack a few days' clothes for me as well! I will take Ezra and Nancee with me, so the Gibbes Street town house can be opened. We'll stay there till I see you hired out and safe." He took Joseph's hand and placed it on his forehead. "Lay your hands on the sick, boy, as God commands! Beg Jesus Christ to give me strength—with forgiveness!"

Joseph's whole being numbed as he shook and prayed. The man was frantic. Maum Bette came, and as soon as she took his place, Joseph started gathering clothes. He hurried, knowing that his errand to the kitchenhouse to get Eric's trunk from the loft might give him one more chance to see Rosa.

————

Brant had never conducted a funeral, though from the time he had been Eric's age, he had been made to stand at somber attention during them just as his young brother beside him was doing now. Brant read the service of burial by torchlight. While the slaves stood around the opened grave, the little body, wrapped in white cloth, lay on a board atop the dug-up earth beside its eternal resting place.

When Brant finished, Hampton Gund said a spontaneous prayer. "We thankyee for the comforts of heaven, Papa-God. Help us all to walk the path of peace, knowin' we all gwine someday be where this child is, leavin' the earth for eternity."

When the little body was put down into the hole and covered with soil, there was a period of wailing. Afterward all the Africans headed back to the shanties in one swirling line across the Hermon Creek footbridge. Instead of crying anymore, they sang, with Parris's voice coming stronger than the rest.

I look down that road, an' that road so lonesome, Lord.
I gwine walk that lonesome road, oh . . .

Brant stayed in the graveyard until they all passed him by.

All I want to know is my sins forgiven. . . .
All I want to know is my soul set free. . . .

Holding Eric's hand, Brant took up the rear. As he looked up into the sky, holding so many stars, he had to agree with Delora's slaves—life was a lonesome road.

He was just at the driveway when a group of young patrollers rode up on horses.

"Hallo!"

The unfamiliar voice clued Brant to know that Teddy probably was not with the riders.

"We all heard the drums and came to see if you folks had been slaughtered." There was spitefulness in the teasing, and Brant felt uneasy. He knew some of these men had stood around him the night Joseph had been plucked from the ditch.

"It was a funeral. By now our overseer has the drums locked away," he explained self-consciously.

"Your daddy's sure a strange one, letting them sound like devils by night and preaching Christianity at them by day."

Brant attempted no justification. Inwardly he, too, disagreed with his father for allowing the drums to speak during the Africans' time of mourning. His daddy, however, saw nothing in the Scriptures against drums, so he had even allowed them to be played at his mother's passing.

"You found out any more about the brandings?" someone asked.

"No." Brant was anxious to see them go.

"Well, we all just rode in to show our support." This time he recognized the speaker as Tyson Clemson from the Young Planters' Club.

"Thanks." Brant sensed he should not trust their motives.

When the men pushed off, Eric squeezed his hand.

"Are they our friends or our enemies?" he asked with simplicity.

Brant waited until the patrol's lights were out of sight. "Really, Eric, sometimes I don't know."

Rosa finished the dishes with Joseph on her mind. That wasn't unusual, for she had thought of him almost every waking moment since he had been carried to the house. From Maum she had reports on his recovery. This satisfied her worry but did nothing to ease the longing in her heart.

Then suddenly Joseph appeared in the dark kitchen doorway as though part of some miraculous vision. He looked well, strong, and ever so handsome. She dared not speak in case he was only a specter.

He came in, dressed in clothes like the master's: white shirt, white cravat, dark brown trousers, and vest—which looked almost gold against his dark skin. He smiled, seeming nervous and awkward, and she felt just the same. The silence was painful, but she could think of nothing to say, though her mind spilled over with both concern and joy. Finally she spent her delight like a coin.

"Oh, it's so good to see you well!"

He looked around the kitchen that had been furnished again. When he touched the rope ladder she cried, "I can't stop thinking how you saved me! And how much it cost you!" It cut her heart that he did not look at her. She felt it might be her fault for having so insensitively rejected him. Reaching into her apron pocket she took out the paper she carried with her everywhere. "I shouldn't have run away," she said, holding the poem so that he could see it. "I should have thanked you and stayed by you."

"I . . . I couldn't speeeak whaaat I felt." He struggled, turning intense, dark eyes to hers. "I stiill caaan't."

"You will. And so will I!"

"Naaa." He pressed his lips together like one fighting a wave of sorrow. "I go to Chaa'leston soon."

"Not to be sold!"

He shook his head. "Hiiired."

Without saying more, he turned and climbed the ladder. She watched and waited until he came down with a small trunk balanced on his shoulder. Instead of carrying it straight out, he put it on the new table Gund had brought in. Hardly looking at her, he handed her the Bible Mr. Callcott had entrusted to him. "Faaa you."

She touched his wrist, not the book. "I can't. If Mr. Callcott gave that to you, then you must keep it. Besides, you love the words of God, while I can scarcely understand their meanings."

"Yooou caaan!" He sounded so urgent that it shamed her.

"Perhaps faith will come," she said mournfully, "but I don't know how if I cannot see you again. Will this be . . . for always?"

Shrugging and shaking his head, he took the trunk again.

"I'll treasure this," she said, holding up the scrap of poetry, "and I will always treasure getting to know you. You helped me in more ways than you can ever know."

He stood looking at her, then slowly walked to the door. He seemed grateful that she came with him, wanting to stay close. She realized that he was holding himself back from touching even her hand. Instead he looked up at the stars while they stood in the doorway.

"God waaatch over you. My praayer. And tooo seee you again."

"Oh yes." Then those stars blurred, and he was gone.

———

Just after ten the next morning, Joseph helped his frightfully weak master step up into the brougham Ezra had waiting at the door. As was Joseph's usual practice, he entered the coach with Abram. Always before, however, he had taken the velvet seat opposite the master, but today he sat beside him to give him support. Standing outside, Brant lingered at the open door.

"I still don't see the urgency of this, Daddy. Surely you can wait a day or two more before taking him to town. Or I can do it for you. I can meet with Mr. Wahl."

"God knows it's something I must do."

The son seemed to feel slighted. "Then I can come with you! Or meet you in town. You should not be in our town house alone."

"I want you here. I don't want anyone—branders or patrollers—trespassing on this property again."

The son resigned. "I'll try my best to keep order."

"I know you will. Joseph, close the door."

Joseph hated being squeezed between these two opinions, but since Abram was his master, he reached to take the coach's inner handle. He felt Brant's eyes of disapproval upon him.

The coach moved through the shade of the magnolia trees. Joseph, unaccustomed to sitting at this window, saw his mama running along the fence, waving and crying. Since the day of his birth, they had never been separated, but now after only a few hours for saying good-bye, he was leaving her—*forever?* When the coach passed the next gate, stout old Maum stood there without expression. Joseph nearly pulled back from the view, feeling that all this was too much to bear. Then he saw Rosa, neither weeping like Jewell nor steady like Maum. Instead she leaned to the fence with her eyes wide and her fingers to her lips like one fighting to be brave.

It was a feeling he mirrored in himself—to be strong as he gazed at her, even while his position made him powerless. His last look at her became distorted as the carriage moved on and he was forced to see her through the edge of beveled window glass.

"You are in love, boy. And she is so trusting of you."

Joseph sat back, for he knew then that the master had been watching him and even feeling his every motion as he was leaning on his shoulder. His feelings felt too private for exposure.

The master spoke again. "I never would have guessed anyone could rescue Rosa as you have. Do you have any idea of what she's been through?"

He nodded, understanding now that Master was referring to her past.

"I feel for you, but it *is* best to move you from here. Brant knows about Mr. Wahl and the rice mill, but he does not know any of my ideas about school. Truthfully, because of the darkness of your skin, my plan may be unworkable."

As much as life, Joseph wanted school. It was the only thing that made his fate now verge on being bearable.

"As of now I know of only one Negro teacher who has the reputation of sometimes daring to teach slaves."

A Negro teaching slaves!

"But I will have to see what he says about your color. If he won't take you as a pure African, then you will just be a clerk."

Joseph could not even nod. To have no choices! To be removed in one day from all he loved! With every turn of the coach wheels, slavery—and his life—seemed less and less fathomable.

Brant concluded an unhappy noontime meal with his brother and distraught sister. Maum Bette came in and curtseyed at his chair. "Colonel Rensler's here, sah. He come to call on you' daddy, but now he says he talk t' you."

Mayleda was like a tiger on fire. "Why is he here!"

"I don't know," Brant said with a glare. "I'll speak to him in the parlor, Maum." He pointed to Mayleda, warning her to behave. She frowned as he left to cross the cool hallway. His neighbor already had seated himself.

"Hallo, Brant. I came to visit you' daddy because I heard he's unwell. I'm quite surprised that he's gone to the city."

"Well, he has, sir." Brant continued to stand while searching for something more to say. "He took his Joseph to town and plans to hire him out. That's the solution we've arrived at, now that the boy is getting well."

"I certainly hope he finds a strong-handed taskmaster. Can the buck speak now?"

Brant didn't know, for he had chosen not to be near him. "I haven't heard him speak, sir," he answered truthfully. "I'm sorry you came all this way. As soon as my daddy returns, I'll tell him you called."

"When do you expect him?"

Brant felt wary. "He might be a few days, Colonel."

The white-haired gentleman leaned upon his gold-headed cane. "My word! Theodore suspects he has the fever."

Brant clenched his teeth, not wanting to hear anything like that. "Perhaps he's wrong, for Daddy is recovering."

"I'm sorry to have missed him. I had a pressing matter to discuss with him. Of course, since the field hands are under your direction now, I suppose it's fine to speak with you."

Brant twisted a button on his coat. "What is it, sir?"

"I'd like to borrow one of your slaves, Rosa, since Corinth is not fit to be a waiting maid at present. I haven't sold off her issue yet, so I've put the wench down in the street. Indeed, I'd sell her off, too, if I didn't need her skills. As it is, I'm only looking for a temporary maid, though of course buying a good one is never out of the question."

"You've never seen our girl—"

"Yes, I have. Perhaps you forget that I was at auction the day your daddy won the bid on her, not that anyone deemed her to be valuable then. Actually, I was hoping to get a fresh look at her during the chapel dedication, but you didn't bring her."

"No," Brant said, not wanting to talk about it.

"Well, do we have an agreement? I will pay you a dollar a day for her work. That's more than generous."

"Yes, sir, it is generous," Brant said, full of hesitation. "But my daddy's not eager to part with his people, so I really don't think I can give you permission."

"That's quite unneighborly, isn't it, since he's willingly hiring out another of your chattel to someone in Charleston?"

"He'd be concerned for her health," Brant said wondering at his own choice of words. "She's very nervous."

"Nonsense! I'm offering to take her into my daughter's own chambers. You all keep her outside. I'll pay you generously and board her well. What else do you want?"

Brant was tongue-tied. From the corner of his eye he could see Mayleda and Maum listening in the hallway as quiet as lizards on a fence. He had tried to figure out some way of refusing the colonel, but being the younger planter and neighbor, he did not have many avenues. "Sir, Ann may not like her. Indeed, I think she won't. The wench's hands and feet are weathered, and she trembles."

"Is that so?" The man slid forward in the chair as though he might be leaving. "Well, then, I suppose the only way to answer the question is to let Annie have her own close look. Will you bring the wench over, or shall I take her now on speculation?"

Brant drew a defeated breath, knowing he was obliged to comply. "I . . . I'll bring her over, sir. Tonight."

"That's very good of you." The colonel beamed.

Having no butler as did the Renslers, Brant showed the man to the door himself. At the threshold Colonel Rensler turned. "You know, son, I still strongly favor a Rensler-Callcott wedding."

"Yes, sir. Thank you, sir." Brant closed the door then and sighed against it. The whole despicable issue of controlling slaves tumbled down on him again. Colonel Rensler was not even to his horse before Mayleda and Maum came at him like birds driving a cat from their young.

"You can't take her off this property!" Mayleda cried. "Daddy would never have agreed to that!"

"Unfortunately *Daddy* wasn't the one being pressured," Brant said. "There was no way out. The colonel is my elder and our neighbor, and he came with a fair agreement."

"Mass' Brant, they gwine gobble her up like sweetbreads over there!" Maum mourned, never one to hold her tongue around him. "It would be better if you just done took her down and slit her throat or done hauled her off to auction."

"Don't you think I know anything?" he fumed at them both. "I'll do everything in my power to keep her here. Now, Maum, you need to help me. I will take her to Pine Woods, but with the worst-looking feet and hands you've ever seen. I'll give Ann the chance to look at her—and to reject her—and then I'll bring her straight home."

———

When it came to giving Rosa any comfort, Bette felt as useless as a butter knife trying to cut cordwood. The girl quaked and shivered at her every touch when Bette rubbed cold ashes into her palms and the soles of her feet to make them look as worn and dry as possible.

"Mass' Brant is sure of this plan, honey," Bette said, certainly not sure of it herself. " 'Sides, *choice* just ain't a word for nobody but the massas, gal. You gots t'go."

"I can't!" Rosa shrieked, doubling over and squeezing her hands to her neck. "Theodore Rensler's taken hold of me twice!"

Bette stood sympathizing and praying for wisdom from heaven. Suddenly a scrap of paper fell from Rosa's sleeve. "What's that there?" she said. Rosa moved like lightning to pick it up.

"Why, that's writin'!" Bette gasped, taking it from her. "You know what would happen to you if'n the massas done found this on you t'night?" She narrowed her eyes to the printing she could not understand. "What's this 'bout?"

Rosa could not be pressed to speak.

"I'm sorry to have to do this, girl." Bette walked over and threw the paper into the cooking fire.

Rosa moaned as though it was her own soul going up in smoke.

"You done been readin' with Joseph, ainty!"

Rosa did not deny it.

"Did that boy go off havin' print on hisself too?"

"Mr. Callcott's Bible."

Bette squeezed shut her eyes. "Ah!" The world would not tolerate black love or black learning.

"You think he'll be punished, even though his master gave it to him?" Rosa was beside herself with anguish.

"Hush!" Bette scolded because she was alert to footsteps outside. In a moment Master Brant came through the door. She grabbed Rosa to straighten her stance.

"Don't worry now, Maum." His small nervous smile did not show confidence. "I'll bring her back in just a few short hours."

CHAPTER 13

THE PINE WOODS MANSION was befitting of her nightmare. Glazed by the light of a broken moon and imbedded like a crystal in the cobalt sky, the two-story house had ten long windows all aglow with lamps. Each windowpane had the appearance of being a facet of that eerie jewel called opulence, which Rosa herself had once known as her own.

Master Brant drove the wagon to the steps of the lower piazza while a Negro man followed them.

"Hi-ho!" the servant called as he closed the space between himself and the wagon bed where Rosa sat. "Who's there?"

When Master Brant looked around, every detail of his bland face was easily seen in the light seeping from the windows.

"Why, shoo! Mass' Brant!" The roughly dressed slave became instantly cordial. "I sure didn't know it wa' you drivin' a wagon!" Rosa was eyed by the black man as he spoke.

The master gazed into the nearest floor-length window where a young blond woman could be seen playing chess opposite a stylish gentleman with brown hair and beard. Rosa felt a chill come over her whole body. She remembered these two. They had been with Teddy and Brant to see her in the fields.

Brant spoke with agitation while the servant held his paired horses. "For goodness' sake, Morrison, it seems that I may not be welcomed here, even though I've come at the colonel's request."

"What, Massa? You think Mista William in there be stealin' you' woman's heart!" The plantation worker laughed while Rosa pulled the piece of blanket Maum had given her around her shoulders. "I says you got nothin' to worry 'bout, sah! Miss Ann do have her bonnet set only for you—same as always."

"And how would you know that?" Delora's young master scoffed.

"'Cause she do never make no changes. I'm still s'pose to run an' tell her whensumever I see you' carriage or horse a-comin'. Which I would have done now, too, 'xcept this wagon fooled me!"

"And just why is she so anxious for a warning?" Brant Callcott sounded hurt and suspicious.

The slave Morrison swung his hand. "Aw! 'Cause she don't never want you just sneakin' up on her, sah. She always want time to fix herself up to look real good for you."

Brant folded his arms, considering what the window framed. "She always looks real good."

"Hah! That is for true, sah!" the slave agreed liberally, which might have been dangerous under other circumstances. However, Brant seemed accepting of the slave's camaraderie.

"Say, Morrison, why do you side with me when it comes to my courting Annie?"

Hesitation suddenly marked the older man's countenance. "Well, sah, 'cause someday I would like to work for you, 'stead of bein' here." His head was down now. "That, 'course, would be afta you an' Missy become husband an' wife. Seems to me some of the colonel's people gwine be moved over to Delora then."

Rosa heard Brant's unhappy chuckle. "I'm not sure I would wait for that, boy. Especially based on what I see in there. Where's the colonel and Mr. Nathan and Master Teddy?"

"I don't know 'bout the older gentlemen, but young Mass' Rensler done rode off afta supper to sell a fowlin' piece to somebody up past Reesers' Plantation."

Rosa's next breath came easier because of that.

Brant nodded. "Morrison, go prove what you said earlier about how Ann reacts to news that I'm here. I'd like to just look in now and see what happens."

"Fine with me, sah!" Morrison tied up the horses and then deserted them. The mansion door opened, then closed, and soon the slave was back. "Mind if I watch too, sah?"

Moments later the slave and the planter were laughing together, for Miss Rensler had gotten on her feet immediately to look at herself in one of the room's oval mirrors used to reflect the interior lighting.

"So, sah, you will think of ol' Morrison onc't you get 'round to needin' a gatekeeper?"

"All right, boy," Brant promised flippantly while jumping down from the wagon seat. "You wait here."

Rosa could see Morrison grinning, but as soon as the young planter was in the door, the gatekeeper's mask of happiness dropped away.

"So how you doin' this evenin', missy? I's the watchman here."

He tipped his cap, and she could see that he was neither young nor handsome.

Rosa's tongue was heavy under the stranger's gaze. Fear of even his inspection made her skin crawl. Looking away, she dug her bare toes into the rice straw strewn around her.

Instantly Morrison seemed duly empathetic. "Oh, gal, what you massa doin' haulin' you over here so late? I done knowed that man since he wa' a toddler, an' a more respectable white person you never gwine see."

She dared to pass him a look of anxiousness. There was noise as people came out. With dread Rosa backed herself into the wagon's darkest corner while Morrison stood by. Just a moment more and a little nimble houseboy was sent up over the wagon's gate. He had a candle and did not hesitate when strongly ordered by the white-haired master to light Rosa's face so that all could see her. As Rosa became imprisoned in that circle of brightness, Brant spoke plainly. "It's like I've already said, sir, my daddy's had her working outside all these years. She's become skittish around white folk, and wait till you see what the work and weather have done to her skin."

Rosa clearly heard the imposing planter's reply. "I believe I have the experience needed to make a sound choice for my daughter."

Then the blond woman called Ann was there to speak for herself. "I can decide. I don't need a committee of *men*!"

Rosa saw and felt other lights defining her. She shielded her eyes and wished she had a way to disappear like smoke.

"Slide on down here, gal," the white-haired master told her bluntly, removing the backboard from the wagon.

Feeling sick she pushed herself through the straw. Hands reached for her, but the first to touch her was the oldest one—Colonel Rensler. She bit her lip, whimpering to herself, for she already knew that abusers did not care whether or not their victims pled or cried. A little way off she felt Morrison still there watching.

"Feel those callouses on her heels!" That was Brant again. "They are as thick as any buck's—you have to agree!"

The young blond woman sighed harshly at Brant. "Why did you wait till it was so dark if you wanted me to see her flaws? From her face and form you have to judge her as being comely!"

Rosa nearly fainted but had the sense to keep her guard.

Brant sounded nervous. "I . . . I brought her when I could. I know you, Annie. I could make this decision for you. She's not really what you need or want."

Rosa shuddered anew as the white-haired man's fingers began to trace her wrists. "Your daddy sure net a bargain. She's turned out to be the hidden treasure from that lot of Aspidae niggers."

Aspidae! Rosa drew a breath of pain. Oh, to be touched by someone who had seen her on the block, almost naked and full of child. She pulled away, biting her tongue so she would not scream. But the man was like a snake, venomous, quick-moving. His fingers bit hers so that she could not escape the light.

"Daddy, you're hurting her," Ann said.

"No, dear. She's just reacting to my knowing who she is."

Roughly he turned Rosa's palms over like a market woman buying meat, to evaluate them.

"She's always skittish like that," Brant said.

"Behavior can be reformed," the other master answered.

"My daddy won't want her marked," Brant said suddenly.

"You need not worry. I am not one to break pretty flesh."

Rosa could not help emitting a frightened cry.

"I think you should stop right now!" Another young woman ran up. "Look how scared she is!"

"Miss Gilman, it's a simple business transaction."

"In New England, to touch a woman could send a man to jail."

"A wench, Miss Gilman!"

"A woman!" Felicia cried. "Please, Daddy, don't let this continue!"

Another man approached the colonel. "This is quite distressing to my family and me. I beg you, let the Negress return to Delora. Knowing Abram as well as I do, I doubt he would want the girl to be here."

"But what about getting a maid?" Ann said to Mr. Gilman.

Brant intervened. "I wanted to help you, and I wanted to show good faith toward you, Colonel, but I think we all can agree that Rosa cannot be put into your house."

The colonel turned and put his hand squarely on Brant's shoulder. The acrid planter spoke with understanding. "I underestimated how great a burden you bear, Brant, in trying to balance your daddy's practices with those of ordinary, business-minded planters. Were it any other gal, I would have taken her out of that wagon and showed her that she dare not have a will of her own. But since your daddy seems to have spoilt all your people during his tragic grieving, I'll not tamper with what has been done. I can only say you're in for hard and miserable times if your daddy does not do something to bring your people under control. First Joseph. Then the nig-ger-preacher Parris. And now this Rosa."

Rosa cringed at every name.

"I'm sorry, sir. I truly did not want to disappoint you."

"Right now, young man, I have concern for you and the future of your property. Do you have any idea how many more are ready to explode against you?"

Brant gave no answer.

Ann Rensler came beside him. "Look, you've come this far. Why not stay and go out on the river, as we were planning to do just before you came. Then the evening will not have been totally wasted."

"I should return," Brant said.

The colonel disagreed. "It would do you well to relax a little." Then he called Morrison. "Boy, put the wench in the barn and keep her under lock and key so she doesn't skip off till the master's ready."

"Colonel, that's not necessary. I should be going—"

"Please. Stay," Ann said.

The tender-hearted woman Felicia protested behind her. "You'll lock her in the barn?"

"There's nothing wrong with that," the colonel answered.

Ann was touching Brant. "Just for a short time?"

Rosa shivered to see him nod.

"All right. Just for a while."

Rosa did not dare to make a pleading glance toward him. Instead, she was obliged to let Morrison help her down after the white folks were dispersed.

"I won't hurt you, gal," Morrison promised. "I have daughters of my own, livin' off here an' there."

Her low voice shook almost like her hands did. "Yes, but do the masters have keys to the barn?"

The Negro would not look at her. "Yes, Missy, they do."

Her face went up to the sky just before she went through the barn door. She thought of Joseph's promise to pray for her. But none of his God's stars were smiling down on her now.

Ann saw Brant worry as the Delora slave was led away. Surprisingly, it was William who stepped forward just then to encourage him.

"I'm glad for another fellow's company. Being reared on the water, I have confidence in handling any worthy vessel, but I have no experience navigating this river by night."

"Our darkie will row," Ann said, feeling awkward in Brant's presence because William still had so little understanding about even the most ordinary facets of southern living. In the beginning William tried hard to cover his ignorance, but since Sunday he seemed to be displaying a negative attitude toward their culture, which Ann found unsettling.

"I think it odd that you don't do any work down here, even when it's pleasurable," William said in regard to rowing.

Brant let the insult pass. "I can't be out long," he said to them all. "My brother and sister are home alone."

Felicia came to Ann's side after going back into the house for a warmer shawl. "Are you certain the Negress will not take a chill? She has nothing but a rude scrap of wool."

Ann answered with impatience, "Yes! How do you think our Negroes survived before you came down to fret about them all?"

But Brant seemed focused on Felicia's concern. "I'm not going to stay long, I promise, Miss Gilman."

As a tight little group they walked down to the family's narrow riverside wharf. Their Negro waited in the rowboat. William and Brant behaved as old friends as they climbed in, then helped the women. Ann sat between the Gilman siblings, leaving Brant to take the lone seat in the bow. They left the shore, and for a long time after that there was no sound except the lapping of water. The silence felt thick and unhappy, so Ann told the boat-man to sing. William was delighted, though the music from this one voice was not as rich as many darkies singing together.

Even so, William, in another strange show of New England manners, thanked the black boy and paid him a coin for what he said were melan-choly Gullah tunes. "Negro music puts me in the mood for reflective poetry," William announced, and he recited a strand. " 'We are as clouds that veil the midnight moon . . . yet soon, night closes round, and they are lost forever.' "

"Oh, William," Felicia complained with sisterly sighing. "Shelley is much too glum a writer for such a lovely night. Besides, I find it unsettling to hear his work when one remembers that he lost his life *drowning*. Can't we just be quiet and enjoy how the moonbeams sparkle on the river's rip-ples?"

"Oh, you're a poetess yourself," Ann cheered her, trying to lighten the heavy atmosphere.

She saw William and Brant exchange the first of many glances, which she feared might have everything to do with her. Finally William said, "If we could put the Negro off, I'd be content to row. I do have *some* expe-rience, after all."

"Well, of course we can if that is what you want," Ann said. Once the changes were accomplished by going to the shore and sending the Negro back, Ann considered the two men. Perhaps William was just too timid to admit that southern life had become disconcerting to him. Since coming home on Sunday to have a long private discussion with his father, Ann had seen him brooding and spending hours reading many of her daddy's plant-ing journals. *"You have quite a life carved out for yourselves down here,"* he would say to her from time to time. *"However, it seems unstable, even wrong, to have it built so much on the black labor. That opposes the ideal of having the liberty to make your own way independently, by your own strength and power."*

"We do make our own way!" she had retorted. But now as she thought back on those uncomfortable discussions, she became very thankful to be in the position to lean on Brant. His presence, after William's, was so warmly familiar. She sighed. Why should she try to manipulate her affec-tions toward William, when she knew it was Brant she cared about? If the evening would just afford her some time to speak with Brant, then perhaps they could put the problems of Sunday behind them both.

By his words and actions William seemed only eager to affirm Ann's indelible feelings toward the southern man. As he rowed, William spoke of shipping in general, of the seas and of school, but never once did he say a thing about Ann. Nor did he give any hint of interest in ever wanting to move south.

Brant initiated no conversation, but after a while he put his arm around Ann's waist to protect her from the river's dampness.

"Are you still thinking of your slave?" Felicia said with an innocence that sounded blunt in the dark.

"I guess I am," Brant said, and immediately Ann felt tension return to him. "I am responsible for bringing her here."

"She'll be all right for an hour," Ann said to them both.

William rowed the small, low-riding vessel so that the oars did not make a sound. Ann found herself in contented awe as she indulged in the nighttime beauty of the vast shoreline owned by her family and the Call-cotts. She and Brant had many reasons to be grateful and to stay bonded as they looked to carve a good future for themselves. She was happy when the feel of his arm around her seemed to prove that he was at rest once more.

But suddenly the quiet was broken by a man's sharp cry for help. It came from along the tangled riverbank. Immediately William rowed with intensity toward shore. Not exchanging a word between them, he and Brant splashed into the knee-deep water the moment the boat touched land.

"What do you think's happening?" Felicia cried as more calls for help were heard, and the women were deserted by the men.

"I don't know!" Ann whispered, clawing the side of the boat and listening. Soon all became quiet. Felicia, having been raised near the ocean, knew how to tuck her skirts and wade to land unscathed. She helped Ann do the same. They clung to each other as they heard an unseen woman's softer but far more heart-wrenching scream.

Felicia dragged Ann toward the point of terror, while Ann tried to think what other woman lived along this piece of ground. She stopped Felicia the moment she saw Teddy's black horse tied to the trees.

"Don't go farther!"

"But someone's been hurt!" Felicia reasoned.

Instead of trying to see anything, Ann fought to turn her friend around. "What's taking place is none of our concern! And the one who called for help was likely the darkie we put out of the boat. He'll be beaten for crying out."

"What are you speaking of?" Felicia demanded as with new determination she pulled Ann back closer to the forest. "If he's hurt someone, we need to help her."

Ann lunged for her friend's skirts, but Felicia got away. Having no choice, Ann ran after her, calling, "Allow the men to deal with it!"

But Felicia didn't stop until she caught up to Brant and William. Then, in a moment, she was wailing into her open hands.

"Get her out of here!" William raged at Ann. "This is nothing for my sister to see!"

Ann pulled Felicia to hide her face in her bosom, but not before she, too, had taken a look at the Delora slave with her dress in shreds and at Teddy, his coat off and his shirt undone.

Even in the presence of other women, Rosa imagined that Brant would be the next to violate her by the way he came at her, lifted her off the ground, and threw her over his shoulder. She had the deepest and ugliest desire to shed her body like a snakeskin. She was repulsed by the feel of her own flesh against this second man who held her against her will. Carrying her almost at a run, Brant raced through the woods and then into the lighted area by the house. They rushed past the barn, where she had first been discovered by Theodore Rensler, who had gagged her and taken her away by horse.

Once into the mansion's yard, Brant literally threw her into the wagon. She groped for a nail, a piece of rope, anything, by which she could destroy herself. Brant leaped behind the reins and drove like a madman. Rosa would have jumped to her death except that each time she tried to stand, she found her strength gone.

She scratched her face and the skin of her legs and arms to war against the sensation that Teddy still held her. The moon above the open road was like a light from hell.

CHAPTER 14

AS SOON AS HIS SON, William, had given a stammering explanation for his sister's hysteria, Nathan Gilman demanded that the colonel show them to a room where he could speak alone to his children. Nathan brought Felicia in first. She was as weak as a newborn. He sat her down beside the warming fire and said, "Darling. What can I do? What I can say to comfort you?"

"Where is the black girl now?" she moaned.

"The Callcott boy put her in the wagon and took her home."

"Ohhh, Father! No! Some woman should be there to comfort and hold her! Ohhh! She must be terrified! I cannot imagine even the smallest portion of what she suffered!"

"My dear, kind child." He stroked her hair. "I'm so sorry that you had to come upon this. I should never have given you permission to be out in the night."

"It was Teddy, Father!" Felicia raged with words so high they broke her breathing. "How could he be like that? We've known him for years."

"He's been taught that it is not wrong," Nathan said with embarrassment and regret. "Oh, don't think for a moment that this could have happened to you."

"He's a pig! Dirty! Rotten! Evil! Oh, how could he? Ohhh!"

He let her sob, crying himself for her loss of innocence.

"I don't want to stay here, Papa! I never want to see him again! I want to go home! I just want to go home!"

"Yes, I agree," he whispered into her damp hair. "We will go, I promise. We will go tomorrow on the first packet north."

When he finally had her settled, Nathan went out to see his son in the hallway. William met his gravity with dry and somber eyes. "I pray you weren't a partner with him in any of this!"

"No!" William vowed. "I find it just as repulsive as you."

"Can you say as God is your judge and witness that you have kept yourself pure all the time you have been here?"

"Yes. I swear it!"

Nathan gave a grateful sigh. "Your sister and I have put in our votes for leaving as soon as tomorrow. And I am eager to dispel the idea of starting any business here."

William looked at him. "Yes, I am too. Ever since Sunday I've been feeling uneasy."

Nathan nodded grimly. "Even if slave labor could work for us, the *morality* of this system would keep me from investing here. I'm going downstairs to tell the colonel my decision, and I'm going to ask him to make an apology to the both of you. I would get Theodore to do it, but I don't want Felicia to face him."

"I don't want to see him either!"

"At some point you will have to ask God for grace to forgive him, as I hope that poor Negress can. But for now I understand your feelings. Stay with your sister."

Nathan found Linford Rensler in his office writing in his ledger. He rapped on the opened door.

"Come in," the planter said. "Have a seat. I was expecting you."

"No, thank you. I hope that in a moment you will see the necessity of coming with me."

"Really?"

"Colonel, my children have both witnessed a rape." He swallowed after speaking with such directness, but he wanted the man to know the gravity of the deed done. "I want you to make apology to them on Teddy's behalf."

The colonel leaned back with his elbows on the arms of his wooden chair. "It was indeed unfortunate. But in a way, my friend, you and your family should be making apology to me."

Nathan was taken aback. "How so?"

"If that darkie rower had not known that your northern children were on the water, he would never have dared to cry out as he did. Even as we speak, my overseers are administering some one hundred lashes to him."

"That is criminal! He discovered a woman being compromised!"

"A *colored* wench, and by a white man, Nathan. That was not his business."

"You mean to tell me he had no right to sound an alarm?"

"Teddy's only mistake was that he took his pleasure with someone else's property. The Negro has no rights!"

Nathan sat in the extra chair. "I want an apology! My children should never have witnessed what they did."

The colonel looked at him. "I'm sorry, I have no apology to give."

"It's for their moral instruction. And if I may say so, you should pull your nephew in, too, and give him a piece of your mind. These young men and women need to know that sexual relations without marriage are an abomination to God."

"I can't say that to him." The colonel paused. "You see, I have sired slaves."

Nathan found himself standing numbly.

"Now, Gilman! Don't go judging us so harshly by your puritanical standards. Every master must decide how he will behave with his possessions. There are plenty of gentlemen, like my neighbor and your friend Abram Callcott, who choose *not* to indulge. It is a very private matter, which we do not speak about to spouses, family, or *outsiders*."

"Private!" The word tasted bitter. "Except for the poor women you terrorize and their own race of men who have no recourse against your actions! Private! Until the children of your sinful compromises are birthed!"

Rensler's justifying smile was wide and thin. "The issues we produce belong to us. Since you have intruded in such an ungentlemanly fashion, I will be perfectly honest with you. It can be productivity with pleasure."

"I and my children will be leaving by the quickest conveyance! I will never invest another dime in the South unless it is to rescue Negroes from this curse you have them under."

Colonel Rensler said nothing further to him. Nathan turned, rushed upstairs, and met his children to pack for home.

———

Brant had driven wildly on the main road, but then on impulse he turned the foaming horses aside so that now he was forced to take the rarely used King's Road Trace at a much slower pace. But his mind still raced as his horses had. What would his daddy say? How could he face his sister? What might the slaves do to him after seeing that another of their lot had been damaged while in his care? It made him angry to think how the colonel had pressured him into bringing Rosa to Pine Woods. And Teddy's uncontrolled and shameless lewdness made him furious, even with Rosa. So many men had taken her. Could it be possible that some Negresses naturally had the demon of temptress brewing in them, as so many of his young planting friends said was true? If so, then he would end that here and now.

Pulling the wagon to a stop, he wrapped the reins around the stake at the driver's seat. He startled Rosa by climbing back into the wagon bed. At once she tried to leap to freedom, but he caught her by the hair, which had been hanging loose since the moment he discovered her in the forest. Turning her away from him so that he did not succumb to the temptation of looking at her himself, he pulled the same knife he had used on Joseph. "I will stop all from lusting after you!" he screamed.

She begged. "I did nothing. . . ."

He felt uncontrollable anger as he began to hack off her hair in thick clumps as close to her scalp as possible. All the while he made himself insensitive to her shuddering. When he was done, she dropped to her knees and tried to crawl away. Brant commanded her to hide herself in the straw. She would not listen but tried to climb out of the wagon instead. Her ghostly cries echoed as he caught her time and time again to keep her from escaping. He was at his wits' end to know what to do when a hot white light arrested them both. Turning, blocking his eyes against its brightness, he saw both Hampton Gund and Billy Days glaring at him, blazoned by their lantern light.

He was speechless to explain Rosa's tears, torn dress, or ruined hair. Now that his anger had been spent on her, he felt only weary regret at the whole horrible chain of events. The overseer and driver traded glances.

"We wa' out lookin' for Parris, sah," Gund said cautiously, perhaps holding to the pattern that no overseer pries into his master's business. "Somehow he done caught wind of the fact you wa' a-takin' Rosa to Pine

Woods." Gund looked with grief at her.

"I did not touch her!" Brant vowed, full of defensiveness. "She was taken by another, and I was powerless to stop him. I cut her hair to end this infernal lusting over her." But neither of the others seemed wholly willing to believe him. Their attention was entirely on her suffering.

"It's the truth!" Brant raged. *Why, Lord, oh, why?* he cried inwardly. "What else can I say! God knows the truth!"

"What do you want us to do?" Gund asked coolly.

Brant sighed, the sense of failure almost overwhelming him. "Take her home. And I want Parris found!" Then he saw their two horses. "Billy, you drive this wagon! I'll go with Gund."

Billy spoke tenderly. "Come on, chile. It's you' Unc' Billy. Look up now. See, I's the one takin' care of you now."

Gund waited until Brant had hold of Billy's horse's reins. He sounded nervous. "Sah. I fear Parris has armed hisself with an ax from the wood-pile."

"Aww!" Brant cried as new disgust filled him because of his slaves. He was already sickened by what his own anger had done. Now Parris might be on the prowl with murder in his heart.

His overseer seemed to stay vindictively silent.

"If you think I am the one who sinned against her, you're wrong, Gund! I found her with another. I blamed her when I shouldn't have, perhaps. But I did not lay a hand on her myself."

Still Gund did not respond.

"I cut her hair. I already said that. Only because I hate the way men crave her. But by law I did nothing wrong to her or to Joseph!"

Gund cleared his throat. "Sah, I think we should work to find Parris 'fore that boy do kill somebody—maybe even one of us."

Hampton knew Parris probably had it in his head to find Theodore Rensler, but to say that straight out could mean that the boy would be hanged, no questions asked when found. So he tried to guide the inexperienced young master while at the same time keeping every option open for bringing Billy's son home to him alive.

"I'd say he's out in the open an' down by the river where he can move by the light of the sinkin' moon."

Master Brant easily agreed and skillfully rode out in front of him to one of the fishermen's trails that followed the river. Hampton felt sure it would benefit Parris to find him before any patrolman did. He feared that the big young slave might be riled up enough to murder anybody who'd try to stop him from avenging Rosa's distress.

The young master pulled his horse to a standstill as they came to the next opening in the trees. Hampton listened and looked, wondering what the planter heard or saw. Without a word Brant reined his mare tightly into a low place filled with shadows. Hampton followed him in. The blackness around them magnified the moonlight shining on the river. Then Hampton saw the gray-capped creases on the otherwise black water, indicating a boat or canoe was riding upstream. At the same moment he heard voices and then shouting from the shore. It was likely there were men on land and men in the river who knew one another. He watched them come together. While the boat pushed to the riverbank, others on foot pressed down to the water's edge.

Hampton strained his eyes to the limit. A tall, bulky form emerged in the midst of the two boisterous groups.

"It's Parris!" the slavemaster decided just as Hampton came to that conclusion.

"It is, sah! And they must be patrollers."

The groups combined to form one circle. The moon was strong enough for Hampton to see human outlines with cudgels raised.

"They'll kill him!" Brant's voice was suddenly loud with prediction. He then drove his horse out, firing his pistol as he rode. Blindly, Hampton followed.

———

Bette was out of bed the moment she heard a wagon in the driveway. Stumbling across the unlighted room, she held to the door's latch momentarily, bracing herself for what she would meet outside. For the crime of running off, her boy might be dead. Going to the edge of the porch, Bette saw her husband in the lantern light. She ran to him, but instead of finding Parris, Bette saw Rosa, blue dress torn, her hair hacked off, and her face swollen by more than just her tears.

"Where's my son?" Bette screamed. Because Rosa had been harmed, she had no hope that Parris, as the girl's avenger, would come back alive.

Billy was like stone. "I dunno. Mista Gund an' me done found Rosa with Mass' Brant. I was told by him to bring her back here while he an' Mista Gund stayed out to search for our boy."

"Mass' Brant done this to her?" Bette raged.

Billy ignored her flaming indignation. "You take her down to Negozi.

That's the only place she wants to be!"

"Oh, baby!" Bette reached for Rosa, but the girl, holding the fragments of Miss Oribel's dress around her, dashed off alone.

"Don't you let her out of you sight," Billy warned. "She's to the place now where she will do harm to herself."

"You gwine back out to look for Parris, ainty? You not gwine let two *white* men come 'pon him first!"

"You go care for that girl, an' I'll see to Parris." His face was a mixture of anger and agony. When Bette did not move, Billy spoke with the cold authority given him as driver. "I says, woman, go after her! She done been taken an' used."

Bette still wasn't thinking on Rosa, but she turned and headed down the street. It was a night of evil. Even now Parris's soul might be separated from his body and gone from this earth.

In Negozi's house Bette found Rosa on her knees and howling like a wounded animal in front of the old woman's fire. The stiff, withered aunty had already shooed everybody away except Abiel, who stood silent as a crooked walking stick in the corner. Negozi's glazed eyes were black and as dry as her skin when Bette came in. Bette explained to the other woman that which needed no explanation.

"The buckras have been drawin' they pleasures from this child." Her bitterness was as wooden as her words. "This time it wa' Mass' Abram's own flesh and blood."

"No! It was Rensler! Rensler!" Rosa screamed.

Bette and Negozi continued to meet each other's gazes but with more anger and less personal hurt to know their own master had been cleared. Bette went and knelt beside the distraught woman, taking every care not to touch her.

"You back safe, honey. It's all behind you now!" She thought again of Parris, but this was trouble enough to keep her busy.

Rosa's moanings changed. "I cannot live like this!" Without a moment's warning she threw herself face-first toward the blaze. With miraculous speed Bette and Negozi trapped her. They pulled her back to safety, but not before the room filled with the sickening odor of singed, smoking hair.

"Let me die!" Rosa wailed. "Oh, let me die!"

"You know you ain't the one to pay for this!" Negozi said, her face as hard as leather. "Let the devil have his way. Let the right one be drug off to his grave."

Bette knew what the other was thinking, for Negozi still practiced the ancient heathen art of conjuring, learned in early womanhood from African spiritists.

"I won't have you addin' evil to evil," Bette warned her, holding so tightly to Rosa that the girl was free only to chew her fists in her terrible drive to destroy herself.

"The power of both human an' demon spirits done been given to us!" Negozi reasoned, rising and reaching for the sweet-grass basket that always hung near the hearth. "If only I had a itsy-bitsy slip of fingernail or a knot of his hair, I'd make a real potion. Then ol' Buckra Massa would be dead inside a week."

"Stop!" Bette begged. "We all're Christian now. Mass' Abram don't want no more hoodoo what sides with the devil."

"An' we don't want no rape, do we!" Negozi shouted back with gold fire reflecting in her eyes. "But we still get what we don't want! Now let those massas get the same!"

"The Bible don't say nothin' to bless no conjurin'! It's the devil's work."

But Negozi moved with the independence of a cat. "Here's goofer dust I done collected the night we dug the baby's grave."

"Abiel!" Bette cried, remembering that Negozi's Christian husband was there. "Make her stop her foolishness 'fore God's condemnation falls 'pon us all!"

The small man in the shadows was reluctant to come nearer. "It is ungodly, woman," he said to his wife but stayed exactly as he was.

"An' that's not?" Negozi's hand flashed toward Rosa's exposed and quivering shoulders.

The girl's piteous begging quieted them all. "Please help me. I can't stand myself. I must die."

Negozi's fingers worked like spiders' legs. After stirring together mysterious dark powders, she uncorked a small vial of amber-colored fluid. "Oh, to have somethin' what belong to him—"

"I have this!" Rosa gasped.

Before Bette could take hold of her, something like a stone was passed to Negozi. It was a gold button torn from the gentleman's coat.

"Dear Rosa!" Bette pleaded. "Don't be a part of this. I knowed it's in you blood to believe that revenge is the answer, but as God is the Lord, chile, I says you mustn't give you'self to this, no matter how bad you done been hurt."

Rosa only widened her eyes as Negozi hunched down beside her. Bette smelled the vinegar and herbs as the button was dropped inside. Suddenly two huge dark hands appeared over their heads. Bette screamed as she looked behind herself.

"Oh, Billy! Lord! They be conjurin' an' I cain't make 'em stop!"

"Shut every mouth!" In the blink of an eye her husband had the bottle and the basket wrenched from Negozi's hands and thrown into the fire. "Mass' Brant an' the whole beat company's a-comin'. They got Parris. Now don't none of you say a word!"

It was only moments before her son was pushed through the doorway. Bette collapsed in anguish right next to Rosa, who was doubled over with her shorn head buried in her arms. As Parris was forced in, Bette saw his shirtless body glistening with sweat and blood. His arms were tied in front of him. His right eye was battered shut. Overseer Gund was gripping his right elbow, and his own daddy moved to take his left. One of the company of white men spoke after Massa Brant came trailing in behind the others.

"Tomorrow will be the start of his forty days, Mr. Callcott. But we're putting him into the chains tonight."

Bette had no idea of the man's meaning until others from this hateful party latched on to Parris's wrists and ankles the thickest set of shackles Bette had ever seen.

"Forty days, Mr. Callcott. And if he ain't broke then, arrangements will be made with the slave court in Charleston."

"That won't be necessary. I can deal with my own."

"Like you did with your Joseph? Letting him go just moments before Dr. Rensler was finished up right with him?"

Bette saw the anguish in Brant Callcott's eyes.

The patrolman continued. "I warn you, Callcott. Either you get your niggers under control, or the patrol will soon have jurisdiction over them all."

"There will be no more problems!" Brant sounded as breathless as a child awakened by nightmares. Just then Parris, stunned and wobbling dizzily, must have caught sight of Rosa crumpled on the floor. He bellowed and fought his new chains. They shook and clamored like broken glass while he raged.

"What's been done to her!"

White or black, nobody answered him. Showing no fear, Parris churned his thick bent arms like paddles on a waterwheel. Gund was thrown off balance. His daddy was swept to his knees as Parris kicked left, right, and even behind him. Scrambling to their feet, Gund and Billy knocked Parris flat. They pinned him, while half of the white intruders cursed and the other half laughed. With cruel harshness the commander of the patrol, who was not Rensler, pulled his pistol. "It would be best to put an end to that bull now."

Bette emitted a biting scream as the man reached down and used the butt of his gun to club her son to unconsciousness.

"So this is the nature of your daddy's finest nigger-preacher, is it, Mr. Brant?"

Brant's lips opened, but no words came out. Gund and Billy stayed at Parris's shoulders, even though he was as limp as cloth.

The tension on Brant's face was as clear as ice.

"Delora will continue to be watched!" the patrol spokesman warned. "You tell your daddy that! Tell him we don't need no more converted niggers raising up axes against the innocent." Then he looked down on Parris directly. "And if we ever find him roaming again, I swear this group will have him flayed and burned from the feet up as we lynch him."

Like seafoam the men disappeared, except for Mass' Brant, who continued to look at all his people in that room with small stony eyes. "Well, you heard them, didn't you! You all want violence, then violence will come back on you!" He stared at Parris. "Forty days he'll be in chains! Now let that be a lesson to you all that there are powers at work outside this plantation that are beyond my ability to control."

From her place on the floor, Bette noticed when Parris's eyes fluttered open. Immediately her son fixed his vision on Rosa, who glanced furtively at him. Mass' Brant's concentration was on the overseer.

"Gund! I'm holding you responsible for maintaining order. You will lose your job if you fail."

Bette saw Gund give a quick look to Billy. "Yessah. As long as that beat company don't come back, we can be at peace."

"Then be at peace, so they don't come back!"

Mass' Brant walked out and Billy stood, releasing Parris. Bette's heart was in her throat, for she feared her boy might rise up and strike the slaveowner still within reach. But Parris just lay there, and in a moment he started sobbing with his eyes shut tight. Bette wrung her hands until they pained. Her exhausted husband glanced between their son and Rosa, who had crawled to the farthest, darkest corner and cowered there like a homeless orphan.

Suddenly Billy was on his knees, raising his fists toward heaven, even though Gund was still there. "Oh, God, don't you see none of this? These are our children of the next generation!" Each word struck like a hammer on an anvil. "How long will you wait 'fore you rescue us? How long?"

PART TWO

A

Work

of

Redemption

CHAPTER 15

THE CITY CLERK'S bald head looked bright in the light of the court-house windows. Abram Callcott watched the man study the name on the paper and then look up at him as he stood in front of the desk, holding his cane and leaning on Joseph's arm for support.

"Morning. Mr. Callcott," the city worker said, checking the written reference once more. Then he tipped his pencil. "Boy, don't just stand there. Fetch a chair for your master."

Joseph moved one of the well-worn seats away from the wall, and Abram sat down. The clerk continued with some uncertainty.

"Is *this* the one you want hired out?"

Abram sensed the need for caution. "Yes. I want him put under the supervision of Mr. Wahl, the foreman at Grafton Mills."

The man showed no interest in the explanation. "I see you own property along Ashley and also on Gibbes Street. You will be at your town house through the fever months?"

Abram hated the term, for it reminded him of grim disaster. "No. I keep to my plantation year round, for that, I believe, is a master's duty." He felt the clerk judging him to be a fool.

"Then no one occupies the Gibbes Street house?"

"My son might live there," Abram admitted, "if he secures a position in Charleston for the summer." It was something he and Brant had talked about because of his boy's fear of fever. Now, however, he was not sure he should agree to it with Joseph already here, and he was not certain of being strong enough physically to do without Brant through planting and harvest. He thought he saw Joseph fidget slightly.

"Your son's name?"

"Brant Melvin Callcott. But it's not certain that he will move to town."

The clerk traced along more of the handwritten lines Abram had prepared according to the city's requirements. "Your agreement with Wahl extends from today to the end of the year."

"Yes, with the option to extend it, even by letter, if my health does not permit me to return to see him in person."

"The position you specify here is order clerk."

"So it is."

"Why the change of occupation? It's obvious that he is a manservant."

Abram shifted in the chair. "What is *obvious*, man, is that I am not well and that I will not need a waiting boy forever."

The clerk touched his desk. "I don't want to pry into your business, sir, but it is my duty to tell you that you may not dispose of insolent help here in Charleston. The auction blocks on Chalmer and Market streets are for that."

Abram drew himself up to this civic plebeian. "I demand apology. This boy is a model worker."

"You needn't be defensive," the man said, shaking off the challenge, "any more than if I were your physician daring to speak to you about suspected illness. My duty is to help you. Unruly chattels cause their owners social embarrassment, financial obligation, loss of productivity, lawlessness, and legal entanglements. Often on Saturday nights the jail and workhouse are filled up with them. So—"

"So!" Abram pulled at his gloved fingers. "You have no cause to question my intentions."

The clerk tapped his pencil to the desk. "Just so you understand that whatever flaws your boy brings with him, Charleston will see them magnified."

Joseph, standing at his side, slipped Abram the first of several worried glances. This made Abram choose his words carefully, more to reassure his tender slave than this brutish bureaucrat. "He is a God-fearing Negro. Now, may we move on from here? And quickly!"

The clerk gave an abrupt chuckle and shuffled the papers. "Where does Mr. Wahl reside?"

"Smith Street."

"The boy will stay there?"

"Why is that of importance to you?"

"It's required that I record the darkie's place of residence."

Abram sighed. "He'll live on Anson Street." There was a very good reason for this, which he would never tell the man.

"Then who will be in charge of him if the foreman is on Smith Street and the mill blocks away?"

"Mr. Wahl, thank you!" The day before, Abram had been to Grafton Mills to work out everything, including how Joseph might attend a Negro school on Anson in the evenings after his duty to Wahl was fulfilled. "The foreman's made arrangements for him to be housed with other Negroes of whom Mr. Wahl is guardian. The free colored woman who rents the house is virtuous, and she holds three nominal slaves who are her kin."

Abram did not see why he had to give these details. The city was full of free colored persons and also of nominals—slaves owned by free sympathetic individuals of color. Since slave manumission was forbidden by state law, being owned by a free family member or friend was the closest any South Carolinian bondsman could ever come to having liberty.

When the clerk frowned, Abram felt the need to make his case clearer. "All four colored residents of the house are members of Cumberland Street Methodist Church where Mr. Wahl attends." Abram was keenly aware that Joseph was learning all this about his future secondhand.

"The free Negress's name?"

"Last name is Haskell. That is all I know."

This information was scribbled into a margin. "Is Joseph the only name the boy answers to?"

"Yes." Abram knew Kwash, Maum's nickname for him, but this man didn't need to know of it.

"Now, this one can read and write, can't he?" The man kept adding more notes to the page. "Otherwise the mill wouldn't put him in a clerk's position."

"Yes, he can." Immediately Joseph touched Abram lightly on his back.

Looking to his slave, Abram recognized the worried puzzlement on his face, and rightfully so, for Joseph did not *yet* know how to write. As soon as they were away from here, he would explain everything, but now was certainly not the time to do so. Feeling more unwell by the moment, Abram added, "Mr. Wahl came to my town house yesterday to make an inspection of the boy. The gentleman needs none of this information."

"This is for our records, not the employer's. Exactly how tall is he?"

"I don't know! Look! You're not going to find him wandering the streets."

The worker snapped his fingers. "Bring the stick."

An old darkie received the command and moved from a corner stacked with dull-looking books. He held a pole, nicked with marks, and stood it at Joseph's shoulder. " 'Bout seventy inches, sah."

"Twenty years old, you have written down here. And just about as black as you can find them nowadays, eh, since we've stopped bringing them over by boat." The man chuckled.

"Get this over with," Abram begged, the room beginning to spin. His hands numbed, and his cane clattered to the floor. Instantly Joseph was at his knee.

"Saa, he neeeds waata!"

Abram stayed alert enough to know that the old Negro brought a drink and that Joseph held it to his mouth. Never had he felt closer to the boy. The youth's concern for him remained even after his spell was over. Abram just sat there, gratefully squeezing the dark, graceful fingers that had supported him. "I beg you, clerk, let us be on our way."

"His wages will be sent to you by the employer?" There was no hint of compassion.

"Yes."

The man continued writing. "He will have no money of his own?"

The weakness in Abram's mind and body continued. "No money of his own."

"If the city needs to contact you, it will be through"—he flipped back to see the name—"your son Brant."

"No!" Abram coughed. "Mr. Wahl will oversee everything! Whatever you do, make that perfectly clear on this record!"

"Mr. Callcott, owners are financially responsible for any disciplinary actions taken by the city. If your boy—"

"I do not want my son involved in any way." Abram had no strength, but anger and exasperation kept him going.

The clerk raised both eyebrows very knowingly. "I see." He blotted his inked work. "This full document will be kept on record for the aldermen who supervise the city wards."

Abram wiped the perspiration from his forehead with his fingers, then Joseph offered a handkerchief pulled from Abram's own coat sleeve.

"There's just one more thing, Mr. Callcott. The city keeps a written description of all distinguishing marks a slave carries on him."

"He has none worth mentioning," Abram proclaimed. Indeed! Joseph had been subjected to enough indirect insult. There was no need for everyone to know him scar by scar.

"That is untrue, sir!" The sour clerk wrote again, with fury. "He stutters like one muted manually. Has he a tongue?"

"Of course he has a tongue!"

Those fingers snapped again.

Abram tried unsuccessfully to rise in Joseph's defense. "I don't want him inspected!" It was useless. The old Negro sauntered forth and, with the skill of a slave trader, pried Joseph's mouth open.

The clerk moved from his desk to better see the injuries. "Cuffee, show the rest of him."

Swiftly the black man parted Joseph's clothing, lifting the shirt to his neck while lowering the trousers.

Abram had strength only to hang his head, suffering his own kind of humiliation at his slave's exposure. He did not watch while the boy was turned around calmly and callously until the clerk saw the cross and circle on his flank.

"*Call-cott!*" the clerk said, recognition lighting his face. "Now I know that name. You're the one who started that society for preaching to plantation darkies up along the Ashley. And Mr. Wahl, isn't he the secretary of your club?"

Abram refused to answer until Joseph was unhanded. In bitter silence he watched his pained servant rebutton his trousers and tuck in his shirt. "No, Mr. Wahl is not secretary." In truth, Wahl was treasurer.

The clerk put down the papers. "You should have started with this brand mark, sir. I must advise against putting the boy here. Your aggressive evangelism efforts have caused reverberations even in this office. Gentlemen have come in demanding to know what registered servants have masters in your group."

"They come, and you do not arrest them? These records should be private! A Christian master has moral obligations to his darkies!"

"I am a clerk, not a policeman. I don't control what happens. But those involved with the Cross and Circle branding are in the city, and if that were my property, I would keep him home."

"Are you saying this registration does nothing to safeguard Joseph? Have you set this whole system in order only so you can arrest the unruly *colored* element? Where is justice if I do not have the freedom to put my trustworthy servant out to work and feel secure that he will have the city's protection?"

"Of course the city enforces its laws for the citizens! But tell me something, sir. How long did it take for him to receive that branding? And why did *you* not prevent it?" He did not wait for answers. "In the city things can happen very quickly. If a company of whites spots him alone and, recognizing him as one of yours, takes him down, he is not allowed to defend himself. If he should happen to survive and even knows who attacked him, you will have no recourse for recouping damages, because persons of color cannot bear witness against white men in our courts." The man folded his hands calmly. "Of course, the decision is still yours."

At that moment Abram was so furious he could have suspected this clerk for involvement in the violence done to Joseph in the laundryhouse. Still, one glance at Joseph's somber face told him his slave wanted to stay regardless of the risks. To benefit his loyal bondsman, Abram tried to communicate a mood of courage.

"The agreement is already finalized between the mill and me. Mr. Wahl will exercise wise and careful use of him."

The clerk remained expressionless. "If that is your decision, please rise. Raise your right hand and repeat after me, 'I do solemnly swear that this Negro is my property, is of the age and condition respectively stated, and is here for hire. So help me, God.'"

After the oath was taken, the papers signed, and the court fees paid, the clerk neatly lettered Joseph, *servant of A. Callcott, St. Andrew's Parish* into the city ledger. Then he took a square copper badge with the words *City of Charleston SERVANT* and the number *648* tooled upon it. Using a pin, he pulled some threads through the hole punched into one of its corners, securing the tag to Joseph's person. "You lose that, boy, and you'll meet your ward's alderman straightway. Every time you set foot into the street, starting today, you have that on you and a valid pass from your employer. Lacking either will get you leather on your backside. That's exactly what happens to every darkie who's found out after curfew, too, which is set at nine o'clock."

Though Joseph seemed steady, Abram saw trouble in his rapidly moving, downcast eyes. "Come with me," Abram said, eager to pull him from this injurious environment. "We're finished here. Help me to the carriage."

Abram slowed to a halt when they were away from the courthouse and under a shading Pride of China tree. "You don't have to go to the mill, boy," he said, still holding to Joseph for support. "I'll put you to work at Delora, though it can't be in the house. You heard everything said there. I did not know it would be like this when I decided to bring you here."

He saw and felt Joseph's momentary indecision. He realized then that until this week he had never asked Joseph to make a decision concerning himself.

"Sah, yooou said about wriiiting. I waaant thaaat."

Abram then had second thoughts about his whole plan. Joseph seemed too eager, which was what Wahl had said after seeing him yesterday and listening to Abram's ideas. *"A push for independence always follows increased knowledge in the darkies,"* Wahl had warned him. Now Abram feared he saw that too. Brant already was of the mind that Joseph had stolen private information from them. Was it possible that his strong affection for the boy had been hampering his judgment? Could Brant have correctly guessed an insatiable drive for independence in Joseph, while he stayed blind to it?

He felt the urge to rein Joseph in and control him here and now, right as they came to the moment of decision and release. But he also remembered that he had soaked his choice to come here with prayer. Obviously what he was about to do had very little earthly wisdom in it. The importance, however, lay in knowing whether or not this was truly God's will. He stood by his earlier decision of learning a Negro's real capabilities before he died.

"Joseph, if you get yourself into trouble, you will mar not only my personal reputation, but that of the whole Gospel Society. You see how the unsaved world is looking for ways to make fools of us who entrust the Word of God to black folk. You are my property, even here, and thus my representative. You better behave yourself, for God knows your heart, even if I and Mr. Wahl cannot."

Joseph gave him a strange look that combined both unrest and sincerity. "I waaant school, saaah—"

"Then you need to behave yourself completely!"

The boy gave him silence with lowered eyes.

Abram braced himself for what he had to say next because of his decision to hire him out. "Then you are no longer my manservant." He pulled away to emphasize the necessary parting.

Joseph seemed dismayed and almost terrified. Abram made his own way toward the carriage, relying fully on his cane. Joseph followed, but Abram did not look back. After years of having this boy, he was giving him up. It was not an easy price to pay, especially when the end result might ruin the slave and bring him grief. Because of Wahl's reflections, he began to think that education without freedom could prove to be a cruel fate for Joseph, and he loved the boy too much to think about being the cause of his unhappy end. Yet for himself, he needed to know just how much a Negro could learn.

If Joseph failed in school, he could be glad for that, for then he could be at peace with things as they were. But if the boy were successful? Then there was the possibility that he might ruin Joseph's temperament for subservience for good. And that would be tragic, for there was no way to free this African from his lifelong status as a slave. Once more Abram turned to him.

"If you do not want it to be this way, I will take off that badge and restore you to myself."

There was both grief and adventure in Joseph's face. "I will staaay in Cha'leston."

The repercussions of that one decision were swift and painful. When Joseph reached the carriage door, Master Abram dismissed him coldly. "Don't even touch that latch. You now bear the tag of a menial laborer."

The change in Master Abram was too sudden for comprehension. "But, saaah, you neeed heeelp!"

"Get up in the driver's seat next to Ezra! I left my manservant, Colt, at home."

The words cut like a knife. The separation was based on the rigid practices that kept strong walls standing between all classes and races. As a common worker, Joseph could never think of riding in a gentleman's carriage. His hand touched his badge. He saw privileges he had once taken for granted fade. The hurt stung and swelled his throat with the venom of rejection. He climbed with reluctance to the wooden bench beside Delora's coachman. Fortunately, the gracious and wise uncle asked him no questions, though Ezra eyed the new badge hanging over Joseph's heart, now heavy as a nail-keg lid.

At the master's shout Ezra clucked to the paired chestnut mares and boldly drove them out into the traffic of the bustling sandy street. The world was alive with a confusion of smells, from sea air to the human offal collecting in corners and gutters. It was filled with noises, too, both beastly and mechanical. Up to now Joseph had spent very little time in the city, and he had never ridden outside a carriage, exposed to all its sights and sounds. One of the first things to impress him was the presence of so many unescorted colored persons everywhere. Many of them were as dark as he and Ezra.

Male hawkers and female vendors cried out their wares. Each was shadowed by a huge bundle—be it firewood, fruit, or fish—balanced on the head, just as plantation workers carried the makings for their masters' profits at home. But these were free men and women, or at least nominals, earning cash for themselves. It was easy to see that not all city Negroes were simple laborers. In shop windows and open doorways, Joseph spied brown and black barbers, carpenters, tailors, and shoemakers as Ezra drove by.

Children, in a mix of colors, shouted and played in front of brightly painted houses. Within an arm's reach of the coach there were slow carts and overstuffed drays, filled with sacks of cotton and groaning like gluttons in the oncoming lane.

"Now you on Tradd Street," Ezra spoke to him suddenly as he turned the horses right. He made some of his customary noddings, which were a familiar part of his quiet, easygoing way. "This here road take you right down to Grafton Mills 'fore it takes you to the same old river what done run past Delora maybe early this mornin'."

So Ezra knew exactly where Joseph was going. In a few moments his older companion turned into the beaten-down yard of a three-stories-high sooty brick building, balanced like a charred red block on the edge of blue-green water.

Joseph jumped down, his gaze fixed on the choppy waves that churned the river and the first arm of the sea swelling the harbor just to the south. From standing beside Master Abram through the year-round series of fund-raisers, fairs, and balls, Joseph knew of the Grafton father and sons who owned this place and were made rich and powerful by its profits.

At this moment, however, the business looked more like a sawyer's operation than a place to hull and pack rice. Huge piles of slabwood cluttered the landscape around the high belching smokestacks. Awkwardly Ezra came down behind Joseph. Abram now needed him to be both footman and driver. Joseph knew enough from his experience outside the courthouse to let their owner approach the nearest door alone, relying on his cane. Ezra had to nudge him to make him follow.

"Get you'self in there."

Within the first room, dull with dust and hedged by drab walls, Joseph saw Mr. Wahl busy at a desk. The foreman came around and took Abram on a tour of the sprawling property. Joseph followed them. The man shouted every word because of the din of whirling machinery that flicked and twitched at them from every side. It was a mind-boggling array of shafts, pegs, and bars, all in motion and interconnected.

For the first time ever, Joseph watched machines make boards. On plantations all such work was done by hand. He stood in awe, not only hearing noise but *feeling* it vibrate through his ribs and skull.

"Right now most workers are building tierces out of oak and willow," Mr. Wahl yelled, pointing to about two dozen men whose black skin was powdered gray by the sawdust that filled the air like gauze. "Each of those containers will hold six hundred pounds of clean rice once the milling process starts in earnest. Beginning today, Joseph will work in this room, since all the orders for hulling and packing are taken here. See those two mulattos in the corner?"

Abram nodded.

"That's Peckory." Wahl still pointed. "And the older one's Harris. They both can read. At present I have them figuring out the number of packing containers that will be needed. They compile the materials list and then pull the right woods so that the other workers can peg or hoop the various crates and casks we'll use later in the year. Of course, they're also keeping track of the sawmill orders."

Already the airborne dust was prickling Joseph's windpipe, but he stifled his urge to cough.

"What about his living situation?" Master Abram yelled. "The city clerk asked so many questions, it worries me."

"Come on, let's go back to my desk." Wahl motioned as he spoke. "Then we can hear ourselves again."

Joseph took one more look at all the machinery. His heart sank, thinking back on Delora's quiet elegance. For the hope of school, he was subjecting himself to this.

At his desk Mr. Wahl had notes prepared for Abram. "As I mentioned yesterday, Joseph will be housed with a Negress and the slaves she holds. Her dead sibling was a good and faithful Negro stevedore who drowned while working some years ago."

Joseph's ears still were ringing.

"How close will that put him to the school?" Abram's question warmed him immensely. "It seems to be a more dangerous proposition than I thought, given how the city watches over them even as our parish patrolmen do."

"Just two blocks away. That's why I arranged the housing with Miss Gail. He'll stay in the cellar with her sister-in-law Allis, who is a laundress, and with her two sons, Tag and Luck. They are all good darkies."

Abram seemed relieved.

Wahl gave his first command to Joseph. "Boy! Step away! I will take a word with your master alone."

Joseph did as he was told and moved to a place that seemed satisfactory to the owners but also was close enough for him to continue hearing. From his slight upward glance he saw Wahl's hand on Master Abram's shoulder.

"I'm speaking to you as your friend and one who mourns your losses and your present illness. Are you sure you want to take the risk of schooling him? Nobody—brown or white—is going to welcome it. All night I've thought about the outcome. You're heading him and yourself toward trouble."

Joseph put his head straight down after Abram caught him looking.

"I'm not sure I could live—or die—in peace with any other decision but this one. I want to see what a full eight months of classical learning will do for him."

Joseph's heart was palpitating. *Eight months of school!*

"Horace," his master went on, "regardless of his progress, don't write to me about it except in the most cryptic of ways. For I plan to tell Brant nothing about the Negro teacher. I don't want my son put in any position where he'd think of lying if questioned. I feel it will be safer and fairer for everyone if he does not know—at least for now."

"I understand what you are saying, but it's not just your son's reaction that concerns me. As elections approach, there's a growing population of Secessionists here who ardently oppose all forms of Negro education. And you already know the strong resentments some hold toward colored evangelism. It's a poor combination. . . ."

"These are risks I will take, but keep me informed and let me know how he's getting along. I can take him home if that proves necessary."

Joseph heard Wahl's murmur of agreement.

"Joseph! Come now!" Wahl's order was more sharply edged than any that ever came from Abram's lips.

"Be reasonable with him, Wahl, and clear about what you want him to do. Then he will do it. You will never have to lay a hand on him. Feed him well, give him rest, keep him healthy—"

"Yes, I will, Abram. You have my word. I trust the clerk already informed him of all the city codes."

Abram sounded weary. "For his own protection, please be sure he understands what each of the laws requires of him."

"I'll do that this evening," Wahl said while shaking hands.

Then Abram turned to Joseph, his voice welling with compassion. "You honor Mr. Wahl, and do what he says. Remember, he's not only your supervisor—but also your protector." His cool, shaking fingers stroked Joseph's hand. "It is hard for me to say good-bye. You stay good, do you hear?"

Joseph dared not to answer him, for he feared revealing his tumultuous emotions. Being transferred between slaveholders as though he were only a horse or a mule bubbled up ugly pustules within him. He felt used, powerless, and angry, but at the same time he was stretched by the weight of his love for the master who was leaving him.

Mr. Wahl waited until Abram Callcott was out of sight. "I am a fair Christian man, and like your Mr. Abram, I, too, know I have a Master in heaven expecting the best from me. You will get what you deserve here—peace for peace, but swift confrontation for rebellion."

He waited until Joseph had nodded.

"Come, I'll show you how to take your noonday meal, and after that you will work till the conch shell is blown at five o'clock."

CHAPTER 16

WHEN TWO DAYS HAD PASSED without word from Master Abram, Joseph's vision of school began to perish under the heavy toil of his new employment. The two other literate slaves, Harris and Peckory, were masters at deciphering any merchant's or broker's handwriting. They could manipulate figures in their heads to estimate quantities, and they understood currency so they could write out bills. Joseph, on the other hand, knew none of these things, nor could he make even one intelligent mark with pencil or pen.

Friday's work drew to a close, leaving him feeling childish and unworthy of his dream to become an educated Negro. Since the day he had first witnessed Theodore Rensler's coming to Delora to doctor the family, Joseph had entertained wild notions of being a doctor himself in order to aid worthy persons like Abram and his own colored folk. But now those thoughts were like hot sand sifting through his tired, chafed hands.

Harris noticed how low-spirited he was. "You look like you have everythin' the matter with you," he said with concern. "You want to talk?"

Joseph shook his head, not wanting to air his silly plans.

Harris was twenty-five years old, with a slave wife and three children. He had helped Joseph greatly on both days and had promised to stay by him while he learned the details of the work. As good as that was for Joseph, Peckory balanced everything with his negatives. Brash and single, shameless and selfish, he had made the first eighteen hours miserable for both Harris and Joseph because of Joseph's slowness. Not wanting Harris to share his abuse, Joseph had tried earlier to declare that he could cope on his own. His lame tongue, made weak by fatigue, however, had not made him clear, so now he tried again. "Haaarris. I caaan beee alone—"

"No, siree! You a brother in the Lord an' a companion worker. I'm gwine stick with you. Don't you pay no nevermind to Peckory."

The conch shell blew, and despite Harris's words, Joseph walked out from work waiting for no one. It was painfully clear that his life as a houseboy had made him naive, and in order to survive, he had much to learn. If he couldn't even decode the script of working men or write his own name, how could he dare think he had the intellect to be a scholar?

His gloom kept up with him until he'd left the mockery and noise far behind. Yesterday after work and in the predawn of today Mr. Wahl had escorted him to and from the mill. But this time, in the comfortable air of early evening, he traveled alone. And freely. There was no master anywhere to demand a thing from him. No one to control him. Joseph headed east, then turned north on his mile-long walk to Aunty Allis's kitchen. Like a starving man stumbling onto a storehouse of food, he grew almost frantic in wanting to possess every sight, every sound, every smell in the salty air around him.

There were businesses, walled gardens, and storefronts on Broad and King and George streets, all of which he savored. He knew where he was, where he had been, and where he was going because he had taken notice of the city's street signs while Mr. Wahl had been his chaperone. Now as he walked he planned. Tomorrow he might explore the entire length of Tradd, which would take him to the Cooper River wharves. The day after that he might wander through the marketplace, and the next trip, he might make a slow perusal of all the grand homes on Meeting Street. His eagerness was like that of a spoilt master's child set down amid a mile-high stack of Christmastime presents.

Everywhere he went there were Negroes freely going about their business just as he was. He began to identify with them, and so with himself in a new and different way. Out here in the sunshine he was not Abram's or Wahl's *boy*. Away from the mill he could be his own possession. That put a spring in his step. He even dared to think again on a surname he had privately devised for himself a long time ago. The last name he would choose for himself would be *Whitsun*. He liked the sound of it and its meaning, since it came from the page in the prayer book that coincided with the day of his birth. *Joseph Whitsun! Joseph Whitsun!* His feet could fly to that rhythm.

His chin moved higher. His stride widened, and his first bite of freedom became intoxicating. It caused him to smile and tip his flat, dusty cap to every old aunty who passed him by. Oh, and better yet, it made him grin inwardly at every young colored lady going about her mistress's work. For certain, these lovely girls saw him, too, for many came as far as their masters' gates and with soft dove-eyes gazed upon him. However, each woman's attention made his mind flee straight back to his last view of Rosa from Master Abram's coach. Perhaps he would find his way back to her.

Joseph opened his mouth, holding his sore tongue to the air. Maybe it would heal, and they could carry on a natural conversation after his eight months here. Then she could come to know him, and he her, in that deep and wonderful way he had longed for during his gruesomely imposed silence, which she had so selflessly helped him endure. He reasoned with himself. *Why should I fall prey to mild flirtations, when back at Delora there might already be a hope for love?* His whole being tingled. Yes, he would save his eyes and heart for Rosa! Right there on Church Street he made a pledge before God to keep faithful to the possibility, no matter how small, of putting himself at her side once more.

By midwinter, perhaps, he could go home and find her waiting. It was a risk, of course, for perhaps he never would be sent back at all. But even if his lot were to stay here, Joseph had heard from his mama that trusted servants were sometimes allowed to visit other places and plantations. He set it as another goal to so please Mr. Wahl that someday he could walk up Delora's lane, head high, and show Rosa he was doing well. In the meantime he needed to use his days wisely, to learn and become mature in every way. Then, perhaps, Rosa would be as glad for their reunion as he.

His one meal of the day, served at the mill, was behind him, and the curfew would not sound till nine o'clock, so Joseph had no reason to go straight to the cellar at the back of Aunty Allis's kitchen. With joy renewed he proceeded through the bright city until the streets were filled with shadows and streaked with evening sunlight. Only then did he go to Anson Street. It crossed his mind to save time tomorrow to look for the Negro school.

Going up to Miss Gail's property, he entered by way of a wooden gate in the hedge. As he had already observed, paint in Charleston was used mostly to brighten the street side of houses. In the backyards there were sheds and drab, two-story brick slave quarters. Typically, these dwellings looked as worn out as the people they served. Joseph went up through a thriving vegetable garden and entered the unpainted, one-story clapboard kitchen built up tight against the back brick wall of Miss Gail's house. A rough door led inside, and it was standing open, ready to welcome in the evening's cool air.

Going in unannounced, Joseph found the thin, middle-aged Aunty Allis crouched down and sorting laundry with quick hands into different baskets lined up on the hard dirt floor. At a simple marred table near her, Tag and Luck, her two sons, sat facing each other on backless benches, eating fish and rice out of wooden bowls with oyster-shell scoops.

Joseph had met the younger boy, Tag, the previous evening. The boy had been dressed then just as he was now in a shirt covered with soot, a stark contrast to the fine white clothes spread out everywhere around his swinging feet. From Mr. Wahl, Joseph knew that Tag was one of the Negro children paid by the city to light its streetlamps. The boy had been quick to warm up to him at their first meeting, so Joseph had already heard him boast that he could climb the posts, clean globes, and either light or extinguish a flame faster than any other in this ward.

Luck, the son he had not met, was a strong, bulky man in his prime. Again from Wahl, Joseph had information that this slave worked the long, uneven hours of a stevedore, loading cargo for Grafton Mills as his daddy had done before him. Wearing only baggy slave-cloth trousers, Luck had powerful arms resting on either side of his bowl. Instantly Joseph surmised that this fellow, like Harris and Peckory, could become either his ally or his foe. By size alone Luck was intimidating. He and the rest of his family were dark "ebony" Negroes—one of Peckory's demeaning terms for Joseph.

When Luck showed no interest in him, Joseph greeted only Allis and Tag. He felt stiff and keenly aware that they all had been thrown into living together without choice.

"Lucky, this here's Joseph, the plantation feller what works for Graftons now," Allis said to her older son.

She spoke pure Gullah, which Joseph knew, but Master Abram always forbade him to speak.

Luck blew against his bowl. "So what he do? Spit shine the massas' boots?"

Joseph decided he must speak for himself, though his tongue was aching. His soft hands and new clothes were enough to make Luck think he did no significant work. "I sooort woood, but sooon I will fill ooorders."

Luck showed surprise and disgust at his stammering, and immediately Joseph was sorry to have exposed his broken words.

"Set down for supper," the woman said.

"Oh, nooo thankyee, ma'am." Joseph grew more uneasy, for among Mr. Wahl's admonishments there had been one to not take any food from this poor black family. "I eeeat at the mill."

She was indignant. "Mass' Wahl ain't got no say over this here kitchen. Now you set you'self down afta' workin' hard all day!" She filled a bowl for him, and he, always hungry on slave rations, did not complain.

Tag, so talkative the night before, seemed silenced by his older brother's presence. And Luck, though showing Joseph no more animosity, had no words for him either. Joseph took his cues from them and mutely ate. Still not used to chewing without full movement of his tongue, it took him quite a while to finish off the large portion of peppery fish and rice, but he did so with relish, since this aunty's food was more like Maum Bette's than the mill's bland soup had been. Allis soon went back to her washing, and Luck leaned farther in on the table toward where Joseph was seated on the bench beside Tag.

"Bet you can read, ainty? Bet you have to, to be fillin' orders."

"Yes. I caaan some." Joseph toned down his English and concentrated hard on moving his tongue.

Allis was back in a flash, like a cat with claws extended. "You'all not gwine say one word 'bout readin'. I don't want no book learnin' in this house. Is that understood?"

Joseph thought about the Gospel Society Bible that Master Abram had told him to bring. "I haaave a Biiible, ma'am," he said, deciding it was best to be honest.

"Then you keep it to you'self," she answered quickly. "My boys ain't never gwine touch nothin' like that! It don't matter if it be the Holy Word of God. Nobody's gwine learn to read here!"

"Yessum." In three different tones, there were three sober affirmations by those who sat at the table. Joseph, feeling nervous, excused himself.

Leaving the bowl behind, he walked the length of the kitchen to the shallow set of stairs leading down into a narrow cellar dug below Miss Gail's portion of the house. The dank space was only partially below ground. It had two barred and shuttered windows that looked out on the front at street level. At this time of the evening almost no light came in, and no provision had been made for more.

Shuffling across the cellar's bricked floor, he went to the spongy, moss-filled tick that was his bed. It lay under the left window, between the room's south wall and the leather-covered trunk Abram Callcott had loaned him. The container from Delora was lavish compared with the poverty of Aunty Allis's dwelling. The night before Joseph had met Miss Gail Haskell only briefly. He believed that Aunty Allis and her sons did have rooms in Miss Gail's house for sleeping. He himself, however, had been invited to go no place but the cellar and the kitchen, nor did he think that would ever change. With so much work to do, and no servants of their own to do it, he understood why Allis and her sons spent so much time near the woman's work, with her irons, soaps, and kettles.

Joseph opened the window's shutters and took his Bible from the trunk. Its interior odors of lavender sent him off into reflections of Delora's chambers. He was homesick for the familiar and for his mama and Bette. Again he thought of Rosa. Before Brant's attack he had enjoyed Sunday afternoons doing no work but sitting in the presence of his elders, Ezra and Billy. He longed to have those men near him now. Except for what he had learned from them, he knew almost nothing about other African people. Having lived so exclusively with the master, Joseph felt like a stranger here, even though his color matched everybody else's in this house.

Glumly he decided that loneliness would be part of the price he'd pay for daring to seek education. Yet there was a grand side to being lonely— he need be obliged to no one but himself. Content, he turned to the window and put the Scriptures on his lap in the deep purple light. Closing his eyes, he beseeched the Holy Ghost to quicken the study of God's Word to his heart. He had never prayed such a prayer, yet he felt the unction to whisper the same words Master Abram used.

Settled in body and spirit, Joseph started reading where he had left off the night before. *For God hath not given us the spirit of fear; but of power, and of love, and of a sound mind.* Those were amazing, stirring words that were not revealed to slaves in the masters' oral catechism, which fed Christianity to them by measured and guarded spoonfuls. He saw then that reading the Bible was like holding a ticket into heaven. With it, he could poke around everywhere in the Almighty's chambers, instead of having white folk tell him what holy doors were closed to him.

Under his fingertips was the entire Word of God, and he read it like a thirsty man finding a deep well. *Be not thou therefore ashamed of the testimony of our Lord, nor of me his prisoner: but be thou partakers of the afflictions of the gospel according to the power of God. . . .* Joseph put his hand over the page as if to trap the words in place. *Power!* Twice in one short reading that word had leaped out at him. He was excited beyond measure, believing that perhaps this is what it meant to have God's Word quickened to his heart. If so, then God was hearing and answering his humble prayers!

Wherein I suffer trouble . . . even unto bonds; but the Word of God is not bound. As Joseph read this, he felt down his leg to the line of scabs where Rensler's leg iron had worn away his skin. He knew what it felt like to be a prisoner. There was no power in being trapped. Yet Paul of the Scriptures wrote about power while he was in irons. It was a mystery Joseph desperately wanted to understand. *Therefore, I endure all things,* this believer Paul went on to say. *For if we be dead with him, we shall also live with him; if we suffer, we shall also reign with him. . . .*

Joseph didn't think the Word of God could be more applicable to him than this, but then his eyes fell upon the closing line. *Study to show thyself approved unto God, a workman that needeth not to be ashamed, rightly dividing the word of truth.* The message was like heat from a furnace. Inwardly Joseph cried, *Is there power just for enduring? Then I will endure as I did before! But if there is a command to study, then, God, you must open some way.*

"What you doin'!"

Joseph's eyes snapped open to the reality of Charleston. Tag's small face was pressed between the iron bars set in the glassless window. "What if some pateroller done saw you in there!"

Joseph realized he had been incautious to sit in the only patch of light. He was used to rural isolation. "Yes, Tag. Thankyee!" he gasped, hiding the Bible in his mattress at once. Mr. Wahl had warned him that the ward patrollers could search anywhere, even to the point of breaking windows and doors to make unannounced raids in *any* Negro's home, be they slave or free. Reading within view of the street could have harmed this family. He closed the shutters sheepishly while Tag went off with his lamp rags in his hand.

Joseph's mood swung from rapturous prayer to oppression. The room took on a soft new glow with the shutters closed, a sure sign that Tag had lighted the town's lamp outside. Joseph lay down, his hopes for finding power through prayer drowned in remorse about even deciding to be in Charleston. He was a slave—a slave forever! Nothing more.

A little while later Joseph awoke in the sickly yellow lamplight. Someone was descending the cellar stairs! On his mattress Joseph feigned sleep, thinking wildly what he could do if this were the city patrolmen coming for him. He lay motionless and watched through squinted eyes. His heart beat like a hand pounding on his chest but quieted the moment he decided that the muscular prowler must be Luck. When the other young man boldly crouched beside him, Joseph put his pretending aside and sat up, not knowing what to expect. Luck spoke with intensity that felt almost solid, like iron.

"You hear'd of bro' David Walker?"

"Nooo." Joseph was apprehensive and groggy from his rest.

"Man, you can read. Still 'n yet, you don't know?"

"No."

"He done laid down he life for speakin' the truth, even to white ears."

Joseph's uneasiness grew to be fear. "Hooow do you knooow about him?"

"I am a seeker of truth," Luck proclaimed with dignity. "An' when I find it, I holds fast 'cause I don't care what it costs. Truth be truth, an' I be out to know it. I gots copies of what the bosses call the 'Walker Pamphlets.' From what I hear'd, the po'lice gwine pay up to a one thousand dollar just to catch somebody in this here town—be he black or white—with he hands on even one of 'em pages." He rocked back proudly. "And right now, I done gots myself more than fifty of 'em pages hid in Aunty's house."

Though impossible to see them Joseph looked around. Luck made fun of his insecurity.

"Bro' Walker wa' murdered for printin' 'em, so it's folk like me what's gwine keep he word alive. He weren't afeared to say things like they is—how God's gwine flash down judgment if this nation don't repent of treatin' women, children, an' men like they wa' beasts."

Joseph judged Luck's ideas to be dangerous. "Thaaat's why your maaa forbids you to read," he struggled. "I heeeard about all the city's ruuules. Yoooou have whaaat's called 'incendiary liiiterature,' and you can be whipped or fined or taken tooo the workhouse!"

"Sure 'nough, Mista New-comer!" Luck treated him like a cowardly child. "Haven't you thought it all through yet? There's a law for *everythin'* concernin' the black man 'cept breathin' an' breedin' more of he own color! Rules ain't gwine keep me from fixin' on the truth. They gwine push me to freedom!"

"But you caaan be arrested!"

"Ain't liberty worth some price to you, *houseboy*? My daddy wa' a free man with the same dream as mine. Sometimes he done work twenty hours a day 'cause he had this notion to buy he own wife an' he own chilluns to free 'em from they white owner."

Joseph looked at him sadly. When children were born of a free man and a slave mother, the law declared that the offspring would be slave. "I heard your daaaddy drowned," he said, trying to show compassion.

"He did." Then Luck surprised him by laughing sharply. "The massas put him out in that storm on purpose, I am sure. 'Fore that happened, though, he got he money saved. But then the state go an' makes 'nother law, sayin' there can be no more manumissions even with you' own *massa's* approval! So all that liberty money my daddy done got? 'Fore he died he made *hisself* into a *colored* slaveowner, buyin' us for a big swollen price, an' then ownin' us—he own flesh an' blood—to hold us close!"

There was a moment then when confidence seemed to slip in Luck, and he looked away. Joseph now understood more fully the meaning of the word *nominal*, which had been cropping up everywhere.

"But now I's workin' on his first dream—to see this family freed!" They were seeing each other well in the low light now.

"You reeeally think escape is pooossible?" Joseph asked, honestly amazed. "On plaaantations, you hear of men running off to taaake some rest in the swamps. But as far as I knooow they're always brought baaack. Once a slave visited us with his master and half his fooot was cut off for running. How dooo you plan to do aaanything better?"

Luck leaned very close. "It's our black feet what step on those boats to load 'em up 'fore they go back north to the land of freedom. Maybe I can put my mama in a barrel an' my brother in a sack while some rich abolitionist is down here but lookin' the other way. You see, they plenty northerners what talk 'bout hatin' slavery. Yet 'n still, they keep on comin' down here to make their profits from our sweat an' blood. Howsumever, if I can find just the right vessel, I do believe I can sneak my family aboard. But to find that right vessel, I needs know how to read. An' you gwine help me."

"I don't undeeerstand."

"I done a'ready know the names of some northern sea cap'ns, to hear 'em, but not to see 'em in writin'. Howsumever, onc't you learnt me, then I can find 'em an' they ships by the names chiseled on they bow. That way, I can get my family on board an' keep 'em all quiet till we out on open water. I judge we wouldn't be turned back."

"I can't belieeeve you're reeaally thinking this!"

"All I need is them names an' a right knowledge of schedules. Anybody what can read can have that just by lookin' into the *Mercury* newspapers, secretlike, for ship departures an' destinations." He paused. "God must have sent you here."

Joseph was appalled. "Your maaama made us promise. And boooth my master and Mr. Wahl warned me not to find trouble."

Without a word Luck crawled to the window and easily pulled out a loose shutter lath. His actions let in a streaming band of light. Next he rolled back the top of Joseph's bed and removed two bricks from the un-mortared floor. In a moment he had a paper. "Here's a page of Bro' Walk-er's writin'. It's incendiary all right. As incendiary as hell, 'cording to what the buckras say. But to me—an' just maybe to you—it's the sweet new breath of heaven blowin'. 'I am the way an' the truth, saith the Lord.' Through this brother's writings the *way* an' the *truth* has come to me."

Joseph read only the first line. "This speeeaks of murdering the mas-ters!"

Luck pointed to the window. "Out there, they can tie you up an' whip you for just 'bout anythin'. They can do it just 'cause you a black man lookin' too pleased with you'self. They can do it 'cause you wear shoes what they think are too fine for nigger feet. No matter which way you try, man, you ain't gwine please them all 'less you find some way to bleach out all that color God gave you. I'm not for lettin' 'em kill me over somethin' simple. If I'm gwine suffer anyway, it gwine be for somethin' good. They not gwine bruise Luck just for some itsy-bitsy notion. No, sah! It gwine be for freedom. I gwine either get it or die on the right road tryin'." He tapped the bottom of the paper. "Now you read 'em last lines. There."

Joseph's eyes fell just where Luck's finger pointed. "It's too dark to read," he lied.

Luck huffed his anger. "It's not too dark, an' you know it! You' just scaired an' way too much like them. But I don't need you to say this part of it. Since I can't read—yet—I have it memorized." He sounded just like Parris preaching a Sabbath message, except he confined his passion to whispering.

" 'They chain an' handcuff us, an' our chilluns, an' they drive us 'round like brutes. Then'—hear me—'they go into the house of the Lord of justice to actually return thanks to Him fa' havin' aided them in their infernal cruelties inflicted on us. Will the Lord suffer His people to go on much longer, takin' His holy name in vain? O Americans! Americans! I call God, I call angels, I call men to witness that your DESTRUCTION is at hand an' will be speedily consummated unless you REPENT.' "

"A blaaack man wrote that?" Joseph cried. He had been compelled to read along with every word. "It's teeerrible, but beautiful! Did masters let him gooo to school?"

Luck frowned. "You got the ignorance of a rat raised inside a box! He wa' a freeman in Boston till he wa' killed. But I have prints of his papers, so even afta' he death—God rest he soul—I'm bound by my own pledge to tell he stories."

Joseph considered the real danger of sitting and talking like this. "Luck, I think whaaat you're doing is goood, but I don't waaant any part of it. I didn't come heeere thinking of reeebelling."

"Since you done held that paper, you a'ready part of it. You just like so many other house niggers I done meet. You got all you' sense an' sympathy blanched out of you. You *white*! In every way but color."

"Nooo, I'm not. I . . . I'm just not looking for a fiiight with them! I have a chance to go to school, but I mustn't be caught doooing anything wrong or the chance wiiill be lost."

Luck crossed his arms against him. "What it like, boy, bein' so content with you'self that you blind to the truth that hundreds—no, thousands—of you' brothers an' sisters are, at this moment, staggerin', dyin', an' bein' raped?"

Joseph grabbed Luck in his rising anger, "I haave suffered! You want scaaars to prove it? Well, then, look at my toooongue. And feeeel this!" He yanked up his shirt and pressed Luck's hand against his branded side.

Luck pulled back, amazed. "I . . . I never would of 'xpected as much just by lookin' at you."

Joseph sat back in silence while confusion wailed inside him. On the plantation there had been no talk of freedom. Duty to master was always equated with rightness and with the surety of getting into heaven. But in the city he already saw how things were different. He had never heard of black men writing down their opinions, let alone finding some way to publish them. And he had never known that freedom might be waiting for him on some distant shore. In the chaos of all his hard wondering, Joseph became aware of an outside sound, a horse being ridden through the street. "We'll beee caught!" he cried.

Luck muffled him, then hid the paper under the floor again. The sound of the rider faded. "I hope you understand. You done a'ready broke the law by seein' that pamphlet. Anytime they want to arrest you from now on they have cause."

"I had nooo choice! Yooou forced me!"

"You a'ready committed a crime just the same!"

"But I . . . I didn't ask to see it."

"Still, you guilty by the white man's opinion of you."

"The moment you leeeave I'll destroy it, I promise! I don't want to be caught!"

"I got others where you cain't find them. And every so often I get more deliveries through a white man what plays the part of a broker's assistant dealin' in goods like coffee an' rice."

"Pleeease, I don't want to be in trouble."

"You a'ready is if they find us 'fore I learn to read. You want to save you' neck, then you teach me—startin' t'morrow. What do you think the paterollers will say if they come here now an' find literature, knowin' you the only reader in this house?"

"How would they knooow! I wooold say nothing!"

"You' work tag. An' mine. The courts know all."

In the darkness Joseph touched the cursed piece of metal.

"You teach me to read, and I take the blame," Luck promised. "You leave me ignorant, I see that you bear any an' all accusations what come this way on 'count of my mission."

"You are haaateful!" Joseph almost screamed it.

"I care little what you think right now, buckra boy. You do it, 'cause you know you have to. I could even turn you in myself an' get on they good side, if you push me to that. But it don't have to be like this, neither. Just as easy, I can treat you like a brother."

Joseph clasped his knees. "Gooo, please."

"Too bad you don't like my company, 'cause I know 'xactly where you can hear 'bout slaves freein' theirselves to head north. Too bad you don't have no stomach for it. . . ." Luck paused, as though knowing what kind of lure he was reeling out to Joseph. "Unless, of course, you want to change you' mind."

"There are laaws—"

"For true!" Luck stood. "Shame how folk of color can't come up with legislations of they own. The first one on my list would be 'No black man can just hide hisself out of fear.' You a disgrace to *my* race, boy!"

"I dooon't want to be caught."

"You could learn somethin' t'night, an' the risk would be 'bout as slim as findin' an eel in the grass. That 'cause the meetin's right up here on Anson Street, so till curfew you have a good travel pass. Even if 'em paterollers come, they can't haul us off, for we's in our rightful place 'cordin' to our tickets."

Joseph groped for his shoes, which he had taken off for sleep, but then he realized that the police could know him if they saw him. "But they'll seee my foreman's name on my pass."

"They go mostly by badges—" Luck pressed a loose copper work tag into Joseph's hand.

"I already haaave one."

"Sure you do, man! But you use this one if you gwine come with me. It's current, with the year nicely pressed 'pon it."

"It's cooounterfeit?"

"Nope. A real number off a real Negro—God rest his soul in glory! One of my friends works for the city coroner. When he's sent off to receive the dead, he takes the poorest of the darkies' badges off of 'em 'fore he carries they stripped bodies in. They have neglectful owners what never come to call for their corpses or their badges. That give folk like we a little extra help for gwine out by night."

"Then it *is* dangerous to be doing this."

"Ain't you learnt nothin' from me yet? You a black man in South Carolina! That makes it dangerous to breathe! Don't you ever ask you'self why they don't allowed such meetin's? 'Cause they knowed what these abolitionists have to say is truth. They *is* a land of freedom for the darkie, an' it is reachable!"

CHAPTER 17

THE BROWN MAN'S FISH SHOP stood just inside the city limits on the southwest corner of Anson and Boundary streets. Tonight there were no fish in the seller's barrels, though the place still smelled of them when Joseph and Luck entered the dark one-story shanty. With no explanation, both of them were handed heavy half-made baskets and enough loose rushes and palmetto butts to weave them to completion. Joseph had no experience with the African art of basketmaking, but the other men, including Luck, sat right down on the benches and odd assortment of chairs to take up the work that generations of craftsmen had done before them.

Dumbly Joseph joined the rest of the company, numbering less than ten in all. Without uttering a word, the men started plaiting reeds in the smoky light of tallow candles. Eventually Luck whispered to him, "This is somethin' you should be learnin'." His hands moved over Joseph's to show him how to grasp the raw plants to form a basket coil, but Joseph had no interest in it. Beginning to fear he had been tricked, he looked around, wondering about the program Luck had promised.

The fishmonger among them was a tiny clabber-colored man who sat as straight as a pole on the sill of the one shuttered window facing the street. Adding to the smoke of the burning candles in the interior, a hazy vapor rose from the glowing cob pipes clenched between the teeth of most of them. Joseph noticed with sudden apprehension that Peckory was the youngest of the smokers and sat on a bench by the door. Joseph dropped his head, but not before the mill worker named him publicly.

"Hey there, Eagle! Never in my life did I 'xpect to see you here!"

Joseph did not acknowledge him or the ugly nickname, for the word "eagle" meant "vulture" in the city. With a nervous glance to Joseph, Luck questioned the relationship between them. Flimsily hoping that Peckory might think he was mistaken, Joseph pretended to be fully involved in twisting the dead plants. At the fishmonger's designation, two men were sent outside as sentries to warn the others at the first sign of danger. Moments after these men left, a white man walked forth among them like a colorless ghost drifting out from the cobwebs. He looked as young as a boy and was dressed all in black.

"This here's Tom Diller," the fish seller said with respect. "Believe most of you know him."

There were nods and casual intimations of greeting, which made Joseph think the whole roomful of colored men trusted the bland-looking stranger. Without delay Diller started talking in a squeaking, unpleasant voice. "I will be quick this evening on the subject of our colored brother, James R. Bradley. But first, since the hour is late, let me announce the next meeting in this series on how to alleviate yourselves of slavery. It will be ten days hence in the shed behind Jack's grog shop on Duncan Street. Now may God bless you and inspire you with the information you are about to receive." The man actually raised a hand as though giving some sort of benediction.

The Negroes continued to weave and listen to this man who sounded half preacher and half auctioneer. "Brother Bradley was born in Africa and sold into slavery right here in the auction houses of Charleston." There was a murmur of assent, for every man present could relate to how the tale began. "Gentlemen, from these very streets James Bradley was carried off against his will into slave territory due west of here."

Joseph moved in his seat, for he had never heard a white man call colored men "gentlemen."

"Mr. Bradley owned nothing but his determination, his faith in God, and the skill of his two hands."

The white man's style of storytelling was not as compelling as a Negro's, but still his hearers called to him as though he were one of their own.

"Do tell! That's right!"

"My friends! Our brother James, though in bondage, had a vision for liberty! By night, he started plaiting discarded cornhusks into work collars for horses. Eight hours a collar. Two collars a week. And he earned himself a grand sum of fifty cents apiece for them."

Joseph felt the grass between his fingers. So this basketmaking was more than a ruse to fool patrollers. There was a silent message to be spoken to their souls by it. Plants were free and obtainable. That was the connection to be made. As with this brother James, weaving could put coin into even a slave's hand. Joseph began watching how the baskets were made.

"Eventually, our slave brother earned enough to buy a pig and a sack of seed corn, which he planted and harvested in secret after working his twelve-hour days for his master. Though he was weary, though he could have been frightened and discouraged, he continued until he could feed his sow's first weaned litter on corn that he had raised himself without one extra dime. Slowly, he expanded both his crop and his pig-breeding operation till he had saved up for himself three hundred dollars."

There were audible gasps.

"Listen to me, men. This brother told me in person after he had come into Ohio that that was the amount he needed to buy himself free. Now we *all* know it is a crime against the heaven for *any* man of *any* color to have to purchase *his own body*!"

"Yes, indeed! Amen! So it is!" The quiet undercurrent of comments rustled as persistently as the bending grasses.

"But, brethren, until the House of Slavery falls, such unnatural and unorthodox actions must be taken! This very night *hundreds* of your sisters and brothers are traveling northward. At this very hour certain known Quakers, Mennonists, Methodists, and Baptists are waiting to receive you with the Christian kiss of fellowship. Now is the time to consider your choices. Now is the time to arm yourselves with a plan. You work for merchants, shippers, and railroaders. You are all closer to the path of freedom than you might know. Consider Mr. Bradley! Currently he attends the college—*with white men*—that I came from, and he even heads up the antislavery society. Think on that, friends, and on what you could be doing instead of suffering here. In our next meeting, I will lay out plans."

Tom Diller raised his high voice slightly. "Until then, pray for the cause of freedom! Consider that God knows you have the right to pursue life, liberty, and happiness, which has been promised through the Declaration of Independence to *all* men in America, the land of *freedom*!"

Joseph had never heard of such a declaration, and he was pondering it when the sentries outside started kicking the door. Instantly Tom Diller vanished back into the darkness as though he might have been a phantom after all.

"Keep weavin'," Luck muttered. "An' don't act scared!"

The door opened with a loud cracking sound, and seven men in riding clothes spilled in like milk. Joseph was surprised to see that two in this group of raiders were persons of color. The older of them was white haired, pompous, and gouty as he took his strides. The other, nearly Joseph's age and build, looked uneasy and hung just inside the entryway.

"I want to see identification from them all!" A man spouted.

He was the city patrol captain, Joseph guessed.

The elder mulatto marched directly up to Luck. Before fingering the stevedore's badge, the fair-skinned Negro pointed to his reluctant colored partner to move up to Joseph. With the boy coming toward him, Joseph glanced quickly to see other patrollers spreading out to confront each slave individually. Without warning, the captain grabbed the fishmonger off the windowsill and threw him to the floor. Joseph flinched when this happened and again when the brown boy reached out to examine the tag on his shirt.

"It's just baskets, sah, an' teachin' the next generation!" the shopkeeper panted as he lay on his back, his head slightly raised. "That's all we doin' here!"

"You know the time, ol' cuffee?" the captain said, menacingly pressing a heel to the shopkeeper's chest.

"Yessah. 'Bout quarter till the hour of nine o'clock, I 'spect. It weren't never my plan to keep nobody afta curfew."

The captain, certainly a planter by the quality of his polished silver timepiece, checked the Negro's guess.

"Honest, we was just 'bout to clean up, sah," the shopkeeper said, still helpless to get himself up.

Joseph's heart beat hard enough to shake his vision.

The captain let the fishmonger lie as he looked around at all the patrollers. "The only way to keep the nigger honest is not to trust him. Now check those tickets and write down all the work tag numbers. Hold any that do not have valid identification." In the soft light his blanched face looked as hard as ice. "Darkies, you all will stand and keep your hands in plain view till I tell you that you can move again."

Joseph was beside himself. He was trembling, but then he saw the hands of the young dark patroller quavering too.

"Your pass! Your badge!"

The mulatto's demand was devoid of both timidity and compassion. As Joseph showed his ticket, he kept his hand on the bottom of it to block Wahl's signature. The boy wrote down the number on Joseph's false tag. The patrol captain walked near them like a buyer taking a precursory look at a slave for sale. Joseph started licking his dry lips, but one squint from the young brown patrolman told him it was better to make no move at all. He feared what would happen to them all after Mr. Diller had been found. They could all be charged with plotting insurrection, which, according to Harris and Peckory, was considered by white citizens to be the most heinous of slave crimes.

Now Joseph knew why the subject had been on Peckory's mind. He turned just in time to see his mill acquaintance dragged out through the door. Two others were also taken away while the captain thoroughly checked every corner, bringing his own lantern to aid his cause. Unbelievably, Tom Diller had disappeared.

"Whether or not your abolitionist is with you, we all know what you have been doing here!" the captain exclaimed, going back to the fishmonger, now on his feet. "When we find that Yankee, and we will, we'll make it most unpleasant for him. Then we'll come back and get you all. Now you'd better run boys, 'cause we can catch niggers that are out after curfew."

Joseph's legs and hands were jelly when the colored patrolman, showing smooth skin and large eyes, gave him back the dead man's badge that had been pulled from his shirt. Another moment and Joseph saw that Luck had also been cleared. Together they fled the shop like skittering crabs.

"What are coolored men doing in that patrol?" Joseph gasped after they slowed for their first moment to unlatch Miss Gail's gate.

"They rich slaveowners, an' they do they time with the po'lice so's as to stay in good with all the white folk." While he panted and spoke, Luck's troubled eyes moved to the street.

Joseph turned, thinking they had been followed. Instead he saw Ezra, and in the street, Master Abram's coach. The old Delora slave came up and grabbed Joseph and held him by twisting one of his ears.

"Where you done been the last three-quarters of this here hour?"

Joseph did not struggle under the pain inflicted by the normally gentle uncle who had known him all his life. Luck edged away. Joseph stayed, speechless and sick in his stomach as he looked at the brougham's windows, dreading his first clear glimpse of the man who said he owned him.

"He's not in there," Ezra told him sharply. "He's ill an' exhausted from tryin' to make a place for *you* in this city, an' he sent me with a message instead of comin' hisself."

"Whaaat message?" Joseph begged just as the bells of St. Michael's struck out the hour of nine o'clock.

"I ain't sayin' nothin' to nobody as irresponsible as you!"

"Ezra! I neeever left Anson Street, and I waaas back by curfew. You are my witness!"

"Where you been?" Ezra unhanded him.

Joseph put his lips together before speaking. "At a meeeting. I . . . I heeeard about a slave goooing north."

Ezra shook him by the shoulders. "You fool! Not out of Delora two days, an' this! You want to kill you' massa? Break his heart? Boy, shame on you! Afta all he done for you."

"I waaasn't plaaaning to run. I waaas just curious."

"Yeah." Ezra let his eyes go wide. "Just like some mouse sniffin' 'round a cat. No problem! No danger! No harm in that!"

"I just wanted to hear aaabout the North."

"An' who, pray tell, was qualified to do the tellin'?"

Joseph felt justified. "A visiting aaabolitionist."

"Lord, have mercy!" Ezra cried. Joseph swung left thinking the older man would strike him. Instead the driver slapped his own thigh. "You cannot do this ever again! Those abolitionists aren't nothin' but the new generation of trappers. Don't you know that? In the days of my daddy an' you' granddaddy, white traders took little trinkets an' lured our black brothers into they boats, promisin' 'em glass an' red cloth, an' then kidnappin' 'em by the thousands instead. Now it's the northerners what's comin' down here. They want you to believe they love you' skin—'cause they want to carry you off to pull their carts an' coaches! They don't have no beast of burden up there."

"Thaaat's wrong!" Joseph dared.

"You the one wrong! Believe you' old uncle! I care 'bout you! What you think a *white* man wants with you? It's worser up there than down here. Now you got a good massa, as good as they come. You run or disappoint him, you gwine kill Mass' Abram for sure! He don't hardly eat nor sleep since he done let you go. I'm gwine take him home t'morrow an' put him back unda' Miss Mayleda's care."

"So you want me to cooome back with you?" Joseph guessed. "That's your message."

Ezra grunted. "I think that's how it should be. Howsumever, nobody's askin' me. Here. I'm to give you this little note. It has an address for one Mista Daniel Alexander Payne, a colored schoolmaster, an' the time of you appointment t'morrow."

"Yes!" Joseph grabbed at it, almost ripping the piece because Ezra still held to it.

"Now, you wait a minute! I'm not givin' you nothin' till you promise there won't be no more foolery like I seen t'night. You go to work, you go to school, an' you come straight back here every day, an' then you go to church on Sunday. You swear in the presence of God to do this, then you can have it."

"I swear! Ezra, just giiive me thaaat. I waaant nothing more than schoool!" He was shamed by Ezra's frowning.

"You'll not be like this, Joseph! You need think on more than just you'-self. You wouldn't be gettin' no chance at all if it weren't for ol' Mass' Callcott. So don't you be selfish—only grateful an' watchful, even by you' prayers. And don't you cause Delora any more grief by layin' old Massa in his grave."

Joseph was humbled. "Yes, sir. You caaan trust me. And I wiiill pray—daily and twice thaaat!"

Ezra still eyed him distrustfully, yet now he gave him the paper. "Onc't you read that, you destroy it, an' don't you tell nobody about Mista Payne. 'Cept for Mass' Wahl, nobody but Mass' Abram an' me know anythin' 'bout this—the Callcott chilluns included." Ezra's mouth still looked soured, but his eyes turned kind. "Now I gwine be a-prayin' for you too."

"You give my love tooo my maaama and Maum," he called after the man had turned to leave. "And tell the girl Rooosa I say 'hallo.' "

Ezra shook his head contrarily, but then he smiled.

It pained Joseph to see him leave, taking with him the last remnant of what felt safe and familiar. He fought the sudden hollow fear that he might never see Abram Callcott alive again. "Unc'!" he shouted loudly, since Ezra was now across the street at the carriage. "You teeell them all I'll cooome seee them. Maaaybe at Christmaaas time."

"All right, then," Ezra called back. "I take care to save you a good-size piece of Maum Bette's Christmas pie. Now you watch you'self an' get on inside!"

––––––––

Upon rising Saturday morning, Brant checked his daddy's still empty bedroom. The man had been gone since Thursday, and Brant worried because there had been no word from him. Going downstairs and outside into hot humidity, he started toward the stables to get a horse so he could ride out to fulfill his obligations to watch over the plantation. He pondered his daddy's illness and wondered if he should go into town to check on him. On the other hand, he was hardly eager to face his parent after what had happened to Rosa at the Renslers' place. Day and night since Billy had brought her home, Mr. Gund had given Negozi leave to stay with Rosa so she would not kill herself.

Lost in thought, Brant nearly stumbled into Theodore Rensler before seeing him in the driveway, his horse already tied to a ring outside the barn. Facing him for the first time since the bedlam Teddy had caused at Pine Woods, Brant found himself loathing this man who would not control his passions even out of respect for his neighbors. "I am not pleased to see you," Brant told him directly. "You've caused me more trouble than you can know, and it makes me question your motives even as far back as when you so freely gave me counsel concerning Daddy's boy."

"You have no reason to be bitter," Theodore said haughtily. "One of the reasons I'm here is to present a written apology."

"The damage is already done," Brant said, walking past him to reach the stable door.

"We want your daddy to know the whole story. That it was not your decision to have your slave there."

Brant looked back. "I drove her there."

"Perhaps I should speak directly with your father, then I can assess his physical progress also."

"He's still in Charleston, if that's any business of yours."

"My word! Brant! The man is in no condition to be alone."

Brant sighed, feeling he would never again confide in Teddy. "If he's not home soon, I'll ride to the city."

"I'll leave the note with you." Teddy took it from his vest.

Brant stepped back to reach the paper. It was addressed from the colonel to his father.

"I'm sure you'll be happy to know that the black boy who mishandled

Rosa has been flogged and sent off to the Kentucky traders," Theodore reported.

"You're daft! It was you I saw with her!"

"Oh yes, but only after that darkie so rudely and so quickly availed himself of her. You know how they are with their lusts."

"You're lying! I heard him call because of *you*!"

"Yes, when I pulled at him and hit him, he came away with his claws still ripping at the poor gal's clothes."

Brant stepped away, dumbfounded. "So that's your story now!"

"Yes, as it was from the beginning, for it is the truth." Teddy smiled. "The boy's sold, and that's why I came to deliver the letter. It explains everything. Your daddy will not need to be concerned about that hot-blooded buck coming after your wenches. It also tells why the colonel was so desperate to find a replacement for Ann after Corinth was delivered. And it clearly states why he persuaded you to let him have the yellow girl that he remembered your daddy purchasing a few seasons back."

"Why are you willing to go along with these lies?"

Teddy shook his head as though Brant were the dense one. "You make it too hard on yourself—this planter's life. You can have what you want. You are in the position to control."

"All right. I'll believe that." He pointed to Teddy's face. "Get off my property."

Teddy raised his hands in mock fear. "Fine. But first let me ask you a question. Why did you keep Joseph's reading a secret from me?"

Brant's mouth dropped open.

"I was in Charleston myself just yesterday. As captain of the parish beat company, I do have access to the courthouse records of any parish slaves who are living in the city. I even know Joseph's work tag number. That was a bad move to take him to town. Once a slave can read, he's trouble everywhere."

Brant could not tolerate the thrill his once good friend was showing in tracking down the Delora servant. "Why do you get so much pleasure from inflicting cruelty on this weaker race?"

Teddy shrugged rudely. "Mostly because my neighbors are so lax on the critical issue of slave control. I read the report on your Parris, and I know that Sub-Captain Clemson sentenced him to forty days in chains."

"It's almost thirty-nine days now. Believe me, I'm counting."

"Why do *you* take so much pleasure in trying to protect them? Just whose side are you on, Brant? Do you want your own darkies to be the first ones to rise up and slit your throat in the night?"

Brant was silent, for he could not deny that he feared Negroes, even those living on his own property. "I told you once to get off Delora land."

"That's not kind of you, especially since I'm almost like a brother to the one you say you love."

"Teddy, don't start on that. If the colonel has not *already* decided that I am unworthy of Ann's hand, then I'm certain that you can press him just a little more to make that decision."

"I'm *for* you! Don't you think I want the properties merged?"

"There'll be no merger, and likely there'll be no marriage either. If you want to go courting business, then start to make William Gilman your bosom friend."

"Ah, you haven't heard. The Gilmans have gone back to Boston for good. For you that must be very good news."

"What would be good news is to have you stay away from here. I may not be the religious fanatic my daddy is, but I do believe in truth and chastity. And I'm beginning to see the wisdom of choosing friends who honor those virtues too."

"You're hardly the man to preach on virtues." Teddy reached into his vest again. "My uncle has also written you a letter, outlining the anguish you have brought to Ann regarding her purity and character."

"What! You can't be serious! I have never even kissed her!"

"Abandoning a southern belle can be just as devastating in our society as taking her prematurely. For months you've been distancing yourself from her, and people are talking, especially after they observed your cool manner at the Sunday dedication."

"I was distancing myself before either you or the colonel could demand me to do so. I know you are at total odds with what my daddy is trying to do in converting slaves. I did not want to embarrass your family."

"However, you ended up embarrassing us all the same. Of course, some were surmising that Ann's affections had gone to William, since he was the only eligible escort at her party. But when news gets around that he has left, then the rumors will focus on one thing only." Teddy raised his eyebrows. Brant had no idea what that could mean. "That you had already compromised her and made her unfit for marriage to anyone else."

"That is a lie, and you are its mouthpiece! My integrity is known. You cannot threaten me to cling to her by making me fear you. I don't understand you. What business is it of yours?"

"Read the letter. In time, the man is always forgiven for impropriety, but the woman remains a spinster forever."

"Ann is as pure as I am!"

"It is appearance that matters here. Not actuality. There is my uncle's old friend who still may be willing to take her—"

"Stop speaking of vile relationships. I love her with a pure love. And you of all persons should know that!"

"Then, by all means, we'd better start working together. If you do not marry Ann, it will be your loss and mine, since Pine Woods may never come to me if that other man claims her."

"You're willing to do anything to have your own way!" Brant fumed, stunned by the news that Ann might be headed toward matrimony with someone else. Teddy was heartless to think of her only as a pawn.

"Be honest with yourself, Brant. Everywhere you turn, things are out of control. I can help you, and both of us will benefit if you love Ann as you say."

Brant was voiceless for a moment. "I have failed, yes. But I still have morals. I'll not compromise them anymore, even with you. I'll believe there is an honorable way to rescue Ann and prove the rightness of our love. Now, Theodore, I'm telling you: Stay away from my property and stay off my land."

CHAPTER 18

JUST BEFORE CLOSING TIME on Saturday evening, Peckory showed up at the mill with a grim Mr. Wahl walking right beside him. Coming into the loud stifling room where Joseph and Harris had worked since five that morning, Peckory had his shirt off and tied around his hips. The other workers didn't waste a glance on him, but Joseph could not keep his eyes away from the fresh seeping welts covering the man's back from neck to waist. Peckory's lips were pulled away from his teeth, a pure sign of his great discomfort. Yet when he saw Joseph, he lighted into him without delay.

"Boss, I swear I saw him there!"

"That's not possible," Mr. Wahl returned, looking toward Joseph with worry. "The patrollers wrote down the numbers, and his tag matched none of them."

Joseph feared guilt would be written all over his face. He forced himself to reach for more staves from the piles in front of him. The foreman stepped closer and called him to attention. Then he made Peckory turn his back to him.

"There now, boy, I want you to have a close look at what happens when one gets caught being out at night. It ain't a pretty sight, eh?"

Harris came up behind him, kicking Joseph in the heel to get him to at least dip his head. "No, sir," Joseph responded.

Mr. Wahl left the three clerks alone. Harris had not one bare thread of sympathy for Peckory or for what he called Joseph's "dumb shanty antics."

"You both caught up in the notion that somebody else can tell you how to beat the massas. For God's sake an' you' own, hear me out. No good can come of it." His stern fatherly look flew at Joseph and then at Peckory. "Peckory! Man! The day's gwine a come when that man's gwine tire of you' defiance. They're gwine take the skin clean off you or else sell you."

Peckory fought back with tight jaws that scarcely moved. "Long 'fore that time comes I be breathin' the fresh air of freedom."

"Listen to me, Joseph." Harris condemned their fellow worker with his pointing. "There's what happens to fool-hearted, uppity *nigras*!"

Peckory growled back. "You can just stay here, Harris, an' let them decide if an' when they gwine sell away you' wife an' chilluns. Or you could ask Eagle, here, 'bout this road to freedom, for he done hear'd the same talk as me."

Though Harris showed disappointment in Joseph, he did not question him. Instead he pushed Peckory to turn around again. "Lookee! Twenty fresh lashes atop all the old ones. You want to be like that, with the price of you' hide gwine lower every time somebody decides to cut you again? If you want some happiness in this life, then don't fight battles what you cain't win. Think whatsumever you want 'bout the buckras, as God be you' judge, but don't you cross 'em. It'll only get you this!"

"Why didn't they take *you*?" Peckory squinted over one battered shoulder. "How come you' tag number never showed up on that list?"

Joseph pulled away like a cornered rabbit.

Harris took up for him. "Let him alone."

"Heah! I'm leavin' for the North soon," Peckory boasted as the sound of the machinery continued to cover them. "Soon, Harris, you'll see I ain't no loser. Fact is, I'm kinda proud of Eagle here. We beyond just curryin' for they wretched favor, like you is."

The other man shook his head, appearing sorry for Peckory. "Don't let him p'suade you, son. You think this all over for you'self. Mass' Wahl make his people stand up an' take they own lickin'. Still 'n yet, he 'bout as fair as they come. Most anyplace else, you be mistreated. But here, you gets only what legally comes to you when you don't mind they printed laws."

Feeling trapped and blighted, Joseph had had more than enough of them both. He made excuse to go for wooden hoops stashed in one of the dusty corners. He longed for the conch-shell's trumpeting sound. For his sanity he needed to be out of here and back into the natural air of the streets. But more than that, this next blast would release him. He had someplace to go, and that was to meet Mr. Daniel Alexander Payne.

Joseph found the building set back within the closed yard of a wood-frame house. With trepidation he went through the gate, took the straight brick path, and knocked on the door. An evening in May never seemed hotter or more likely to steal his breath than this one did while he waited. He had never had the privilege—or the dilemma—of making his own introduction, and that only made his anxiety worse. Soon a young, light-skinned Negro opened the door. Joseph found himself as dumb as a scarecrow staked up in a field-slave's pea patch.

"Good evening," the calm male said. He appeared no older than Joseph and had a thin face with prominent cheekbones and a head of woolly hair that outlined his ears and ended at the joints of his neat, narrow jaw.

Joseph stayed frozen, in part because he could not tell by the man's manner or dress if he was the teacher, a student, or the teacher's servant. The man spoke into Joseph's racing silence. "Are you inquiring about school?"

His tension burst. "Yeees, sir!"

The man's smile brought relief to Joseph, and his sharp bright eyes showed that he welcomed having direct vision with him.

"You are Joseph."

"Yeees, sir!" He sounded like a horn blast again.

"I am Teacher Payne." The man stepped aside in the hallway. "Come in. I was expecting you. You are right on time."

"Thaaank you, sir." Finally Joseph was in control of his injured mouth and its volume. It was so peculiar to be on his own business, yet he felt elated as he walked into the cooler, darker corridor. The two of them seemed to be entirely alone. Payne conducted him into a modest-sized, well-lit room, where large windows cast the early evening light down on many well-polished desks. Teacher Payne, who was shorter than Joseph, led him to a seat and politely invited him to sit down.

Joseph moved awkwardly. He had never sat in the presence of a free man, nor had he ever been in the social presence of a free *black* man before. Rays of bright sunlight streamed down on them both as though angels might be watching. Joseph took a look around. There were maps and charts and paintings on velvet, all of which represented a world entirely new to him. There were also many mounted specimens of wild birds and animals, some of them beautiful, some of them ghastly.

He was still gawking at the odd decorations when the young teacher put on a pair of green-lensed glasses. "Like you, Joseph, I have not always had a teacher to guide my quest for learning. One of the first things I did in trying to study science was to watch a solar eclipse. Do you remember a few years back when the sun grew dark in the middle of the day?"

"Yes, sir!" He could have said much about his memory of that odd natural event except that he was reluctant to reveal the limitations of his tongue. From what the man said next, however, Joseph wondered if the teacher might actually be trying to set him at ease.

"Soon after that eclipse I started having trouble with my eyes. Whole pages would look black to me. Now I understand that the intensity of the light ruined some of the mechanisms of my vision. This ongoing infirmity I won for myself because of my natural curiosity." He smiled. "I thought you might be able to relate to my frustration."

Joseph moved his tongue. "I dooo understaaand, sir."

"I know you do." The teacher then went on to explain that Master Callcott had already told him about his years of secret study and the culminating tensions between him and Brant that had robbed him of his fluid speech. "Try not to be embarrassed about the way your words sound here." Payne looked at him warmly. "What you're suffering now is a mark of your dedication to learning."

Joseph was humbled and at the same time honored to hear a learned man speak well of his moonlight endeavors. The young teacher opened a book on the desk in front of him.

"You will stand whenever you are called upon to read or answer questions, for that is the proper etiquette of a classroom. Please, let me hear what you can make out of the first paragraph, starting on the left."

Joseph looked at him helplessly. He had no idea what a paragraph was. Payne seemed to read him instinctively. "Look at this." The teacher moved so that he could point into the book. "The paragraph is a grouping of sentences or lines. See how this indentation and this spacing marks one whole collection of thoughts?"

As though encountering a sun too bright for his interior soul, Joseph had to close his eyes. He was receiving instruction in broad daylight—and at a school with a teacher. Incredible praise welled up in him toward God. "Yes, I see!"

For a long moment Joseph's nervousness threatened to disable his brain as well as his mouth. But he stood anyway, and as he forced himself to say the first words, his thoughts were pulled into line with the author's. " 'The ooostrich is the laaargest of birds. Traaavelers who have seen them in their native land aaaffirm that theeey can be as tall as a man on horseback. Some, which have been brooought to Eeengland, are seven feet high.' " He stopped and smiled. "That is the eeend of the paragraph, sir."

Teacher Payne stepped back. "Yes, it is! You read very well! This is from a sixth-year student primer, and there's many a white man studying in seminary who has a hard time with some of these same words! But do you comprehend what you read? Tell me, what have you learned from this short section of the discourse?"

"Thaaat the oostrich is thh laaagest—" Joseph stopped, dropping his head. His nervousness, joining with the fatigue of having worked twelve hard hours, threatened to make a response impossible. A tremendous fear of rejection and failure hammered him until he again looked at the patient man.

"Don't give in. Work at this. God has His reasons for allowing this struggle, and I do not believe it is by accident that your master was compelled to bring you here. You have learned so much on your own, and already I can see you are gifted for this work. Believe that you can accomplish so much more now by being with me. Please. Try again."

Joseph's eyes stung with gratefulness, but still he struggled with the feelings of being unable and weary.

"This is a rare opportunity for the both of us. If I had my heart's desire, *all* persons in this city, regardless of the depth of their hue or their place— rich or poor, slave or free—would learn to read so that they could know the wonders of our God and His creation. But so few in your circumstances are ever allowed in through this door."

The hurt within Payne was obvious, even as he pointed energetically to things around the room.

"This is the place where I envision knowledge combining with a love and fear of God. School is the place where Christ himself can untap all the wellsprings of our minds and spirit."

Joseph was encouraged by the man's great vision. He tried again.

"These birds can be seven feeet tall, sir," he said clearly.

"You even understand the measurements. Good!" Payne's eyes were lively as they looked over the rim of his dark glasses. "Now! What do you think? Is the information true?"

Joseph stared at the words. He knew about birds only from seeing them, and none had ever been as tall as a man on horseback. Though he feared Mr. Daniel Payne less now, he still desperately wanted to show that he was smart and could be correct. Yet dishonesty was the mark of a fool, his conscience told him. What should he say? "I know nooothing aaabout such creatures," he admitted finally. "But I believe whaaat I have read, for you are known to beee a man of faith, and I dooo not think you would waaaste time on books that did nooot show truth."

Payne sat on the bench of the desk in front of him and shook his head with definite satisfaction. "So! You weigh the trustworthiness of the text against the trustworthiness of its owner!"

"Yes, sir!" Joseph delighted in this sudden sparring of wits. He relaxed. "Now tell me, please, sir. Is it true?"

"Listen to how clearly you are speaking! That, I think, reveals more than even your countenance does of how you delight in mental exercise. You showed wisdom to speak out of your best judgment and with pure honesty. And yes, the descriptions are true. Do you know the word *philosophy?*"

"No, sir."

"In its purest form the word means 'love of wisdom.' You do know what *wisdom* means?"

Joseph thought of the proverbs Master Abram read daily. "Yes, I thiiink I do."

"Let me show you how you can know for certain." He got up and brought back one of two large volumes from a table that served as his desk. "Even teachers must have teachers. And here is the life work of a teacher whom I feel I know but have never met. His name is Noah Webster, and I have been his pupil through the miracle of books. Books, Joseph, minister with equability and can be used by all who can read. The printed word will never hedge on you or modify what it has to say because of your status or your color."

He opened the heavy volume on the desk in front of Joseph. "This is called the *American Dictionary*. Mr. Webster worked for twenty-five years to compile the meanings and spellings of these seventy thousand words so that I—and you—and all other educated persons can draw on the wealth of his labors."

Joseph reached for it. Payne had called him educated.

"Yes, do! Turn the pages! In part, this is what your schooling will be about. I am not to be your *only* teacher or even your *best* one. A real part of learning is learning how to learn."

Then Joseph found himself holding his head instead of the book. For the second time that evening he felt like crying out of joy. "How fast caaan I learn to learn? How long will it take?"

"Only a lifetime." Payne smiled. "But for the serious student I recommend three hours of work per day. I continue to do this myself, rising at four each morning for my own studies, devotions, and exercise. Then I get to my other daily labors and, of course, to the business of teaching school." He went back to the book. "We spoke about wisdom. See the entry here? The kind of wisdom I want all my students to focus on is this."

Joseph read aloud from the dictionary, looking where his teacher had pointed. " 'Wiiisdom is true religion; the knowledge and feeear of God, and sincere and uniform obedience to God's commands. This is the wisdom which is from above.' "

Payne looked at Joseph mildly just as Joseph covered his mouth with his hand. He had slipped on two words only. It was like a miracle of grace that his speech was coming back with his concentration on reading.

"You are ready for this kind of work!" Payne was animated with excitement. "Starting on Monday, each of your school days will begin with a study of the Scriptures. After that I will give you instruction in language and mathematics. Of course you will learn to write, for Mr. Callcott has given me permission to teach you. Then, at the close of each evening, you will have an hour or more to study here on your own, since it would be unwise for you to take books out onto the street." He touched the metal tag on Joseph's shirt. "There is no reason for you to have to display that in here. By the city ordinances it is permissible for you to hang it on a cord around your neck, and I suggest you do so. Then when you come in here, you can tuck it away. All I ask of you is that you show the respect due a teacher by his student."

Joseph unpinned the badge, just for the huge pleasure of doing that. "I wiiill, Teeeacher Payne." His eyes drifted upward to the maps he saw near the front of the room. "Those are draaawings of lands and seas, aren't they, sir?"

"Yes."

"Where is the laaand they call England? I have heard the Callcotts speeeak of it. They have faaamily there."

The teacher went forth and pointed. "This is where Charleston lies along the seacoast of North America. A ship must sail across the Atlantic to this point here. If you come closer, you can see the principal cities. Here, for example, is London."

Joseph moved to the man. "When peeeople speak of the Noorth, sir, what dooo they mean?" His speech showed how nervous he was to broach the subject.

"This is Charleston. When a boat leaves port and goes this direction, it passes the coastlines of other states in the union of states called the United States of America. We, as persons of color, are not considered citizens of this nation for which we spend our sweat and labor. Yet the line of true slavery stops here." He pointed just inches above the dot showing their city. "Above that line, on this eastern coast at least, no man, woman, or child can be a slave."

"Have you beeen up there, sir?"

"No, and if I ever go, I will never be permitted to reenter Charleston. But my father's people were from New England—up here. My father told me when I was very young that he was born in the slave state of Virginia—here—of free parents. However, he was kidnapped, brought to Charleston, and sold as a slave. Eventually he saved a thousand dollars and bought his freedom."

Joseph's breath whistled as he considered it. "We cannot dooo that now, sir. There is a law against it."

Payne showed concern. He left the map and came back to stand beside his desk. "Sit down. For our mutual safety some things must be understood right from the start. I am here to teach you what I *may* teach you—and that is to write, to read, to think, to study, to find resources, to use your observational acumen, and to direct yourself to God as a servant worthy of His kingdom. Under the threat of imprisonment, fines, and having my free status changed to slave status, I cannot discuss certain issues in life—slavery included. But if our tongues are muted by these rules, I hope you know my continual prayers are for you and for all others in your circumstance. However, do not ask me to compromise on the regulations. To maintain the freedom to teach at all, I must maintain the city's rules."

Joseph nodded, envying Payne's free status but also seeing for the first time that many limits were placed on such men also.

"I think you should know about my regular students who are here from nine until three. Most are *brown* youths, young men and women from the wealthiest and most influential colored families in Charleston. The majority of these people practice slave keeping, so that is the reason I choose to educate you on my own time and not with the others. It's best for both of us that you have no contact with them. But that is in no way a reflection on you or on how I will treat you as my student."

Payne brought his hands together. "My conviction is that God has made us equals, and that He will never hold you in higher regard than He does now. Slave or free, He judges us only by our relationship to Him. Yet, I must say that I do have concerns for you learning as a slave. For I see education going hand in hand with freedom. I am not sure what learning without liberty will do for you." He looked at him. "It could be very painful."

Joseph lightly closed his eyes. "Then I wiiill welcome this kind of pain."

He found his teacher touching his shoulder. "A famous man from England once said that knowledge is power. So by that philosophy, Joseph, to some degree you will be empowered by your studies. What you are learning, compared with what you are experiencing as a bondsman, will be contradictory. As a Christian teacher, I can warn you that power can be employed either for destruction or for good. In this classroom I challenge my students to commit themselves to a *sanctified* knowledge—submitting first and foremost to Christ as their teacher. The power He gives through knowledge will always be glorious. That's a promise from the Bible, so you can take hope in it as a believer. As far as you are able, use what you learn to confer blessing on others and to be armed with the thunderbolts needed to crush Satan's strongholds."

Joseph could not look at him anymore and lowered his eyes. He wanted to honor this man, for he was so moved by Payne's confidence in him.

The teacher was gentle. "What is it?"

His voice cracked. "Juuust yesterday I was stuuudying the Bible and praying about how I, a slave, could knooow the power of God. And now, sir, you are speeeaking about this very thing!"

Payne seemed deeply touched. After some hesitation he said, "I will dare to say a few comments about slavery just this once, though it could cost me all I have. I oppose it not because it enslaves the black man, but because it enslaves *man*. God created man, and according to the eighth Psalm we are all made just 'a little lower than the angels.' *Man* created

slavery, which hurls individuals down from the elevated position God or-
dained for them."

He paused. "You know what I mean. God himself never took the liberty to bind a human's will. Yet slavery will dare to do it. 'Ye are bought
with a price,' Scripture tells us. And that is not speaking about any slaveholder's money, but rather the precious blood of our Lord and Savior,
Jesus, when He died to rescue us from sin and return us to His own holiness. Ultimately, Joseph, you do belong only to God."

Joseph raised his tearing eyes.

"I think we must hold to the conviction that God will be victorious.
After the darkness, the sun must rise! Even in the darkest of darkness,
God's sight is not hindered from what is now and what will be. His eye
will forever be upon those who seek Him, to strengthen those who are
fully committed to Him."

"Then yooou believe that slavery wiiill end someday?" Joseph longed
to be hopeful.

The teacher showed glumness. "I cannot say. What I do know is that
no man will be able to flee the bonds of tyranny without education. For
that reason I think you must use your God-given opportunity, regardless
of what lies ahead."

"Then I wiiill, sir. That is a pleeedge I have already made to my God.
And now it is one that I also maaake to you."

The teacher smiled. "Thank you. As long as you are permitted to come
here, I pledge to do my best for you also. Now we will begin with a time
of prayer."

CHAPTER 19

SUNDAY WAS RIGHTLY NAMED, for the sun shone brightly. Corinth had been put back into service around the house. Her baby was kept in a kitchen crate, where Ann's daddy allowed it to be suckled four times each working day.

In the early afternoon the servant had carried out Ann's sandalwood-inlaid escritoire so that she could write letters under the live oaks between the house and the river. When the wench went off to nurse her infant, Ann stayed alone in the flower-perfumed breezes. Taking out pen, ink, and paper from the portable desk's narrow drawers, Ann began a letter to Felicia, the first since her friend had left for that distant and now seemingly very unfamiliar world called Boston.

4 May 1834
My dearest Felicia, who stays in my heart closer than a sister,
    Within a day we will be moving to our town house in Charleston.
How I continue to regret the deep disagreements raised between our

fathers by that ugly incident which occurred just nights ago. 'If there be any comfort in love,' as your Gospel says, please restore my joy by letting me know you hold nothing against me because of the practices of men over which we women of the South have no control.

Father and Teddy assure me with the earnestness of saints that it was the darkie rower who touched the Negress. I will not question them, for to rail against actions denied, dear friend, is like going before the sun to tell it not to rise. Anyone here knows that mental sickness can result from prying into affairs over which one has no control. However, you must know that I cannot live with the pain of your rejection. Please tell me you do not hate me just because I am born a planter's daughter.

Loneliness has settled back over my chambers like a sullen fog. I do not see or hear from Brant, though yesterday Teddy did carry a letter to him. I fear Brant is punishing me with isolation because of his displeasure toward my family. That's odd, because just a week ago he had said almost this same thing to me—that my family must be wanting my separation from him. What a sorry mess!

After writing this to you, I am determined to write to him. I continue to be thankful that he shuns the lewdness that Daddy and others wink at. They don't understand that licentiousness is like murder to the female soul. I have reached the conclusion that if Brant's goodness is the result of Christianity, then I may be able to embrace that faith more readily than all this faithless deception around me.

Teddy tells me privately that Abram Callcott may be dying from the same disease that claimed Brant's mother and brothers. I long to comfort Brant. I would try to give him everything he needs as a wife. Do you continue to think that your God has a plan and a reason for all things— even suffering? I wish I could think so, but at present I do not.

Please write, with or without your daddy's blessing! Rely on your Christian duty, if you must, but forgive me. Cannot our loyalty transcend the philosophies rending our two societies?

Your loving, mourning companion,

Ann

Remember to send your letter to our house at South Bay.

As she held her correspondence for a quick rereading, she saw Morrison approaching almost at a run.

"I think he a-comin', Miss Annie. I just done seen he horse past the gates an' go up 'long the road. He could be a-cuttin' in through the woods."

Ann felt herself blush. "Maybe Master Brant is just out for a Sunday ride." Still, she reset and retied her bonnet.

"I don't think so, missy. He done have row 'pon row of 'em sweet yellow jessamine vines drapin' down 'cross he horse."

Brant did? That concerned her. Maybe he was going courting somebody else, upriver. She cloaked her worries in her chiding. "Bet it wasn't even Brant you saw. He's as unromantic as a frog."

"Sh-sh-sh! Child!" Morrison looked straight out behind her into the forest that bordered the yard. "He is a-coming."

"Then you get out of here." She brushed back her hair through the ribbons that tied under her chin and folded her hands in her lap. "I'll meet the gentleman alone, thank you." Just then Corinth came back to her. "Master Brant's paying an afternoon visit," Ann said, feeling the flightiness in her voice. "You get us something nice and cool to drink, but take your time."

"Yeees, missy," Corinth dragged out her words to show that she could be slow moving and resentful. Ann had the grace to forgive her this time, for Brant was almost there. She could hear his horse breaking twigs.

Soon a fragrant, natural necklace of flowers dropped around her shoulders as though falling out of heaven. "Brant!" She did not have to feign surprise at the gift.

He took some time to tie his horse to a sapling. Then he stood like an awkward servant beyond her blanket. "My father thinks I am on my way to Charleston to move into the Gibbes Street house," he said. "He and I had a long talk when he returned from the city. There might be a summer position for me in the Grafton Mills countinghouse. He's agreed to let me move into town, with Ezra and Nancee to be my help."

"Oh, that's wonderful."

He frowned. "I thought you'd think it foolish and demeaning for me to take a job with commoners."

"I wasn't thinking about the work, but only that you'd be in Charleston, as I'm going to be." He seemed truly surprised at the warmth of her response.

"General Wilton Morton directs Grafton shipping, and the man just happened to meet up with my daddy while he was in town. Then he mentioned that he was looking for a planter's son to do some work for him during the busiest shipping months."

"Brant, I love the idea—if it means we can see each other." She fingered the flowers but could not get him to say anything about them. "You know, this is hardly the shortest route to the city, going *south* by going *north*."

He smiled. "Some men will go around the globe in search of the girl they wish to speak to."

His response delighted her, for it had been a long time since she had seen such easy humor in him. Folding her full pale green skirt more closely around her knees she invited, "Sit down."

Brant did so, but just at the blanket's hem. He seemed unaware that his strong rugged features overwhelmed her. Though he was every inch a man, she could be tempted to describe him as beautiful, with his gray-blue eyes and his thick, wavy hair already bleaching from the strong spring sun. Windblown and smelling slightly of horses and leather, he showed his worry by wrinkling a brow. It made him look dashing.

"Annie, I've come to talk to you about a lot of things. So just listen and don't make light of me, no matter what you think at first."

His intensity was frightening.

"You know that in the past I've been ashamed of my father and of the way he holds on to the things he thinks are right. But last night when he came home from Charleston, I decided to tell him the truth about what happened to Rosa. And even though he was angry—as he had a right to be—he showed me compassion and forgiveness."

"You weren't the one wrong! It was Teddy!"

He held up his hand to stop her. "From the day I started having problems with Joseph, I've been wanting to leave the plantation. What's amazing to me is that Daddy is willing to let me go for the summer so that I can sort out my feelings and decide what I want to do with my life."

"You're just going to the city," she said to clarify what she had thought she understood. "You're not leaving Delora?"

"Not yet, but that may come."

She found herself suddenly as serious as he.

"That's why I'm here. It's only fair that you know my decisions and my indecision too."

Fearing what he had to say, she watched him form a sad, distracted smile. "I know I have a duty to my daddy and my family, but I'm not sure if I must stay with Delora to fulfill it. My daddy's ill. . . ." His voice trailed off.

Ann brought his hand to her cheek. "Oh, I'm sorry you're facing this kind of sorrow again."

His eyes showed more determination. "It may not be fever. In fact today he seems fine. Otherwise, I would not even think of leaving him. I detest the stubbornness that makes him want to stay at Delora while every other planter moves into town. But I'm not going to argue that point any-more. In fact, I think he entertains a sad premonition that this might be his last summer—"

"Oh, Brant. This all must be so hard on you."

His smile showed gratefulness, as though perhaps he did not feel so alone when sharing his thoughts with her. "I'm not sure what I will do with all the responsibilities directed toward me, but I think there are some things I must not do. I know this may sound childish or even irreverent to you, but in the first hours of this morning, I made a covenant with God to seek Him fully while I am alone in Charleston. I must know why I live and why I'm here!"

Ann felt very timid of soul, yet instantly she agreed with him. "I feel that way too!" Her eager response seemed to shock him. "Do you believe that God grants *personal* guidance? All the time Felicia was here she kept saying He does."

"Yes, I believe it, but divine forgiveness must come before divine di-rection. That's what I saw last night when I faced my father in fear. His forgiveness gave me hope that I can find purpose without utterly disap-pointing him. I also began to think more about God's forgiveness and that maybe I can be put on the right way if I desire to have God's will done more than my own."

Ann had never heard Brant speak like this. "You've given this much thought," she said, in no way belittling him. "I wish I were at the place where I could trust that God was active in my life."

"I did not sleep a wink last night, Annie. I was on my knees, begging God to clear me of so many, many things! And always as I spoke, I con-tinued to ask, 'What is God's will concerning you and me?'" He handed her a letter in her daddy's handwriting. "I suppose you know about this."

She read it, her mouth dropping a little more with each line. "Oh, dear! Teddy and Daddy never said a thing to me. They never asked if I felt shamed! Nor did they tell me that they thought I'd been disgraced! I can't believe this!"

He took the paper back, and his face looked pained. "I don't think it's true. I pray it's not. You must know my motives and my affections have been virtuous. And the delay of marriage has not been my will—"

"I know. I know." She touched his sleeve.

"I'm here, Annie, because I want you to understand me, even if no one else cares to or can. My affections are not with property or the kind of life we lead. I want to find the right way. My hope is to find peace—"

"Oh, then help me to find it too!"

His eyes were bright and intense. "Do you mean that?"

"Yes, I do!"

"This morning I decided I could honestly ride away from everything without regrets. Everything—but you. I had to come talk with you and tell you that even if I leave Delora, I believe I will love you always."

She kissed his fingers and kept them at her lips.

He continued. "My daddy's always saying that true love means sacrifice, but I fear that in this case I must sacrifice *you*—because I do love you. I think I may decide to go away."

She sat dumbly as his words sank in. "You can't leave! Don't you see that I want to find peace just as much as you? What course will I have without you here—a woman alone? You can leave. You can travel around that globe if you want. But what can I do? Stay here and be at the mercy of Daddy's will and Teddy's."

His eyes opened wide. "Would you sacrifice everything, even the plantations, to be with me?"

She drew back, feeling tears of fear or worry. "I don't know why you think that rightness has to be coupled with leaving. If that were true, then plantations would already be devoid of all good Christian men!"

"I must find God's will and not be afraid to do it."

"Well, how does one do that? And how can one know when he—*or she*—has found it?"

He lowered his head. "I'm no theologian and no minister. In fact, I've been awfully neglectful of the Bible. But Scriptures say that those who have submitted themselves to Christ have the power of the Holy Spirit dwelling in them to strengthen them and give them direction."

"Then you think you have to believe in Jesus and all that the church says about Him before doing anything else?"

"Yes. I don't struggle with that at all. There have been times when I wanted to scoff at my daddy's rules, but I cannot deny his Christianity as the only immovable anchor in my life."

She bowed her head. "I do doubt the need for faith in Jesus."

He sighed. "I don't know how to lead you to faith, Annie. Indeed, I never expected to be talking about this with you. I came to say good-bye, to give you my explanations so that you would know I do love you—"

"I need you, Brant!"

This time he was the one who took her hand. "If you honestly want to know what is right, then I think God will show you—no, us!—what is right. That's the faith I'm going on now."

"I want to have peace," Ann said truthfully. "I don't respect the way Daddy and Teddy conduct their business. That I know. If someone could show me sound reason for believing that the Bible is true, then perhaps I could come to trust it as you do." She paused. "Will your daddy let us see each other in Charleston?"

Brant shrugged sheepishly. "I don't know. I never asked, because I thought this would be the end of it."

She looked into his sadness. He had faced so many crises. She could forgive him for his trepidation concerning the future. "If we can be together, then let's just take each day as it comes. I don't see any reason to try making all your decisions now."

He moved from the blanket to the grass. "True, yet I think you should decide now if you could love me if I weren't a planter."

She believed in that moment she would do anything to keep him from slipping away. "I do love you, Brant, for who you are inside." She moved to him and drew a finger across his chest. That was true. But she, for one, was not ready to believe he would have to desert the planting life to find his own best. For that reason she repeated what she had said before. "Let's just take one day at a time. If God has a way, then let Him reveal it."

His smile looked slightly cautious and disbelieving.

Just then Ann's daddy strode down through the ancient trees. Her thought-consumed courtier saw him and stood awkwardly, for there was no righteous protocol in sitting out here hand in hand without even a Negro as chaperone. Yet Ann's daddy didn't give the slightest hint of displeasure, which made her think that, regardless of what the letter to Brant had said, he had not changed his mind about wanting Brant to be her husband. Yet now she felt resentment toward him and fear, since marriage to his aging friend had been brought up in the correspondence to Brant.

"Why, Mr. Callcott!" Her daddy's eyes twinkled as he surveyed Ann's floral festooning. "It seems you've come to make amends."

The comment made Ann furious, but Brant faced it boldly. "No, sir. It's more that I came to 'speak the truth in love.' "

Her daddy chuckled, perhaps a bit impatient with him for that sturdy comeback. "Well, then, I suppose you'd better come into my office and explain yourself completely."

Ann felt Brant's uneasiness. She, of course, was not asked to join them. That made her feelings toward her young man soar all the more. He had dared to be honest with her, and now he was daring to go before her daddy.

She waited until both men were in the house, then pulled out her letter to Felicia and in the margin wrote a note with flair. *Brant has just now brought me flowers! And Daddy and he have gone inside to talk in private! My dear sister, do pray for me!*

Brant followed the colonel, wondering with every step at the rightness of his being there. Under different conditions this could have been the home of his wife and father-in-law by now. It was a familiar place, for he had spent much time here in his childhood and adolescence. The head male servant, Clarence, came out quite formally and walked with them, closing the doors behind them after they had gone into the planter's study. The room was cluttered with hunting and fishing tools as well as all kinds of memorabilia from the war between Great Britain and the United States two decades earlier. Resting over everything was a lingering grayness caused by tobacco smoke.

Brant glanced with worry to the colonel, who motioned easily for him to occupy one of the comfortable chairs placed in a circle around a low table. The slavemaster sat down, too, and offered him rolled-up tobacco, which he refused with boylike awkwardness.

"How's your daddy?" Colonel Rensler asked him.

Brant stayed guarded. "He is better, sir."

The colonel leaned back, his thumbs together. "I'm glad to hear that. I hope he received my letter and took its meaning rightly. It doesn't please me to be at odds with a neighbor."

Brant said nothing.

The colonel sighed and came toward him once again. "You're a fine young man, Mr. Callcott, and I fear you're under a heavy load of both expectation and responsibility."

If that was an open door to speak against his father, Brant decided not to take it. With tension he said, "Sir, I thought you wanted to speak about Miss Rensler."

He was not sure what would come next, but he did have the presence of mind to breathe a small prayer for divine help and protection.

"Let's not be guarded with each other," Ann's father said. "What are your intentions regarding my daughter?"

"Sir, that has much to do with my daddy's wishes—"

"It's not your daddy's answer I'm asking for. But yours!"

Brant searched his soul, and the colonel made it harder.

"If you're not interested in marrying her after dragging out the courtship for so long, then I'll dismiss you after reprimanding you severely for destroying her good name."

"Sir, I do love her! And from the time I've known what marriage was, my hope has been set on having her as my wife."

"Get to the point!"

"That is the point, sir, but I'm not sure my daddy will ever consent to it. And besides that, there are now some things that I must decide—"

"You are rejecting her!"

"I am not, sir! I am just unsure of my future. I . . . I may end up leaving Delora, perhaps as soon as after this harvesttime."

Suddenly concern, not hardness, marred the older planter's face. "What makes you say that? Worry over your daddy's health? Your family finances? Tell me, what has you so troubled?"

Brant could not fathom the change in attitude. "I'm not asking for help, sir. I'm just trying to explain the truth. I . . . I'm not sure the planting life is for me."

"Have you told this to Annie?"

"Yes, just now. I came in a spirit of fairness, Colonel Rensler. I cannot believe I've damaged her reputation, as you say I have. I told her that I love her, which is true. But I might not be preparing well for the life I expect she wants to lead."

"And what did she say?"

Brant paused, wondering just how daring he had the courage to be. "I guess you need to ask her yourself."

The man frowned angrily.

Brant spoke in his own defense. "Our relationship has been pure, Colonel. She has been my angel, especially since my family's tragedies, and I have never once been unchaste with her. She deserves the best. But the best may not be me."

The man kept eyeing him while lighting a cigar for himself. He watched the smoke swirl into the air. "Son, what exactly is it that has you so unsettled?"

Perhaps there was no wisdom in saying it, but Brant did anyway. "I don't have the tolerance to govern slaves. You know yourself what a mess I've made of things."

"Honestly, I don't." The man shook his head. "Have you ever considered that you're being much too hard on yourself?"

"If you were *my* daddy, you wouldn't say that. I am responsible for putting Delora into turmoil three times in two weeks."

"Ill men say harsh things, son. If your daddy's spoken roughly to you, he will regret it once he's well. The truth is, you've been doing the best you can in the midst of some very difficult and touchy situations."

"My daddy knows that too." Brant's defensiveness came back. "He's forgiven me for what's taken place, but that doesn't change the fact that I hate dealing with slaves. That's one reason I am going into Charleston. Annie knows this. General Wilton Morton of Grafton Mills may have a position open in shipping."

The colonel's nod seemed good-natured. "The general's a fine man and certainly only looking for the best to assist him."

"I haven't secured the position, sir."

"It's a worthy goal, nonetheless."

Brant breathed just a little easier. "Thank you."

"As for not enjoying your contacts with Negroes, that's quite understandable. That's why strong overseers are so important. They're your buffers. They keep the peace for you." His cigar had gone out, so he lit it again. "Are you sure I can't interest you in a smoke?" When Brant refused again, the colonel sat back and drew his own to glowing brightness. "Brant, I will do whatever I can to help you. Ann likes you, and so do I."

Inwardly Brant questioned why he had dared to send him the scathing letter. As though peering into his mind, the colonel answered his unspoken thoughts.

"I apologize for what I wrote to you. I was trying to make you see the gravity of the situation. My daughter's not getting younger, and everyone in our circle of friends knows how much time the two of you have spent together. At her party there was talk that William Gilman might become her husband, and then I still have my friend who presses me. You can see how devastating it is for all to be guessing why she's suddenly being passed over by everyone."

Brant looked down. "I want to marry her. I'm struggling with how terrible it would be without her, but perhaps that's just how life must be. For her sake, however, I would beg you to let her marry for love and not just for security."

The colonel stood and walked to him, the smell of smoke growing stronger by the moment. Brant was going to stand, too, but the man told him to stay as he was. "Be brutally honest with me on two matters, Brant. What will be necessary to remove that unfriendly wall your daddy has built between us? *And*—what can I do to help persuade you to stay on as Delora's next master?"

Brant looked up, still too cautious to be grateful for the show of concern. "I'm not sure of either answer, sir," he said after a long hesitation. "I'd like permission to see Ann while we're both residing in Charleston. If you don't want it to be in public, I understand. I ask permission to at least come to your house." Then he thought of another thing because of what Ann had said outside. "And I'd like Ann to have the freedom to attend a good church this summer, since she, too, seems to be doing some honest questioning about faith."

"Is that so?"

Brant felt terrible for breaking Ann's confidence. He covered with an honest statement. "I think it would help my daddy to know that Ann is going to a Christian church."

"So she can be converted like one of his black heathens!"

Brant cringed. "So that we might seek the will of God together, sir, concerning our futures."

"Your daddy will think more highly of her if she goes to church, won't he?"

"No, sir. Not if he thought she were doing it just to appease him. He'd find that hypocritical. However, if she went out of true curiosity and with your real blessing, then, yes, I think that would make a difference."

The man went back toward his seat. "Say, Dr. Bachman's congregation? Would he approve of that one?"

Brant must have looked as dumbfounded as he felt. "Why, yes! My daddy respects that pastor very much."

The colonel laughed. "You judge me as one who has no interest in religion, but that's not true. I'm for whatever creates unity and stability. And in some cases, I'll admit, religion does that. Your daddy, who is my friend, has been through the fire of trials, so why shouldn't I do what I can to help him see his older son happily married while he's still alive and well enough to enjoy that? In fact, I'm going to have a talk with him father to father. I'll ask him to give permission for the two of you to attend St. John's together."

Brant's mouth parted. "Sir, he doesn't know I came here today. He thinks I went directly down to Gibbes Street."

"Then this will be our secret," the man said glibly.

Brant's stomach tightened. "But there's still this matter of my uncertainty about Delora, sir."

"Let's just think about Charleston." He looked at him sincerely. "You do have a fine legacy in Delora, so it's only natural that I'll take the side of helping you *not* to despise your inheritance. But all in good time."

Brant thought about the merger of the two plantations and wondered if the colonel's motivations were as entangled as Teddy's were in wanting to see the lands joined. He said nothing about that worry, however, for he was also thinking on Ann. What she had said was right. As a man, he could make a decision to walk away from his present occupation, but as a woman, she was controlled by the men in her life. If possible, he decided, he should rescue her as well as himself from whatever proved to be un-godly. And he should nobly guide her to whatever was right. Unfortu-nately, he did not know the boundaries of those two kingdoms yet, even for himself.

Colonel Rensler leaned into the silence of Brant's pondering and put a new cigar into the upper hem of Brant's dark vest. "Here. Take this. Keep it for your wedding day."

———————

Early the next morning, after his first night on Gibbes Street, Brant stood in the front office of Grafton Mills. With his best beaver hat in hand, he waited to be seen by the manager of shipping, his father's friend General Morton. The gentleman arrived, and Brant recognized him by his thin-ning gray hair and the short fringe of white beard not quite wide enough or long enough to curtain his double chin. There was a brief greeting spo-ken between them, then the man led him back to his secluded office. Cocking one cool eye at him, he sat down, leaving Brant on his feet.

Brant was overdressed, for already he had glimpsed other workers in shirt sleeves and loose, disheveled ties. He felt tempted to blame his father for this error, since he could have better prepared him.

The general showed a slow smile. "I was happy to speak with your daddy last week. I admit I was surprised and concerned about his health."

"Yes." Brant was not eager to engage that kind of talk.

The other man seemed sensitive to his reluctance and let the topic pass. "The Grafton family and I are ready to put our trust in you. We all feel the Callcotts have an impeccable reputation, and we've been looking for someone who cannot be moved by bribes, no matter how lucrative. Once I have you signed in, I'll take you upstairs and explain the work we have for you."

Like an unproved hunting hound led on a leather strap, Brant followed the aging man once the initial paper work was done. He knew through his father's narratives that General Morton had managed all of the Graftons' shipping for years. Like Colonel Rensler, this man had retained his officer's title from the war against England, which they had fought at sea.

Upstairs there were desks and a dozen or more harried-looking workers seated on stools. The general took Brant to a free spot beside a dirty open window. Brant could smell the ocean as heat exuded from the sun-filled work yard below. There were Negroes, thick and shiny as bugs, hauling sacks and rolling barrels.

"Here is the situation." General Morton pulled Brant's attention away from outside. "The men in here are the watchdogs for this company. They keep track of the profits from our two main commodities—rice and lumber. In this room one can find a record of every barrel and every board sold, exchanged, or shipped within the last five years. But now, with increasing political tensions, we're finding it necessary to maintain even more detailed accounts. We need to be on the constant lookout for seditionists and smugglers, and most especially, we want to catch any secretists who are bringing contraband publications in on northern vessels. And, of course, we're always checking for those who would sneak out of port with unauthorized, live, *ebony* property."

Brant nodded with understanding, though his heart was sinking, for even this work, he saw, hinged on slavery.

"The docks you see from here are the interphase between two increasingly different and antagonistic cultures—that of the North and the South. But for the sake of business we must continue hosting Unionists who come down here to exchange their goods for ours and ship them home."

"How am I to be of help?"

"I choose to call you the *counterpoise* to any illegal actions being staged down there. By that I mean you will balance any unlawful exports or imports with a strategy all our own. The idea was mine initially, but I needed a stronger, younger man to carry it out. From this day on, Mr. Callcott, I will be supplying you with many different kinds of figures. Some of them will appear redundant, at least at first, for I will give you facts on the same cargo, or exchanges, but recorded from different points of view—namely those of sea captains, independent buyers, and inspectors. Some inspectors are employees of our company, but some are paid by the federal government, which also patrols this port. Your job will be to point out to me even the smallest of discrepancies in any of the reporting or sums you see."

Brant feared inadequacy, since he had never been an eager student. The man opened several sets of books. "Here is an example. These are supposedly identical records on a steamer called the *Swiftlight* that tied up at

Grafton's Wharf April twenty-fifth. A federal employee called the collector of the port compiled this one. This one is from one of our own inspectors. You see the difference."

The man had his finger on the answer. "Yes," Brant said. "The recorded
tonnage is more on the federal inspector's sheet."

"Correct! The difference may have been only a bookkeeping error. Or
it may have been fraudulent reporting. It's impossible to tell once the ship
has sailed. Here's a second error."

Again, Brant saw it quickly. "Your inspector counted ten less barrels of
housewares ceramics than did the federal man."

"Right! And again it's too late to account for the difference with the
ship already back out in open waters. However, just days later, the city
police found a pottery barrel containing antislavery essays from northern
newspapers."

"So you think the *Swiftlight* could have brought them in?"

"That is the kind of thing I want to know for certain!"

Brant was intrigued. Perhaps he could be happy working at a desk with
figures instead of with sweating, breathing slaves. General Morton went
over the details of his first day's investigations, then left him with papers
and record books stacked up to the level of his elbows. Brant felt nervous
as he sat down, for he wanted to do well.

Through the open window he heard the black laborers joking. Despite
the enormity of his tasks, he looked out again at the slaves, the *primitives*,
as Colonel Rensler often called them. He could almost envy them their
simple, carefree living contrasted with the stress and uncertainty planters
and businessmen felt each day. Untying his black silk cravat and opening
his stiff collar, Brant realized he would be cooped up here for an entire
summer.

For the first time, his Delora horses would remain unridden except by
grooms. His hounds would stay locked in their pens except when they
were exercised by Negro boys. And his best firearms would hang silent on
their wall racks, gathering only dust. Leaving the wilderness and his family
was a dear price to pay for the privilege of being one step removed from
plantation slavery and the summer fevers. The major conciliation, of
course, was that he would have the summer with Ann.

CHAPTER 20

AS ALWAYS IN MAY, mosquitoes made life miserable along the Ashley River. So when a stiff breeze came off the ocean that Monday to announce the coming of rain, Abram took advantage of the change in weather to move outside, knowing that the pesky biting insects would be dispersed for a time.

Once Colt had him situated comfortably on the second-story piazza with hot tea and his daybook, Abram dismissed his lazy servant until suppertime. Sitting alone, keeping his book closed, Abram faced the wind, thinking. Since coming back from Charleston late on Saturday, he had felt the continuous unpleasant sensation of being a stranger on his own plantation. In large part this was due to all the misery that had befallen his people during his few days away. Sunday morning had given him his first look at Parris. His best worker was battered physically, with sagging shoulders and blackened eyes. But there was injury of the heart, too, brought on by the humiliation and weight of the patrollers' chains. In front of all of Abram's other darkies, Parris had refused to both sing and pray at the chapel's Sunday service. Abram had let the disobedience go, troubled deeply that his lead convert seemed robbed of faith because of his mistreatment by other planters, many of whom were church-going men.

He had not believed the beat company's testimony about Parris's prowling—that is, until he had visited Rosa with Negozi. Hampton Gund had gone with him and affirmed that she had not eaten since her attack, nor did she plan to even if forced.

With a sense of obligation he opened his journal now and jotted down notes concerning his two slaves' brokenness and the distress it caused him. As a bookmark to this place in his business diary, he had Colonel Rensler's recent letter. How irresponsibly the apology had flowed from Linford's pen! How pathetic the events that caused Parris to be shackled and Rosa to starve herself into oblivion after being raped by one of Rensler's spiritually neglected Africans! Abram's fingers curled. Where was God's justice? Why did the righteous suffer injury and sickness while the arrogant reigned supreme?

Despite feeling poorly, he closed the book, stood, and walked to the railing to look over his property and the dark, gray river. It was raining, and he felt himself a weak, sin-sick man with no unction to pray. Yet pray he did, for he was beyond being governed by his feelings. *Oh, God, have mercy on us all! Perhaps, Father, I could have protected Rosa and Parris and even Joseph if I had been a man of more constant prayer. Forgive me!*

He squinted against the pain in both body and spirit. Oh, if he only had the chance to start again, perhaps those yonder fields would still be wilderness. Was Delora plantation truly God's plan for him and for his father before him? Could they be blessed financially, yet spiritually deceived? Was guilt the right response to slavery, or had it been God's design all along to use masters in America to deliver the Gospel to the neediest of those in the nation—her slaves?

Again he closed his eyes. Was his confusion caused only by physical weakness, or was there something more? He thought of Joseph and missed him desperately. He wished he had not parted on such cool terms with him. Instead, he should have undergirded the innocent Negro with indications of his love. As soon as he was well enough, he would make another trip and share his real feelings with the boy. Until then he did not have to wait for Wahl's first report to believe that his servant was doing well. Neither did he need any evidence to assume that his experiment at the school was truly providing an education for him.

Abram's encounter with Daniel Alexander Payne had been both convincing and convicting. The free Negro schoolmaster was thoroughly a gentleman and clearly a genius to have educated himself in so many disciplines before reaching his quarter-century mark. How could any white man of intelligence be duped into believing that Africans lacked mental qualities after meeting a Negro like Daniel Payne? Yet if Brant had not unveiled Joseph's reading, then Abram himself would still be ignorant of such qualities in one of his own.

Cool raindrops hit his hands, though his face and body remained protected by the overhang above. He was not sure what his new understanding would mean for himself, for Delora, his family, or for his slaves. All he knew was that he had the responsibility to walk in the light as God was in the light. Bette came to him just then, her lightweight shoes tapping on the porch wood. He turned to her curtsey and to the trouble in her eyes. She knew all about Parris and Rosa, so he thought this reason enough to explain her dismalness.

"The colonel's here, sah. He askin' permission to come up an' see you."

Inwardly Abram tried to repent of the dislike he harbored for the man. "All right. Show him hospitality." He left the banister and came back to the chair and sat down. The other planter arrived on Abram's private porch within moments. He walked with a fine, ivory-headed cane, though having no physical need for one. Abram glumly, even bitterly, assessed his peer's vigor.

"It's going to be quite a storm if this wind gets any stronger," Colonel Rensler said.

"Indeed." Abram crossed his arms against the breezes.

"I hope I'm not disturbing you."

"Sit down." Abram pointed to a wicker seat.

"Abram . . ." The man held to his cane and did not move. "I've come out of honest concern for you. I know we've slipped out of making neighborly visits with each other, but I'm convinced that now's the time to renew the practice. I'm here to see what I can do for you before I leave for town."

"Then thank you for coming." Abram again pointed out the chair, and the planter availed himself of it.

"Oh, you old hard Callie!" Rensler gave a sudden hearty laugh as he candidly used the nickname that had been put aside for decades, ever since they had stopped riding and swimming together in the river as youths. "You're not happy to see me. In fact, you're struggling inside that great big

Christian heart of yours to find even one scrap of charity for me." He shook his head as though content with himself. "Haven't we known each other long enough to be truthful? Let's drop our southern gentlemen facades and just say what's on our minds."

"All right." Abram said it numbly, for he had no feelings about continuing the conversation. "I am angry about Rosa."

"Even after my letter! I sacrificed my boy to the auction block just to make *you* happy after he saw your wench and took advantage before anything could be done about it. You know perfectly well that no other planter but you would be offended over such a small event."

"The offense was against Rosa, not me!" Abram snapped. "You know her past. You know I brought her to Delora only to protect her. Brant should have taken no liberties to let you look at her, and you should have known better than to request that she be transferred to your house."

"On the contrary, I believe I was right in my offer. I thought it was a perfect combination—you had a wench you doted on, and I had a daughter with a heart to pamper some new servant."

"You did it behind my back!"

"No. The timing reflected the coming of Corinth's unwanted issue. And I was anticipating the Planters Hotel Gala. I couldn't wait until I had the chance to see you face-to-face."

"My overseer says your nephew tried to take advantage of the Negress twice—in the field and in the laundryhouse."

"My! To have poor white mongrels set upon us! Yes, Theodore looked her over when he saw her, I'm sure. He wouldn't suggest that I put Ann with any lash-scarred gal."

Abram sighed, seeing the discussion was getting him nowhere.

"I came not just for your sake, old man, but for the sake of our children. A talk about Brant and Ann is long overdue. It's been cruel to them and unseemly to others for us to be giving them no direction."

"Brant knows my direction! A marriage between him and Annie is bound to failure, and I have told him so. If that's what you've come about—"

"I beg to differ. Goodness, Callie! We've reared them almost like siblings, and they're still the best of friends. There's no doubting they feel perfect for each other after all these years."

"Starting out together does not mean that two young persons will end up together. I've given this my closest attention. They have grown up to be very *unlike* each other."

"How can you say that?"

Abram hesitated. "There's the difference in our faiths."

"Ah! You still consider me a backslidden heathen."

Abram said nothing, though his mind went back over many things. Soon after Oribel's death there had been a parting of ways between this friend and himself. He had risked talking to Linford about his newfound commitment to making Jesus Christ the center of his life, but his companion of a lifetime, armed with Teddy's college texts, had mocked him for being so provincial in an "era of liberal universalism." Basically Linford had come to believe that mankind had outgrown its need for a savior. But now the man was speaking as though they saw things eye to eye.

"I don't reject faith, just some of the popular pathways to it. I don't want Negroes in the celestial city with me. And I'm not patient with anybody who says I must be a worm before God will make me a butterfly." He pulled his chair in closer to Abram as the rain poured down more heavily. "Finally, I do not like the weeping and wailing of your present-day revivals, for they make the white worshiper look and sound exactly like your hooting, dim-witted Negroes." He brushed a raindrop from his knee. "However, what I cannot deny is that Christianity *in general* does give morality and substance to civilization. I see it in the way your son conducts himself toward my daughter, and as the daddy of a precious girl, I am grateful for that. So much so that I am planning to enroll Ann in Dr. Bachman's catechism class this summer."

Suddenly Abram took notice, and the other planter laughed. "Don't look so surprised! We Renslers do know we have souls. If Ann wants to believe that God has spoken through Jesus, then I can be tolerant, so long as she's under the tutelage of someone like Bachman. I'm not for emotionalism, but I'll respect a pure and sincere rendition of the Gospel."

Abram felt some excitement. "When and how did such interest grow in her? Brant has not said a word about it!"

"Ah, that's regrettable." Linford's face softened. "Perhaps that's more telling of *his* current religious demeanor than hers."

Abram took that as criticism and found it difficult to be gracious. "Linford, have you not thought that this may just be pretense on Ann's part? Surely she knows by now how I feel about Brant's marrying outside the community of faith."

Rensler appeared more than slightly insulted. "All I can tell you is what I know. I spoke with her last night. As soon as we move into Charleston, she wants to start attending Dr. Bachman's classes. As an infant she was baptized in that church, so I will support her. Will you also give her a chance? You're the one purporting, 'Christ first, Christ only.' "

Abram leaned back wearily.

"I thought you would be pleased as a mule in a hayfield! Where's your zeal gone, Callie? Or is it only slave conversions that you rejoice in now?"

"Lin, you have a very hard tongue for one still claiming to be my friend! Of course I'm pleased. But I am cautious, too, because I think I know young minds. I see danger here. Perhaps we are being manipulated by our children. I'm not going to make an about-face concerning marriage just because of this report."

"Ah, Abram! These last years have rendered you so pessimistic. And here, you're the one who's supposed to be full of joy and goodwill toward others! Why, then, am I the only one feeling the need for celebration? I'll tell you why! Because I believe these two are right for each other!"

"You would be happy if your daughter accepted the Gospel and claimed Jesus Christ as her sole Savior and Lord?"

"Of course, man. I've never been against it. It's just that I respect people who lead with their heads, not with their emotions. I'm not for spiritual pretending, but I'll even go with my daughter to St. John's if she wants me to. Is that permissible by your standards?"

Abram looked to the banister where he had wrapped his hands just minutes ago. The chill in the air was stronger than before. *Oh ye of little faith!* He quoted the scriptural admonishment to himself in silence. Perhaps his few prayers for this man were being answered, and he was not even being grateful. At that moment he repented and breathed a new prayer for his neighbor. "I'm glad you came, and I'm happy for the news," he said, willfully turning himself to a different attitude.

Linford smiled.

"Brant has moved to the city for the summer," Abram told him. "He has a job with General Morton, helping to police exports and imports for the Graftons."

"Is that so?" Linford seemed both surprised and pleased. "Then perhaps he would like to go to church with us."

"I'm sure of it," Abram said without much enthusiasm.

"It's going to make for a lonely summer for you, Callie. Can't you think of moving to the city, just this once?"

"Delora is the center of my responsibility and my home. And . . . well, it may be the last crop I ever see to harvest."

Linford seemed grieved. "How can I help you?"

"Prayer . . ."

"What about your younger children? Don't you worry about exposing them to the dangerous miasmas?"

"I have no choice. I'm not for letting them live under Brant's lone supervision, and I don't want them only in the servants' care."

The other man kept frowning. "What would you say to letting Eric and Mayleda spend the summer with us?" He brightened. "That could be beneficial all around, for Ann needs something to occupy her time, and she could easily tutor both of them from her course work at Pemberton."

"I . . . I don't know what to say." For himself, Abram immediately disliked the unexpected offer, but for his children's sake, he considered their isolation and the lack of feminine touch in their lives.

"Well, think about it." Linford grinned. "We can be ready to receive them at a moment's notice. I know Annie would enjoy Mayleda's company most especially."

Abram let his eyes drift from Linford. Losing Mayleda and Eric too! Was this offer one of Providence or temptation? Was it a sign that he would lose his ability to hold his family together? He had a strong and sad foreboding concerning death. "I will think about it, Lin. Be certain that I will."

The colonel stood. "Let me send Teddy over to have another look at you. You need medical attention. That is as clear as the nose on your face. None of us wants to lose you, friend."

Abram remembered the ineffectiveness of all the doctors who had cared for his family, Teddy included. Instead of comfort from Linford's easy words, he felt worry. If he died, this man could be a controlling factor in his children's destinies. For a moment he felt totally helpless. "I shall call for another doctor if I must. For now, Theodore will continue to stay away."

"Entirely your choice," Linford shrugged, "though I thought you'd see Christlike forgiveness to be the order of the day. It would do you good if you could bring yourself to doctor with Teddy. He has good training—"

"I have standards and rules that I will maintain." Abram brought himself up even while fighting the feeling that he was deteriorating and losing the battle for both life and his family.

Linford set his high hat on his head, then tipped the brim. "Yes, you have your own ways. That is for certain."

Abram stayed in his chair, letting the wind toss him as the other planter bid him good-day. When he finally heard Linford down on the driveway, he stood and made his way to the rail to look over the edge. Below, Rensler sat on his leggy, hot-blooded stallion. He dashed away up the sticky sand driveway, just as Teddy would have done, setting a reckless and merciless pace for the horse in the rain.

––––––––––

After only two evenings, Joseph had already found Payne's school to be a glorious refuge. Reluctantly leaving the school building just minutes before curfew on Tuesday night, he was compelled to run the whole two blocks to Miss Gail's gate to avoid the patrols. He walked into the kitchen where Aunty Allis was working by the fire. Though younger, thinner, and lighter on her feet than Bette, she still reminded him of Delora's maum because of her nonstop industry.

"Where's Luck?" she said the moment he walked in.

"I don't know, ma'am." Joseph's eyes widened as his mind went to the whipping that Peckory had taken the day before. Had the patrollers some-how tracked down Luck too?

"Have you been at the mill this whole time?" She questioned him as though she were his mama.

"No, ma'am." He confessed this with reluctance, because he had been warned by Wahl not to say anything to anybody about his attendance at school. But he knew the secret was already out, because he had told Luck. What surprised him next was that Tag spoke up about him while he was sitting at the table shelling peas.

"I know where he come from, Mama, 'cause I done saw him go there just afta five chimes from the clock this evenin'."

The mother commanded Tag to tell what he knew. "He done been to the colored schoolhouse." He grinned like an imp.

"Joseph, you—!"

"It's aaall right, ma'am!" He tried to reassure her. "Both Mr. Wahl and my master know I . . . I am going there."

"Why did that man put you into this house?" She was halfway between screaming and crying.

"I am keeping it a secret from everybody!" Joseph promised.

"If'n my seven-year-old chile can find it out in just one day, then how long you think it gwine take 'fore the aldermen an' the paterollers know?"

"But it's not illegal, ma'am. If anybody questions me, I will tell them to taaalk to Mister Wahl. He knows all about it."

"They gwine accuse us all of learnin' off of you!" she fretted. Her hands were drawn out of her wash water, a sure symbol of her worry. "They gwine think Luck the one gettin' instruction! They gwine find ways to abuse him just like they did his daddy for knowin' how to read." She was wailing.

"I will not teach him, ma'am. I promise—"

"It don't matter what you *will* or *will not* do, but only what *they* think you doin'!"

"I promise on a staaack of Bibles, ma'am, no one will see me going to school."

"I follow you, easy!" Tag said, destroying his argument.

But Allis wasn't listening anymore. "Where is Luck? For true, don't you know?"

Joseph was struggling to think of a way to calm her when Luck strode in. Immediately Allis's tears were traded for rage.

"Where have you been?"

"Haulin' home a load of groundnuts, Mama." Luck looked very pleased. "There wa' a buyer on the docks t'day, an' I did some extra on-the-side work for him. He done paid me in this way." Luck pulled in a bulging burlap sack as wide as a wash kettle and almost as high as his waist.

She was amazed. "He done give you all that?"

"Yes, indeedy." Luck smiled. "So, t'night some of the fellers an' me gwine wrap these up into neat, small bundles, so's we can sell 'em door-t'door an' on the streets."

"That sack's free an' clear? You sure of it?" she asked, worry in her voice.

"Ma, of course. I'm not fool 'nough to sell stolen goods."

She slipped her hands back into the water. Joseph could see she was thinking by the squinting of her eyes.

"How many bundles? An' how much you gwine ask for them?"

"We'll figure all that out t'night. Now don't you be worryin' when you see the man comin' in here directly."

"What! The buyer? An' he be white, I guess!"

"Sure, Mama, but—"

"Don't you but me! You tell what's gwine on here, an' you tell it now, as God be listenin'!"

The heat of her agitation was intense enough to drive Joseph back to the nearest kitchen wall. Tag, too, was tremulous, but Luck stood his ground.

"He gwine bring us some scales. An' he gwine stay with us like he wa' our overseer, so's we have the freedom to finish the job without paterollers comin' an' findin' us not bein' supervised by any white man, as the law requires."

"What he be askin' in return for all this 'kindness'?" She was squinting again.

"Nothin'! We done already helped him. Like I says, we done unloaded special cargo for him."

She seemed dubious, but after a while she took Tag by the shoulder and went up into the main house. Joseph started to the cellar, but Luck came to him.

"Mista Tom Diller's back on Anson Street." His voice was lower than the crackling of the diminishing fire in the wide open fireplace.

Joseph stayed near the wall. "I'm not going to hear that man again."

"You don't have to, 'cause he's the one what's comin' here."

Appalled, Joseph immediately brushed past Luck to the cellar stairs. "What about your mama, your brother, your aunt? You're putting them aaall in danger!" he said, taking the first step down.

"They won't s'spect nothin'. An' neither would you, if you hadn't seen the feller a'ready."

"I waaant nothing to do with this! Yesterday I saaw a man at the mill whipped for being at that meeting Friday. And I'm not going to risk having my flesh look like that!" His tongue was aching as it had not done in a while.

Luck scoffed. "The bossman wa' real sure to show you the marks, ainty? Don't you know he done that just to scaire you?"

"It's not because I'm fearful. I'm doing what I think is right."

Luck went and opened the sack with a knife as Joseph spoke. Several handfuls of sand-colored peanuts fell out to the floor, but what Joseph saw in Luck's hand was a newspaper.

"We gwine wrap these up into two sheets. The outside just gwine be an old piece of newsprint from Cha'leston, but the inside be different."

Joseph glimpsed the large print on the paper's banner: *Liberator!* Instantly the name told him it was contraband. "I don't want anything to do with this!"

"Sure! You been somebody's boy so long you don't even know how to be you' own self. Oh, you love you' massas! Scum! You don't even deserve to *know* how to beat slavery once an' for all." He shook the paper in his hand. "But this here's the printed voice of the American Antislavery Society. Down here it's called the most dangerous document ever to show up on our shores."

"Why do you bring it here when you can't eeeven read it?"

" 'Cause there's plenty what can! An' I'm not selfish like *some* folk I know. I want to give the message of hope."

"This is too daaangerous, too fruitless!"

"Mebbe. Mebbe not. But one thing I do know—it would be a whole heap safer for me if I did know how to read. As it is, I am as dependent as a blind man on this northerner. But if *I* could read, *I* could be in control . . . an' better able to watch out for myself an' my family."

"Luck, I am nooot going to teach you."

"That's too bad, for someday it might mean the difference 'tween life an' death for me."

"You can saaave you'self just by stopping now! Tell this Mr. Tom who-ever-he-is to staaay out of here! He can't know what it's like to be a slave."

"For true, but that don't mean he can't help us neither. We gwine 'stri-bute these papers unda the guise of sellin' groundnuts to our neighbors. An' if the paterollers be lucky enough to catch us, well, *you* be hauled off with the rest of us."

"I won't be involved! Do you hear me?"

"You *a'ready* involved, just by knowin' me an' livin' here."

"Then I'm leaving."

He laughed out loud. "To where? You go out on the street, the patrol will catch you for sure an' have your backside cut by mornin'."

Joseph ran into the cellar, then came back with his mat. "I'll leave this house to staaay in the yard. I tell you! I have too much goooing to risk all because of *you*."

"Don't I know that." His voice sounded hollow. "But you the only priv-ileged nigger here what's been allowed to go to school. An' that's not hel-pin' the rest of us, nohow."

Joseph's breath caught on his rough tongue. "Don't hooold it against me. I was told by my master whaaat to do and not do."

"Hmm. You's a slave through an' through."

"No! I just dooon't want to risk what I have!"

"Ahun! You doin' fine for now, so why worry 'bout any of the rest of us?"

"I dooon't mean it like that."

"Yes, indeed, you do. 'Cause if you meant it any other whichway, you'd teach me while we still had a chance."

There was a soft rapping on the door, though it was already opened. When Luck went and pushed it wide, Joseph glimpsed a white face. That was enough for him. He hurried by the unwelcomed northerner and went outside to the farthest, darkest corner of the walled, leaf-cluttered yard. With frustration and worry he sat down on his mat. He begged God to rescue him, to show him what to do. The last thing he wanted was to be entrapped in a plan for insurrection that he cared nothing about.

The light from the kitchen continued for hours. He ended up sleeping under the stars, since the illegal project took most of the night. Tag woke him before dawn as he set out to extinguish the streetlights.

"What you doin' here?" he asked.

Joseph looked up at him, too confused to say. When he got up, he left his tick right where it was and hurried off to work, putting the incident out of his mind.

It did not surface again until late that afternoon when Peckory approached him with an all-too-knowing grin. He offered Joseph a handful of groundnuts taken from a newspaper sack. Joseph said nothing while refusing him.

The moment his mill work ended, Joseph fled to Payne's school.

On Friday afternoon it rained so violently that Billy and Mr. Gund had to let all the field hands go in early. Negozi came back to the row of shanties, saying it was on her mind to make a goodly supply of sweet, warm hoecakes in those precious idle hours so that all who dwelt under her roof might eat them. After nearly a week without food, Rosa was ravenous. She did not trust her endurance by staying inside even to smell the dry cornmeal, which itself would have cut like metal in her hollow stomach. Miserably, she traded going back out in the rain for the dry interior, thinking that this might be the hour when she would go insane.

Abiel was on the sagging porch mending his circular fishing net. Slipping by him, Rosa had no trouble getting away to the drainage ditch close to the place where she had found Joseph. She had held hopes that in starvation, life would simply drain away without creating anguish. She had started her hunger strike thinking only of death and its end result—safety from this world, rest, and sweet reunion with her only joy from this life, little Kulo. But now she was stuck lingering . . . and living.

She was dizzy, hot, then cold. The rain coming down on her scraggly, matted hair only added to her torture. Looking longingly at the mud around her, she considered filling her mouth with it. But she resisted the temptation by telling herself if she kept herself hungry for just a few more hours, then maybe she finally would ebb away.

Like the Africans, she crouched instead of sitting, hiding herself in the weeds that glistened with rain jewels. Even with the abuse to her body last week, her monthly cycle had remained unbroken. The small flow of blood she had discovered that morning told her that at least she would not have to birth a buckra's child. Evidence of an empty womb challenged her to rethink her plan for escaping life through death. For an instant she gave into her natural inclination toward self-preservation and sucked the rain from her fingers.

The next thing she knew, Parris was parting the weeds and putting himself down at her side. Every day since the rape he had sought her out. She should have heard him coming by the terrible clinking of the chains he dragged along with him.

"You need come in an' find some pro'tection, gal," he said softly.

Why should she? She was hoping to die as quickly as she could.

"Rosa, you must try to conquer this longin' for death."

She looked away, more set than ever on ending it all after seeing those hateful shackles locked around a man who had risked himself on a mission to avenge her.

"No matter what you think, this here ain't hell. But I am sure there's gwine be a hell afta this life on earth." He had said these words to her every day since they had put him into irons. "I don't honestly know if I believe in the massa's sort of heaven no more. But it don't take no god to make a hell. Buckra men can do that! Girl! Think on what you doin'! You don't know if dyin' can be in you' favor or not. No man nor woman has ever crossed River Death an' come back to talk 'bout it."

"Go away."

Parris never lingered, and he never argued with her. "A'right. Just so's you know that as long as you still on *this* side, I gwine see you an' care 'bout how you doin'." He raised his head with dignity but kept his eyes away. "You keep thinkin' on the things I say to you." Then he stood in the rain.

When he left, she got a morbid sense of satisfaction by looking down at herself. Truly she was changing. Oh, how she longed for that day when there would be no more fullness in her breasts, no more viable womb beneath her caved-in belly, and nothing comely to the hard, brown skin that would cling to her skeleton like paint. She curled her head against her chest and put her arms up over the wet carpet of her hair. Parris was right in that there were terrors to be faced in both living and dying.

But still she pressed herself toward the latter because of her repeating nightmares that men of all races were taking her again and again. Because she could not overcome or overpower these fears, she stayed with her plan to at least overcome and destroy herself to be away from them.

Inside, her mind was pounding. With Negozi's help she had continued to conjure against Theodore Rensler. What scared her now was that the planter was still alive and well while she was on the horrible route toward dying. Was it possible that the devil had already taken control and had turned the conjuring back upon the conjurer? She feared that greatly—to be trapped inside her own evil. By hating Rensler so much, she felt as though she had tapped into a root of poison. But instead of being able to destroy the buckra with it, the poison seemed to be destroying her. And what of the hell she hoped for, the one where Rensler would be there writhing and rotting forever? What if someone or something was working the same black magic on her to trap her there forever? What if Satan himself delighted in her scheme? What if demons were the ones driving her to such anguish and such a loathsome end?

Parris had warned her that the darkness after this life might be ten thousand times darker than the darkness she knew now. He had challenged her more than once to think what would happen if death did lead to hell and if hell were worse than life. Then what recourse would she have? Would there be a second death to save her from eternal burning? Parris thought not. And neither did she. Into her weak, wet hands, Rosa began weeping. The fear of death—*timor mortis*—had truly come to her.

Suddenly she grabbed at reeds growing up through the scummy water. Frantically she yanked them out by the leaves and crunched down on their gritty, bulbous roots. "Oh, God!" she cried, not knowing if there was a God. "If death is even worse than this life, then let me go on living!"

CHAPTER 21

FOREMAN WAHL'S CALENDAR changed slowly until August arrived. Then the mill's huge two-hundred-fifty-pound pine pestles were set in motion in anticipation of the barges, flatboats, and wagons that would soon bear down on Charleston from every direction with their loads of unhulled rice. Joseph now understood the foreman's wisdom of having trained him in the spring. There would be no time for questions or errors now. Orders would be taken hourly, and he could make no mistakes with the handwritten assignments that often looked as foreign as Teacher Payne's book in Greek.

Even this first morning of the month was busy. There was no time for talk or for Peckory's quibbling. Joseph scurried between jobs, making certain that every rice merchant remained confident and pleased with Graftons' operations.

Hurrying by the most recently installed pestle, he smelled something unusually hot. Smoke was curling from a shaft overhead. Shouting for someone to find Wahl, Joseph climbed a nearby ladder to the next floor and alerted workmen there. He grabbed a piece of metal and started ripping up boards at his feet to expose the overheated machinery. Soon others rushed toward him with leather buckets and doused the smoking junction before the mill dust could ignite and explode. The crisis was over almost as soon as it had begun.

Joseph came back down to the main floor, shaking. He had just saved the mill from disaster, and Mr. Wahl did not forget him. At noontime Joseph was put at the head of the line and given extra brown bread. Then while he was eating, one of the Grafton sons came to meet him personally.

"You're a fine boy," he said as Mr. Wahl stood nearby, beaming. "For your good service, I'm giving you some coin and letting you off to spend the rest of the day as you please."

Joseph looked to Wahl, not believing the young owner. But the foreman took the money and pressed it into Joseph's hand. Joseph was so taken aback that he stood fingering the dollar's worth of silver even after the white men had walked away. Peckory, Harris, and others came up, congratulating him and teasing him for being such a "bright Negro."

He was close to being surly with them, for having earned something for himself was a moment of wonder, one he wanted wholly for himself. In all his working days he had never had so much as a half cent of his own. Now here he was holding *his dollar*. No one had to advise him what to do. Immediately he went outside and, in the shadow of the mill, separated out ten cents for the Cumberland Street Church collection plate and slipped that in his shoe. Then, gripping the remainder of his godsend, he headed straight for King Street to the bookstore, where he knew every item in the window by heart.

Within a half hour Joseph had exchanged his precious earnings for three treasures—a pencil, a blank notebook, and a small bound volume of English poetry. Heading quickly to Miss Gail's, he found Aunty Allis filling pails at the city well. He tucked his purchases into the loose waistline of his pants so that his hands were free to help her. She worried about seeing him. "What you doin' here at this hour?"

"The bossman left me off," he answered, still almost in heaven and thinking numbly on how he had just walked in and purchased a book—for Rosa. "And now I'm on my way to school early!" He felt as liberated as his tongue, which had healed almost fully during the long summer's weeks.

She shook her head wrapped in yellow-and-orange cloth. "Someday, somehow, they gwine find you out. I know it!"

Joseph didn't heed her anxiety. He was excited about having extra hours for study. Yet Maum Bette and his mama would have flailed him had he, a young man, neglected to first fill this woman's kettles. With many rapid trips, he served her. Then, rushing inside one last time, he exchanged his sweaty clothes for those he kept just for school. Emerging from the hot kitchen and feeling respectable, he was in the street just as the steeple clock struck three.

He gave no thought to what he was doing except that he was getting to school early—and with his own book, notebook, and pencil. When he opened the school yard gate, four light-skinned youths, all on the edge of manhood, quickly met him. Before Joseph could even decide what his re-action should be, they pinned him roughly to the school yard wall.

"What are you up to?" the largest of them grilled him as another fingered the loathsome copper badge of bondage hanging by a string around his neck. A third kept him immobilized while the fourth stole his things. "Blackie slave!" they taunted. "You think you're coming in here—for school?"

Joseph had no time to answer, for Mr. Daniel Payne marched up to his tormentors. The teacher was young enough and light enough to look just like one of them. He was smaller than they, yet fiercer than a shrew.

"Unhand him! This is ungentlemanly and un-Christian behavior. You all should be ashamed of yourselves!"

Immediately the students scattered out the gate like chickens from a coop. Joseph's eyes trailed them, for he was quite sure one of them was the same youth he had seen on patrol in the fishmonger's shop. Before Teacher Payne could say anything, Joseph dropped his head as though this man were his master.

"I'm sooorry, sir," he stammered, though his mouth was healed. "I didn't consider the problem of coming early."

Payne picked up the books and pencil and gave them back. "Go inside."

Joseph was nervous, for he thought he heard disapproval in Payne's voice. In the classroom the teacher pointed for him to take his usual seat.

"Those four stayed behind to help plan a trip out to Sullivan's Island in search of reptiles," he explained. "They were wrong in how they treated you. I hope you know that."

"Yes, sir." Joseph looked up cautiously. He could see anguish on his teacher's face.

"They've been taught to be protective of brown-society privileges.

They model their parents' opposition to slave education."

"Yes, sir." The words were extremely painful.

The teacher looked at Joseph's new notebook. "What need have you of that?"

Joseph's hands grew hot as he clung to it. "I . . . I hoped to copy some information."

"What! Maps? A geography text, perhaps? Do you know I will lose my school if someone discovers you doing this?"

"Oh no! I never thought of copying that sort of thing!"

Payne frowned. "Then what?"

Joseph paused, realizing that maps and geography could help him plan an escape. "I . . . I was hoping that you might have a book on medicine." He stopped again, feeling foolish for his idea. "It would be for my master's sake, sir, to do what I can to save him from yellow fever."

The teacher removed his protective glasses. His eyes were compassion filled. "Forgive me." He looked away. "I was as wrong as my students were to prejudge you." His fingers knit together after he had put his glasses away.

Joseph was moved by the man's humility. He sensed that something very deep was troubling the spirit of this one whom he had come to admire and respect above all other men.

Payne looked to his meager supply of texts lined up against the wall. "Books are expensive and difficult to obtain even for white men. I don't have any on medicine or even on sciences. That is why I am putting together my own study manual based on the things I observe firsthand." He stroked his chin with one thumb. "You may read as much as I have, for that will at least give you a first look at animal anatomy."

"You would not mind my doing this?"

His smile showed weariness. "No."

"Then you don't think me foolish?"

"Never!" Payne walked behind him. "Tell me something, Joseph. If you were like the students you just met outside—free and endowed with material wealth—what would you do?"

Joseph felt a great uncomfortable weight in contrasting himself with those others. "I . . . I think I would study to be a doctor, if that were possible."

Payne came around and faced him. "Why would it not be possible?"

Joseph dipped his head.

Suddenly the teacher was adamant. "It is a worthy dream! No one should have the right to sway you from it."

"A worthy dream—for them!" Joseph dared to look up at his instructor. "An impossible one for me!"

The teacher put his hand on Joseph's new notebook lying unopened upon the desk. "You cannot say that for sure, since no one knows the future. If the yoke of bondage were lifted, then you could do it. You could! You have the Gospel. You are receiving education. And you are one of my most gifted and dedicated students. Oh, Joseph, I desire you to know that the true freeman is the one whom the Lord sets free. I cannot promise a thing about the future, but don't let discouragement ever keep you from pursuing the highest endeavors possible. Let others be the cause of your inability to reach a goal, but don't be the cause of it yourself."

Joseph dared to look at the young philosopher fully. Payne smiled before getting papers from his desk. The man returned and began to speak about himself.

"I committed my life wholly to Christ just a few years back, when I was eighteen. Soon after that, during a time of ardent prayer, I felt as though someone actually came and laid His hands upon my shoulders. Deep within my soul I heard God say, '*I have set you apart to educate yourself in order that you may be an educator of your people.*'" Payne's countenance was glowing, looking dark and rich in the afternoon sunlight. "That is why, in part, I dare to take bondsmen and bondswomen as students. I believe it to be God's call."

Joseph could feel his own spirit soaring.

"When I got up off my knees that day after hearing God speak, I was still the same poor brown city orphan as before, having to do carpentry and tailoring just to keep myself fed and clothed. But I began to pray for books. . . ." He put his hand toward the shelf. "God provides! I started studying in the predawn hours because my days were not my own. I made tables, racks, even corset stays for women's fashion—anything!—to sustain myself." He smiled as though it was good to remember these hard times. "God calls. God gives. It is seldom easy, and within the bonds of slavery it must seem impossible. But if you can catch even a glimpse of what you are to do, then pursue it!"

Joseph's mind flooded with the events that had brought him here. He knew that his determination to read and the awful slicing of his tongue had been the start of it. He remembered the April sunrise, and suddenly he was fighting tears. "No one has ever talked to me this way, sir. At times

I do think I am hearing the voice of the Lord, but then circumstances destroy my hope."

"Joseph! Listen to yourself!" Payne said with wonder. "You have spoken all that is in your heart so clearly. Even in the slow but steady healing of your tongue, God has graciously intervened, for you've told me that it was the parish doctor's plan to keep you mute forever."

"God has healed me!" Joseph rejoiced, daring to say it for the first time. "Yes, He has!"

In full introspection Payne brought his thumbs to his lips. "My own colored teacher, Mr. Thomas Bonneau, started a library for Negroes here in Charleston. I will go there tomorrow to see what kinds of medical readings I can find." There was a mischievous sparkle in his eyes. "I will! But only if you will do something for me. I want you to start taking regular examinations . . . like this one I am preparing for my advanced students."

Joseph touched his chest as the papers came to his desk. "You want me to take tests, just as they do?"

"Absolutely. Our talk today has set me thinking that someday you may need a written record of your accomplishments. Besides, I believe you are ready to expand your horizons. Tell me. Have you ever dreamed of knowing any of the other languages I have here? Greek or Hebrew or. . . ?"

"Oh yes! Latin!" That was the language of Rosa's strange-sounding poem—the same one he had just found reprinted in the volume he had purchased for her.

Payne laughed at his enthusiasm. "Well, I am very glad I asked! Let that be your incentive to do well on your first examination. You may take it next Saturday evening when no else is here. If you do your English and composition correctly, I promise you a Latin lesson."

"Then English and composition is what I will study until our regular lessons begin!"

"No doubt!" Payne tapped the desk with much good humor. "You do that, and I'll be back to share a Scripture reading with you and to start your regular instruction promptly at a quarter past five." The teacher left beaming, and immediately Joseph became engrossed in his work. He hardly knew when Payne was gone and when he had returned.

That evening they went through their normal regimen of classes, then Payne left him alone again for his final hour of independent study. Eventually the other man returned to light a candle.

"Watch your time," he said. "It will soon be curfew."

"I can't believe that!" Joseph looked up to see how dim the room had become during his hours of concentration.

"You had better leave now!" the teacher said.

Joseph put away Payne's books, then slipped his own new purchases under his shirt and into the small of his back. Payne watched him with concern.

"Joseph? That scar . . ."

"Yes, sir?"

"Was that made by those who oppose preaching to Negroes?"

"Yes, sir. It happened at Delora before I came here."

Payne's worry increased. "I know there are individuals of that persuasion here in Charleston."

"Yes, I know that, too, Teacher Payne." Their gazes connected for a moment. It thrilled Joseph to see the admiration and warmth so transparent in the other Negro's eyes.

"You need to be very careful. Especially if you're going to take your books with you."

"I will be, sir."

Payne walked with him as far as the gate. It was still quite light when Joseph started out, but before he had gone one block, the bell of St. Michael's started chiming. That set him to running. Seven . . . eight . . . nine . . .

Suddenly a swarm of patrolmen rounded the corner, their stamping horses filling the air with dust. The frothy steeds turned in on him just as he put his hand to Miss Gail's gate.

"Check his ticket and his work tag!" the captain roared while Joseph stood, his hands to the wood. The boy ordered down to do this was the same youth he had seen in both the shop and the school yard. The nervous young Negro demanded both kinds of identification while the white men and the older brown man stayed in their saddles.

"This is his place, sir," the boy tenuously called up to the white leader.

"I want his tag number anyway!"

Joseph glimpsed what seemed to be the brown youth's sorry look, and the captain did not miss it either.

"Philip Handsome, the whip will come to you, boy, if I find out you're taking up for any of your colored cousins."

The other youth demeaned himself just like a servant for the moment. "I have his tag number, sah! Charleston Servant, six-four-eight."

Joseph shook, for as Philip turned him around, there was no mistaking that the other youth felt the books hidden at his waist. Yet this Philip

Handsome said nothing to the men haughtily waiting over him. When he finally was released, Joseph stood frozen until the patrol was away. He was left with the very odd feeling that he might have just met a friend among his enemies.

Luck met him at the kitchen door. "You' massa's here!"

"Mister Wahl!"

"No. You' plantation massa—a Mista Callcott!"

"Which one?" Joseph cried, his nerves still on edge from what had just happened in the street. "I saw no carriage."

"I dunno!" Luck snorted, nearly having to pull him inside. "He up in Aunty Gail's sittin' room, an' he been there half 'n hour." Whatever was the cause of the visit, Joseph thought, it could only be made worse by the fact that he was coming in after curfew.

Luck pushed him to get him moving and likely he felt the books in his shirt just as Philip had. Having never been inside the main house, Joseph climbed the few interior stairs to the second floor, entered a dark hall, and then found his way to a bare, lighted room. Shaking every step of the way, he almost cried his relief to see Master Abram, not Brant, seated in Miss Gail's only half-decent chair. Instantly he felt poor and shabby in his master's presence.

Approaching the gentleman while keeping his head low, Joseph saw how much older and thinner Abram looked. The slaveowner must have been assessing him in the silence too.

"Don't they feed you, boy?" These were the first words from his mouth.

Joseph looked up. "Mr. Wahl gives us our meal a day, sir."

"That is not enough!" Abram slipped to the edge of the seat and took hold of Joseph's wrists by making circles around them with his fingers. "I will speak to Mr. Wahl the moment I leave here! Now tell me, what else should I know? How are you? Tell me everything!"

Joseph felt awkward yet relieved, as though part of home had been brought to him quite unexpectedly. He did not know what to say, for he was having a hard time believing Abram had come just to see him.

Still holding on to him, the master said breathily, "You've spoken a clear sentence to me already. Your tongue has been restored! God has answered my prayers!"

Feeling the quaking of his master's hands and their bony deathlikeness, Joseph had concern for him. He had kept his pledge to pray for this man daily. "Sir, you are still unwell."

A familiar cloaked smile came back at him. "I am feeling better now than I have all summer."

Joseph's time of separation had not ended his intimate understanding of this man. Abram was still struggling with illness, though he chose not to mention it.

"How is it going at the mill?" The man turned the attention back on him.

"Fine, sir."

The man shook his head and then smiled more broadly. "It's better than fine! I was there this afternoon and heard how you saved the building from disaster!"

Joseph could not deny that he liked the praise, but he did not acknowledge that openly. "Anybody would have done it, sir. I was just the one to see it."

"And to act quickly and wisely." His master voiced his pride. "Mr. Wahl is very well pleased with you." His pause was brief. "And how is school?"

"I like it, sir," Joseph said, wondering if Abram had been to see Teacher Payne too.

The man looked around the deserted room. "I would like to hear you read."

"Except for private devotions I do not read in this house, sir."

The planter's frown seemed full of understanding. "Yes, I suppose that is wise, considering the aldermen's opinions in this city. Where do you keep the Bible I gave you?"

"In my mattress, sir."

"I want to see where you stay."

Joseph was hesitant to intrude on Luck and Allis by bringing a white man into their world.

"Is something wrong? Is there something you are hiding?" Abram inquired.

"No!" It was distressing how easily his master could distrust him.

"Then show me where you sleep."

"Yes, Master Abram." Joseph felt bitterly aware that he had no choice. "Come this way."

Joseph led him down unstable stairs to a smoky, drab shed having stained whitewashed walls and a huge blackened fireplace. The dirt-floored room was deserted, but Abram still could feel the presence of its people, for a black caldron was steaming over the fire, and there were chipped pottery bowls on the table, as though the residents here had departed in haste at his coming. His boy led him down another short set of steps to a cellar with clay bricks on the floor. In one corner, his former houseservant had a thin, moss-filled tick. Beside it sat Eric's chest, still packed in perfect order. There was no light in the room except that which shone from a streetlamp through an open glassless window.

Abram trembled with the unsteadiness that had been afflicting him all summer. He relied more fully on his cane.

Instantly Joseph noticed and apologized, "I'm sorry, sir, there is no chair down here."

"That's all right." Abram lightly braced himself against the damp wall. "Will you read for me now?" He was aware that he had made his request into a question. Master to slave, he should have simply stated his desire, yet this moment seemed too unusual for that.

The first thing Joseph did was to close the shutters, obscuring the light somewhat. For a second Abram experienced fear. What was this boy doing? Then Joseph pulled away one loose lath to give them some light and much more privacy. Kneeling down on his bed, he uncovered the book as though it were a precious, ancient manuscript. Abram saw the way Joseph kept it wrapped delicately in one of his clean shirts.

"What do you want me to read, sir?" Joseph asked as he stood.

Already Abram's emotions were swelling. "Whatever you choose," he managed awkwardly.

Quietly Joseph turned the papers. Abram let himself remember that this was his *African slave* facing him with the Bible. His throat closed and his eyes burned at the sound of Joseph's very first word, for this was August first, and Joseph had chosen to read the first chapter of the book of Proverbs. Each word was perfect as he went through the chapter on how a young man must obtain godly wisdom. It moved Abram so that he could scarcely breathe.

Intellectually and spiritually this young man could easily be his son!

Joseph hid the text away and then hastened up the stairs without asking, coming back with a bench to put against the wall.

"Sir! Please rest! What more can I do for you?"

Abram was moved by Joseph's compassion. The boy's serving heart stripped him bare and put his sin and blindness before him all the more. "I want nothing! What I wanted I have more than fully received. You have proven how wrong I've been! All that remains now is to know what must come after repentance for belittling you and your kind all these years!" He put his face in his hands. Had he ever doubted that he would see manly capacities in Joseph after releasing him to this? If he were honest with himself—No! Then why did the boy's accomplishments strike him so hard now? Because they were proof of something he had allowed himself only to speculate before—the equality of their races!

The young man looked at him with sincere questioning. Abram grabbed his wrists again. "You can read! You can think! You can pray! What am I to do as a master because of this?"

"I don't know, sir."

Abram shook his head, despairing at Joseph's pure honesty. He stated what he thought was right to do. "I want you to keep working at the mill, and I'll continue paying Mr. Payne to have you in his school. I will speak to Mr. Wahl about having you stay on in Charleston permanently."

Then he saw the muscles tighten under Joseph's smooth cheek—a sure sign, as it had been since his boyhood, that something was troubling to him. At one time he never would have asked—why should he, as master? But now everything was in the state of change. "What is it? I know that what I've said upsets you."

Joseph seemed amazed. "As much as I love school, sir, I was hoping to be brought home in December. I miss the others, and . . . well, I'm eager to see Rosa."

Abram should not have been surprised, but he was, and he chided himself for that. Where would this new understanding of the African mind take him? And how long would it take him to fully accommodate the simple truths he was seeing now? Of course! If a black man can pray and think and reason just as a white man, then his ability to love and hate must be equal too. Of course the boy might still think of Rosa. He realized then that Joseph knew nothing about what had happened to her.

He forced himself to look into Joseph's earnest face, not knowing what to say. "She's unwell."

Joseph pulled away to hold his hands together. "Please, sir, write a pass for me to visit home! Others have told me that permission can be granted to make visits to other places."

Abram closed his eyes. Joseph spoke of Delora as home, though having known it only as a slave. Nothing could have moved him more deeply, yet he said, "It would not be good for you to visit. Trust me. She desires to see no one."

"Then for *my* sake, please let me go!"

What if this were his son—or Rosa his daughter? The question harangued him. But they were not his children. They were his slaves, and he was obligated by law and convention to treat them as such. "Joseph," he said cautiously, not knowing how to make right sense of all he was feeling. "She will never be well again."

Joseph's worry gave way to ferocious demanding. "What has happened? You must let me see her! Can you not understand why I need to be with her?"

"Yes, I can," Abram confessed glumly. He weighed the next thoughts in his mind. Should he tell the boy what had happened? He feared that rage and the possible use of violence would be the only recourse opened to Joseph if the truth were spoken. Abram tried to pray, but immense walls suddenly seemed in his way. "Joseph," he said, striking out in light of his own uncertain wisdom, "I cannot let you go home, but this is what I will do. As soon as I am back at Delora, I will go to Rosa. I will tell her of your distress. I will see if I can bring her to you. That I promise before God. If I can, I will bring her to the Gibbes Street house and then come personally to bring you to her."

Joseph covered his face with his hand.

"Mr. Wahl needs you too much right at harvesttime. And it's likely that once she turned you away at Delora, your grief would be more poignant than it is even now."

The African turned his back on him. That was not to happen, but Abram let it go. "I'm coming back to Charleston within a week for the Graftons' Rice Ball. If I cannot persuade Rosa to come before then, I'll speak to you on Saturday, for I need you as my waiting man that evening." He had to trust Joseph to be listening, for he still could not see his face. He made another consideration just in case things might change even in one week's time. "I have not been well, and I think you know that," he confessed. "I'm not sure if it's still the lingering first stages of fever or something else. Usually I keep to my bed. That is why I have not seen you till now. However, I'm coming to this party because I have a serious obligation. In June Miss Ann Rensler became a Christian, and I'm going to finally give my consent to Brant and Annie's marriage."

The boy now looked at him with something close to fear.

"She truly has been soundly converted. Even Miss Mayleda says so, for the girls and Eric have spent most of the summer together."

Joseph still seemed unnerved, and then Abram considered the deeper reasons why. "It will not change anything for you, I promise! You can continue with Mr. Wahl—even if I die." He took a breath. "You will never fall into Rensler hands. I have changed my written will so that Mayleda will inherit you. Not Ann and Brant." To speak about him as chattel cut Abram to the core.

Joseph leaned against the wall, and Abram's heart went out to him. Better than ever he understood the incredible circumstances every slave faced because of this most basic question of ownership. "My goal is to live," Abram assured him. "My goal is to continue doing the best for you and all the others under my care."

He could see the African hold his breath while he pushed himself to stand straight again. A moment later Joseph reached behind his back, pulled up his shirt, and uncovered a small book from his waistband. He handed it to Abram.

"Today I received the first money I ever made in all my years of work," he said coolly. "With some of it I purchased this for Rosa. Do I have your blessing to give it to her through you?"

Abram felt as numb as Joseph looked. "Yes. I will take it to her, I promise. No one but the three of us will know."

Then Joseph dared to reach under his shirt again, this time to expose a pencil. Good judgment would have told Abram to confiscate that immediately, but he only watched instead. Opening the book Joseph began to write on the first page. Abram's heart fluttered. By his own doing he had allowed Joseph to learn this skill! In one more way he saw how education had cut his control, and he saw how dangerous Joseph would seem to the whole slaveholding world around them. "You must *never* let anyone see you with paper, book, or pencil!"

"I know, sir." He looked up, pausing as though expecting Abram to take it from him. When Abram did not, Joseph sighed audibly and went on with his writing. Though Abram did not demand it, Joseph left the page open so that he could see the short inscription he had put there. *Dear friend—Let this gift be the evidence that I will love you always.* Wisely Joseph had neglected to use any names.

Searching for adequate words, Abram drew the book to himself. "Originally, boy, I came here to say something I had neglected to say outside the courthouse back in May. I care for you, Joseph. I love you, boy!" It took him a moment to go on. "Now I fear I have made a terrible mistake, for in this society, where can your knowledge lead you?"

"I will have faith in God," Joseph said with only a moment's hesitation. "Whatever is ahead, I will be grateful to you, sir, that you made the way for me to go to school."

Abram had to press the book's cover hard against his chest so that he would not drop it with his trembling hands. Joseph reached and took both the book and cane. Abram nearly wept because of the strong, confident servant who still so freely gave him aid.

"How can I help you home?" Joseph asked with concern.

"Ezra is around the corner with the coach."

"Then, sir, with your permission I will take you to him."

———

Brant had been pacing the first-floor study of the Gibbes Street house, wondering where his ailing father was and why he had said nothing about going anywhere after excusing himself from the Renslers' table following supper in their South Bay home that evening. The moment his daddy came in, supported heavily by Joseph, some of his questions were answered, but a thousand more grew in their place. Joseph actually lifted Brant's daddy in his arms and carried the man up to his bed.

Brant ran up after them but refrained from saying anything. He waited to go into the room until Joseph had his father undressed, in his night-clothes, and put to bed. His father's condition was too troubling and so was the former servant's unanticipated presence. Weak as he was, his father tried to voice an explanation.

"I went over to Anson Street to see how Joseph was getting along. I had an attack of palsy there. He helped Ezra bring me home."

Brant gave the silent slave a quick glimpse that was half grateful. A large part of him wondered what was going on, for Joseph was dressed much too richly for mill work. "I thought you said he was hired out to Graftons to pack rice."

"He is, son."

"I don't believe that! I see his clothes! I think he's wearing one of your own good shirts."

His daddy exchanged a glance with his boy, as they had done so often in his chambers. It made Brant feel outside their secrets once more.

"I'll tell you the whole story," his daddy began. "But you must understand. I was thinking of *you* when I withheld this information."

"What information!"

Again he looked at his slave.

"Joseph *is* working twelve-hour days at Graftons'. If you don't believe that, you can go see him at his work. However, after his job, I am allowing him to go to a Negro school."

Brant threw up his hands. "How can that be! You never even chose to send *me* to school!"

His father's face crumpled. "It was an experiment at first. To see exactly how much a bright young African can know."

"And just what have you found out?" Brant was fuming.

"That Joseph learns and reasons and thinks and feels just as we do. I am sure of that now."

"And what good does that do?" Brant demanded, furious that his daddy had done all this behind his back.

"It does no good," his father said wearily. "But it is the truth, and as Christians we are obligated to know the truth and then to act on it."

At that Brant saw Joseph stir in his place.

"I want him out of here! I promised Ann that we would never let him back in the house because Teddy told her that he's prime insurrectionist material."

"That is not the truth. You know that, son."

"How can anyone know what he might do? And how will you stop him now? I suppose you have let him read *and* write *and* cipher during all these months of secrecy?"

His daddy did not deny it. "Brant, I didn't tell you because I never wanted Theodore or anyone else to pressure you about it."

"But now I know!"

"And now you will not tell."

Again he saw Joseph move, perhaps with fear.

"I'm not sure what I must do next!" Brant spouted in truth.

His daddy's eyes drooped shut. "Part of me is as sorry as you to learn what I have. But, Brant, think! With so many Africans and mulattos embracing the Gospel, this must be God's next step: to instruct us white believers that the colored man is equal to us."

Brant focused totally on the boy, who had his head down. His daddy went on.

"He knows the danger he's in because of the skills he has acquired. However, Brant, now a burden is put on you also. To keep him safe, you must keep this knowledge of his schooling to yourself. And when I am no longer able to do so, then you must do all in your power to protect him as a brother in Christ."

"I would be a fool to speak to anybody about what you have done!" Brant raged, continuing to let the whirlwind of his feelings show. "The patrol! The city police! Our neighbors! They all would drive us out of

South Carolina if they knew. Even now, many of them are working hard to pass legislation that will make *all* Negro education illegal. And they won't wait for a law before coming and rounding us all up!"

"We must move by faith," Abram said. "I'm going to let Joseph continue his education. And now I'm depending on your support—even if my illness or death puts the burden on you."

"I will sell him first rather than continue this!"

"Brant, you will not have that opportunity. I have met with our attorney, and Joseph will be given to Mayleda when I die."

Brant was dumbfounded. "This is not the day to see things just as you *want* to see them, but as they really are! He could destroy us, or others will be bound to destroy him!"

His daddy looked at his slave. "Not if you two help each other. He can serve you, and you can serve him with protection. Now write a ticket so that he can go back to Anson Street. And write one for Ezra to transport him by coach. It would not be safe for him to be out there walking alone."

Brant's mind filled with anger as he searched for pen and paper. *Let him write his own pass! That's what educated Negroes do—for themselves and others! And when they are caught, then they are beaten or hanged! So let it be with Joseph.*

All the while Joseph stood looking at his father with sorrow that showed itself like pain. *They love each other.* That was undeniable. Brant pulled himself together to act as responsibly as he could. He dropped the pass on the bed for Joseph to pick up. "You head for home!"

Brant could not escape Joseph's silent dignity even then. Brant saw how his hands had been roughened over the summer and his shoulders broadened. The slave left wordlessly after bowing to the man in bed. As though savoring every one of Joseph's footsteps, his daddy stayed quiet until the front door closed.

"Go to the table over there," his daddy said and pointed. "There's an article from the *Southern Planters' Journal.*"

Brant went and easily found the slip of paper.

"This is about a state Supreme Court judge who favors manumission in rare cases," his daddy explained. Brant looked at him as though light had been blasted in his eyes. "Yes, Brant. I'm going to start the legal process to see if Joseph can be freed."

CHAPTER 22

EARLY ON SATURDAY BRANT hurried into the quiet but already stuffy rooms of Grafton's deserted offices. He was there to do a few hours' work, after which he could put his mind fully to preparing for the most important evening of his life—his public proposal of marriage to Annie.

For twelve years the Graftons had hosted a ball on the first Saturday of August at their premier estate where their grand house overlooked the Cooper River. It was close enough to Charleston that the night lights from the city shone like stars from their property.

The ball was anticipated by all the low-country planters and their wives, and most significantly, by their energetic offspring who embraced the evening as their opportunity to prove themselves to be society's most promising young gentlemen and ladies. At the tender age of ten, Ann had forthrightly proclaimed to the yet-unromantic Brant that one day they, too, would have their engagement announced within those Grafton halls. Tonight, only nine years later, Brant was out to fulfill her dream.

His daddy was coming out of seclusion to join the colonel in making public their future wedding. Ann's faith in Christ, though new, was bearing fruit. On their weekly Sunday visits to Delora, she continually raised his daddy's spirits by reading to him or playing the piano, which had remained silent since his mother's passing. Ann was teaching Mayleda and Eric to play, too, and whenever they showed off their unsteady little tunes to her father, he was moved to grateful tears. It was incredible how things had changed. Finally, Brant's hopes and his father's were being reconciled. This marriage was going to be good for them all.

In the presence of more than two hundred guests, Brant would ask for Miss Ann Fox Rensler's hand. Though this night was to be the fulfillment of Ann's dream, it was but the beginning of his. Sitting at his desk, Brant felt his mind was as full as the ledgers in front of him. Besides affirming the marriage, the two patriarchal planters had also reached an agreement on a second crucial issue—that of merging their two plantations. As it stood now, the Callcotts would be under no obligation to consider partnership until one year after the wedding day. At that time, the Callcotts could decide either for or against joining the properties, depending on how the family relationships progressed during that first year.

The terms of the legal contract both surprised and pleased Brant, for there had been sleepless nights when he had worried that he might lose Ann because of his father's cautious attitude about bringing the businesses together. Teddy's harsh methods of control made Brant feel wary, too, but now it seemed Brant had God's blessing in marrying Ann without immediately having to face the merger. As to whether or not he would stay a planter, this summer in Charleston had convinced him that he probably would.

Working at the Grafton countinghouse with common men had opened his eyes to the disadvantages of not owning property. Males who did not inherit family land and wealth supported their households solely by wages. That put them at the mercy of the economy, the markets, their bosses, and even their own health and strength. Disaster could instantly make them worse off than slaves, for darkies were usually fed and sheltered even after their productivity ended.

As for what his marriage would do to Theodore, Brant felt at ease about this too. Teddy would inherit his uncle's plantation. And since his prestige in medicine and his influence in politics already added substantially to the way folks viewed him, Brant could find no reason to regret that Theodore might never be the proprietor of more than one property. Brant, himself, was growing comfortable with the idea of caring only for those Africans his father had bred and trained. Delora Negroes, at least, should have no complaint. Only Joseph continued to unsettle him. Unfortunately, he was obliged to think today about that slave, for his daddy had written asking that he fetch Joseph that afternoon to serve as their waiting man that evening.

"Workin' hard, ainty?" The sudden question came from behind Brant and was posed in such a way as to mock the African Gullah. Turning, he saw Teddy and General Morton.

"Yes, I am, Dr. Rensler," Brant replied quickly and proudly, for his job here made him feel confident in Teddy's presence. It surprised Brant that Teddy was with Morton. It had not occurred to him that the two might be friends.

"What are you working at, Callcott?" the general asked, sitting down on one of the workers' stools.

"I'm checking the reports on vessels that have tied up within the last twenty-four hours. So far, sir, everything seems in order." Of course, that wasn't saying much, since Brant had daydreamed his way through the morning.

"The company's certainly found the right man in you."

Brant was glad Teddy witnessed the compliment. The ill feelings between them were slowly giving way as the two men faced the reality of soon becoming extended family. After a nod from General Morton, Teddy tossed a crumpled piece of newsprint onto Brant's desk. "There's a clue for you here," he said.

"Yes!" Brant agreed after only a cursory reading. "This paper was printed by northern abolitionists!"

The general chuckled warmly. "See! I told you he's developing a fine nose for ferreting troublesome business, Doctor."

"Thank you, sir," Brant said. "Where did you get this?"

"From two illiterate darkies selling groundnuts in the Neck," Teddy said. "The arrest came after a merchant on Marsh's Wharf spied a white man shouldering cargo. The police checked vendors in that area, and sure enough, they came up with this." He chuckled harshly. "However, we still haven't caught the northern instigator who's been bringing the papers in. He can be as careless as an albino crow on the waterfront and still get away."

"The darkies protect him," General Morton observed. "Once he gets in with them, he's more like a gator submerged."

"This is the closest we've come to grabbing him." Teddy pointed to the paper. "Several of us patrol captains have banded together with the city police since we've been finding abolitionist literature even in the parishes."

"Our best guess is that maybe as many as ten or more Negroes are involved in distributing northern papers," General Morton put in. "The first two monkeys we caught were hung up by their wrists in the work-house overnight. The master there got them to talk, but only after plying the lash for hours. The police will track down the others they've named as soon as we catch the Yankee scum."

Brant imperceptibly ground his teeth. His new decision to live as a planter had not increased his tolerance for torturing bondsmen, no matter how misguided they be. Even now he thought back to Joseph's writhing on the toolshed floor. As a Christian, he could not wish such suffering on any kind of flesh.

"With your help, we can get this fellow," Teddy said, showing that he already had some of Brant's reports in hand. Brant's glance went to his supervisor.

"Your friend here has just been appointed as a new representative to city council. At a special session this morning, he presented the Young Planters' Club's concerns over slave-control laws that are being neglected at present."

During the past weeks Brant had missed all club meetings, in part because of his busyness, but also because he now questioned some of the organization's harsh disciplinary practices used on slaves.

"We want to see full compliance with the Seaman Acts already in the law books," Teddy said.

"The Graftons agree in full," Morton put in.

"I . . . I'm not familiar with these acts," Brant confessed, reluctant to say so, yet knowing that he would fail if he tried bluffing his way through the entire conversation.

"See!" Teddy said. "*He* does not know about them, and yet he works with wharf regulations! That's further proof of what we've been saying."

Brant feared disappointing his superior. "I am sorry, sir."

"No apology needed," General Morton affirmed. "The entire city's been lax concerning these laws."

"But no more!" Teddy declared. "That must be the message now if we are going to stop abolitionists. Basically the Seaman Acts require that all captains turn their Negro sailors over to the custody of city officials when-ever their vessels come into port. That way all nonresidential darkies can be sequestered, preventing communication with *our* Negroes."

"It's pure common sense to do this," Morton said. "Exchanges between colored sailors and stevedores can be common and subtle. The Graftons and other shippers will cooperate with the police," Morton said. "From now on, every colored boy from outside Charleston will be most unhappy when his ship arrives here. And you, Brant, will have a new category starting Monday. Our own inspectors will indicate the number of colored workers they count on every vessel. You, then, will check this figure against the captain's log to make sure that all colored sailors are being turned over for confinement."

"The city can lock up *free* Negroes, even if they're from northern states?" Brant asked, wanting to make sure he understood.

"That's the law!" Morton was adamant. "And starting Monday it will be universally enforced."

Teddy nodded at every word. "Most of the ships' owners and operators will be unaware of your comparisons. We want it that way. Then if any of their colored workers are slipping through, we can confront them quickly and directly."

Morton touched Brant's already crowded desk. "I know it's another heavy responsibility, son, but an important one."

"Yes, sir." Brant buoyed himself to look sharp in the bedraggling heat.

Teddy slapped Brant's back as though to cut through his soberness. "General, do you know that by Monday you will have this bachelor replaced by a gentleman anticipating marriage?"

Mr. Morton was put off only for a moment, then he smiled and extended a congratulatory hand. "Brant! You haven't said a word! That's grand! Will I be surprised to hear the lady's name?"

Brant knew his face was coloring but hoped it looked like a natural reaction to the heat. "No, sir, I guess not. Dr. Rensler knows because he is nearly her closest relative."

"Well, then, my congratulations to Miss Ann Rensler too!" Morton was intimate enough with both families to know the relationships. "The announcement will surprise no one, I am certain."

"Ah yes, there is *one* who will be surprised, I hope," Brant countered lightly, his nervousness about the evening starting then. "That's Ann! I've already proposed in private, but it's been her dream to have the announcement made public at the Graftons' ball. So our fathers are both coming, unknown to her, and I'm going to ask for her hand again."

"A charming plot, man! And the date for this wedding?"

"Next spring, I hope, sir, since winter will soon be upon us, and she's wanting to have some guests arrive by sea." Brant stopped short of mentioning the Gilmans, for no northerners were favored in this shipping crowd, even though the Boston family's vessels still came in ladened with northern goods.

The general assured him in a fatherly sort of way. "It's good to let the women take the lead in wedding plans, for indeed, it is their most precious day." There was awkward silence then, broken by Morton. "Say! You should not be wasting your time here. I demand that you close these books. In truth, I don't want to see you again till that gal of yours is on your arm at the dance this evening."

"Why, thank you, sir!" Brant's smile was quick in coming. "I guess if you command, I must comply."

"A drink at the Planters Hotel in celebration?" Teddy suggested with sudden merriment.

"I'm not sure about that," Brant said, feeling squeezed between his superior and his friend, for both he and Wilton Morton had the reputation of being temperance men. "I think I'd just rather spend the hours alone at home."

The general beamed his approval, and Teddy seemed to have no hard feelings. Brant breathed with relief as Theodore spoke again.

"I have something else to tell you. I stopped by Delora yesterday to check on your father."

"Yes?"

"I prescribed a medicine for him that might strengthen his nerves for this evening's excitement, and what do you know! He agreed to let me treat him."

Brant could be gracious because of Teddy's concern. "Thank you for that!"

The general waited for Brant to stand, then he ushered them both through the doorway. "Until this evening," he said.

"Until this evening," Theodore agreed.

Brant was glad when the others had parted. He was ready to savor the anticipation of the evening by himself as he walked back to Gibbes Street.

———

Hours later, Brant reluctantly went after Joseph and entered the unfamiliar mill's oppressive heat. Mr. Wahl, who was one of his daddy's Gospel Society friends, led him through the deafening noise and then outside to a dirty compound. Slaves were lined up to receive a late-afternoon drink of water. Wahl pointed to a worker who was away from the others, cupping his hands to wash his face at a rain barrel.

Brant had a hard time recognizing that the African was Joseph until Mr. Wahl led him closer. Then he was arrested by Joseph's narrowed, apprehensive eyes, which never looked directly at him. Brant pulled out the note his father had sent him. "I am here to fetch him for the ball." He showed Mr. Wahl his written evidence.

Unbelievably, Joseph dared to speak, his voice whole. "Sir, I am *never* to be given over to him."

Brant could not believe his ears. "What right does he have to question me?"

Wahl frowned at the Negro. "None." But then he spoke a kind word to the African. "Don't be afraid, boy. Your Master Brant does have his daddy's instructions in hand." Wahl turned to Brant. "He fears you because your daddy told him he would have no contact with you. But fear can be a good thing for keeping them in order."

Brant felt only slightly comforted. As soon as he had Joseph out in the street, the Negro slowed his step and dropped his shoulders, a darkie's way of voicing defiance without words. Brant was unnerved, for certainly the slave had learned such tricks from the vile company of primitives he now kept. "Look lively or I'll tell my daddy, and he'll not even take the time to see you!" Brant wielded the threat like a switch, and it worked, for at once Joseph picked up his feet. At the barbershop, Brant turned in and Joseph followed.

While one free colored man shaved Brant, he paid another to shave Joseph and oil his skin. Then they set out again, a groomed but uncomfortable pair.

Joseph had the ugly feeling of not being able to recognize himself as he trailed Brant Callcott through the hot, hazy streets. There had been hard days of millwork when he wanted nothing more than to be back as a houseboy, but now he saw how much extra bondage came with the "privilege" of being well fed and dressed. It felt like poverty of both heart and spirit to be dutifully following a white man's heels again. The only thing that kept him going was his slim hope of being reunited with Rosa once he arrived at the Gibbes Street house.

The first servant he saw when he came into the yard was Aunt Nancee, Ezra's wife. The kind, plain-looking woman ran and hugged him, kissing him as though he were a son. Joseph warmed to her touch like a turtle in sunshine. She restored a little of his sense of still having family and home, though now he lived almost completely on his own. "Joseph! Honey!" Her hands went around his waist. "Goodness! Don't them city bossmen feed you nothin'?"

Joseph grinned into her sweet motherly worry. "More now than they did a week ago, Aunty," he said, letting his tongue slide naturally into Gullah. "The family I'm with now gets coin every week to let me sit at their table." From the corner of his eye he could see Brant scowling, maybe because he dared to speak the African Creole easily and proudly. Indeed, he had a new, full sense that this was part of who he was.

"Get inside!" Brant's order was predictable. Once the cool, high-ceilinged house surrounded them, the young master snapped again. "Unc' Ezra has laid out clothes for you. Get up to the second bedroom and dress yourself properly." As Joseph slipped past, Brant reached out and took hold of the slave tag hanging at his chest. "Hide that inside your collar. Tonight, I don't want your 'jewelry' being seen."

Joseph felt that Brant was trying very hard to be commanding. It crossed his mind that disobedience here might not be as costly as it was with Mr. Wahl, who kept a whip hanging in every room of the mill. Though defiance just for defiance's sake could earn him nothing, he inwardly felt agitated to fight, just to prove that he had a brain and feelings too. Yet when he was alone in the upstairs room, he stilled himself with thoughts of Rosa. He would not risk sacrificing any chance to be permitted to see her. When he started to undress, Brant came by and locked him in. "You'll stay there till I'm ready to take you to my daddy."

––––––––

Hours later in the humid twilight, Joseph rode toward the gala, clinging to the Callcotts' carriage like a footman. A new shock had beset him during his idle time inside the locked room. This was to have been the night of his first examination, and now he had no way of telling Teacher Payne where he was. The trial of being taken away without warning twisted a funnel of resentment inside him.

The command to take off his mill clothes and put on formal livery had racked his emotions in ways he could not have imagined months ago. Now, instead of taking pride in how the master dressed him, he felt shameful disgrace. It was better to live like that barber who had shaved him—poor and uncertain of what whites might do to him moment by moment—than to live on the crumbs of the luxury that cost his race so dearly. He considered Rosa and what price she had paid—or was paying—to make Delora wonderful to planters.

When the coach stopped outside the Renslers' South Bay house, Joseph saw Corinth come to the porch with Ann. Eric came out, too, already dressed in his nightshirt. He gave him a casual boyish wave, which Joseph was hesitant to acknowledge, considering the eyes that watched them. Then Miss Mayleda appeared dressed in pearl-colored taffeta with her hair piled high off her shoulders. She looked far different from the caring, smiling child he remembered. Tonight Joseph would be careful not to look at her at all, for the transformation he had dreaded for so long certainly had taken place.

Applying himself to duty, he got down and held the door for the women and the maid as Brant got out to greet both his sister and his wife-to-be. Next Brant called a brief good-bye to his brother, left in the company of other servants now on the porch.

Joseph heard bits of conversation. Colonel Rensler and Theodore had taken their carriage to Delora to give Abram transportation. Worry began to cling to Joseph just as tightly as he held to the coach after it was set in motion again. Outside heaven, most of Joseph's earthly help came from Abram. Everything would change the moment that man gave up his life. For a countless time Joseph breathed fervent prayers for his master, which really were prayers for himself and all Delora slaves.

Standing in isolation over the rear wheel while Ezra drove, Joseph rode through town and into the Neck of Charleston. When he had alighted on Grafton property, he began to look for a chance to speak with Corinth. Perhaps the aunty had news concerning Delora people. At least twenty years older than he, Corinth was someone Joseph had known all his life because their masters had spent much time together. But they found no time for talk as they held to their roles of properly attending the beau and the belle of the ball. Since Master Abram was not there yet, Brant took Joseph for himself.

The huge, luxurious home was aglow with orbs and candles. In the dazzling lights a gentleman Joseph did not know came to Brant and handed him a card. Brant paled before revealing the contents to Miss Mayleda, who was standing in awe over the grandeur of her first Grafton ball. "Our daddy's collapsed on the way to the party. Teddy's forfeiting the evening to go back home and stay with him."

Instantly Miss Mayleda broke into tears. "Brant, we must go home! Oh!

Bring Joseph, so he can help care for Daddy."

Then Joseph heard another feminine voice.

"Oh, Brant, what do you think we should do?" It was Ann.

"He could be dying!" Mayleda cried again.

Joseph saw Brant reread the letter.

"Teddy assures me that he is stable, and that the crisis is under control."

"Oh, Brant, if you don't go, I'll find my own way!" Mayleda threatened. Joseph's heart was sinking too.

"All right. I'll call Ezra to take you home, and then Uncle can come back for Ann and me. Tell Daddy that we are coming, but first there is something important to be done!"

"What can be so important?" his sister demanded, looking and acting more like the Mayleda Joseph knew.

Brant drew both of Ann's white-gloved hands to his chest. "Tonight I'm proposing to you—here."

The mistress's mouth opened demurely. "Oh, you trickster! How wonderful you are!"

Brant's eyes shifted to his sister. "I'm going to stay long enough to make that announcement. This is very important to me, and I know Daddy will understand. You tell him we will be home before midnight. I'll make sure Ezra has the coach back for us by then."

Joseph fully expected to be called into service, but one of the Grafton servants was engaged to make the proper arrangements.

Just before Mayleda left them, she suddenly came near to Joseph's side. "I want to take him, Brant. He could be a comfort to Daddy."

"No. I'll send him back to the mill with Mr. Wahl, for I see that he is here."

Immediately Joseph felt the hollowness of Miss Mayleda's leaving. Oh, if he were a white man now, he would choose to be at Abram Callcott's side within the hour. He began to entertain an idea that he had previously dismissed every time it had entered his mind. But now it appealed. There was no millwork on Sunday. Perhaps it would be possible to forge a pass so that he could have an hour to see both Abram and Rosa. Tomorrow, he might just try . . .

Joseph was called from those thoughts when he and Corinth were told to follow the master and mistress upstairs where all the carpets had been covered with sailcloth to make a dance floor. Brant and Ann were satisfied to be alone, so Joseph found his moment to speak with Corinth as they stood along the wall with other idle slaves.

"Evening, Aunty."

She covered her mouth. "You can speak! Lord o'mercy! Nobody on Pine Woods would ever think that afta all them stories Mass' Teddy done told 'bout you an' him."

"I trust you are well!" He found pleasure in giving her a nod of respect.

Her eyes flashed vehemence, but then she quickly regained the indifferent composure carried by his people as defense against both hurts and punishment. Joseph understood the look but not the reason behind it until she spoke, no trace of her pain showing on her strong, round face.

"I done birthed my baby boy back in the month of planting"—her eyes blinked dryly—"an' the ol' colonel, he sold him off just last week so's my teats would dry up in time for me to be here lookin' respectable."

Her suffering put a pit in Joseph's stomach. "I'm so sorry, Aunty." He turned partway around to the pairs of rich, white dancers enjoying one another. Two worlds suddenly seemed to be meeting and spinning, with enough violence to rip the human fabric from them all. *His* Brant and *Corinth's* Ann were out there laughing while he and Corinth stood just yards away engulfed in a system run on grief and toil. Joseph waited until he felt Corinth's mourning subside. "Say, I want to ask you about a pretty gal from Delora named Rosa." Joseph hoped he sounded calm, though his heart was racing.

Corinth would not show her eyes. "I don't know her."

"She's light-skinned with fine green eyes—"

"I done said I never hear'd her name!"

Joseph put his hand almost to the woman's hand. "Aunty! You do know something! I can see it in your face."

"I don't, so don't you be talkin' like this now. You keep you' mind on you' massa. That's all we good for here." She pulled from him and straightened her skirts.

He stepped after her. "If you know something, tell me. Bad or good!"

"A innocent Pine Woods black man done got his back split open wide an' his body sold south, takin' the blame for young massa compromisin' some Delora brown girl."

The words hit like bullets. "Rosa! Teddy Rensler!"

She acted like a maum. "Joseph! I know'd you shouldn't hear that now! Don't you lose you'self by you' anger! There ain't nothin' to be done! Push it out of you' mind!"

He felt a desperate cry well deep within him. When it surfaced, it was not so much pain as hate—for *every* white man! It scared him to find himself so enraged, but now those dancers whirled like laughing, senseless *murderers* in his mind. How many of those gentlemen had stolen a black man's love? How many of those ladies heartlessly put their maids through hell by selling their children or denying them the comfort of husband and home? Whatever the masters wanted, they could have! His vision blurred, not with tears, but heartbreaking distress.

With those dimmed eyes he saw Colonel Rensler stride into the room. The man went immediately to his daughter and Brant. They spoke a long time outside the range of Joseph's hearing. Then the dignified, white-haired slaveowner conferred just as privately with his Grafton hosts. After that, he called aloud for everyone to come together around the young breathless couple.

"As many of you know, Mr. Abram Callcott fell ill on his way here this evening," the colonel said to the group. "Fortunately, my nephew, Dr. Theodore Rensler, was there to give him immediate attention. Mr. Callcott is now resting comfortably at his home, and Dr. Rensler is with him."

There was muted gratefulness that could be felt.

"His daughter, Miss Mayleda Callcott, has gone home. Early indications are that he may have suffered a stroke. Dr. Rensler will know more once Abram has had some rest."

There was corporate hushed breathing, and Joseph's insides felt as though they were being torn from throat to waist. He closed his eyes. How he wanted to be at Delora.

"Brant Callcott, however, has remained at the party with his daddy's blessing, for this was planned to be a very important evening for us all. Abram and I were prepared to make a wonderful announcement. But now I will take the responsibility of bearing the news to you all myself. Mr. Callcott and I would like to announce the engagement of my daughter and his son—" He extended his hand. "Mr. Brant Callcott and my own dear Ann!"

There was applause, and at the colonel's beckoning the couple came closer to him. The man turned them both around and put a hand on each of their outer shoulders. "The future Mr. and Mrs. Brant Callcott of Delora." Again, individuals surrounded them with clapping. Brant blushed and Ann looked radiant.

Corinth distracted Joseph by touching his waist. "Praise be!" the woman murmured. "I been a-waitin' a long time for my move to Delora."

Joseph looked at her blankly.

"All of us at Pine Woods feel the same. You got good massas for you'-

self. Anybody would be mighty proud servin' Callcotts 'stead of Renslers."

Joseph said nothing. He knew many servants took pleasure in boasting of who owned them, but it could never be that way for him anymore. There would never be *anything* worth boasting about in slavery after his small taste of freedom.

The Negro fiddlers struck up a new tune, and the white world spun with gaiety once more. It stayed in motion until most were too out of breath to lift another step. Then Mr. Clemson, the sub-captain of St. Andrew's Parish Patrol, grabbed one of the black musicians' bows. Tipping it out beyond the genteel crowd he pointed to the watching colored help. "What do you all say about turning this into a Negroes' flopdoddle ball for a time?"

The slaveowners, glistening with light perspiration, smiled and laughed at their waiting men and wenches. Among aristocrats, it was a great form of entertainment to see darkies dance.

Miss Ann came to Corinth. "Joseph will be your partner."

Corinth seemed willing, but Joseph stood his ground, even though the colonel was there shadowing his daughter. "What's wrong with you, boy?" the colonel said.

Joseph let his eyes slip warily everywhere until he fixed them on Brant. His owner's son came toward him. Remembering that Corinth had said Pine Woods thought him mute, he did not say a word to give his speech away.

"Your darkie's balking," Colonel Rensler reported.

"That's only because my daddy never lets him dance," Brant explained uneasily. "He has never allowed any frivolous behavior in him, so now I'm sure Joseph believes he cannot and should not dance."

Several other young planters were around Joseph now, Mr. Clemson included. "My word, man!" Clemson said. "A nigger's born with music in his heels. Step on out here, cuffee, and bring your 'lady' with you."

Joseph's mind flooded with thoughts of Rosa being led and forced against her will by a condescending white man just like this one speaking to him now. The white smiles turned his fury red. How could he dance to entertain men who so often trapped and harmed his kind? He stood frozen.

Colonel Rensler spoke haughtily, "Boy, maybe you're too dull to understand. Tonight, you dance."

Joseph looked to Brant. Agitated and frowning, Brant said, "Sir, please. I don't think he does understand. Please let it pass. My father's ill, and perhaps the boy's only trying to do what he thinks is honorable."

The colonel countered him sharply. "You think he can behave *honorably*! My word! Look at my Corinth! And that one! And now that one there! They're all copying your ugly monkey-boy's same defiant posture!"

Joseph was so frightened he felt his pulse in his hands.

Mr. Wahl appeared in the crowd. At the same time one of the Graftons came through to give every Negro the same ultimatum. "You all will dance—in here or in the street!"

Then the house owner called for certain men to get their canes. "This one's already made his choice!" he announced while Joseph panted and stared at the floor, realizing it was too late to change his mind, even though his nerve was wearing thin. "He will dance, with some good practice down in the alleyway. Now take him away! Whose boy is he?"

"Mine," Brant admitted, almost inaudibly. "Please, Mr. Grafton, there's a misunderstanding. He's confused. My daddy, his master, is not here as expected—"

"Confused or not, he's caused this trouble. We'll not be too hard on him for just nigger stupidity."

The house owner spoke to a few men from the Planters' Club. "See that the men already outside don't do permanent harm to him. Now, Master Callcott, you are welcomed to stay here, since this is your lady's special night. The matter will be dealt with properly."

Ann was there and laced her arm through his. "Oh, Brant, do trust them to do what is right."

Brant knew that might be wise, considering how he was in the employment of the Grafton family and maybe already at odds with most of the club's young brotherhood. Yet he thought of his daddy. Had that man been here, he would not leave any Delora slave alone to be disciplined by others. For that reason he gently pried Ann's fingers. "I'll be right back, darling. This is something I must do, since Daddy's not here." Brant was encouraged to see Mr. Wahl coming with him.

Joseph had already been half driven and half dragged from the room. When Brant and Wahl got down in the street, they found the slave fenced in with walking sticks. Brant prayed, first that Joseph would not do something stupid like raise a hand to defend himself. Then he prayed that they might not kill him, for this group loathed every form of Negro disobedience. No law was needed to assign a moblike spirit to them. While music drifted out overhead, one man, then three, then ten struck at Joseph's feet, knees, and shins, making him career and leap to avoid as many of their blows as possible.

Colonel Rensler called merrily to Brant when he saw him. "Your boy can dance after all!" A chorus formed that sickened Brant.

Here now monkey! Here now crow!
Higher, higher! Up you go!

Canes clattered. Shouts rose.

Brant staggered, pressing himself in rather weak-heartedly until he saw blood on their sticks. "Let him go! He knows his error now!"

Another shouted. "Does he?"

Brant lost sight of Joseph when he dropped to the street. Fearfully parting the heated men, Brant got close to Delora's beaten slave. Joseph's shoes and trouser legs were split in a dozen places. In a moment Mr. Wahl was down beside him. "They've really wounded him!" Brant grieved while the foreman began to examine Joseph's feet and knees.

"Enough dancing for one night," someone rudely said, and eventually the crowd was led away.

"What shall I do, Mr. Wahl? I know no doctors here, and my carriage is home with my sister."

"I'll take care of it," Mr. Wahl said. "I can't spare him. I'll get help for him. I need him back at work by Monday."

Brant did not know what to say. He didn't even know what to feel or think.

"Just a piece of advice, young master." Mr. Wahl turned to him. "Next time, make sure your servant knows what is expected of him, or you are one who stands to be disgraced."

"I *have* been disgraced—by countering Mr. Grafton," Brant guessed dismally.

"On a normal evening I would say yes. But the Graftons can be gracious. Perhaps they understand the worry you're under with your daddy ill." He took hold of Brant's arm as they stood up together. "Go in. Apologize to your hosts, and then find your lady. By my letter of agreement with your daddy, I'm under obligation to care for the boy, and I will."

"Thank you." Brant weakly brushed the dirt from his knees. He looked at Joseph, hating him as much as ever, but feeling deep sorrow because of him too. Tonight he had publicly committed himself to Ann, and in doing so, he had also committed himself to planting and slaveowning forever. That was a sorry thought right now in light of what had happened.

It was like walking on broken glass. Like having iron nails claw at his heels. With more than half his weight supported by Wahl's shoulders, Joseph wobbled in a daze of blackness to the coach that had rolled near them. His white foreman opened the door, and Joseph crawled on his hands and arms to pull himself inside. The man sat on the bench. He curled on the floor. Papers and cardboard were put under him so his blood would not stain the coach's carpeting.

That was all he remembered until he woke up in Mr. Wahl's stable behind the foreman's house. Wahl was still with him and another man also—one with black hairs growing from a mole on his chin.

"Do you honestly think you honored your master by not dancing?" Wahl asked.

Joseph did not answer. His mind was on Teddy Rensler and on what he had done to Rosa. He clenched his teeth as the man with the mole poked him and painted ill-smelling medicine all over his flesh from the knees down.

"You *will* be at work on Monday. If you think you have any reason for anger, boy, think again."

Joseph lay still, beginning to understand how violence could do its work. A slave could come to the point of not wanting to suffer any more pain and start compromising everything just to have peace. Joseph felt he was almost to that place now—having been muted, then branded, now caned. Perhaps the next time he would be their "good boy" and trade his last shred of dignity to do anything he was told—give in, so they could be satisfied he really was the animal they took him to be.

The physician assured Wahl that no bones had been broken. Joseph grabbed at the straw he lay in. He could not let himself be reduced to nothing. Thoughts of defeat were more painful than new injuries. Wahl's doctor bandaged him and left, but the foreman stayed.

"This is the last time you'll cause trouble in my presence, whether or not Master Brant is with you."

Joseph kept only one picture in his mind—Rosa being held, being shamed, being hurt. He quelled his sighing. His suffering was nothing compared to hers. Wahl departed. He pulled at his ears because of the excruciating inner agony. Could anyone having liberty ever imagine the torments of those who had none?

His distress fanned the hatred within. It broiled in his heart, threatening to sear all conscience, including what he had learned from God's Word about mercy and grace. He lay there hating and hating and hating until he remembered Mayleda's kindness and Abram on his bed of affliction. Again he heard his master pleading, *"If slavery be sin, forgive the children."*

Joseph thought of Luck, who wasted no time struggling with forgiveness. That brother was pressing on to find a route to freedom. *"Break from whites. Do what is necessary to save yourself and those you love. Pick what you will die for, then put your life into it."* Raising his head, Joseph looked down across his wounds. For now, his plan to write a pass to see Rosa was as useless as his stinging, swelling feet.

He set his jaw against the many things that tortured him. When he finally let himself sob, it was first for Rosa, but then he went on, crying out to God for himself. He feared that hatred—either given or received— might consume him unless the Christ who had died for *all* men came— even here to this stable—to rescue him, a lowly slave.

CHAPTER 23

ON HARD, SWOLLEN LEGS Joseph suffered through Monday, driven by the hope that he would have strength at the end of the day to go to Payne's school. During the long work hours, Harris worried over him like a hound with only one surviving pup because Peckory was absent again. Since Joseph had only the cut pants to wear, the lumpy, scabbed-over swellings were in plain view. Only Harris asked him for details. The others, it seemed, were too accustomed to seeing fellow slaves battered to have curiosity or sympathy.

Harris kept making Joseph pledge that this had nothing whatsoever to do with Peckory's secret meetings. Privately Joseph worried that the rest-less clerk had gotten himself into trouble again with the secret abolitionist visitor. Peckory had already been flogged once. His discipline would be even harsher the next time the patrolmen caught him. Fear and punish-ment or giving up his vision to live and react as a man—were these a col-ored man's only choices? Joseph mulled the question over as he hobbled about trying to do the work of two. Harris was the only other clerk working with him on the endless pile of orders.

The moment the quitting horn sounded, Joseph fled the mill. Dragging every ounce of his physical torture with him, he limped out into a steamy summer downpour that painted everything a drab green and gray. Black children were happily dancing in the shower. Despite his discomfort, their voices and energy lifted his spirit. In the slick, wet streets he pressed his way, but when the town clock struck six he was still blocks from Anson Street.

Joseph decided then against taking time to change his clothes. Instead he went straight to the nearest public well to wash his face and hands, even though there was a law against it, and headed directly for the school. He wanted to tell Teacher Payne why he had missed the examination on Saturday.

When he finally arrived, he was met by eerie silence that increased when he went inside. As usual, everything was in perfect order, but for the first time since his starting there, Payne was gone. This troubled him because his instructor was a model of punctuality. Soaked to the skin, Joseph took his seat, too weary to do otherwise. He sat for a while worrying and praying. As Luck had told him, no man of color was ever safe, and that, he knew, included Daniel Payne.

The rain slowly tapered off, and the room grew lighter. Joseph took the liberty of limping to the windows and opening them so his clothes would dry. When he sat down again, he leaned forward, allowing the stirring breezes to reach his back. More time passed, and he considered that he should leave in case the teacher was already in trouble. It would do him no good to have a bedraggled, abused slave found in his classroom. He pushed himself to stand, and at that moment Payne came through the door.

The small-framed teacher said nothing as he hung up his walking cane, hat, and cloak. When he turned, Joseph saw he was holding a small silk bag about the size of his fist. Noticing his demeanor, Joseph thought the teacher was either ill or in anguish. Immediately Joseph put aside his own woes. "Sir, I am sorry. I was wrong to have let myself in."

The other man focused on him awkwardly, as though forgetting that Joseph should have been there. Then he showed grave concern by walking closer to look at Joseph's bare legs and quaking stance. "Sit down, my brother! You have been beaten! That's why you missed school on Saturday and church on Sunday."

Joseph took his seat gratefully. He longed to speak, but he saw that the man was already weighed down with burdens of his own. His teacher sank to the chair beside him.

"Were you taken by the proponents of that Cross and Circle campaign again?"

"No!" Joseph realized that his anger was still like a wound breaking at the surface. He bit his lip, fearing he would cry or scream if he spoke a word of his own distress.

"Then this was done because you attend my school!" Payne concluded wrongly.

Joseph was surprised by the false connection, but of course the conclusion was sensible. "Oh no. I was hauled off to work at the Grafton ball, and there I was caned because I would not dance to entertain the 'gentlemen.'"

Payne turned away. Joseph had never seen the teacher dejected, and he had never seen him as he was now, nearly losing his elegant poise. "You are the one who is ill, sir," Joseph worried. "Do not think on what has happened to me." His teacher's distress filled him with new sorrows.

"Yes, I am ill!" Payne shivered noticeably. "If sickness of the heart is illness, then indeed, I am ill! Gravely so!"

"Mr. Payne! Someone you love has died!"

"No. But some *thing* I love is dying!" Under his rain-spotted glasses he pressed his fingers to his eyes. "It's the call I thought I had from God." His thoughts visibly hardened his bony cheeks and narrow chin. "There's a strong move in the next political election to close all Negro schools. I've known that. But what I did not know—until today—is that all the gentlemen I hoped would stand with me in defense of what I'm doing are going to desert me. Including Bachman." Payne's voice was tremulous. "I was at his house yesterday, and what I heard and saw convinced me that he will be like the rest, consumed with one matter and one matter only—that of shoring up the South so it can stand on its own and protect slavery at any cost."

He got up and went back toward the rack where he had hung his cloak. "I should not burden you. You have had enough pain."

"No, teacher. Any way I can serve you, I will."

After much hesitation Payne slipped on the flowing, rose-colored robe he often wore in the classroom. "Yesterday Dr. Bachman suggested that I may want to leave Charleston—to teach in Africa! Can you believe that? All of them now think that *another* continent is the only place fit for educated, American-born men and women of color!" He faced Joseph and his breathing was shallow as he came back to Joseph's desk. "They say it's *Providence* that has me moving out of the South! Providence! Do you hear them? Blaming the Almighty One for the sin-ridden way of life that blights even their Christian brothers!" He struck the polished wood. "God have mercy on their souls! And on ours, if this furnace of affliction does not burn itself out!"

Joseph stood quietly. "I will go, sir. Doubtless you want to be alone. I am hardly a worthy confidant."

He was surprised by Payne's sudden response. "No! Indeed! You are— if you feel well enough to stay."

"I do, sir."

He drew back, clapping his hands lightly but with tension. "I regret that I am so readily showing you my weakness, but Joseph, all last night I thought I would go mad with the burning certainty that they still have no idea *who we are*!" He leaned on the furniture. "Even wealthy *colored* men see reason to keep this present culture viable—even though it means relegating their darker enslaved brethren to treatments worse than those due animals!"

"You don't have to explain much to me, sir," Joseph murmured. "But why do light-skinned colored men—like your student Philip Handsome— side with the imposing race?"

"Because they lead lives similar to those of white slaveowners. Because they, too, have status and wealth to lose if slavery is eliminated." Sighing, he put his hands behind him. "Today I spoke with some of my students' parents. Not *one* of them is willing to say publicly what he thinks privately. I should not be surprised, I guess, for even the few white folks who once wavered on the rightness of slavery now are silenced by their fears. No one dares to counter the majority's will because they know there may be terrible retribution."

He paced. "Oh, Joseph, do you see how the time is already here when Christians will have to choose between what suits them personally and what is right according to the precepts and will of God?"

Joseph grieved with the man, though not completely comprehending all the reasons for his anguish.

"Last night I felt beyond faith," Payne confessed, taking off his glasses. "I was sleepless with questions. Where is God? How long must this go on without the Creator's intervention?"

"I know, Mr. Payne. Last night I was sleepless too."

The teacher wiped his face with his open hand like a man who had been crying. "Forgive me. I should never have verbalized such unbelief! God forbid that I should draw anyone toward disbelief."

"Then what is the answer to our suffering, sir?"

Payne looked at him with warm humility. His answer was slow in coming. "*Hate* sin. *Love* God. That's what keeps being pressed on my heart as I pray. There is a small, calming voice when I choose to believe that I hear it. It says to me, 'One day may be like a thousand to the Lord Almighty, but *one* day slavery will be brought to an end.' I think that must be the promise of a just and loving God."

Joseph hung his head, not knowing if he could submit to God's will if deliverance was still to be such a long way off.

"You might think it strange, but all this soul searching started because of a simple errand yesterday. I went to retrieve a magnificent orange and yellow moth from Dr. Bachman, who had been rearing it for me in his laboratory. I was planning to kill it and put it inside this bag and bring it back to mount for the students. Instead, I kept it alive overnight, then I walked to the countryside and let it go."

The man looked weary, like a Negro who had been worked from dawn to dark. "I have sat many times in the gallery of Bachman's packed church, which serves more blacks than whites. I have been greatly moved by this man's preaching. Without a doubt he *knows* we are brothers in Christ. Yet now?"

Payne's feelings at that moment became too deeply buried for Joseph to know the whole meaning of his sudden pausing.

His teacher sighed and started over. "Upon my first meeting with Dr. Bachman, *he* was the one who offered to raise this most unusual caterpillar that one of my students had brought to me. I was invited into Bachman's home to see the creature when it emerged from its odd cocoon. And there the man received me warmly. We spoke nearly as colleagues. I was even invited to sit in his parlor with his wife and daughters. I listened to music played on their piano."

Joseph moved uncomfortably, for such interaction between the races was unheard of.

"I see now that I was too hopeful. As a theologian, Bachman concludes that we both are redeemed creatures in Christ. As a scientist he holds fast to the unpopular truth that we are all descendants of Adam and Eve, regardless of race. Yet today he spoke to me of colonization! Of my moving to Liberia—because of the color of my skin! Perhaps I should have countered him with his prospects in Germany, since his blue-eyed, yellow-haired ancestors are from there."

Joseph felt himself grin sadly, despite their common grief.

"The white man's plan, I believe, is to rid America of its entire skilled and learned colored population and, at the same time, put bans on education so that every succeeding generation of Negroes in America will be dominated by ignorance." His thumb pressed his lips. "Therefore, while Bachman and others may be our brothers according to the Gospel of Jesus Christ, they remain part of that world that willingly and consciously attempts to break us. I just can't understand it, based on what is provable about us." He stroked the surface of the desk. "I built this one and several others. Have I been teaching for no reason at all?"

He looked around the room like a man envisioning disaster. "From the very beginning I have done everything I can to promote a classical education among our people so that gentlemen like Bachman could learn the truth of our equality. But few have dared to visit this classroom. And even fewer have dared to look at the facts they could obtain here." Some of his intensity waned. "I guess releasing that moth gave me an odd sense of justice. At least *something* from this schoolhouse has gotten its rightful doorway to freedom. . . ." His voice dissipated; his weak eyes welled. "I had always hoped this school would be a refuge and a wellspring for our people."

"But it *is* what you hoped for, Teacher Payne!"

"For how long?" he mourned. "Until this state separates from the Union? Until the next legislature is seated and the representatives adopt one more law to press down the man of color?" He rubbed his face as he had done before. "If they are successful in passing the legislation currently being drafted, then my work will be cut off within months. I tell you, until yesterday I never wavered from the hope that with equal education we would rise naturally to our rightful place. Until yesterday, I had faith that a few Christian men of both races would valiantly stand together and speak for what is right, as God sees the right."

Joseph's head went down, sharing Payne's heaviness.

"If they can banish all colored teachers and close all schools, then they will have seized the day!" Payne mused.

"That cannot happen, sir!" Joseph said with sudden boldness. "As long as there is even one literate Negro, there will be at least one teacher, for everyone who has learned can teach."

Payne stared at him. "You would be so determined, even if writing and reading became illegal and punishable by fines and whippings?"

"I would, sir! After the caning, I lay thinking for a long time. A man must have things worth living—and even dying—for. And learning, also teaching, if needed, has become that important to me."

Payne got up and walked to his lecture table. He came back with a journal and some papers. "I promised you this." Smiling, he handed him a thin, soft-bound volume. "It's a copy of *Southern Planter*. It contains an article on the treatments of all known types of 'summer fevers.'"

Next he showed Joseph the examination from Saturday. "It is nearly eight o'clock, my friend. Are you interested in taking this now, or should it wait until tomorrow?"

Joseph felt extremely sober. "I am not fitly dressed to be a scholar."

"Dress has nothing to do with intellect."

"Then, yes, allow me to do the examination now, sir, for only God knows if there will be a tomorrow."

"All right." There was a small amount of brightness in Payne's face. "I will give you one-half hour. Then I will review your progress."

————

Joseph finished the examination before Payne came back to check on him. He started to stand, but the other man insisted that he stay seated because of his legs. While the teacher looked down over his work, Joseph tensely endured the silent scrutiny. Finally Payne looked at him.

"You need to improve on your handwriting and your spelling, and that will take much practice."

"Yes, sir," Joseph responded glumly.

The teacher's eyes stayed on him. "Other than that, you have done a fine job. A very fine job, indeed!"

Joseph was breathless. He hardly trusted himself even to smile, but his eyes met Payne's, and in that moment they mirrored appreciation for each other.

"Let me guess," Payne said, his face glowing. "You want to study Latin, even though the time is short."

"I do!" Joseph laughed, then curbed his enthusiasm. "But, sir, only if you want to start that now."

Payne showed him a Latin text. "We have only ten or fifteen minutes. There is no need for you to rise when you give your answers."

"I appreciate that, sir."

Soon they were sitting next to each other, two heads bowed over the one common book. Joseph still had Rosa's strange Latin words burning in him, demanding inquiry. But he kept his silence because it was clear the teacher had an introductory lesson already planned. Almost immediately Payne opened an English book he also had with him. "While you were taking your examination, I continued to pray concerning our despair. As I did, I remembered this challenging line of Latin from the journals of John Wesley, that famous evangelist who preached even to the plantation slaves of South Carolina. Here, I've marked it." Payne removed the ribbon from his opened volume. " *'Nudi nudum Christum sequi.'* "

The words, of course, were a total puzzle to Joseph.

"Translated it means, 'Naked to follow a naked Christ.' "

Joseph looked at him with embarrassment, for even the translation did not mean much to him.

"This, I believe, is part of the answer to our struggles," Payne concluded, his poise nearly restored. "Are servants expected to have an easier task than their masters?"

"No, sir."

"Have we any right to claim *anything* for ourselves when the God of Heaven came to earth to redeem us, not even demanding that His own life and dignity be spared?"

"No, sir, I guess not. But Teacher Payne, it's the *colored* Christian man who is always sacrificing! Never the white!"

"Yes, for now at least, that seems to be true. But one day justice will prevail, because *God* will be the judge of all." Payne looked at him. "For that reason we must fight the temptation to return evil for evil. *Hate* sin, but continue to *love* God, for He is willing and able to deal with sinners." Just then there was a noise at the window. Payne was first to see a face peering over the sill. "Ah, just a curious boy from the streets."

"No! I know him. It's Tag!"

Payne gave permission for Joseph to go to window. He had to call Tag's name to make the child willing to show himself again. Tears marred the smudged little countenance.

"Oh, Mama thought you was dead, for the paterollers done been roundin' up all Luck's friends!" Then Tag eyed Teacher Payne and would say no more.

"This boy is from the family I live with," Joseph said.

"Are you in trouble, Joseph?" There was compassion in the teacher's question.

"Not that I know of, sir."

"I can't hold you from going back there, but I can warn you about the company you keep. Your accusers can level guilt by association if any of your acquaintances have been arrested."

"Yes, sir," Joseph reflected glumly. "I know that. But still, I sense it's my duty to go to reassure Tag's mother."

"Then go, knowing that I will pray for you."

As quickly as his sore legs could carry him, Joseph hurried to follow Tag. The boy, however, did not lead him home but to the backyard of another city house. "Luck's in here," Tag said, opening the only door to an unused smokehouse. And indeed he was in the dark, acrid interior, hiding with five or six of his abolitionist-minded friends.

"So, Joseph." He knew Luck by his voice. "Now you, too, are here."

Joseph coughed against the smell of ash and smoke. Once the door was closed, there was no light at all.

"Somebody's done struck him on the legs," Tag said, sounding almost boastful of Joseph's injuries.

"How many took you, an' how much wa' you obliged to say 'fore they let you go?" It was a harsh, accusing question.

Joseph weighed what sorrows might have brought them all here to hide. "I don't know what's been going on. I was taken back into my master's service on Saturday and then caned by some of his friends at the Graftons' ball."

"Ahh!" There was puzzled, uneasy sighing.

"Then you weren't with those arrested an' held at the workhouse?"

"No. Who was arrested and taken there?"

It was Luck's voice that answered. "The city knows 'bout the newsprint an' the packages. An' mostly that be Mista Diller's fault. He becomin' so unwise an' so eager to keep things in he own hands, instead of trustin' 'em to us."

Another voice joined in. "He always be talkin' 'bout gettin' us all to the free states, but then he keep makin' every decision by his lonesome self."

"I think he just done come down so's he could go home an' boast of all he done for us po' black slave folk."

"For true!" Others agreed with the speaker Joseph did not know in the dark.

"It's almost like he wa' usin' us for he own gain. Maybe like God, the big boss be keepin' score, an' He be a-claimin' us as treasure in He crown of glory."

"I don't think so." Luck got in again. "He come down, sure 'nough, 'cause he do hate slavery. He big problem, howsumever, be that he ain't got no better opinion of any of us than our own buckra massas do! That's why he always a-thinkin' 'bout *his* way being the only right one. He got no clue how we might know a thing or two to help we'selves."

"Ahh-hah!" Others in the pitch black agreed forcefully.

"Why are you all here?" Joseph dared.

" 'Cause the po'lice are out to find an' torture us all," Luck explained with fury. "They think that the white boy will put he head up, if'n he thinks that we all have got ourselves in trouble. If they can catch we, then they can catch him. That's the long an' short of it."

Someone added his opinion. "Our purpose now is to get out of Cha'leston, an' quick."

"With our families."

"If they catch even one of us, then that could lure Diller," Luck explained. "We all like bait now, but if'n they get him, then we all be like chicken necks tied to a line an' et' up by 'em crabs in the waters."

"We all will be 'cused of insurrection an' hung high if they find us or him. An' our women an' children will be sold off to others, for sure."

Joseph swallowed the best he could.

"You still our best hope, friend!" Luck touched him.

"How!" Joseph countered.

"We all know the names of cap'ns and vessels what might be safe to carry us to freedom. Howsumever, not a one of us can read, so's there's no way for us to know what vessels are where in Charleston ports."

"I still don't see how reading can help."

" 'Cause then we can pick up the discarded papers, secretlike, an' find out what ships an' cap'ns are here in town. Those schedules are printed every day, ainty! So even from here, we can work our plans, since we know those vessels' names."

"I can't teach you all to read in just one night!"

"We only need know ten or maybe twenty words."

Joseph felt dizzy. "That's still impossible! It's dark. I have no tools." Then he remembered the pencil and notebook still damp and hidden in his shirt. And he had told Teacher Payne that teaching was something worth dying for.

"Maybe you can use the charcoal in here," one said while another opened a tin and blew lightly on the hot uncovered coals. They dared to ignite tinder and then kindling, punching out some of the log building's chinking so that there would still be some good air to breathe.

"This is our one an' only chance," Luck told him with drooping eyes that Joseph could now see. The other men were just as intent on him as Luck.

"I'll help you all, just tonight!" Joseph pledged quickly.

The men nearly cheered. In the light Joseph saw that Peckory was not among them. Being literate himself, maybe he had worked out his own plan to freedom.

"I want to say something to you, brother." Luck patted his shoulder. "One of the things we all learned from Mista Diller was something a Virginny white man said concernin' freedom."

Almost like a class reciting in Sunday School, the men spoke together once Luck had them started. " 'Is life so dear? Is peace so sweet as to be purchased at the price of chains an' slavery? Forbid it, A'mighty God! Give me liberty or give me death!' "

Joseph's whole body chilled.

"That'll be our cry!" Luck proclaimed. "No matter what they do to us, they'll not get one other thing off our tongues but that! Give us liberty or death."

Joseph felt small in the midst of their determination. Slowly, and to the amazement of them all, he pulled a book of paper and a pencil from the waistband of his trousers.

"God be praised! Where'd you ever get that?"

Even little Tag was on his knees expectantly as Joseph sat with pencil poised. "What names do you need to know when you see them in print?" he asked quite breathlessly.

They all spoke at once, then Luck took charge. "A steamer called the *Anotta* under a cap'n named *Cramer*. Takes goods back and forth to Cuba."

"Another's the *Columbia*."

"Then there's the *Swiftlight*."

"And I think we all can trust the Pennsylvanian called *Coulter*," a big man with a crooked nose spoke up. "But I sure don't remember the name of he ship."

"Also, any vessel comin' in from Gilman's Shipping Company be safe, I think!" The talk went back to Luck.

"I know that name!" Joseph gulped, pausing from writing furiously. "He is my master's friend! And part of the Gospel Society!"

"Well, you got that all down?" Luck pushed, taking no time for extra talk.

"I don't know. I'm not good at spelling," Joseph admitted. "I don't know if I have all of them just right."

"Try you' best, bro', 'cause you the best we got." Luck affirmed him with a nod.

After they had rattled off a few more ship names and captains, the men told Joseph to list all the days of the week and the names of all the familiar wharves so that they could recognize the time schedules printed in the city's papers. When he had everything recorded, Joseph tore the page from his notebook and handed it to Luck with trembling fingers. Then he hid his paper and pencil away.

"You should come with us!" Luck said. "It's likely they all have you tied in with us, which can only mean trouble for you onc't we gone."

Heart pounding, Joseph considered it. "If I run, I need to take the risk of going home to Delora Plantation first. I should take somebody with me." And that, of course, was Rosa.

Luck grasped his hand. "I think it would be death for you to go home. The only right way to run is far, far away." When Joseph gave no response, his friend bowed with dignity. "This might be farewell—forever. Thank-yee, my brother!"

"I . . . I'm sorry I didn't do it sooner, Luck," Joseph said feebly. "That first night in the cellar, I just couldn't imagine either the *depth* of slavery or the *height* of hoping for freedom."

Luck nodded with a kind of caring understanding. " 'Give me liberty or give me death!' Now you do see!"

"Yes, maybe I do," Joseph said. "May God watch over you all!"

"And you, too, brother."

Outside the church clock started to chime the curfew hour.

"If you not staying, you'd best go!" Luck counseled. "The house be dark, but you can sleep there, I s'pose. The women done went into hidin' in case it be our night to run."

They smothered the fire, and Joseph opened the door alone.

He was unsure what to do. He might be a marked man if he went back to Luck's house. However, he could be trapped by patrolmen if he had no home and stayed on the street. He almost decided to go back to Payne, but he knew that could bring real trouble on the man. In the end he limped on to Aunt Gail's gate with legs that were on fire now that his wounds had been covered with stinging ashes.

Suddenly a white man stepped out right in front of him alongside Aunt

Gail's hedges. "Where have you been? You smell like smoke, boy!" The speaker was Wahl.

Joseph had been too strongly warned by Abram Callcott to dare to mar his soul with lies. "I was just coming home," he said weakly, not having to feign how much each step pained him.

The foreman asked him no other questions. Then Joseph saw that Harris was there also, with Joseph's trunk on his shoulder. The whole place was dark. "Do you know where everybody is?" Joseph asked, wanting to know what the white man knew.

"The patrol came and raided the house last night. It was by God's grace that you were at my stables, or you'd be in jail."

Joseph looked at Harris, who did not look at him. But he did keep on carrying his chest, freeing Joseph to struggle with his walking as they headed on foot to Mr. Wahl's dwelling.

"From now on you will sleep in my barn," the foreman said. "And you know I'll keep my eye on you!"

When they finally were home, Harris handed Joseph his small chest of possessions. "Peckory's dead," the Negro said in a throaty whisper.

Wahl heard Harris and intruded on them again. "The city will see that your days are numbered, too, boys, if the police have anything to prove against you."

Joseph was stunned to quietness. Wahl separated them and sent him inside the barn for the night. Glad to be resting in the straw but sick with horrible wonderings about Peckory's demise, Joseph examined the contents of his trunk. Everything had been searched through, for all was in disorder. The Bible was missing, either left behind in his mattress or found by now.

This would have been the best night to flee for his life, but his legs, still swollen like sausages, gave him no choice but to languish immovable in the dull moonlight leaking through the loosely shingled roof overhead.

A thousand times he thought he heard the patrollers coming for him. It was a night without sleep.

CHAPTER 24

NIGHT AND DAY JOSEPH was in fear because of Peckory's merciless fate. He and Harris did not even dare to speak about it.

Only after his tender flesh wounds healed did Joseph start believing that perhaps he would be safe. The whole ordeal left him feeling permanently wary, a scar on his emotions and soul like the scars he carried on his body.

While he was walking home to Mr. Wahl's after church the first Sunday in October, a coach pulled up beside him. Immediately he eyed it with apprehension. It was the Callcotts' vehicle, and no one seemed to be inside. But Unc' Ezra and Aunt Nancee were in their Sunday clothes seated side by side on the driver's bench.

"Take ahold," Ezra called to him and pointed to the footman's place. "We don't have much time, but Miss Mayleda wants to see you 'fore she leaves the town for home."

Surprised, Joseph got up. He rode through the streets and through the open gate to the Gibbes house yard. His cloak of constant uneasiness thickened when he jumped down. Ezra encouraged him.

"There ain't nobody here but Missy."

Nancee led him inside, where Mayleda awaited him.

"Joseph!" Mayleda's voice in the unlighted hall had a tone of urgency and secrecy. "I didn't think Brant would approve of my wanting to see you, so I told him I was coming here to collect some things—which I am—but then I sent Ezra around to find you. I hoped you'd be at church."

"I was, miss," Joseph said with much caution and with his eyes held down.

"Oh, Joseph, I have so many things to say, yet probably they mean very little in the grand scope of what is likely to happen. First, I want to speak about Daddy."

"Yes!"

"He's so unwell. The palsy has claimed his whole right side, though most days he's alert and able to speak, which Dr. Bachman and others say might, in and of itself, be a miracle. He's not welcoming to doctors because of how little they were able to do for Mama and my brothers."

Joseph was too sorry to even express himself.

"I know it's a terrible burden, not only for us children but for the servants also."

Joseph was surprised by her insight. "Yes."

"Let's see! We have so little time. I know you are in school! My daddy told me. And I know your tongue is healed. He told me that too. And for all that I am well pleased."

"You are." He breathed it as a statement but felt it as a question.

"I must know! Are you willing to come home and care for Daddy again if Brant will trust you?"

"Missy, that is not for me to say! I am a slave—"

"Oh, you are more than that to me!" She dared to touch his hand. He drew back, knowing what a touch could cost him.

"Don't take me wrongly!" She stepped back too and put her hands together. "I am here to speak to you friend to friend. Can it still be as it was when we were children?"

"I don't see how, Miss Mayleda."

"That's because of the terrible environment we are in! There's nothing morally wrong with our being friends! By Bible terms we are sister and brother. Oh, Joseph, I'm not going to have many opportunities like this one, but I want you to know that I support your freedom."

"My freedom!"

"Why, yes. Has Brant never come by to speak with you? Has Mr. Wahl said nothing?"

"Miss, I'm not sure what you are speaking about!"

"My daddy's petitioned the State Assembly to see if they will vote to release you upon his passing."

"Release me! As in manumission?"

"Yes! You didn't know?"

"No, ma'am!" Joseph could hardly fathom that their talk was real.

"Oh! I suppose Brant has his reasons! Perhaps he is afraid of Mr. Wahl's reaction. Daddy's been unable to write letters, and such news would be far too dangerous to put through the mails until the legislature's decision is final."

"Miss Mayleda, forgive me, but I don't see how a body of slaveholders will ever vote to free a slave."

"I know it would be rare, but there's a state Supreme Court judge who supports manumission in cases where the servant has been loyal in service unto his master's death. And you have been that to us, taking care of my brothers and my dear mother. And now, if you would care for Daddy—" Her voice broke with a sob.

"Dear Miss Callcott, I would come home to help whether freedom was talked about or not, for nobody has ever been better to me than Master Abram."

"Oh, I want you home. Things now seem so dangerous in Charleston. And every word I've said about the petition is true! Living within the confines of Delora until this summer as Eric and I did, I could never have imagined human hate and fear being so strong as it is. A few men daring to have friendships with colored freemen have died mysteriously in this town, and I've seen how even the Renslers deprive and belittle their help. Once we drove past the city workhouse, and I heard slaves scream and cry. Believe me, if I were grown and not a woman, I would escape this life."

He looked at her hands. "Just like a young running slave?"

"*You're* not thinking of running, are you? It's too dangerous! And you would break Daddy's heart. In his fevers he calls for you, Bette says. That's why it is my request and my fervent prayer that Brant will let you come home—unless you truly do not want to be at Delora anymore."

"If I could help your daddy, I would come," Joseph answered soberly. He felt a commitment to this man and to dear sweet Mayleda that went far deeper than slavery.

"I hoped you would say that!"

"But I'm not hoping for manumission, and neither should you. From what I've seen, ma'am, the world is too cruel for that."

"There's still a God in heaven. Daddy's changed his will so that you will come to me when he dies. I pledge, as God is my witness and judge, I will do everything I can to get you out of slavery, whether or not the state grants you manumission."

He was touched by her compassion but hardly hopeful. "Miss, in Christian kindness you could do one thing for me. Tell me truthfully . . . how is Rosa?"

Her smile was bleak. "Yes, of course, I should have said. Daddy came home very weak that day after you gave him the book of poetry. Eric and I have been staying with the Renslers all summer but visiting Delora on Sundays. Quietly Daddy give the book to me to give to Rosa. When I went down into the street, she wept over it. I think you should have hope."

"But how is she!"

"Thin. Weak. If anyone besides God deserves recognition for keeping her alive, it must be Parris. Mr. Gund says that daily Parris finds her to encourage her."

Joseph felt the weight of what she said and dropped his head. "I'm glad someone is able to do something for her." Already he mourned his loss of her in a way he had not done before.

"We mustn't linger. If we do get to see each other at Delora, please know that my coolness toward you will only be for the safety of us both."

"I understand, miss."

"Look at me, Joseph! You will always be more of a brother to me than a slave. Can you believe that? Your friendship has been so genuine, your person noble."

"If you find no offense, Miss Mayleda, then I will say you have been a fine Christian sister to me."

She smiled her smile at him very quickly, then picked up a small box of possessions from the hallway. Joseph carried it for her to the carriage.

"Whatever Missy had on her heart to say to you in there took way too long," Uncle worried, looking at the worn watch he carried. "Mass' Brant's gwine be over here any minute lookin' for her if I don't drive her to South Bay directly."

"Then you do that, Unc'," Joseph said, already heading to the gate. It would not benefit anyone to have him found on this property with only the master's daughter here. "I can walk through Charleston nearly anywhere on Sunday. It will be no problem for me to head home on foot."

Ezra nodded. "You take care!"

"Yes, sir. You do the same."

By the time he was back out on the street, everything felt unreal to him. Had he really spoken about a slim chance for ultimate freedom? Had Mayleda really offered her friendship—forever? Had Rosa really cried over his book, then been comforted by another man? It all made life seem as unstable as the wind and as unsteady as the sea.

He found himself reaching out to heaven as the clouds released their stored-up torrents of rain in hard, stinging drops. As had happened so many months ago in the sunrise, Joseph now sensed God speak to him in the storm. He'd have to face his future just as he had to face this driving rain—pressing on, taking no shelter, for there was no way over it, or under it, or around it. The only way was through.

———

By now Brant was becoming adjusted to being engaged and having his formerly independent ways intruded upon. Almost every night Ann wanted him to stay after supper and sit on the porch for conversation. Tonight was to be their last night in the city, and again they sat side by side looking out over the moon-sparkled water after a day of rain.

As usual, Ann wanted to discuss details of the wedding. "What do you think about flowers?"

Brant chose to tease her. "Flowers! Oh, he may come, though I do not know him personally."

She smiled over their evening cups of coffee. "Well, you do know his wife, Petunia."

"And the children!" he said smugly. "Daisy and Begonia."

Ann laughed. "You have been pretty patient with me, dear. Have I bent your ear every night with wedding plans?"

"Indeed you have." He turned his head and held his ear so she could see how crooked it had become. Then he added mildly, "But, darling, you have been so *pretty* through it all, I hardly mind the agony associated with my state."

"Honestly, do you think roses would be nice?"

"Yes, by all means. Invite them."

"Be serious!"

"I am! Have whatever flowers you want, just as long as I am the one getting you."

Corinth stepped up to pour more coffee, and neither of them refused. She was there for more reasons than just to hold the serving pot, but Brant made certain the slave would have no cause to be concerned about their actions. Ann's commitment to faith had made their courtship a hallowed blessing. Though he counted the days until their union, he was content to wait to touch and kiss her until Ann was his in God's sight. But waiting didn't mean that he could not sit with her and enjoy the sweet, heady communion of her companionship.

Whenever Brant let himself relax like this, he could almost believe that all was right with the world. His wife-to-be was like a beautiful canary with her bright dress and lovely voice. She had become so tender since her conversion after one of Dr. Bachman's powerful Sunday sermons. Even while busy with wedding plans and tutoring his sister and brother, Ann now made time for church meetings and afternoon teas with other young female believers.

Sitting close beside her, Brant experienced regret that his mother had not lived to see this, the answer to her prayers. From his boyhood, he knew she had continually petitioned heaven for a believing wife for each of her sons. That Brant was the only one to reach that privilege put him into silent, humble awe. Eric came out and sat beside them. As usual, Ann showed no resentment at his wanting their company. In fact, she spoilt him a little by giving him a sip of the sweetened coffee in her cup. He smiled and stayed near her, somewhat to Brant's regret.

Teddy's horse came into view under the streetlamps that formed a gold line between the waterfront and the ornate iron gate. Brant surmised that he was coming to talk him into slipping off for a game of whist at the Young Planters' Club. As usual, Brant was ready to refuse, since he truly enjoyed Ann's company more than sitting in a smoky clubhouse bantering about finances and political unrest.

Ann's cousin was barely on the porch before he made a tense announcement. "Alderman Kennedy's calling a special meeting. It seems some low-class scoundrels took offense this afternoon at seeing that darkie teacher Payne walking like a gentleman with a cane. They struck him down and brought him in, and he's been jailed for hours. Now that the news is out, however, the incident is causing quite a rub, for there are some white church folk who do not want him held for trial, even though Payne broke the law by boldly resisting the ruffians—"

"I hardly want to hear it, Teddy. Ann and I are busy with other things."

"But you need to hear it, Brant. Some clergymen are at the courthouse ready to speak in Payne's defense. They want him released because of his reputation within the brown community."

"I don't have any interest in the fray," Brant told him. "If you stay with us, we can offer you a much nicer evening. I can even make you into a quick connoisseur of the latest wedding fabrics. And over coffee too."

The other man did not smile. "You need to be there! Those against Payne compiled a list of the Negroes he has wrongly influenced. One of the names they've posted is a registered slave called *Joseph*, owned by one A. *Callcott*."

"No!" Ann panicked.

Brant was out of his seat. "I'm sure it's not that serious!"

"Don't bet on it, my friend. Remember the connection being made between slaves in this town and those who had been in cahoots with the abolitionist Diller. A while ago the city patrol took one of those trouble-making niggers out to the hanging tree, and he had been a clerk at Grafton Mills."

"Isn't that where your daddy's Joseph works?" Ann cried.

Brant grabbed his hat. "Where is this meeting?"

————

Alderman Kennedy was in charge of the podium. As Brant and Teddy slipped into available courthouse seats, Brant took a look at the sour expression on this notable lawyer's face. He was the same attorney who had written the death sentence for Charleston's last colored anarchists, including Denmark Vesey.

As was often the case with accused Negroes, Daniel Payne was not present to hear any discussion of his fate. Coming in on the middle of things as they had, it took Brant a few moments to capture the essence of what was being said. The room was like a volcano, with tempers bubbling and erupting all around them. The windows had to be sealed, regardless of the oppressive heat, so that brown and black eavesdroppers could not hear a word. No Negroes were in the chamber.

"It's time this town stop catering to half- and quarter-breeds! Treat Payne like what he really is—a plain and simple nigger!" The man who spoke this in the alderman's presence had his coat off, and he mopped sweat from his mouth and chin, appearing to have already contributed much to the controversy.

Another commentator rose. "Again, I disagree! Belittling any civilized brown man will only work against us. For the sake of our future security we must continue to woo the 'copper' businessman and leader. If they sense too much dislike from us, then it will push them to organize slaves against us!"

"Here! Here!" and "Nay!" were vented all around them.

"I say let Payne go!" A third man stood in the simple dress of a white commoner. "I'm not ashamed to say I go to church with that colored man! He's a decent feller—more decent, to be sure, than those troublemakers who were out for sport and dragged him into controversy just because of a walking cane!"

"Which he used as a weapon of defense!" someone roared.

"Yes, defense! To save his own head!" another countered. "That should be allowed! Even for darkies! I'll speak for Payne also!" This voice of affirmation came from right behind Brant's seat, but he did not know the well-dressed gentleman, who could have been part of the city's clergy.

"He is no threat in our society," the man went on. "At best, he has only a Negro's small brain. He's pantomiming white education, so let the affluent brown men adore him. They are our real bricks of balance. Either we keep the rich brown men with us by mild concessions—like freeing Payne—or we lose them to add their weight to poor niggers, like Mr. Newman has already said."

"But Payne's school sows unrest in *black* men and *slaves*!" someone spouted. "Unlike other smart brown folk, Payne shows no exclusive respect for the privileged colored class that rescued him as an orphan. They would have done better to let him starve as an urchin in the alleyways!"

The argument kept spinning, one strand at a time.

"He's got rich and dangerous colored connections. The Bonneaus and Holloways—"

"All the more reason for us to use *him* to teach them all a lesson they cannot forget!"

"Nay! All the more reason for us to use caution!"

"He is a Christian, not a troublemaker!"

"He's a nuisance!"

"A demon with brown skin and a white man's mind!"

"No, a fool and a charlatan!"

"I say he's a genius, and maybe it's time we look at that!" This was said by the poor church-going man who had spoken earlier.

Alderman Kennedy pounded the podium. "I will give my assessment at this point, gentlemen. Payne is a half-breed with strong ideas and a plan that *can* be hazardous. He believes with all his heart that he can educate brown and black alike. It is undeniable that he is teaching them to write and read. Now history proves that darkies can and will wield mental tools, whether or not they have the sound intellect needed to sustain wise choices. For that reason, I maintain Payne does make our own colored population more threatening—to itself and to us. Therefore, I say we must consider the most logical and effective approach to closing his school."

"Agreed!" There was unity.

"Let's hang him!" someone cried.

Kennedy waved his hand. "Please. Just allow me a few moments to explain some things in our favor. First, do remember the upcoming elections and the power of the ballot! If you want to fight the encroachment of the Negro on this society, then *vote* for strong, intelligent leadership that can lead you in this pivotal battle." There was applause. "Along with strong leadership must come the prudent use of law. Consider the Seaman Acts. Since we've turned our attention to practicing what our legislators have been preaching for almost a decade, there's been increasing quiet on the waterfront."

Chuckling, Teddy leaned to Brant. "Ha! That's a premature statement. It's not peace but the sword we promote down there."

Brant found no pleasure in any of this, but Kennedy kept going.

"Let me say for the record that I fear how some of our more revivalist churchmen promote the false notion that a person of color can receive a *type* of noble, innocuous education. Sirs! Education of any sort for darkies can be no wiser than handing a shackled nigger his own set of keys!"

Cheers actually rose, which made Brant's blood chill, for they all were rallying against people like his own daddy.

"You cannot promote study without a corresponding loss of control! So let us employ *leadership* and *legislation* to put an end to colored *learning* everywhere in this city, in any backwater shanty, or on any plantation!"

There was more applause, and the lynching-minded attendants called out again. "Let's pick the night to string them all."

Mr. Newman rose and dared to frown at everyone. "That's ungodly counsel, Mr. Kennedy, and you know it! I beg you to remind this group that we also have a Judge in Heaven who listens to our every word. Besides, you have no idea what Payne is teaching. I know you all have gone through the records of other Christian brown men who are Payne's friends, and even there you've found nothing that is threatening. I believe if you make the same thorough examination of his school, you will find the very same thing."

"We're planning for that, man!" Kennedy said. "After next Saturday I will be able to tell you exactly what Mr. Payne is teaching. Quite some time ago one of my servants heard from a student of Payne's that the teacher was looking for swampland where he could send his older boys in search of reptiles."

There was laughing. "Ain't that just fittin' of darkie learning!" someone chimed.

Kennedy quieted the room. "Right after I learned that, I sent one of my boys over to Payne's schoolhouse with the invitation that his little band of 'scholars' could come over to my Sullivan's Island estate. Believe me, my sons and I will be there when they arrive to ask them some very pointed questions."

"Then you have to let Payne out of jail to go back to his school," one of the best-dressed men reasoned. "That's the only way to work your scheme."

"He could flee," the man beside him worried.

"Not Payne," a third man said with assurance. "He's convinced he has a *call from God* to teach *our* darkies."

"*A call from God!*" Teddy was the one to shout it loudly. "You mean like Turner's call during the solar eclipse to murder women and children? Or Vesey's call to overpower us all?"

Alderman Kennedy had to shout to plead for order. Brant had gooseflesh because of Teddy's words. He truly began to see the possibility that Joseph could be hanged once they got so far as to decide what should be done with the students. But then at the alderman's decision, the talk was cut off. They went back to some previous conclusions. It would be best to trap Payne with the full strength of the law so that all Negro schools could be closed by legal methods. And to obtain that full strength, it would be helpful to know exactly what Payne did. Then the law could be written to ban his work completely.

"We are right to let Payne go back to his classroom temporarily," a prominent fellow alderman agreed. The crowd became docile and spent in the airless heat. "Then we will effectively target our legislation and send him packing for Africa—or some other foreign, heathen land."

"Such as Connecticut or New York, you mean!" Laughter rippled through the room.

Brant stood. "Teddy, I'm leaving."

Teddy followed him to the nearest door. As Brant pushed it open, General Wilton Morton joined them. "Say, I need to have a word with you two. The *Swiftlight* is in harbor, and there's every reason to believe that Tom Diller's been working on board as a bogus textile purchaser."

"Then we'll get him!" Teddy said with force.

"By now, the 'getting' should be 'got,'" Morton said. "But I'd like you to go down there if extra help is needed."

"Sir, we'll go," Teddy said.

"I don't think I will," Brant ventured quietly. "It's been a long enough evening for me. Miss Rensler is waiting—"

"You know, I never expected things to work out as they did," the general said, opening a piece of paper he had with him. "We found this pushed through the cracks on Marsh's Wharf, where the *Swiftlight* is tied up. What do you think, Mr. Callcott?"

Brant reviewed the ash-smudged sheet where the names of ships, captains, wharves, and dates had been penciled in rows by a shaking hand. "These are some of the same steamers and operators we've been suspecting," he said.

"Yes." The general looked at him oddly. "How do you think this writer knew that?"

"It's obviously a list made by some literate darkie."

"Obviously, Mr. Callcott. Is it possible that one of your own Delora slaves has been involved?"

"No, sir!"

The general smiled. "I'm not accusing you. Nor am I asking you to discount it so ferociously. Whatever the case, this list helped us to be on the lookout for Negroes trying to escape by way of these different vessels. And sure enough, it took us to Tom Diller himself. I thought you might have had the savvy to actually plant the information among the Negroes by using a Negro."

Brant said nothing while Teddy looked over his wire-rimmed spectacles. "You don't seem happy, Brant, yet you spent your whole summer working toward exactly this kind of event."

Brant despised Teddy's smugness. Did he know what kind of anguish this would cause his daddy if it was found that Joseph was involved in any way? Or did he just want to see Joseph put to death and out of the way?

"I suggest you stay close to your town house through the weekend, Mr. Callcott," General Morton said. "After the Kennedys have had time to confront those schoolboys, the next step might be to take them before the slave-court tribunal, perhaps as early as next week. Your Joseph is likely to be among them, since it's known by all that he's been going to that school by night."

A slip of the waxing moon peeked through the shanty window like God's half-opened eye. It kept Billy awake by its steady, unblinking scrutiny. After a long while of being made uncomfortable by it, Billy got out of the high featherbed and slipped on his pants and shirt.

Mass' Abram's sickness had sentenced him to the life of an unmarried man, since Bette lived up in the big house now to care for the planter day and night. That, in itself, was enough to make an old husband's sunless hours lonesome, for Billy found much comfort in having a soft, loving wife. Yet it wasn't so much Bette's absence, but the sure sense of God's *presence*, that made resting impossible for Billy tonight.

He went outside, muttering to the Almighty as though God were only a patient bossman. "A'right! I know! I should be the obedient one when it comes to listenin', Lord. But, Sah, I'm just plain tired of bein' knocked down an' havin' everybody 'round me in that 'xact same po'sition. I am sorry, Sah, but—!" He stopped on the porch. If he were sorry for real, then Billy knew that he would change. Rubbing his face, he turned his eyes up to the stars spread like silver dust over this land called America, maybe one of God's most troublesome spots on earth.

"Sah," he started in again to justify why he had been done with praying and singing since the patrollers had come to put his son in chains. But his cry of protest changed when he felt no heavenly disapproval but only deep divine love wanting to soak him in its knowing. "Oh, Papa-God!" he moaned, daring suddenly to vent out all his misery and sensing once again that faith was making him more of a son than a slave to the Master of Heaven. "Oh, Papa-God, help me, for my heart is nigh to breakin'. Any comfort in this life 'bout to end, Sah, onc't Mass' Abram goes on to see you face-to-face."

Out in the quiet street, God drew so close Billy could hear Him within. *You pray that my will be done on earth, Billy. Don't be like the disciples sleepin' in the garden of agony or like those foolish maids what don't keep 'nough oil in they lamps to burn through to the final hour.*

"Lord God Almighty!" Billy called aloud, his knees weak as a child's because he felt his God so near. "Forgive me for desertin' the watchman's tower!" Wonderfully he sensed holy love, instead of holy condemning fire. At once he set out toward the little old prayerhouse beyond Hermon

Creek. Back in the days when Billy's daddy had been the driver for Delora, the elder African had been the estate's most fervent pray-er for a whole generation of people, both black and white. That's how Billy, as a child, had become a pray-er, too, first at his daddy's side and then in his daddy's place.

Over the course of time, his own son, Parris, had been coming up to do the same—that is, until patrollers had beat him down so hard. As a boy Billy had never thought much about either the humiliation or harm brought on blacks by whites, but now there wasn't an hour when he didn't consider such things. In the beginning there hadn't been many events to shake Billy's faith in God. But after his own son had been jerked around by white men who professed to be Christians, it seemed like he'd lost the desire to ever speak with God.

Reaching the prayerhouse, he already had considered how unwise it was to hold his own opinions up higher than those of the Most High God. Now, again, he saw how foolish he was to hold out for something—or somebody—more trustworthy than the Lord. No matter what, from now on he would pray and he would listen, even if the outcomes did not suit him in this dry and weary land. The little prayerhouse, all covered with vines and under big trees, had been built over a mysterious boulder his daddy had found about two stone-throws from Hermon Creek. When his daddy had been young, he had come out to that rock to pray, and there he had felt the presence of God rain down upon him with the warmth of sunshine, even on the darkest, dampest nights. Kneeling against that rock, his daddy believed he had heard God's voice directly. *"Lead my people in prayer an' praise, or someday this rock will cry out against you an' your descendants."*

You couldn't see the rock now, for it was under the floor, but Billy still felt an amazing anticipation as he pushed open the humidity-swollen door. To perfectly follow in his daddy's footsteps, Billy should have called for all-night prayer in this shanty that very evening, because Saturday and Sunday nights were good times for the people to come away for prayer.

But since planting time and the start of Parris's troubles with the law, Billy had neglected to call anybody together for even one night of spiritual watchfulness. "Well, Lord, I'm back," he muttered sheepishly, still fighting the hard memories of what church-going patrolmen had done to his son. He found a likeness between this old shanty and his soul. Both were the temples of the Lord, and both were pretty sorry structures, considering the power and glory of the One they were so privileged to contain. The building's insides were as dark as a cave, so he slipped his shoes across the grit-strewn wooden floor, thinking on all those times folks had danced and shouted and whirled and fallen to their knees, meeting the God of Heaven in this humble place.

By touch and memory he sat down where he usually sat on one of the four worn benches that lined the walls. Leaning forward, he put his elbows on his opened legs. He let his hands and head hang limply near his knees. He began to pray, and it wasn't long till he sensed that there was more than just his own breathing pumping out a rhythm in this place. He was not frightened, exactly, but it seemed irreligious just to say "hallo," so he pondered the experience for a moment more and then whispered boldly, "I believe the Lord be in this place."

The response was strong and female. "Let all the earth keep silent 'fore Him!"

"Bette! Gal! How you get the time to come here?" There was tantalizing pleasure in finding his wife here.

"Miss Mayleda." He could hear the smile in her voice. "She done never forgets our nights of prayer. Watches over her daddy, so we all can come down."

We all? The words set him to listening again, and then he knew that even the two of them were not alone. "Who the others?"

A quiet voice. "Sista' Jewell." *Joseph's mama.*

A rough one. "Bro' Sampson!" *The blacksmith.*

A tired one. "Bro' Abiel, here." *Negozi's man.*

Each answered in turn down the line on one of the side benches he could not see. Billy was ashamed. For three months he had neglected prayer, but not these others. He felt so unacceptable that he just sat there for a time. When no one else led out, Billy realized they all were waiting for him, thereby still acknowledging the authority vested in him so long ago by his daddy. Amid great emotion he lifted a song. In his younger years his voice had had the semblance of his son's. Tonight it cracked with feeling.

> Come, we what love the Lord,
> An' let our joys be known.
> Join in a song with sweet accord,
> An' thus surround the throne.

The ceiling seemed to be pushed off by the strength of their voices.

Let them refuse to sing,
What never knew our God.
But servants of the heavenly King
May speak their joys abroad.

When they stopped, they had all been in the dark so long that Billy could almost make out the others' forms and faces. He stood, and whether or not the others could see him, they also rose to their feet. Each stepped forward until Billy felt the arms of the ones beside him. Then he stepped through them to the center of their swaying, living ring. He started humming, then praying, then clapping, then shouting. Heel then toe, they moved around him like an iron wheel turned on its side and spinning slowly. Like an iron wheel, it had strength and music as it moved. And Someone had put it all together. And it had someplace to go. The folks traveling in this tight group began to lift new songs never uttered before. They danced. They praised and prayed in whatever ways the Spirit moved them.

Bette wailed on account of Parris, who still shunned the comfort of their Holy God. A little later Abiel cried out for the Holy Ghost to "move double-quick" to save Negozi from her voodoo-doctoring ways. Others pleaded with their Lord and their Savior for wholeness, for mercy, for bodily strength. And after a great deal of time there was sobbing from a woman whose voice Billy did not know. "Oh, God, help me! Oh, God, find me!"

Other women moved to the source of the crying. Though Billy could not see them well, he knew they were putting their hands upon the girl to lend support. His heart warmed while his limbs chilled in awe of God's greatness, for he believed this first-time seeker was Rosa, who may have never set foot in the prayerhouse before. What if they hadn't broken the walls of their discouragement and come? What might still be bound and never be loosed on earth as in heaven, if they all had neglected to praise and pray?

Overwhelmed like the rest of them, Billy got down on his sore stiff knees. His mind went to Joseph, wherever he might be. "Lord, save him! Lord, help him! Lord, give him strength in this hour! Oh, Papa-God! Shield him from the meanness of our enemies."

Suddenly there was light, and it was unholy.

Billy and all the others covered their eyes and stayed frozen to the floor. Lanterns were thrust through the door, and those lamps seemed buoyed by demon fingers. Cursing and insults rode in on the air. Billy made it to his feet, then whirled after a flailing stick smashed his cheek and ear. Falling again to the floor, he had enough sense and strength to make sure his burly form was thrown in such a way as to guard as many of the women as he could, including Bette, Jewell, and Rosa.

"You know better than to have any secret nigger meetings, boy!" Some member of the beat company Billy didn't know railed at him. He covered his head and neck the best he could and waited for the next slicing blow. It never came.

"For the love of God, don't strike them!"

The cry seemed familiar. *White*—yet comfortable in its Gullah. Billy pushed the women fully to the floor, then looked with surprise to find Hampton Gund rising from his knees in the prayer circle. "These are my charges! An' I've been with them all the while!"

With almost unbearable gratitude Billy bit his lip and turned his face upward. Mista Gund had been praying with them. Even as they had done their holy begging to be free from every cursing buckra, he had never said a word to stop them. From the floor Billy saw the Delora overseer's red face, and it looked like it belonged to a saint twenty feet tall.

"You let them all pray *against* slavery!" The young patrol sub-captain, Mr. Clemson, came forth to accuse Gund.

The overseer answered, "They are Christians cryin' out to God on account of their sorrows. I will not blame them."

"You simpleton!" the head of the patrol shot back. "They pray against *you!*"

Gund caught Billy eyeing him. Their gazes linked for one incredible moment. "Then let them pray against me, sah," Gund said. "An' God have mercy on my soul if I *am* the cause of any of their tears, for Christ knows I *am* a wicked, wretched man in constant need of my Savior."

Billy saw their white heads wagging. A few of the young planters swore at Gund without reservation.

"You should be tarred as black as they and hanged for letting them have such liberties. Where's the boy, Parris? We'll make use of him again."

"He ain't here." Gund set his hands to his hips. "An' this time you not gwine touch nobody, for this here's a legal meeting 'cause I am present as their *lawful supervisor.*"

The patrolmen laughed hotly. "Well, maybe you should be removed for your lack of competence."

Billy cringed with worry, and Gund showed a moment of flagging too.

"If you have a problem with me, sir, then take that up with my employer,
Gund came back as strong as before. "Meantime, get off his property 'fore
I counsel Mr. Abram to file a complaint 'gainst you all for trespass." Billy
saw Gund put his hand to the pistol in his belt when no one in the white
group moved. "If you all're so touchy 'bout how Negroes pray, then maybe
it's a sure sign that you the ones what should be spendin' time on you'
knees *'fore the dark sun rises* an' judgment catches you all unawares."

"Gund, you can lose your job for this!" the patrol sub-captain warned.
"And we can make sure there's no safe place for you to go."

"I maintain that I did nothin' wrong, an' neither did they. You all are
the ones what intruded on our peace. An' I have the right, sah, to say that
in court."

"You all are niggers. Every last one!" Clemson told Gund before heading out.

Billy could only admire the white overseer in silence until the intruders
were gone. Then he got on his feet. "Boss! 'Cause of you, there wa' no
arrests, no beatin's."

"Yeah." Gund looked like a man in mourning. He grabbed Billy and
took him outside, away from the others and into the moonlight. Together
they watched to make sure the patrol was riding away. "Look," he said,
turning toward Billy when they could finally trust that they were alone. "I
weren't in there to be no supervisor. I came . . . well . . . 'cause I knowed
I needed prayer."

"You gwine tell us to stop since this done happen?"

Gund frowned. "On the contrary. I was wonderin', Billy . . . would you
spend some time prayin' out here just for me?"

CHAPTER 25

ON THE DAY THAT SOME OF THE BEST of the Madagascar rice was being sorted out for next year's seed, Rosa finally gathered the courage to speak to Parris before he spoke to her. The prime African was still Delora's strongest worker, but his time in chains had seemed to permanently bow both his body and his will.

He now went through the days almost as Rosa did, looking exhausted from start to finish. When she timidly came to him on their afternoon break, he appeared to be sleeping under a cluster of hornbeam trees. He was on his back with his head pillowed by the drab wool cap he'd taken to wearing in all kinds of weather. She had never come to him before, so when he opened his eyes suddenly, she was the one to feel startled and uneasy. Standing within his gaze, she was aware of her bony ugliness and bore it like a protective cloak. As he sat up, his stare carried curiosity and open kindness, but there was no trace of that former desire he had shown for her.

Because of that she risked sitting down beside him on the leaves, though far beyond his reach. She had gone back to tying up her head in the dull red kerchief. Compared with this cool, green piece of shade, she felt dirty. "I came to say I know I never thanked you for taking on the whole patrol because of me."

He showed no warmth toward her for her comment. "Yeah, well, a lot of good it done."

"I don't care what it *did*, Parris. It's what it *meant* that mattered."

He scrutinized her, his eyes growing just a little brighter. "And 'xactly what's that s'pose to mean?"

All the pain of her abuse swept over her. She found it difficult to stay and be the center of his focus. "That . . . that you cared what I was going through. That . . . that you tried to help me, even though you could have been killed."

Parris looked away. "Oh, how I wish I had been."

"You cannot let them drain the life from you!"

His pupils dilated and he laughed bitterly. "Just look at *you*, gal! You done got no right to talk to me!"

Rosa put her arms around her bosom. "I'm not going to starve myself anymore. Last week I went to one of your daddy and mama's all-night prayer meetings. I met the Holy Spirit of God."

He laughed again, no less angry than before. "So! You finally got you'-self religion, ainty! An' just 'bout the time when I am losin' mine."

"It's not religion, and you know it. I was hating myself and my life, and yet I was too afraid of demons and devils to kill myself. Your parents and others were having a 'shout' that evening, and when I fell to my knees and cried out for God to rescue me, *He came*, Parris. I felt Him. I knew He was there, though I cannot explain how. I knew He came, person-to-person, just to comfort me." She opened her hands against her heart.

"My! If that ain't first-rate, church-goin' testimony!"

"Don't mock me or your God, Parris! You know Jewell from the house. She stayed with me till dawn and heard me out. I can see how God put us together, for she knows what I've been through. It was the same for her—" Her lips bent hard with remembered agony. "Being just a body, used time after time." She dropped her head and watched herself trembling. "That's how Joseph was conceived, and she can be glad for him, though now she misses him severely. Despite earthly hell, she knows—as I do now—that we both belong to God. And I know Jesus did rescue me from eternal hell by His own suffering and death upon a cross long ago."

"Yeah?" Parris leaned back on his hands. "So tell me, onc't the meat's back on you' bones, how's Jesus gwine help you when the buckra comes 'round for you 'gain?"

In the darkness of his unbelieving, she felt her faith waver. "I can't say. I don't know. But I do know God was there to meet me when I cried out to Him with the other pray-ers."

He swatted a mosquito on his face and lay down, closing his eyes and taking his former position. "That what you done come to tell me? Well, then, I'd like to finish my rest."

Rosa bent toward him just a little. "Parris, all your talks convinced me to fear hell, and by doing so, you saved my life—both physically and spiritually. I can see the reason for the hope you once preached about. And I've come to beg with you. Please! Don't let them steal away those things that they should never be able to take from you. Your faith. Your trust in eternal righteousness. And your love of God."

"Don't preach at me, sista." He squinted and muttered like an old man wanting sleep. "You just startin' down that same ol' narrow pathway what I done already trod. If God hisself wants me to keep believin', then He had better show up and throw a few of my enemies into the lake of fire while I am 'spectating, or He's just a buckra's god!"

Rosa understood his anger. "Maybe God wants to show you a miracle by *rescuing* one of your enemies instead of by *damning* her eternally."

His vision opened.

"Parris, my family owned slaves and treated them worse than the patrollers treated you." She had to cover her face. "Though my daddy was a Haitian mulatto, he used the whips and the chains. He even had his black 'hot box' just big enough to hold a slave man. And whenever he deemed one of ours was disobedient, he'd pen him up inside all through the heat of the day. When I was a young girl, I remember standing under the shade of my parasol and looking across our fence when someone was inside. Oh!!! When my father would pull them out, each one was like a corpse, yet still alive and half crazy with heat and sickness." She shut her mouth and could barely swallow to think on it now. Her father could have owned Joseph or Billy or Parris . . . or even her, if she had not been his daughter, and he could have done that to any one of them.

"I practiced the piano to the sound of women being lashed. At night I often stayed with my mother . . . because . . ." She could hardly get the words out. "Because my father so enjoyed finding his pleasure in our own street."

Rosa was bent by the agony and the guilt of it all. "All these years, since the burning of Aspidae and the death of my parents, I have focused on what had been taken from *me*, a planter's daughter sold into slavery. You can't image the loathing I had for *my* family's male slaves. There was nothing worse for me on the face of this earth than to have our white neighbors round up those black men and *me*! They sold me along with them. No wonder our Negroes hated me and wanted to abuse me rather than give me mercy. My daddy sowed the seeds of hatred in them, and I was the reaper."

Parris looked away. "You don't have to do this to yourself, girl, just for me."

"It's for me also. To remember what pride and hatred do. Day by day I begged the cruel white drivers to see me as *one of them*. The slaves heard my words. I called them pigs. And dogs and much, much worse. Oh, Parris! You could have been chained in with them, and I would have said the same of you."

Weeping overtook her. "It was only after you went out seeking Rensler that I came face-to-face with how much integrity you and many of the Africans have. It was only then that I allowed myself to think on how my father devastated many Aspidae women and their daddies and lovers."

Parris was stoic, and Rosa did not blame him for hating her now after hearing her speak. "I mourned only *my* injuries and *my* losses," she continued, "but never those my family caused. If you cannot forgive me, I understand. But know this, God took the very worst that could happen to a woman, and in a strange way, He used it as the path by which to set me free." She sobbed, rocking softly. "Please, Parris, go back to loving God. Please! For now I see it is the only way to climb out of the sin that entraps us all, whether it is our fate to be slave or master."

From some place beyond the shade, Billy's conch-shell horn blew its warning. In a few moments it would blast again, pushing them back to work. It seemed to waken Parris to reality. "Rosa, be done with thinkin' on others. Talk 'bout us. Under all this load of grief an' guilt, you still one beautiful gal to me." His reach terrified her. Instantly she drew away.

He showed no understanding. "You just testified to bein' changed! An' I'm tellin' you that for as long as this cruel world lets me live, I want to have you as my own."

She looked at herself. "No, Parris, I couldn't."

His frown was convicting. "Bet you wouldn't say the same if I wa' Joseph."

She looked at him, seeing jealousy inside him that she had not known before. "Believe me, I . . . I had no interest in Joseph when I first went to help your mama care for him. From my first moments here all men have been loathsome to me. I went to look at him only out of curiosity because I overheard your parents say he had been banished and mistreated because he had taught himself to read without the master's permission."

She saw the surprise on his face.

"I know! See, that's what interested me, too, I confess. I thought he would be brown like me to have a mind like that. I wanted to know him just because I was hungry to find someone—anyone—with that skill. For I, too, can read."

He squinted at her, now following her every word.

"He probably knew I was looking down on him, and I was. But only for a time, because he won my trust, and then my heart—I'll admit it—by his gentleness and humble ways. In his weakness I saw so much strength. Yes, I think about him now. Yet at the same time I hope that I may never see him again, for I cannot think that I will ever be right for any man. Though God has rescued me, I still fear—" She could not go on.

Parris shook his head. "You remember what I used to say to you? That if it wa' the last thing on earth, I'd find some way to make you smile? Well, I sure didn't mean that as no promise to watch afta you an' save you for some other brother." His eyes spoke to her of hurt, not anger. "Howsumever, if that's the way you want it, then all I can say is that Joseph owes me a heap of thanks if he ever does get hisself back here."

Rosa hid her face. "All I've done up to now is live out of my own selfish pride. I'm not worthy of either one of you."

"Shoot! I know all 'bout that pride of livin'!" His voice was quite subdued. "It wa' pride what been my real slave driver ever since my youth. No matter if it be my singin', prayin', workin', or preachin', I set my mind on doin' all things well in order to make somebody take notice that this ain't just no ordinary black boy they have here."

He lifted his wrists and looked at the ugly marks the iron bands had left on them. It seemed to Rosa that he had no more energy. "It wa' to my shame how I done lived so long for human praise. You right, Rosa. I done let them beat me 'cause I wa' tryin' to live off they approval—not God's." He sighed, then changed the subject. "Can Joseph *read*, for true?"

"Yes." She felt cautious of saying anything because it was a secret that even his parents had kept from him.

Parris bit down on his lip, studying her carefully. "You readin', I can understand, havin' so much white blood in you. But Joseph!"

"Color has nothing to do with one's ability to read or write. I don't know how any of us could have been so easily persuaded to think otherwise."

He answered her with a question. "You think I could learn?"

"Yes, if you had a book or a pencil."

Parris scraped the ground in front of him with his thumbs. "We can use the dust!"

Rosa was amazed by his exuberance—and worried too. "Why are you so interested?"

"How am I gwine live just unto God, pleasin' Him only, if I don't even know what He wants of me? I am a grown man, yet it's only white Christians what instruct me, flippin' through the Holy Word right in my face, choosin' an' skippin' whatsumever pieces I *may* an' *may not* know!" He ran his hands over his head and put on his cap. "Oh, to have the whole Word an' the whole picture of His glory! God knows I would be done with bein' just a Gospel Society 'nigger-boy believer' if I could just read the whole Book, cover to cover, for myself."

His intensity left her breathless. "I'm sorry to say I have no idea what's in the Bible. My parents were no lovers of Christianity, and my mother, when feeling low, dabbled in the magic she knew from her island."

They heard twigs snapping and saw Gund come to look for them. Parris directed his hand toward the rice field as he fit in one last comment to her. "Missy, this here's all the world I done ever knowed."

She smiled sympathetically, understanding his full meaning, for he had already caught the vision. By reading he could know the world beyond his reach.

The dusty overseer stepped between them. "Didn't you all hear the horn? You coming t'day or t'morrow?" Mr. Gund sounded gruff, but at the same time Rosa saw the brightness of tolerance in his eyes. Despite the risks from the patrol for himself and his family, Gund had stayed lenient with them both.

"We a-comin', boss," Parris said, and Gund trusted him, leaving them alone a moment more. Like one trying to coax a wild bird to come to his fingers, Parris slowly extended his hand. This time Rosa found herself reaching back. With a strong, steady arm he gently pulled her to her feet, then released her to walk on her own beside him. Again, her admiration for him swelled because of the consideration he showed her. With reluctance she entered the scorching sunshine. Parris paused before they separated to join their different work groups. His words were halting. "I want to thankyee for comin' to talk to me. With God's help, I gwine be done with walkin' in pride. It gwine be God's way from now on, whatsumever that means an' whatsumever the cost."

The last thing Teacher Payne taught Joseph on Saturday was that Latin verbs change in pronunciation and spelling to show different persons and periods of time. It was a difficult idea to understand. On a slate with chalk he labored to give Joseph examples, then he left him on his own to practice and repractice the same set of words. In Joseph's less skilled hand the chalk screeched, making background notes for every word he tried. *Laudo, laudas, laudat.* I praise, you praise, he praises.

Joseph lifted the white cylinder and studied how it powdered his hands just as the whitewash did at Delora. For the first time since coming to Charleston, he was finding it hard to study. He wondered what was happening to the master's petition for manumission that Miss Mayleda had told him about a week ago. He wondered about his master's health. Should he be home nursing him instead of here? Over the weeks he had put many medical notes in his notebook. Perhaps something from his studies would help to comfort the man who had made a way for him to learn.

Overtop all these concerns he still had an uncertain feeling about his own safety. He had only to raise his eyes and look silently upon his diligent teacher to understand why. Teacher Payne, lost in his work at his own desk, still wore the closed cuts across his forehead and cheekbone as sad reminders of the attack just a few days back that had caused him injury, a fine, and a night in prison. And if that hadn't been enough to distract him, Joseph thought of what more he had learned of Peckory's end. He was hanged for sedition in the swamplands at the edge of town. There had been no jury or trial.

His fingers tightened around the chalk. What had happened to Tag and Luck and Allis? Were they dead, too, or sold away by now? Since the night Wahl had retrieved him from Anson Street, he had heard nothing from the family. With frustration he put down his work. Wasn't this enough to show him how useless it was for a Negro to improve his mind when others still so easily could control his body? He was about to rise and tell this to his teacher when the door opened and the four daytime students scurried in. Payne was on his feet.

"I did not expect to see any of you until Monday morning!"

The young men scrambled to the science table. One of them unburdened his arms of a huge glass jar. Joseph jumped from his desk the instant he saw the venomous water snake curling and rising inside.

"It was a trap, Mr. Payne!" The student who shouted the decree was Philip Handsome. "We weren't on Kennedy property for more than an hour when that master and his son and some others rounded us all up for questioning as though we were bondsmen and they patrollers." As he spoke his eyes slid self-consciously to Joseph.

"They asked us all kinds of questions!" another panted, "and we thought we were right to give correct answers, because we did not want them to say we were fools when it came to science or mathematics."

"But still they called us monkeys and Gullahs and accused us of only wanting this snake for black-magic conjuring," a third student said.

Payne stood near them and very close to the reptile in the jar.

"They told us all that you will 'pay hell' for what you're doing in this schoolhouse," Philip said.

Joseph quietly stood and withdrew to the corner near the door. Suddenly the fourth student pointed back to him. "It's because you educate the likes of him," the privileged brown boy said. "They wouldn't care so much about us, but they worry because you will even teach black slaves!"

Joseph kept his back to the wall like one of the teacher's mounted specimens. Philip Handsome spoke in his defense. "If he can do the work, and he has his master's permission, who are we to judge him? If any our mothers were slave, not free, then we would have the same place he has."

"Not I!" The smallest boy's face was glaring. "My daddy's a planter, and I'm no field-hand darkie! Not one of our slaves is ever going to read."

"There's no fairness in that!" Philip said before Payne could step in. "I've been thinking much about this. How can we be any different just because of the color of our skin?"

"Well your daddy sure sees it different from you," the smallest boy accused. "He knows enough to respect our prominence. You go ahead and be like him—poor and black—if you want."

Payne ordered them all to take seats, though he left Joseph standing. "What has happened today must make you realize that the battle we're in is not just against flesh and blood, but against principalities and spiritual wickedness in high places. *Hate is hate, young men, and hate is not from God.*"

Joseph knew that Payne had his eye on him while he was still trying to make slow progress toward escaping this company.

"The noblest freeman is he whom Christ makes free!" Payne emphasized. "I have told that to each and every one of you. The Scriptures are clear that we are to no longer regard anyone from merely a human point of view. From the beginning of the church, God has been calling individuals from many nations and persons from all classes to be *His people*."

"But, sir, they do not all deserve education!" The smallest student said it like a miniature tyrant.

Payne rapped his knuckles upon his desk. "We will have no more talk about slavery within these walls. You know it is forbidden. Let me warn you all that without humility your talents and learning will be nothing but the accomplishments of the devil!" He raised his brows to show that he would not be mincing words. "Without humility, even faith and love and holiness will quail and perish in the presence of the tempter who is after your souls! The Christian—no matter what his class or race—is called to look upon himself as nothing and upon Christ as his all." The teacher looked directly at Joseph. "Educated, Christian men, you must learn to practice truth."

There was silence. No one else dared to look at Joseph, but Payne looked at them all as though to seal their hearts with his teaching. "You are dismissed, and you will not utter one more word until you are beyond the schoolhouse gate. Even then, you will not use your tongues to tear down anyone."

Joseph felt like a slug stuck to the wall as they passed him by with their mouths closed. Their dark sullen eyes communicated volumes to him.

When he and Payne were alone, his teacher came back to where he was standing. Joseph dared to speak before he was spoken to. "Sir, even before they came, I was thinking that all is useless for one like me. I was about to ask your permission to leave the school—forever."

Payne studied him with a seriousness that embraced much sadness. "These Kennedys they talked about are powerful men. I believe their fears are well founded. With the evidence they collected today, these men may try to construct a legal case against what I am doing here."

Joseph looked at his teacher's worn but well-cared-for shoes. "Sir, I fear it is my fault. Perhaps the city would not be so harsh to you if it had not been for me."

Payne chuckled softly. "Joseph. You are not my first bondsman student. Even your master knew that. I dare to instruct others, even now—bondswomen, black men—in the privacy of homes."

Joseph sighed, feeling that they all were sinking in a pitch-tar vat that would soon have them smothered and dead to this world that white men found so pleasing.

"Your master dared to come to me with his idea of giving you an education. Even if you leave, I will not go back on my original conviction that every Christian should be taught to read the Scriptures so that he or she may know the world God has made."

Joseph shut his eyes, unable to understand the feelings within himself.

"Whether we have one more day together, or three more months to the end of the year as planned, I want you to keep working. In this society they can move us and pen us by many physical methods. But with your faith in God and your learning, you need never let them trap either your spirit or your mind."

Joseph shook his head numbly.

"Why don't you go back to Mr. Wahl's and think on these things," Mr. Payne counseled softly. "Tomorrow, I'd like to go over your entire work record. I think you'll find it quite encouraging."

Despite his dismal feelings, Joseph allowed himself to smile with resignation. He knew he would never want to be away from this man who truly understood him and gave him courage.

"Until tomorrow," his teacher told him as he held the door for him.

"Yes, tomorrow." But even as Joseph said this, the words had a strangely sad and unbelievable ring.

Walking into Wahl's stable, Joseph had no sense of danger until the moment when men, hitherto hidden, revealed themselves from every corner. They laced themselves around him like a fishing net pulled up around its catch. "What!" He breathed only this one word before terror silenced him.

Among his assailants he saw the shadowy profiles of Theodore Rensler and even Mr. Wahl. From the circle that had him trapped, a policeman emerged to pin his arms behind his back. Too fearful and bewildered to keep his eyes from them all, he searched every hateful face. Mr. Wahl thrust a half sheet of paper into his vision. "How dare you play the trustworthy fellow when you assisted those bent on escape!"

Joseph's mouth would not even open. He stood feeling his wrists numb now that they were tied against his spine.

"We don't need his testimony!" someone behind him spouted as he pulled on Joseph's shirt. "We have this!" Joseph's notebook was discovered and thrown open so that the torn-out page he had given Luck fit exactly back into place. The stub of his pencil fell to the floor. They judged him as harshly for possessing it as they would have done had it been a pistol. "What more needs to be proved?"

He clamped his jaw. Any word to defend himself would make his punishment longer and harder. Already he might be facing death like Peckory. Theodore Rensler gloried in giving him a scowl. "I warned Mr. Callcott that you would be worse for not having been broken the first time around."

"He will be taken to the slave court," Wahl intervened firmly, as though for his protection. "For Abram Callcott's sake, I want this carried out in perfect order."

Joseph dared to look at him. The man had sense for only what was right according to the law.

"You were a fool to get yourself involved in this!" There was anger in the foreman's eyes. "If you don't follow Peckory to the same hanging tree, it will only be because the judges have pity for your master."

"Speaking as his master's physician, I don't think it's advisable to upset Mr. Callcott with this news," Teddy Rensler said. "Whatever the court tribunal sets as punishment will be carried out. You know there's no provision for negotiation or appeal on the slaveowner's part."

"I'll take that into consideration when deciding whether or not to contact Abram," Wahl said.

"But Brant Callcott will be called for immediately." That was Rensler's conclusion, and the policeman accepted it.

Then Joseph was pushed from the barn.

———

Ann could not believe that Brant had come in the middle of the night to see her. Morrison had let him in, and Corinth had dressed her and taken her down by way of the dark slave stairs so that no one but the servants would know they were meeting in the Pine Woods kitchen. Ann was already on the verge of tears, fearing whatever had brought Brant here. She found him sitting at the slaves' table, his head in his hands.

"Is it your daddy?" she said, coming to sit beside him.

"No. Joseph's in trouble again. This time with the city."

She struggled with why this could depress him so.

"They sentenced him to ninety days hard labor chipping gravel in the workhouse. If Mr. Wahl had not made a plea on my daddy's behalf, the punishment would have been hanging."

"What did he do?" she said, much more concerned about Brant and his safety than the slave's.

"They said he helped other slaves attempt escape."

"That's just what you've been working to prevent!"

"Yes, and then a *Delora* slave is caught doing it!"

"You must feel terrible humiliation."

"It's more than that! I can't explain it. Or else I'm too embarrassed to."

She stroked his shoulders, his head, his back. He looked up, still lost in his confusion. "I cannot shake the feeling that Joseph is very much like me. As hard as I've tried, and even with the counsel of so many, I cannot dismiss what I know about him as a person."

"Oh, Brant, you can't go back to that again! You'll drive yourself mad. As children, we both related to the Negro's natural inclination toward friendship and affection."

"But what if this is more than boyhood sentiments! What if God is saying to me that Joseph is a *man*, and that as a man—even though he's a black one—he needs freedom just as he needs air and water?"

She drew away, putting her thoughts together. "Regardless of what he *is*, he has broken the law. The loss of one slave can mean hundreds of dollars for its owner. Even a *man* would be sentenced for stealing property. If *you* put someone's slave on a boat and sent him off, *you would pay*. Why struggle so? Maybe this will finally be the end of it. Let him suffer as a man, if you must. But maybe after those days in the workhouse, he will finally submit and do as he is told. Or maybe your daddy will agree to part with him for good."

"But what if slaves should be free, by God's design?"

"Oh, darling! You've struggled through this already! You've brought it up with Dr. Bachman, and what did he tell you! That before coming here he lived in New York, where his servants could be freed. And what did the simple nigras choose? To follow him here! You should hear the talk on this plantation. Morris, Corinth—all of them want to be Delora people, not *free*! Now what does that say, but that you're doing everything in your power to become the benevolent slaveholder God is calling you to be?"

He answered only with his sighing. "Why do I struggle so?"

"Because you are tender-hearted, which is one of the hundred million reasons I love you." She dared to plant a kiss on her fingers and then transport it to his lips. "You are just and fair, my dear. If you struggle so, then maybe you should think of it as parenting. I know you want the best for them. Now maybe even Joseph will learn that the best for him is full obedience to you."

"I hope so. And I hope that I can be convinced of it too."

Whenever Brant's emotions gravitated to confusion, as they did now, hers went to fear. She wasn't sure that she would ever feel secure if Brant refused to wield authority with a stronger hand. But she didn't admit that directly. "It could have been absolutely providential that he was caught just before you were thinking of bringing him back to serve your daddy. Think about it! He could have carried this disruption to your home."

"He'll suffer tremendously."

"Then maybe he will learn! He'll have to, or you're going to have to face the harder decision of what to do with him next."

"I abhor violence. I keep saying that, but there seems to be no solution to it!"

"It comes only with *their* lawlessness. Please don't neglect to keep it all in right perspective."

"What am I going to tell Daddy?"

Ann only prayed, sensing that it was better for him to reach such weighty conclusions on his own. "God will lead you," she said, taking his hands into hers. "We can pray about it now. Oh, I'm glad you came. This is more than I could ever hope for—to have my husband-to-be consider me worthy to share his burdens and to comment on them."

"You are the only one I can tell! Do you know what the parish men would do if they heard me speak this way? They would commit *me* to the workhouse!"

"I wish there were more like you, so set on doing right. Compared with yours, my compassion is small."

"Oh, Ann, don't speak to make comparisons. Your reasoning about Joseph has been right. Yet I still feel troubled. Why is that?"

"Because you're tired and disappointed that Joseph let you down again. And, of course, you dread facing your family with this news. But in that hour you will find the right words to say. I believe that. And I will pray for it."

It surprised her tremendously when Brant suddenly and forcefully pulled her to himself and embraced her. "Oh, there seems to be so little comfort in this life, Ann. What would I do if God had not made a way for us to be together?"

"You'll never have to know the answer to that, darling, for He has made a way."

Then, for the first time in their years of courting, he kissed her on her lips.

———

From the start Joseph had counted his two meals a day of rice and water to help him track the time. Though not present at his hearing, he knew its outcome—ninety days hard labor for the crime of attempting to smuggle "property" out of Charleston.

According to Joseph's record keeping, today was Sunday. He had been here nine days. Since it had happened once to him already, he surmised that on Sabbaths he would be left alone in his tiny stinking cell, walled in by brick and closed off with an iron gate. He was exhausted and continued to lie on the bare, urine-filled clay, dressed only in workhouse trousers. He was cold and hungry, but not so hungry that he would reach for the dirty pottery bowl. His hands were too blistered to serve him. Since the city had no rock to quarry, it purchased stone ballast from New England vessels and then used slave prisoners to break it into gravel. In the process black men were broken, for the hours were endless and the conditions terrible.

Always now he tasted rock dust. Instead of eating, he chose to continue blowing on his burning, weeping sores while cradling his half-closed hands. Already he was having a hard time seeing them as a *man's* hands. Next to pain he realized that fatigue had tremendous power in crushing the human spirit. He swallowed, praying again that he might not lose sight of who he was in God. Looking to the gate, he hoped to catch a glimpse of morning light. Instead he found a white face looking back at him.

A black guard opened up his enclosure with a key and let the white man in. Joseph pushed himself to sit against the wall. That was not sufficient for his visitor. "You can stand, boy!" The man was Mr. Wahl.

Joseph could stand, but he wondered for a moment if he *would* stand, for his struggle with hatred burned as ferociously as his hands. Yet he did stand, for to slouch in another's presence seemed unbefitting of a Christian man. While getting to his feet, he prayed for strength to keep that vision.

With some gentleness Mr. Wahl pulled Joseph's palms to the light of the gate. "I thought this would be so by now." From the sack carried with him he took out long strips of flannel. "This bag is full of these," he said. "Use them to wrap your hands. As long as I get good reports on you, I'll continue bringing you all that you need."

Joseph hung his head. "Thank you."

"Boy, plan to use this time wisely. The slave-court tribunal was set on sending you to the gallows. It was an act of mercy toward your master, not you, that you've survived."

"I am not afraid to die," Joseph murmured softly.

"Well, I hope you are afraid to live, with the attitude you have! No one could have made a broader way for you to be grateful, and look what you did with your little bit of liberty! If you think that proves your kind should be free, then I stand amazed at how sorrily you have been deceived."

"No white masters were cheated by my *offense*, sir, for everyone I tried to help was a nominal slave, owned by others of the colored race!" Joseph spoke daringly in his own defense, for he had nothing to lose. "If I hadn't tried to help them, they all would have been captured and killed."

"Aye! As lawbreakers, for that is what the whole lot of you have been!"

Joseph dared to raise his eyes. "Sir, from the beginning the watch phrase of America has been 'Give me liberty, or give me death.' Why should it be different for those with colored skin?"

"Oh, death will come to you if you do not first come to know that America does not include your kind."

Joseph decided not to say more. Hadn't he heard in one of Payne's devotions that even Jesus was mute when they led him to slaughter? He felt the scars on his tongue. Perhaps the white race would never understand. But that couldn't matter anymore. With God's help he would keep on existing—or die—as a *Christian man*.

"You'll not be allowed to neglect religious instruction," Wahl said.

Joseph looked at him, trying to determine his meaning. The man produced a Bible and a set of Gospel Society teachings. "Get down on your knees, and I will lead you in recitation."

Joseph got down, but it was before his God, not Mr. Wahl. While the man shuffled pages, Joseph found himself already praying for many different things: strength for himself; the wits to continue reviewing all he had learned; courage for Rosa; protection for Luck and his family if they still lived; even an end to the "furnace of slavery," as Mr. Payne had called it.

"The Scripture for today and every day you spend here is Ephesians, chapter six, verse five. I expect you can, and will, recite that now."

It seemed an offense to God that a Christian would use Scripture to degrade and keep another Christian down, yet Joseph dolefully began the familiar words. " 'Servants, be obedient to them that are your masters, according to the flesh, with fear and trembling. . . .' " Even as his lips moved, he considered the tragedy of being given only this Scripture. From having his own Bible for those few precious weeks, Joseph had read all of Ephesians. Why weren't *masters* forced to their knees to say passages like this: "Be ye kind to one another, tender-hearted, as God for Christ's sake hath forgiven you"?

As best he could, Joseph continued speaking one thing while thinking another. Because of God's command, he would try to forgive Wahl for never understanding. Beyond the cell gate there was a rattling of keys. The black jailer came back. "Sah," he said speaking to Wahl, "there's somethin' here the city po'lice want you' boy to see."

Joseph moved his eyes, expecting his next view to be of a tortured Luck, or even Tag, for he knew what atrocities happened in the whipping rooms and on the treadmill that always rumbled in this place. He heard hard breathing, then saw a grotesque pitch-and-cotton covered form stagger in front of the gate. It steadied itself against the bars with a hand as thick and woolly as an animal's. Joseph had no idea of the human's identity—black, brown, or white. He did know that the victim could scarcely breathe, let alone walk or see. Even Mr. Wahl seemed aghast.

"Here's your beloved leader." The white workhouse master now came into view. "You want to honor him as the darkie savior he once proclaimed himself to be, before we throw him in the hold of the next vessel going north?"

Joseph rose in horror. The suffering prisoner showed his light-colored eyes. Tom Diller, tarred and cottoned now. Immediately Joseph pressed against the gate. "What has happened to Luck?" The jailer and the workhouse master pulled Diller away before there could be any answer from his tar-blistered lips.

Sick of heart and unstable of body, Joseph turned his head to the cell. Wahl called him back to attention. "It was good for you to see that. I hope it helps you remember that northern hotheads will never be of any service to your race. Now get back on your knees."

Joseph got down, silently crying out more of his pent up prayers while Wahl continued to speak. When the foreman finally left him, his groanings became too deep for words.

PART THREE

The

Price

of

Freedom

JANUARY 1835

CHAPTER 26

BRANT HAD DREADED THIS DAY. Joseph had been in the city workhouse since October; now it was January eighth. Brant had not visited him once, and now he had to enter the reeking corridor for the purpose of taking him back. Finding the workhouse master's office, he went inside, away from the awful odors and the close sound of whips constantly being snapped. He kept his hands at his sides. It was like visiting an outpost of hell.

When Brant spoke the reason for his being there, a black worker was sent out to bring Joseph to him. Minutes passed and then the shabby slave came back leading a bowed Negro, who had ropes looped haphazardly around his wrists. Brant never would have recognized Joseph, so thin, so gray with dirt, except for the work tag and brand on his bare back.

His slave coughed heavily when the workhouse master ordered him to step up on the wooden block in the center of the chilly room. Brant understood it was to save the darkie turnkeys from having to reach down to the floor to remove the leg-irons. Wearily Joseph got on the block, as though used to the habit. Brant nervously stopped the workhouse master. "May I pay something to have those left on?"

"That's entirely up to you."

The workhouse Negro pulled Joseph to the floor while the city master wrote up a bill, took Brant's money, and transferred the key. Brant wondered at the impulse that had made him do this. He decided it had been his fear that Joseph might just run off from him in the streets. That would bring him only more shame. At the same time he could see the blessing of having Joseph just slip away. Then he would not have to show him to his daddy. While Joseph hobbled slowly toward the cold exterior, Brant found himself thinking more about a plan to let him escape. He would give the key to Ezra, then give the two of them ample time alone.

The Delora coachman was waiting with a rented, two-wheeled mule cart. When they were outside, Brant told Joseph to climb into the cart bed and cover himself with the empty sacks that were there. "I don't want to see more than your face till we get to the wharf," Brant said, his worry sounding angry.

Joseph obeyed.

Brant made a show of handing the shackles' key to the older Negro. "You can unchain him when you get down to the wharf," he said loudly. Without looking at Brant, Ezra took the key and waited for him to untie his horse. By prearrangement Ezra knew to meet Brant at Grafton's Wharf, where one of Delora's dugout canoes had been moored by Ezra the day before.

Brant made sure he lost sight of the cart as they traveled through the streets at different paces. He began to hope that Joseph, with Ezra's help, might flee even now.

Unhappily, minutes later Brant saw the slaves proving faithful and arriving at the dock just after he. He found it ironic that it was their faithful obedience even in trials that was so repugnant to him. Not moving off his horse, he still found himself hoping the slaves would run away. He commanded Ezra to help Joseph into the dugout. The half-starved Negro stayed wrapped in cloth.

Ezra took up the paddle and pushed off with Joseph, who looked like a burnt-out tree stump set in the bow, his face pitted by hollow, sunken eyes. Releasing them to maneuver the brown water alone, Brant heard Joseph cough again and again. He reined his horse away. *Those two could skip off now*, he thought. He breathed a selfish but honest prayer that he would never see them again.

———

Many times in the past three weeks Abram had considered telling Brant that he knew the terrible secret of Joseph's labor in the workhouse. To speak or not to speak about it had become as consuming as his illness while he languished in bed still confined by the stroke that had laid him low in August.

He had learned of Joseph's fate through innocent remarks included in Nathan Gilman's Christmastime letter. Nathan had said that even in Boston he was now receiving chiding correspondence from leading Charlestonians who were eager to tell him why Abram Callcott's branded slave had landed himself in the workhouse and had received the punishment due a heathen criminal. Without exception the writers of these letters had pointed to Joseph's misbehavior as proof positive that Africans could not be soundly converted into benign Christians. Then Nathan had gone on to condemn any civilization that would make it impossible for a Christian master to rescue his Christian slave.

Abram had no way of knowing Joseph's crime without asking Brant. Day and night he kept Nathan's note hidden under his pillow because he now agreed fully with Nathan in his open critique of slavery as an ungodly institution. The shipbuilder's stationery was actually stained with his tears, for Abram had held it by his good hand and read the words many times in the light of the candles Bette provided for him late into each night.

With agony Abram kept waiting for Horace Wahl to contact him with news of what had happened. But no letter or visit ever materialized. The last correspondence from that man had been in September. It had contained nothing about Joseph, but it did include Horace's comment that Negro schools might be closed everywhere after December because of new legislation.

As he lay there, Abram thought again and again on every word Brant had said to him in October. *"Due to circumstances beyond my control, Daddy, Joseph must stay in the city until after the Christmas holiday."* After receiving Nathan's letter, Abram realized that Brant's "circumstances" meant the workhouse prison. Once a slave was sentenced there, Abram knew Nathan was right. A slave's owner could not appeal either the sentence or the severity of the punishment given. Having a withered right hand, he could not even write a letter to Wahl or Bachman requesting that they look in on him.

That he, himself, had received no angry letters against Joseph or the mission of the Gospel Society made Abram guess that Brant was censoring his mail. But even this did not drive him to confront his son. Neither did he confide in Mayleda, for what could his young daughter do? He bore the guilt alone, thinking that whatever Joseph suffered was because of the reckless experimentation to which he had subjected him. But now Abram counted the minutes because he knew that today his slave was coming home.

When Mayleda innocently came in to visit him close to two in the afternoon, he raged at her. "Is Brant not home yet? What is taking him so long?"

She blinked, her face as pale as milk. "He is home, Papa, and Joseph is with him."

"Then why are they not here at my side?"

The girl busied herself with refolding a fresh towel, but then burst into tears. "Oh, Daddy, all these weeks he's been in the workhouse, and you can't believe what he looks like now."

Abram covered his face with his strong hand. "Oh, I've known!" he cried, but she would not believe his confession until he showed her Nathan's letter. "There was nothing I could do!"

Her eyes were fearful. "Brant made me promise not to tell because of your condition."

Abram pushed his head into the pillow, the unlocked secret pouring like a poison-filled vial into the tightness of his chest. Oh, if his boy came back permanently harmed, he would never forgive himself for releasing him to Charleston.

The agonizing wait continued even after the strong light of the short winter day was fading. Mayleda came in with a lamp, but she did not tend the hearth, which was almost out of fuel. Abram realized then that he had seen neither Bette nor Jewell for many hours. "Where are the servants?"

Mayleda had dark circles under her eyes. "Brant has allowed them to spend time with Joseph before he sends him up to you."

"Is he that ill to need attention?"

Her glance skipped to the hallway. "I . . . I think he's coming now."

Brant walked into the room with the slave behind him. At first Abram thought Joseph was wearing clothes tailored for somebody else. His clean shirt was too tight across the chest, but much too wide and draping at his narrowed waist. All of Joseph's flesh, except his downcast face, was covered by the plain livery someone had dressed him in. His hands, held at his sides, were gloved.

Under a terrible suspicion caused by knowing exactly what kind of abuse workhouse inmates endured, Abram broke down immediately. Harshly he dismissed Mayleda and Brant so that he could examine his boy alone. The moment the door was shut, Abram beckoned Joseph to the left side of his bed. "Show me your hands."

Joseph displayed only a servant's pair of gloves.

Abram grew tenser. "Take those off."

For the first time Joseph eyed him. His face, still young and recently oiled, was like a moonless winter sky. Abram was already beyond himself with anxiety. "I know where you've been! Some event put you into slave court and then to the workhouse! Show me your hands!"

With the demeanor of an unhappy, mistreated field worker, Joseph uncovered his hands, ragged and discolored with many broken layers of flesh. Then his whole weak frame shook as he coughed out a series of connected, gasping breaths.

"Oh, Joseph!" Abram was as shocked by his former servant's posture as he was by his broken physical condition. "You're safe now. You're home." Frantic to prove that true, he made Joseph lock the door and cover the keyhole so that no one could intrude. Joseph was obedient but unresponsive to Abram's passion to make him feel close to him once more. "For the past few weeks I have known your fate," Abram admitted painfully. "Mr. Gilman wrote to me about what he had heard of you."

At that Joseph raised an eye.

"It's true. He knew about your suffering, and he admonished me for letting it go on, though I had no choice."

"I . . . I can hardly believe he'd know. . . ." Joseph stammered, uncharacteristic of the quiet, nearly speechless servant he had been through all the years.

"Yes," Abram mused. "Whatever you were accused of, I am to blame. I should never have subjected you to school when all of society was against it."

"Oh, sir. Even if they peeled my skin away everywhere, I would still be grateful to God, and then to you, for learning." His brows wrinkled, showing his extreme fatigue.

"Get one of the hearth chairs for yourself. Bring it here."

He seemed amazed.

"I am done with convention. From this moment on I'll do what I feel is right to do, as God is my judge."

Joseph got the seat, but he sat gingerly on it only after Abram commanded him to do so. Inwardly Abram made new rules for himself. He would only *request* things of the African. And he would not call him "boy."

"Joseph, please trust me enough to tell me what happened in Charleston. By the judgment of the court you have served your time, but now for my own understanding I need to know."

Joseph seemed intent on surveying Abram's own condition. "Have you been in bed, sir, all these months?"

"I have," Abram said softly. "And no one told you?"

"In prison I had no news at all." The familiar muscle under Joseph's eye was twitching.

"I'll explain my situation in a moment. But you go first. Please tell me what sent you to the workhouse."

Joseph appeared uneasy. "Sir, I tried to save some who were bound for execution." He looked at his hands. "I acted too late, I think. They all loved the hope of freedom more than life. That I now understand."

Abram struggled to know what to say. "I do not condemn you. From knowing you, I think I, too, am beginning to understand."

Joseph showed him a look of amazement, and Abram felt the need to go on and explain himself. "Perhaps I now see that the restlessness is not caused by the learning, but only *released* by it. To be restless is *human*. Restless to be free."

Joseph's lips trembled. His eyes were close to tearing.

"Mayleda confessed to me that you and she met in the city."

The young slave's head went down once more.

"She told me she informed you of my appeal to the legislature for a special deed of manumission."

"Yes, she told me, sir, but I do not hope for it. Nor do I wish for it at the price of your own life, for I understand that it would be valid only at your passing."

"It has nothing to do with my living and dying! I am bound to die, and if my release to glory would usher in your earthly freedom, then you must know I would consider that a triumph!"

"Oh, sir! Slaveholders will not vote to free a black man!"

The words *black man* stayed with Abram. "I've heard nothing from the state, but that does not mean we cannot hope and pray."

Again Joseph surveyed his face, but this time with warmth. "I thank you for petitioning the legislation. I thank you for sending me to school."

His formal, courteous language caused Abram to shiver. "What did they have you do in the workhouse?"

"Chip gravel."

"Were you whipped?"

Joseph would not keep eye contact with him. "No. Mr. Wahl thought that would be too distressing to you if I was returned with scars. When they thought extra punishment was necessary, they withheld the wrappings Mr. Wahl gave me for my hands, or they neglected to give me drink or food."

"My dear, dear Joseph!" In trying to reach for him, he revealed the deteriorating condition of his mottled flesh. "How I want you to have refuge and safety. How dismal for me that I cannot promise it, even though my heart cries for it."

"Am I to care for you, sir?" Joseph asked quietly, obviously struggling to hide the cough he had carried home.

Abram felt shame. "I would not ask you to! Over the months I have become wretched company, even to myself."

"I would be honored, sir."

Abram began to weep. "No. You do not know what a vile man I am, inside and out."

"All men are in constant need of grace."

The slave's compassion was too much to bear. "I have longed to have you home, Joseph."

"And many times I have longed to be here."

"I refuse to have it as it was before. I have no right to hold you to servitude. You have more than amply proved your abilities and God's plan to create you for more than servility."

"At school, sir, I was collecting notes on studies about fevers. And, well, I entertained dreams of learning how to care for the sick in the way that a trained doctor cares for them. I know what it feels like to suffer, and that makes me eager to learn to heal. Teacher Payne affirmed my dreams by borrowing journals—"

"A doctor! Joseph, you want to be a colored doctor!" The question came out quite condemning, and Abram immediately repented of it. "I don't doubt it! No, not at all. I believe it! And I could wish it for you too."

"See, then, I have reasons for wanting to care for you," Joseph said. "But the greatest, sir, is that I do love you."

Abram could find no words as he sobbed like a child. "Brant is in charge of Delora now," he said when he could. "The final decision will have to rest with him."

There was worry in Joseph's countenance. He stood and put the chair back by the hearth, a subtle statement that he still knew he had only one place in Delora regardless of the incredible transformation inside Abram's heart.

"I want you with me," Abram affirmed as he tried to smile. "I want to understand you as you are." His pledge made him think of Gilman's letter. More than one sentence in it had been directed to Joseph. "There's a note under my pillow. Would you reach it for me?"

Joseph paused to put his hand back in the glove.

"Please, don't," Abram said, knowing the common aversion masters had when it came to touching Negro flesh. "Put those aside unless they are of comfort to you." Emotion threatened to constrict his lungs too much for breathing. "Dear Joseph, there was a time, even until just months ago, when I believed I had the right and the blessing from God to think I *owned* those hands of yours. Can you ever even begin to forgive me for such ignorance?"

"Yes." Joseph had his eyes closed. "After much struggle, yes, I can, for I can hate the *sin* of slavery while holding myself accountable to being a servant of God's grace."

"Come to me! Let me touch you! Let me feel this forgiveness!" Shedding more tears, Abram kissed Joseph's battered palms as he held them with the fingers of his left hand. "At least in this one room there will be no more master-to-slave commands, but only brother-to-brother conversation."

Joseph nodded with a vague, believing smile. Abram let him read Gilman's letter for himself. The young man started quivering, and Abram asked him, "What is the meaning of the part that reads, 'Tell Joseph as soon as you can that LUCK has been with me all the while.' Mr. Gilman does not believe in luck."

"That is the name of one of the slaves who needed to escape!" Joseph seemed dazed. "I feared him sold south or dead!"

"Then my friend has been illegally exporting slaves."

Joseph would not answer him.

The idea caused Abram to close his eyes momentarily. He remembered Nathan's pledge at his last farewell to invest no more money in the South unless it would help the Negroes' push for freedom. *So, that is why his vessels are still coming here.* Joseph seemed shocked by Abram's next words. "I agree with his cause. Perhaps arrangements can be made to smuggle you out this way if the legislature will not approve my request."

"What about Rosa, sir?"

Joseph's question took him off guard.

"At the earliest possible moment I will arrange for her to see you, but please, don't speak a word about Gilman or his work. It is too dangerous to spread that news further. When I see Mr. Gund, I'll tell him to bring Rosa up to the yard. Then you can see her. She is thin, boy." He smiled glumly. "Much thinner than even you, if Mr. Gund's description is correct."

He saw Joseph look down across his waist to the floor. He was barefoot, and his toes were blunted and raw, surely from being put to work in the stone piles without any protection.

There was a knocking at the door, and then the door latch rattled as Brant called, "Why have you made Joseph lock this, Daddy?"

Abram saw Joseph's intense worry, and he was sorry for his son's reaction. While Joseph hid the letter Abram whispered, "You are truly willing to work in this room again?"

"I am, sir."

"Then open the door. Please."

When Joseph let him in, Brant entered feeling like Daniel put in with the lions. Though their mouths were sealed, he was extremely wary about being with his father and this slave who had talked so long without him. "What is going on here?" he demanded as firmly as he thought was right. "I know Joseph had to be the one to use the key."

"He was," his daddy admitted. "Sit down, Brant, in the chair to the right of the hearth. And you, Joseph, sit down in the chair to the left."

Joseph showed anxiety, and Brant protested. "What are you doing? Pulling me down to *his* level? Or trying to raise him up?"

His father was adamant. "Maybe a little of both. This is my deathbed wish. Sit down. Both of you." Joseph kept standing until Brant was seated. Only then did the slave take the other chair. Brant felt some satisfaction in Joseph's behavior, for he showed more sense about this absurdity than his father did.

"In the short amount of time I have left, I feel I must do all I can to right the wrongs I've committed in this life," his daddy went on, wincing as he struggled to raise his head from the pillows. "I can't change the world or this society or even what I've done these past thirty years. But in this one room I can make changes. That's why I want the two of you to sit together. In the privacy of this place I want you to learn to know each other as *young men*."

Brant looked to Joseph, who did not look at him. Angrily Brant stood and quietly Joseph followed. "There's no purpose in this. I fear you are losing your senses, Father!"

"No! On the contrary, I am just coming to my senses. Brant! Joseph! In the safety of this chamber I want you to forget everything the world has taught you about class and race."

Brant looked at Joseph briefly and was unnerved when the slave's eyes met his own. "Daddy, *nothing* will work for me if I must acknowledge him as my equal even in this small space. My marriage is only five months away. I cannot live a double standard. Either slavery is right even in this room, or it is wrong everywhere."

"It *is* wrong everywhere."

"You can philosophize all you want in bed. But *I* must deal with reality . . . *now*. I cannot dismiss slaves because that is against the law. I cannot take them out of state, because even as their master I am not allowed to free them. And I cannot live without them while maintaining a plantation. So if what you say is true, then we must just live with damnation! We are locked in with no door for redemption or escape."

He thought he actually saw Joseph nod.

"Please," Brant begged. "Don't trouble me with this issue again. I've spoken to the pastor. To Mr. Wahl. I can't cope with indecision anymore."

"Brant, by God's help there must be a way!"

"I've made my peace with it! I will manage Delora according to the laws of South Carolina. If moral men in power want to change them, then so be it. The Scriptures say we must be accountable to the authorities over us. Therefore, *he* must be accountable to the authorities over him. And that is how we will make our peace!"

"You are his authority."

"Then he knows I work by the laws."

"I want him in the house. I desire his help. I've been relying mostly on Bette and Maum, since Colt has been unsatisfactory."

Brant breathed hard. "All right. He's paid for his crimes. Better than ever he should know the consequences of disobedience. He may stay as long as there are no violations of any law."

Mayleda came in. As she so often did, she probably had been listening at the door. "Oh, Daddy, you will get better now that you have Joseph with you."

She dared to turn to the grown African and actually take his hand. "Bless you, dear Joseph, for your kindness, even after all that has been done against you."

Brant bristled, and Joseph pulled away. "You're not a child anymore!" Brant reprimanded her. "He could be punished for *your* closeness."

His father sighed, and Brant felt control spring away from him once more. To curb the sensation he turned away, not watching Mayleda's actions, but trusting Joseph to do what was comely. That gave him the odd sense that this *slave* was understanding him better than even his family. He went and cleaned out his father's desk, giving an unspoken message to Joseph that reading and writing would not be tolerated. When he left the room Mayleda followed him across the hallway to his own quarters.

She spoke while he filled his desk with his father's work. "I meant nothing by taking Joseph's hand except to show my gratefulness. Jewell and Bette had been run to exhaustion nursing him. Now I know Daddy will relax in his care."

Brant sat down and started sorting papers. "That's not the question, Mayleda. The question is, how am I to relax now that he is here? I trust him, and I don't. It's wrecking to the nerves."

"Perhaps he will get his manumission soon," she said lightly.

"May! You understand so little! This year's General Assembly is staunch proslavery. It's likely they'll come here and drive us all out because of Daddy's correspondence instead of issuing any freedom papers."

"I can still hope for a miracle from God."

"Joseph's freedom would come only after Daddy's passing. You're praying for his death when you pray for that African."

"I'm praying for peace for all of us," Mayleda told him. "Peace on earth as it is in heaven."

"I fear there is no peace to be had."

"There must be peace," she said with childlike reasoning. "For God promised that Jesus would *be* our peace."

Brant stood, not having the patience to hear her simple preaching. He went to the door.

"Where are you going now?"

"To tell Mr. Gund what Daddy's wishes are and to take the livery off Colt so he can go back into the street."

She took his arm. "You really don't hate Joseph, do you?"

Brant looked at her. "It's not about hate or about liking. It's about the continuing struggle to hold to what we have."

CHAPTER 27

JOSEPH BATHED ABRAM GENTLY, for he himself knew what it was to suffer. Night was heavy upon them, but still a round little smile animated the man's otherwise nearly lifeless face.

"You are here to stay?"

"Yes, I am, sir." Joseph looked around. His own fatigue was great and he was ravenous, yet there was much to do even at this hour. For that reason he had not touched the supper Bette had carried up to him. The hearth fire was out, and there was no wood to rebuild it. The lamp was smoking and low on oil. There was no more water in the pitcher beside the bed, so he decided first to go to the well. But he did not even get to the door before Abram called him back.

"Brant took the things from my desk."

"Yes, sir."

"See if you can find any paper and a pencil to write the date today and to put your name behind it."

"I can do that, sir," Joseph said, after checking the nearly emptied piece of furniture. "But may I ask why?"

"Conceal what you write under my pillows along with Mr. Gilman's letter. When confirmation of your release comes, I will pay you the same wages Mr. Gilman pays his Irish help. If I die suddenly, then tell Mayleda to write a note against her inheritance for you. Every day, sign your name to this work ledger. Then you will have some money for travel."

The man sounded so sure, yet he had been slipping in and out of delirious dreams for hours. Joseph judged that getting water was more important than the man's odd idea, but still Abram held him till the task was done.

"You're developing a good script," the planter said, evaluating Joseph's writing before he would let him slip it away. "Now, is the library key still in the desk drawer?"

"Yes, sir."

"Keep it on your person from now on. You'll need to get books to read to me, but more than that, I want *you* to be reading. Once I'm comfortably situated for the nights and on every Sabbath afternoon, you are free to use my library. Any and all of it."

"Sir!"

Abram's whole weak being glowed with his thoughts. "I don't want you to stop your education. I have so little time to right so great a wrong. It's my guess that Mr. Payne took pleasure in your work as his student."

"He did, sir." Joseph was hot with embarrassment but also with grief, for the system of slavery had simply yanked him away from his teacher without granting him even a decent farewell. He tried not to sound eager. "Do you know how Mr. Payne fares?"

"I don't. From the beginning the teacher and I agreed it would not be wise to exchange letters. I depended on Mr. Wahl for my reports, but he, too, mentioned nothing." He stopped, suddenly frowning. "You're still wearing the work tag."

"Yes. I didn't know what I was allowed to do with it."

"Take it off at once. Put it in that drawer and wear the key around your neck instead."

The idea was cheering. "Yes, I will! With gratefulness!"

His sudden lightness affected Abram for the better. "Oh, and another thing! I don't mind if you read aloud to Jewell or to Bette or even to Billy if it's done in private. I know how you all sit around the kitchen on the

Sabbath. I want them to see your accomplishments and be as proud as I am."

"Really, sir! But you hardly even know what I have learned."

"That will change. I look forward to having you break the hours of monotony with your narrations."

Joseph's head went down, and he felt the man eyeing him.

"What is it? Are you so wounded in spirit and body that you cannot be happy and at rest even for a day?"

"I was wondering about Rosa. Would I have permission to read with her?"

"That depends on her, Joseph. You know I plan to tell Mr. Gund to bring her tomorrow evening. If she feels confident enough to come to the kitchen on Sundays, then yes, she may cross the driveway with Billy."

Joseph fought what felt like a blow of despair.

"You are so unhappy, aren't you? Why?"

He could hardly believe that the master was asking or that he was ready to say why. "The night you took ill, sir, I met someone at the Graftons' ball who told me Rosa had . . . been . . ." He looked down, then away, unable to speak to another man of a woman's disgrace.

"Then you know." Abram said it as a gasp of grief. "Your mama and Parris and a great outpouring of prayer have helped lead her to Christ, and that, I hear, has comforted her."

"I'm glad," Joseph said with numbness and shame as he admitted to himself that he envied Parris for being near to her. "Perhaps I should not hope to see her."

Abram gave him a smile. "You still love her, don't you? You're a man of loyalty and greatly to be admired."

The windows were dark, but Joseph looked toward them anyway. *A man of loyalty.* The master of this house had said those words—to him! The water pitcher he held still needed to be filled, and his raw hands were still aching from the weight of it, yet he went out to fulfill the simple task feeling a root of hope inside deeper than any he had ever known.

———

His first night in a bed was luxurious after months of sleeping on the workhouse floor. And the next day moved quickly enough, since there was still so much to do. But more than bringing order to the rooms, Joseph's main concern remained with Abram. The planter had declined into terrible weakness from his inactivity and had many ugly bedsores.

Their learning to work together as patient and nurse might have been comical had it not been so heart-wrenching. By evening they had visibly cried together but also laughed together at their common, piteous condition.

Less than an hour after Joseph had served Abram his supper, the master asked to be put to bed for the night. Joseph was surprised, for Abram seemed more alert and rested now than he had all day. While dressing him in a gown, Joseph began to realize that Abram actually had *his* interests in mind. The man wanted to be settled before Mr. Gund's second visit. The overseer had left the room that morning promising to bring Rosa into the yard before eight.

To realize that Master Abram was looking out for *him* upset the steadiness of his hands. He spilled the toothpowder and misplaced the nightcap, two things that seemed to utterly delight and entertain the widower watching him. "She is a fine young gal," Abram told him when Joseph had finally accomplished everything and was putting salve on the tender spots of the thin man's back.

"Yes," Joseph said, finishing his work with trembling fingers.

The master turned of his own accord to look at him steadily. "And you are a fine fellow."

Joseph let his eyes meet Abram's. "I am African and slave; she is brown and should be free."

"Yet she loved you almost from the first."

Joseph felt his mouth open. "How would you know that, sir?"

Abram laughed. "Dear Joseph, your own mama spoke to Maum, and Maum spoke to me. There are not many secrets in this house."

He breathed hard.

"It's your care and humility that have won her, I am certain. The time is over for you to be thinking so little of yourself."

"Yes, sir."

"You've recorded your service for today on your wage sheet?"

"No, sir."

"Then do it! You are not listening to what I tell you. Must I order you not to neglect yourself?"

"No, sir." Joseph smiled.

The master grinned in return. "I have been reduced to almost nothingness in every area of my life except in prayer. My prayers are with you for tonight when you meet Rosa."

Joseph closed the small tin medicine container and held it. "Is there no hope that she can ever be freed? What of her birthright? Does that count for nothing?"

"After she came here, I tried every legal course I could. There's no written record of her birth, and none of the white folk along the Waccamaw would come forth to give testimony in court that could have freed her. It was especially distressing to my dear Oribel that nothing could be done to right the wrong."

"I remember how Mrs. Callcott used to leave the house for the quarters, sir, but I had no understanding of why."

"Rosa's child died just weeks before the fever claimed my own family members. Her baby was the only slave life to be lost."

Joseph breathed in hard once more, not immediately ready to say what he was thinking. "What if the state does grant me manumission, sir? Would you set a price so that I could work to buy Rosa as a nominal? I give you my word that it would only be to free her. I would not make her beholding to me in any way."

Abram's look was kind. "It seems like sound thinking, Joseph, but to be legal you would have to pay a fair market price, and that's high for a mulatto with Rosa's features."

Joseph felt the heat under his skin.

"If you are freed, the law will banish you from the South within days of your release."

"Then I would have no contact with her?"

The master grimaced. "Not after you leave the state. If I could survive and you could be freed, then there might be a chance, for I could look out for your interests. But I'm not sure that Brant would be sympathetic to your wants, and Mayleda's still a child. She is powerless to do anything legally on her own behalf—or yours."

Joseph dared to ask another question. "If Master Brant knew that you favored her release, would he honor your agreement with me? I would work in the North and collect the sum—however large—and send it down in exchange for her."

"I'm not sure how you would do that, Joseph. I want to say that Brant would help you, but that's not a promise I can make. Besides, I don't know how you would safely transport your money, and I don't think Rosa would have a chance at traveling out of the state alone." He paused. "However, let me think about confiding in Mr. Gund. He's a good man, and I believe that deep down within he shares our aversion to slavery."

"Would you think of asking him to help me escape?" Joseph asked impulsively.

Abram's eyes clouded. "The consequences to him would be almost as great as to you if you were caught. Indeed! Death to you. Fines, ostracism, perhaps even lashes for him. It would also be terrible for me if I were implicated."

"Then I won't ask again." *All things must come from God*, Joseph told himself as he covered Abram with a sheet and pulled the curtains partially closed around his bed. It was sobering to think that hundreds of black men and women must have already died while dreaming of earthly freedom. Quite probably that would be the same for him. At the rapping on the door, Joseph went and opened it. Mr. Gund came in, his thick brogans sounding familiar as he walked across the floor to Master's bedside.

Joseph moved the curtains again. "Evening, Hampton," Abram said congenially, though truly fatigued.

"You lookin' extremely well, sah!" the dusty white man said with hat in hand. "An' that must be thanks to Joseph!"

"If I had not been present for his birth, I would tell you that God has given me an angel of mercy."

Gund nodded respectfully. "All is quiet and in good order down in you' street, sah. Only regular winter tasks wa' done t'day." He put his hands behind him.

"You have Rosa in the kitchen?"

Joseph's heart leaped with Abram's question.

"No, sah, I'm sorry to say, but she don't want to come up."

Joseph held himself like a slave refusing to show hurt even in torture.

Gund went on. "Since her first meetin' in the prayerhouse she been a whole lot less skittery 'round others. But I guess this is just a little bit too much for her, sah. I didn't drive her up, 'cause I didn't think you'd want it that way."

"You did the right thing, Mr. Gund."

Joseph made himself busy by going over to stir the hearth fire. Gund's words burned him. He heard Abram dismiss his overseer.

"Well, thank you. Tell Dell and the girls, my best to them all."

Unmoving, Joseph stayed by the fire.

"I'm sorry. I never expected it," Abram said quietly when Gund was gone.

"What is next for me to do, sir?" Joseph straightened.

"Joseph, you don't have to try so hard to hide your hurt." Joseph would have chosen to be left alone, but Abram continued. "So love is equally hard on every man, no matter what his hue? And women of all races are equally impossible to comprehend? Is that your view, as it is mine?"

Joseph shifted his eyes, grateful for the older man's subtle empathy yet angry too. "Rosa has real and painful reasons for her choices that I can understand."

"She does," the other man said with regret. He lay back and drew his face away. "Let's have our evening prayers, and we'll include your dilemma in them. Then you may still be dismissed. Maybe you'd like to take a book to your room or borrow my Bible. Don't give up hope, my young friend. There will be other days."

When his work with Abram was done, Joseph went into the dark dressing room and lay on the simple bed. He pulled off the shoes Abram had given him that day, relieving his sore, battered feet. Resting with his eyes open, he wondered about himself. He had endured the caning, the branding, and the workhouse better than he was enduring his fear of Rosa's rejection. What did it matter? What had he been expecting? What life could be ahead for two slaves anyway?

In anticipation of seeing her, Joseph had already formulated a long list of all the impossibilities he faced. He had done it to guard his heart, and he felt himself in need of that protection now. He could make no pledges to any other, he warned himself, for an earthly master would always declare the right to dominate his life. He could make no declaration of love, for love required commitment, and slavery allowed him to be committed only to the one who owned him. He could make no betrothal, even if Rosa had shown interest, for the rules of slavery said that they did not even own their bodies to give to each other. Ultimately, then, there could be no hope of fidelity or intimacy. God required a sacred vow, but slaveholding deprived them of it.

He clung to the sheet. What had he been thinking? What could he offer her when every divine gift given by God to man had already been stripped from him? He thought about Luck getting away in Nathan Gilman's vessel. Perhaps he should try to do the same for Rosa after Abram died. His throat closed to think that she might want Parris to be smuggled out with her. *Then so be it*, he decided. Regardless of the pain to himself, or the risk, he would do it as proof of his love for her. He had had his own copy of the Scriptures long enough to know *God's* definition of love. It "suffereth long and seeketh not its own satisfaction."

These thoughts pushed him out of bed and to the door. Peering into the master's chamber, he saw that Abram Callcott was asleep in the light of the candle Joseph had left burning. Joseph moved to him, drew the curtains closed around his bed, and snuffled out the flame. Then he did something he had never done before. He sneaked out of the room and out of the house to cross the forbidden driveway and go down into the street.

" *'Timor mortis conturbat me.'* "

When Rosa heard those words spoken she got up onto her knees on the hard sleeping board. Still dressed in her work clothes for warmth on the chilly night, she peered out between the window laths. The young black speaker in the street was dressed in light clothing and looked like a messenger from heaven. She knew it was Joseph. He was reciting her poem with a healed and seemingly beautified human voice.

From the privacy of that boarded window, she marveled at his boldness, at the wonderful, dark outline of his sleek body, at how he had found her. She gripped the rough wooden sill, for she longed to go out to him, yet dreaded it. Every part of her heart told her to move, while every part of her mind counseled against it. She was uncomely and still fearful, and as a slave she could have no hopes of love and happiness ever coming by their meeting. So she watched him from the distance with parted lips. He was more handsome and more courageous now than ever before. It made her proud of him and ashamed of herself. It was that shame, she knew, that kept her from daring to face him again.

Joseph moved off several paces closer to the head of the street and began speaking again. Obviously he did not know which shanty housed her. The music in his precious voice sounded faltering as he started the poem a second time. " 'As I went out on a merry morning, I heard a bird both weep and sing. . . .' "

Like a storyteller with no listeners, he went through every line. His back was lit by moonlight. When he moved once more, his form faded. At that last moment Rosa sprang from the board, ran through the next room filled with sleeping bodies, and freed herself from Negozi's cabin.

" 'This was the tenor of her talking . . .' " It was her voice now saying the poem, since his had died.

Joseph heard her. He turned and faced her. She grabbed her uncovered hair and held her fingers over the crown of her head as he came back and stared at her for only a moment. Then his head went down. She believed he despised her appearance. She spun on bare feet to flee the shame, but he stayed right with her as she moved.

"Oh, Rosa. Wait! Forgive me for coming here, but it was a vow I made to God and to myself to see you again and to say your poetry back to you."

She met his eyes. They were wide with feelings she did not fear nor understand.

He spoke quickly, holding his body rigid. "I promised myself in Charleston that I would learn your poem and the meaning of the strange-sounding Latin in it. Then having done that, I would come back to recite it to you as a gift. That is why I ignored your disinterest in me! I came, just this once, to fulfill my imagination of this moment with you. Please don't hate me for it. It was hope for this moment that carried me through many stark and terrible days."

She looked at him, confounded and unhappy with her own self-centeredness. His hand had come up to his mouth in shyness, and even in moonlight she saw the damage done to his flesh. Until that moment—God forgive her!—she had thought only of her own suffering on this plantation and nothing of the possibility that he had been further mistreated in the city. Without thinking she almost touched his half-curved fingers. "What happened to you?"

He twisted his head. "That's not what I came to speak about."

"Your voice has been restored!"

His grin was wonderful. "Yes. God be praised for it!"

"I am a Christian." She felt the need to speak hurriedly also. "I can now understand your gratefulness. But, please, tell me of your trials." She could feel her own eyes growing tender. She wondered if he could notice that through the darkness, and she tried to hide herself, as usual, by putting her arms around her body. When he would not speak, she turned away.

"Please! Don't go!" He was so intense yet gentle. He did not touch her but held her by his words. "I know what happened to you. While I was in the city, Ann Rensler's maidservant told me."

Her eyes snapped downward as her hands went to her head.

"Rosa. You can't know how this grieves me to see you suffer."

"I cannot stop the fear," she cried her miserable confession. "No matter how much I pray or what I do, the terrible feelings will not go away. That is why I did not come to see you. I did not want you to see me this way. I am worse now than when you knew me last. And I was ruined then!"

"Rosa. Dear Rosa! I do not think so!"

Reluctantly she met his gaze, filled with so much anger and hurt that his dark eyes were displacing tears.

"I'm sorry, girl. I am so sorry. A man has no right, no matter who he thinks he is!"

His head dropped, revealing his training as a houseservant. She was reminded of those who had once waited on her in Aspidae's chambers. It made her loathe every hour of her past all the more. There was nothing in all her dark existence for Joseph to esteem. And there was no hope for a future as they stood beside each other, not looking to each other but lost in their own entangled thoughts.

Finally Joseph dared to speak. "I know you are a free woman. It must make life here seem utterly wicked and impossible."

"Don't pity me. Hate me, instead. My family owned slaves! And for that and that alone, God can damn me if He wants to in the coming judgment. Surely I am worthy of it."

"You had no choice, even as I had no choice to be born enslaved."

"My father ravished other women!"

"You had no choice!"

"No? Somehow I could have spoken against the evil."

"Rosa. Even if you could have spoken, you cannot now go back to change any of what was done. That is why we need a Savior. God promises to rescue us and to remember our former lives no more."

"I cannot forget."

"I understand. To forget is a goal and not always a reality for me either."

Again Rosa looked at his hands. He seemed saddened.

"Mr. Gund says you spend time with Parris. Surely he has explained God's full plan of rescue."

"Yes."

"I think it is the only thing that can give us meaning in this cruel world," he said. "The truth will not convert the past, but it can wholly cut it off."

"Joseph, I am always so afraid!"

"*Timor mortis?* The fear of death. Now I know what you said to me when you gave me water."

"How?"

He was actually smiling. "I went to school in Charleston. I was taught by a colored scholar. Even one hour with him would have been worth all of this." He held out wounded hands that would not fully open.

"My fear of death kept me from dying," Rosa confessed, "but now I think the fear of life will keep me from living. I no longer fear the grave. In fact I would welcome it, for I know that to die means to be safely in the presence of the Lord. But to live? Oh! What does that mean for us?"

"Rosa, I have very little time. I have no permission to be here. So listen. Are you interested in trying to make a run for freedom?"

"With you!"

She saw his nervousness as his lips pressed together. "No. I understand about you and Parris. My idea is to help you both to get away. I did this once before. Tonight that man and his family are safe in Boston."

She was close to touching his hand. "That's why they did this to you? You suffered so that others could go free."

"It was not so heroic." He glazed her emotion with a small, unassuming smile. "I thought my friends had died in trying to escape. I thought I had failed. I know I waited much too long to help them. I would be so much more careful this time." There was a pause as he drew his hands behind him. "Rosa, if it's too hard for you to be here, I am willing to plan some way to get you and Parris on a boat out of Charleston."

"Joseph! No!" She covered her mouth as he stared so intently at her. "If I could escape, you are the one I would want with me. Without a doubt Parris did save my life. And he has helped me. But he already knows my feelings. You are the one I think of day and night." Her arms went back around her. "I am sorry. I can believe you'd find no pleasure in such a confession. Oh, from the beginning I've been so proud. The awful truth is, Joseph, that I first came to you only because I'd heard you could read."

"Well, at least it brought you to me. For whatever reason you came, I will be glad for it. You saved my life. And you've given me joy!"

She began to cry. "I've prayed and longed for you to come!"

He seemed surprised. "Will you think of freedom then?"

"Oh, Joseph, even if we could steal away, the bondage of my fears would go with me. It would be unfair to you to risk your life for me. I am broken and can never repay the trust or love as you are so deserving of."

"I am willing to take that risk along with all the others. I will accept even your hopelessness and your fears and help you to bear them so you will not have to suffer all alone."

She could not believe him. "Have you no fears of your own?"

"I don't know. I was in the workhouse three months, and I think I've been about as low as a man can go. The day before my release—just two days ago—a city patrolman told me that if I ever break the law again, he will personally testify against me and see me lynched." Despite his words, Joseph smiled wryly. "So I guess I have some worries. But I think what I'm coming to fear most is that I might fail God and fall short of His will because of fear. There is nothing for me to love in this world except you. For that reason I feel much less inclined than some, perhaps, to conform or compromise with this world's ways."

He took a step away from her. "I must go. I may be jeopardizing Abram Callcott's health and our futures by leaving him unattended. But if you would just accept Mr. Callcott's invitation, I could see you every evening and on Sundays. I have permission to read aloud with all who come to the kitchenhouse, and that can include you." He showed the key around his neck. "It's to the library. Any book can be ours for the borrowing."

Suddenly she was as desperate as he to speak quickly. "Joseph. Parris needs an education. I've been trying, but we have no time or tools for it. He needs a Bible and the ability to read it. After Rensler took me, Parris went out looking for him with an ax. They caught him and beat him, and then for forty days they kept him in the heaviest chains the parish company has." She watched the thin arch of Joseph's brow distorting. Suffering was such a common bond to them all. "Since then he's given up singing and praying and preaching. I know he still believes in God, but he fears opening his mouth only to be copying the white man's words. What he wants—what he needs—is a full understanding of the Scriptures. We all do! In those reading times can Parris join us? And can you get a Bible?"

"I don't know what's on those library shelves. The Bible Master Abram gave me was lost in the city."

"Do you think Parris would have permission to come?"

"No, and I won't even ask for it. Not because of Master Abram, but because of Master Brant. I feel he's just waiting to find any reason to accuse me of trouble. If he were to find me here now—" His own deep thinking cut him off. "But listen, we can work together to help Parris. Tell our brother this. Whatever I can read to you all, you and Billy can pass on to him. Maybe we can even teach Billy some reading and writing, and since Parris has free conversation with his daddy, then, Billy can pass the skills along to him by night."

"Oh yes. I will see you tomorrow," she promised suddenly. "In the morning I will tell Overseer Gund I've changed my mind."

"Good." But even as he said it, she saw he was miserable.

She reached but stopped short of touching his cheek. "It's not just for the books or for Parris's sake, or for more talk of freedom. If I had any hope of ever loving anyone, do you know it would be you?"

"There are struggles we share," he told her. "In the nights when the pain of my hands and feet kept me from sleeping, I would wrestle with the circumstances of my life. I decided then that for as long as I am a slave,

I, too, must never hope for love. But all the same I could not keep from coming here. So what does that say, girl?"

"That I've been praying for you?"

"Yes! And that you are a reality that goes far beyond all my reasoning!"

"I cannot imagine that you can think you love me."

"Then don't imagine it. Believe it!"

She was holding herself very tightly now.

"I'm not going to touch you. If it would help, I would not even look at you. But know that I do love you, and for this one brief moment I will let myself be the happiest man on earth."

"And I, the happiest of women. Oh, my gentle Kwash!"

"My Dara!" She allowed herself to bask in his smile. Suddenly she kissed her own fingers, then lightly touched his face. By God's grace and this man's patience, she was amazed to feel no fear. At that very moment she could hope of one day being freed and healed.

CHAPTER 28

BLESSINGS KEPT RAINING DOWN on Delora plantation right on into planting time. The unusual peace sharpened Billy's appetite more and more for heaven. Often while walking back from the fields or sitting on the shanty porch late at night, he'd imagine Gloryland and being safe behind those strong pearly gates.

Their little foretaste of the good things of God had everything to do with Abram Callcott living to see another crop put in. And that had everything to do with Joseph being back to help him. The gray-headed gentleman could now sit on his second-story piazza because of the special kind of chair Joseph had constructed to support his weak side. And the man could ride in his two-wheeled dogcart, which once transported his hunting hounds, because Joseph had made a brace so he could travel outdoors.

That Abram and Joseph went everywhere together reminded Billy of the slave Joseph in the Bible who had accompanied old Pharaoh while bringing Hebrew prosperity to that heathen land. Billy had the notion that

God might be blessing them now, while still warning them all to prepare for the famine to come. Billy already knew one dim spot in this unsteady paradise, and that was Parris. He felt for his son as day by day Rosa gravitated more toward Joseph. And he was glad that Parris was not allowed to cross the driveway, for then he would have seen the tremulous gal and the reserved young man with lovers' starlight in their gazes.

Regardless of the permission they all had from the ailing slavemaster to be reading, Billy worried about that continually. He welcomed the thick swarms of insects that were again upon them like a plague. White folks, including patrollers, were less likely to be out and about when mosquitoes were as thick as pepper. Slaves were mercilessly bitten, too, of course, but that seemed worth the privacy afforded them. For weeks Mass' Brant and Mista Gund had been the only two whites Billy had seen.

But soon many folks would be coming here just for the day when Mass' Brant married Miss Ann out on the lawn. To get ready for the wedding, there had been much activity to prepare the house and yard. After the festivity Billy expected that only Abram and his two youngest children would stay on. The newlyweds would travel and then settle on Gibbes Street until after harvesttime.

Swatting mosquitoes, he walked down the center aisle of the new stables to make sure the grooms were doing right for Master Callcott's saddle horses. Content that all was well, he left the barn and went up across the yard to sit in the kitchen with the others. It was a quiet, lazy Sabbath afternoon.

On Sundays Joseph would simply read, but on other days he had started using sharp pieces of hickory charcoal from the cooking fire to write at least one or two Bible words so that Billy could see what they looked like. Then much later, usually about four the next morning, Billy would make those same marks in front of his shanty's hearth to show the words to Parris. By this slow, uneven process Billy and his son were both learning to read the language of the Scriptures.

The moment Billy stepped up into the kitchen, he felt the smoky relief of a green-wood fire. Joseph was seated on one bench, while the women—Jewell, Bette, and Rosa—shared another. The old backless chair had been put against the wall and left vacant for him. He went and sat down. The young man stopped his reading from a narrow volume that was titled *The Young Freethinker Reclaimed*. Joseph grinned at him, for nothing pleased the youth more than these reading times. "I just got finished talking about what a freethinker is, Billy," he said. "According to Mr. Webster's dictionary in the library, it's the name used for anyone who dares to say that Jesus Christ isn't also God and Savior."

Billy settled back on his seat. Joseph stood and brought the book to him. "Maum Bette still doesn't believe you can read," he said, almost like a friendly challenge. "So while you were absent I told her the last name of the pastor who wrote this book. Now, Billy, will you kindly tell your wife the writer's name."

Billy looked at the small thin page Joseph held before him. He narrowed his eyes to bring the print into focus. "Why, that's *Bald* an' that's *win*, so's the name is Baldwin."

"That's right!" Rosa was the one to cheer him, while Bette only hummed and looked at the ceiling. "See, Maum! He really knows, and Parris is learning too," Rosa said. Her passion brought her to her feet. In her brown dress and turban of red, she looked as pert as a poppy flower.

Billy chewed on his pride. "I could even teach you, old gal!" he teased Bette with a happy spirit. Though his woman's eyes did not find his, he liked the deep purple he could paint on her cheeks with his chiding. Meanwhile, Joseph seemed most taken with Rosa, now standing right beside him. Billy caught Bette's eye then, and Bette caught Jewell's, and they all savored the tender, youthful romance they were witnesses to. By this time all of them knew that Rosa could read and write, though she never volunteered to do so. Maybe it was because Mass' Abram had never directly given her permission, but more likely it was because she loved Joseph's voice and his writings on the floor.

Billy handed the book back to Joseph, who went to his seat. The boy hadn't read more than a few lines when Rosa ran to put a hand upon his shoulder, a very unlikely move for her. It stayed there like an eagle's talons. Then Billy saw why. Master Brant, Miss Ann Rensler, and her cousin Teddy were all standing and watching through the open door.

Ann lifted the hems of her skirts when she entered the hot, hewn-log kitchenhouse. While they had been in the yard deciding how the slaves' serving tables should be arranged, Teddy had heard the slaves joking and teasing about books. Brant had tried to draw them away, but Teddy had instantly led them in. True to his nature, her cousin would not let any slave matter in the parish rest or go uninvestigated, for he hated darkies, and maybe even secretly feared them as most of society did.

Ann knew all the slaves they found inside, and it did not surprise her that Joseph was the one holding the book, since Brant had confided in her why he had cut the boy's tongue a year ago. What she didn't understand was why they were so boldly grouped together. Brant stood beside her and spoke uneasily. "This has not been going on without my permission."

Ann saw her cousin's anger rising.

"There's no formal law against it, Teddy. It gives my daddy some peace of mind because the houseservants still have their religious instruction, though he is too unwell to do it. And it's no secret with any of these that Joseph can read."

"They are gathered without supervision!"

"Only five of them. On a plantation that's not against the law."

Ann kept herself away from the bare walls while her cousin walked along the hearth. He scraped his boot over some of the dusty marks on the floor. "And do they also have your blessing to conduct a school here?" he said arrogantly.

Delora's big burly driver spoke up even before Brant could. "Mass' Rensler, sah! This here's the Sabbath an' we don't do no work on this day."

"I'm quite sure of that!" Teddy spoke back. "But say I had come yesterday. Then which of you all would have been scribbling on these boards?"

The driver stayed respectful but also full of himself. "Sah, you can come any time, any day. I tell you, you won't find none of us doin' nothin' like that."

Teddy refused to banter with him. "I guess not, now that you all know we're on to you! There *is* a law against Negroes teaching Negroes, and the punishment starts at fifty lashes."

Ann blinked, for she had grown more and more disappointed in Teddy's delight in always threatening such severe abuse.

"Woowheee!" The black driver made his eyes as wide as plates. "Never done hear'd nothin' 'bout that, sah!"

Teddy's glance flashed to Brant, who gave a tense explanation. "With daddy being so sick and our wedding on the way, I just wasn't keeping up with all the changes in the law. I just found out about the new legislation last week when we both dropped by the Planters' Club."

"And still you didn't control your boy!"

"The law has to do with teaching, not with reading. But now the folks here know. There will be no instruction of any kind." Brant looked at his people, and they seemed ready enough to heed even his mild warning.

But Teddy took the matter into his own hands, even though Tyson Clemson had just been elected captain for this year's parish patrol. He went up to Joseph and tore the book away. "You black snake. When something like that shows up"—he pointed to the marks in front of the hearth—"you know who's going to take the blame."

Brant looked at the boards. "It's very hard to say if those are letters the way the floor's been rubbed."

"And why do you think it *has* been rubbed?" Teddy asked with chiding.

"I don't know," Brant replied coldly. "But I don't want you starting any new grassfires for me right now. If our colored folk were doing wrong, then they know better now. I have a wedding to plan and my father's illness to deal with. So don't do me any favors by dragging Delora into some legal battle now."

Ann saw a muscle in Joseph's face twitch. The black boy put his hand upon it. Teddy clucked his tongue. "Months in the workhouse, and still you don't have it right! Boy, I feel that yet another day of reckoning is coming for you."

"Stop it, Teddy," Brant said.

Teddy looked down at the spine of the book in his hand. "Your daddy once lent this same book to *me*! What does he think? That I am as simple as a nigger and as easily deceived?"

Brant took the book from Teddy and spoke to the houseboy. "Go inside and stay with my daddy."

The slaves did not look at one another, but Ann quietly feared what they might be thinking. Compared with her daddy's own, Delora slaves were compliant and helpful. She resented how easily Teddy could carry the harshness of Pine Woods here to this quiet place. "Let's go outside," she said.

Instead Teddy strode in front of all the remaining Negroes. "Need I say again that the punishment for one nigger teaching another starts at fifty lashes?"

"No, sah," Billy Days spoke for them all.

Teddy stood toe to toe with the huge driver. "They all are just waiting down at the workhouse for that *reading* Delora houseboy to be sent back."

"Don't harangue them!" Brant said, leading the way to the door. "You've said your piece. I'll speak to my daddy. They all will stay within the law."

Ann had a squeamish feeling about how her cousin gleefully eyed the girl called Rosa. It had been months since she had seen the wench in the moonlight. The girl looked bony and sun-scorched, and she hated that Teddy gave his attention to her anyway. Under his gaze Rosa shook as though he were touching her physically.

"Let's leave. Please," she said to Brant.

"There's one more thing you all should know," Teddy said, still lingering. "The state's going to stop Negro education by every means. Now if *any one* of you wants to earn some reward for yourself, you can do so just by reporting any darkies who dare to teach. There's coin in it, for sure. And if any arrest can be made on account of your testimony, then you could earn for yourself manumission, free and clear."

The black driver Billy dared to sigh. "Sah, I have a hard time believin' all that business could be written into one law!"

"Be sure that it is, Uncle," Teddy replied. "If anybody here reports a violation and the culprit is committed, I will personally escort that teller to the boat of freedom."

Again, Ann saw Teddy look directly at Rosa. In the same moment there was a stir in the loft that served as a partial attic above them. The Callcotts' former houseboy, Colt, climbed down a rope ladder. Ann knew Brant's frustration with him, for he was always going off to nap or hide. But now with uncharacteristic poise the tall, ugly, three-quarters hand gained Teddy's attention. Her cousin laughed openly, for he knew all the tricks young slaves used to curry favor. "Why, sure, boy, that goes for you too! You come forth with information? I'll send you north free."

"Colt. You get back to whatever Maum had you doing," Brant intervened, "and don't you even think about supper for as little work as you've done these last few days."

Finally they left the smoky house. Teddy took the liberty of speaking to Brant like an older, angry brother. "Where is your sense, man! The tools for destruction are in your kitchen."

"They're happy," Brant said, not making eye contact. "There's safety in that, for contentment makes them harmless."

"Your Joseph was penned up for helping slaves to freedom, and the city house he stayed at was filled with abolitionist papers. And still you let him read!"

Ann took Brant's arm. "You never told me about any papers!"

"I know," Brant confessed, "because I didn't want to worry you. There's no proof that Joseph ever saw them."

"And no proof he didn't!" Teddy countered.

Feeling torn by their opinions, Ann walked a little ways from both of them to where new flowers had been put in along the path. Teddy was the first to approach her. "You're not going to be safe here, Annie. My recommendation is that you call the wedding off until Brant guarantees that his people are under better control."

She looked at him in disbelief.

"Someday a riot could start here, and the master and mistress of this house will suffer first. Ann, you could be murdered!"

"You!" Brant came up, rage distorting his face. "If I thought there was even a hint of danger here for her, you know I would go to any length to change this practice. However—"

"You cannot entertain darkies as children, Brant! There's a demon side to them."

"They've been warned of this new law. That is enough. They will not do us harm unless we follow *your* mistakes and make them think we hate them."

Ann inwardly smiled. This was not the same uncertain beau who had draped flowers around her neck last year. And she was not the same piteous, selfish little woman either. "I think Brant is absolutely right," she said, believing it was her place to stand beside him. She pointed along the path. "After all their work is done, they come out here every day after supper to plant flowers for our wedding. That would never happen at Pine Woods, and you know it. I like the way the Callcotts keep their darkies, and how the darkies seem to truly love them in return."

Theodore remained unswayed. "I fear for you, cousin."

Brant waited until Teddy headed off without them, then he took her trembling hand. "I felt your partnership just now! Oh, Annie. Few things could have pleased me more."

Without Teddy present, she was more open with her worries. "Do you honestly trust your daddy's boy without reserve? Doesn't his past in Charleston worry you at all?"

"It does, but he's suffered for those actions. And now I honestly know that Daddy could not live on without him."

"But being right in the bedrooms he *could* slay us all."

"I detect no violence in him."

"Brant, can you promise that no harm will ever come to us?"

"Such promises are impossible. You know that."

His earnestness met hers. "What will you do with him after your daddy's gone?" she asked.

He frowned at the thought. "I think the boy should be content to live a quiet life in our street with Rosa. I plan to offer him one of Daddy's slave certificates of marriage."

"You could sell him, and then we all could rest."

"I won't unless I must, for I fear that he could fall into very bad hands. He's proved himself faithful, and to reward him for that can be encouraging to all the slaves. In fact, I'm thinking more on a whole system that would run on rewards instead of on punishments. That, I guess, is why I took so little offense at what's been going on in the kitchen. If they ever did cause trouble, of course, then I would forbid their meetings."

"Do you think Joseph was writing on the floor?"

"I don't know. But now he has been warned."

"You know Teddy will alert the patrol."

"Yes. I thought of that too."

She grasped his hand because of the concern on his face. "Even so, I think you were right in what you said. I will trust you, Brant. I will."

————

The clock stuck one and Brant was still alone in the downstairs study, the burdens he carried too heavy for bed. In the dark hallway he could almost make himself believe he was seeing a specter of his mother as she appeared in her youth and in the portrait right above the mantel. But then Mayleda walked in, dressed in a thin white gown. "Oh, Brant, for a moment you looked so much like Daddy."

"Really?" He choked back tension. "Well, for a moment you looked like Mama when she was young." They both cast their eyes to the dark portrait above their heads. "What are you doing up in the middle of the night?"

She sat down on the rug at his feet. "The lights are still burning in Daddy's room. I guess I'm frightened and sad because I'm certain he will die. Eric sleeps soundly—but I cannot."

"I know, sweet sister." He held her head on his lap as she leaned against him. "That thought has been keeping me up too."

"Then you'll have Delora all on your own," she said with a maturity past her years. "Do you feel ready for that?"

"No," he admitted. "But we'll still have Gund and Billy. And it's not like this is coming as any surprise. God has been gracious to give me all these months, for Daddy and I have talked about nearly everything."

"It's good to hear you giving the credit to God." She smiled at him, but then her face darkened. "Brant, when you marry Annie, you won't put me and Eric aside, will you?"

"Oh, Mayleda!" He suddenly felt quite fatherly. "You don't ever have to fear that."

She started to brush back tears. "I don't, really. I just wanted to hear you say that you love us. And love me."

"I will love you. I do love you. Oh, this must be hard for you."

"No harder than for you," she sniffled. "I'll love you, Brant. I'll stay by you."

"I know you will, you little crab and shrew!" He stroked her hair, marveling that he could touch her and feel so protective of her. "Ann and I have talked about it, May. She knows she's in line to become almost like a mother and an older sister to you, and she takes those responsibilities gladly."

Mayleda's dark brows rose to warn him of honest, troubling thoughts. "I'll tell you now something that I wouldn't have said before. There was a time, years in fact, when I didn't really like her. But now I like her. I can love her like a sister, unless she's going to steal you away."

"No. I want to travel with her after the wedding—I'll be honest about that. But by October we'll be home to stay. Daddy's condition seems unchanging. I hope it's safe to think we can spend the summer away without having to say good-bye to him forever."

Now she really shed tears.

"I'm thinking of taking Ann north to see the Gilmans, since the two fathers are unwilling to let their daughters be together for the wedding."

"You'd go to Boston!"

"Hush, now! Don't you tell. Mr. Gilman's already mailed me steamer tickets, but I'm not going to say anything to Annie until after the ceremony. She's still hoping against hope that Felicia will be here."

"Then you'll be gone a long time."

"Yes, until October. But you and Eric will be with Daddy and Maum Bette, and the colonel will open his bayside house to you two as well."

"Oh, but that's so long!"

"Not to Annie, it won't be. Please, give me this leave, and I promise you will have us back for good."

"You're not afraid to leave Daddy?"

"I am, but I don't think he'd want us to wait when we have the opportunity to go north now. Things are getting so ugly in politics that it may soon be unwise or impossible to travel. There now, if all your fears and questions have been answered, you should go to bed."

She stood and kissed him on the cheek. "You are just like Daddy. More and more each day." She seemed very womanlike. "If all your fears and questions have been answered, then you should go to bed too."

He laughed. "I will . . . soon."

Her steps faded, leaving him to stare at the portrait of his mother. A small framed sketch of his father in his twenties was on the mantelpiece. It was thought provoking to see the pictures of his parents as young as he was now. He wondered what his father had felt like when the cloak of Granddaddy's responsibilities had been passed along to him. It made him suddenly want to be near the man for a while. He decided to go up to sit with his ailing parent for the next few hours.

When he came to the top of the stairs, Brant heard low moanings and also an intense Negro prayer. "Oh, Lord of Heaven, help us now—in Jesus' name!"

Frightened, Brant rushed in on a most indelicate scene. His father was on the bedside commode weeping. Both of the gentleman's bare arms were draped across Joseph's shoulders as the slave struggled to hold him upright. Indignant at the care, Brant demanded, "What are you doing to him!"

"Oh, thank God! I couldn't reach any bell to call for help!" Joseph cried. "He's desperately ill and has lost every ounce of strength! I need help now to get him moved to bed!"

Brant did not even think of calling another servant. Letting Joseph guide him he worked with him to bring the frail, thin body to the mattress. Then he cried, "I'll get Ezra to ride for Teddy!"

"No! Stay!" His father groaned.

Immediately Joseph began to meticulously wash up the foul-smelling waste that covered the man, the floor, the sheets, and the pillows.

Brant stayed fixed at the bed, holding his father and staring into his glazed light eyes. "You need a doctor!"

"No. You."

But Brant saw the worry in Joseph's face. "What do you think's happening?" he dared to ask the servant.

"The end is coming," he said softly. "Your daddy knows it."

"Daddy! I need to get Teddy!"

"He . . . can't . . . help!"

Brant was frantic. "Don't talk! Save your breath."

"Stay!" His father said again, though Brant had not moved from holding him by his shoulders.

"I am. I will." Again he looked to Joseph, who was wrapping up the soiled linens and attending to the chamber pot.

"May I leave you with him, sir?" the slave asked, sagging with either tension or weariness. "I just need to go for more bedding."

"Yes, of course," Brant said, but without indignation. It was apparent now that Joseph had been competent, though momentarily overwhelmed, in his nursing. Brant watched the dark man he had known all his life slip from the room. He had hated that form for years, but now he could feel nothing but gratefulness for it. He heard Joseph's familiar cough in the hall. He reflected that he knew nothing about the servant's health. He had trusted Joseph to care wholly for his father, but now seeing the slave so exhausted, he repented of his carelessness to know how Joseph was feeling. He rested his father against the pillows. "How are you now?"

There was no answer, as though his daddy had lost his voice. Brant turned back the top hem of the one clean sheet Joseph had laid upon him. His parent smiled briefly, then closed his eyes.

"It's more paralysis!" Brant cried, seeing how deathlike stiffness kept his father's shoulder off the bed.

"No." His father stopped a groan by holding his breath. "It's pain. It will get worse from now on. Put your hand to my nostrils. Am I bleeding?"

Brant's fingers trembled as he did so. "No! It's just your perspiration. See!" With the sheet he dried the beads of sweat on the wrinkled upper lip.

A sigh closed his father's eyes again. "There may be bleeding. And then I may lose my senses. Oh, explain to the children when that time comes!"

"I understand!" Brant managed before he clenched his teeth. It was like revisiting the site of his family's deaths. His mother and brothers all had bloody mucus and had grown incoherent before they died. Now his father was anticipating the same terrible end for himself.

Joseph returned with clean sheets and a glass of chalky liquid. "What are you bringing him?" Brant protested, his sense of protectiveness aroused.

"Lime water and milk with a little wine mixed in. It will settle his stomach. Before you came, sir, he vomited black blood."

Brant felt his eyes grow wide. He took the glass. "What right have you to decide what medicine you will give him?"

For the first time that night he saw his father and the slave exchange one of their deep connecting glances. Joseph's words came slowly. "In school I made a study of miasmic conditions."

"What! So now you are some kind of hoodoo doctor!"

"No. I collected information from real medical journals. I tended to your brothers. God knows, I did not want to be as helpless with your daddy as I was with them."

"Don't fight him," his father moaned. "What do you think has kept me until now?"

With reluctance Brant held the glass so his father could drink. When it was empty he set it down. "What now?" he asked Joseph with resignation.

"Hope and pray that he can rest."

"What of the future?"

"Only God can know, sir. About two weeks ago he had a similar spell and recovered from it well."

"You never told me!"

Joseph's stare seemed empty.

"You never asked," his father whispered.

Brant was stung by conviction. It was true that he had avoided his daddy's sickroom as much as possible, while at the same time continuing to be jealous of every minute Joseph had spent at his side. Now he saw his foolishness on both accounts. He should have been there, and he should not have resented anyone who would endure what Joseph did to keep his father alive and comfortable. "I want to know how you are," Brant mourned aloud.

"My entire abdomen is cramping and burning!" Tears came with his daddy's honesty.

"Well, what can be done for that?" Brant questioned Joseph.

"I don't think it's treatable," the slave said sadly. "It's part of the terminal stage. Your father knows that."

"He knows! He knows! Why do you keep saying that?"

Again there was a moment of silent communication between the aged man and the worried slave. Then Joseph reached under the mattress and showed several sheets of letter paper. "The notebook that was taken away from me at Mr. Wahl's contained my medical information. As much I could recall, I rewrote here."

Brant examined the legible writing. "This is your work?"

"Yes."

"Do you know there's a law against colored folk practicing medicine on whites?"

Joseph seemed grave. "No, sir, but should I be surprised?"

Brant dropped the papers. "What else do you need to do here?"

"Nothing, sir, but to watch him closely every moment."

"I can do that! You are dismissed to your quarters."

It seemed hard on the servant to be sent away, but he bid his Master Abram good-night, then went into the dressing room, closing the door behind him.

"It's kind of you to be here," his father mouthed with little breath. "I have been sick most of the evening. I'm sure Joseph needs the rest."

"Why didn't you call for me?"

His father appeared anguished. "I . . . I suppose because I know how the other deaths affected you. And I did not want you to see me in all my repulsive weakness." He smiled blandly. "But I'm glad you came just when you did. I have been foolish to be secretive. Time might be short, so I am happy you are here. I am. I am."

They sat in silence, Brant feeling like a foreigner in this small portion of his own house. After a time he got up and went to the bookshelf where Joseph kept his father's Bible. Bringing it back to the chair beside the bed, he read Psalm 23 out loud. " 'The Lord is my shepherd; I shall not want. He maketh me to lie down in green pastures; he leadeth me beside the still waters. He restoreth my soul . . . .' "

When he finished, the room was deadly quiet. His father was asleep. After replacing the Bible on the shelf, he went over to the dressing room door and opened it without knocking. It was completely dark inside, yet he heard Joseph immediately rise to his feet.

"Have you no candle?"

"No, sir. Not tonight."

"Then step into the light."

While Joseph did so, Brant struggled to follow through on the feelings that had made him go there.

"You need me, Master Brant?"

Brant saw then that Joseph's face was swollen, his eyes glistening with tears. "No," Brant said, hiding the emotion that Joseph's personal, private grief stirred within him. All doubts about the rightness of the slave's motives were laid aside. "I just came to say thank you. Thank you for all you've done."

Joseph didn't move except to lower his head. "Yes, sir," he said, then seemed to struggle to hold his shoulders still when a fit of coughing attacked him.

"What about your health? You've been coughing for months."

Joseph looked at him warily. "When Master Abram gave me permission to order medicines for him, he gave me permission to order some for myself."

"Then maybe you should take time to doctor yourself," Brant said, not making light of the African's abilities but showing true concern.

"Your daddy needs constant watching."

"I can be with him. You need rest. Take it."

Joseph smiled cautiously. "Thank you. I will until you call for me."

Battling sorrow Brant looked back to his daddy's bed. "I plan to keep a vigil tonight. If you want to join me, I would be happy for your company."

Their eyes met again before Joseph put himself back into the darkness. Brant's emotions were troubled in a different way, and he could not feel aloof from the slave anymore. One Scripture crossed his mind that simplified the understanding of his feelings now, but made his future seem impossible. "Love is the fulfilling of the law."

That's what Joseph had shown him by his dedication. And that's what he felt obliged to begin showing in return.

CHAPTER 29

ABRAM AWOKE TO TWO FACES in the candlelight—one dark, one light, but both looking worn and weary. Still, it seemed a sign that heaven had come near. Both Brant and Joseph were sitting on the chairs beside his bed. Because he had moved his eyes, Brant moved also.

"Joseph, he's alert."

"I see!" Joseph said, just as pleased as the son.

"Daddy, can you hear me? Can you speak?" Brant touched Abram's shoulder.

"Yes," Abram said after a very long time of trying to remember how to make the word. He shifted his eyes. There was light on the horizon outside the closed eastern window. His rest had strengthened him. Remembering what day it was, he spoke to Brant. "You are to be with Ann today, son. To pack her things and practice the music for the ceremony."

Brant smiled back at him. "Yes, but I will stay with you instead. We'll send a message."

Abram tried to prove his vigor by moving his good hand. "Go. This is an important day for you both with the wedding on Saturday. There's nothing you can do for me here, but there you can give my soon-to-be daughter a kiss from me. Take Mayleda and Eric, as you planned to do, for truly, I am better."

Abram saw his son look to Joseph for advice.

"I don't know, sir," Joseph spoke with dignity. "As I said yesterday, he went through something like this before and then recovered well."

"I can say!" Abram reasoned with them both. "Look at me."

Abram noticed that Joseph seemed more rested also. "Master Brant, I could send a messenger to call you home if he does not do well."

Brant took no offense in Joseph's suggestion. "We will do that, then."

Abram closed his eyes to the sweet scene of Brant and Joseph talking. Suddenly he felt ready for his eternal home.

———

Bette came up in the afternoon while Joseph was warming Abram's ice-cold limbs with tepid water. "There's a gentleman downstairs what wants to come see Massa."

"Is Master Brant not home yet?" Joseph said, speaking for Abram, whose eyes were closed.

"No, he ain't, an' this gentleman just won't go 'way."

Abram spoke then. "Who is he?"

Bette curtseyed and shrieked in one motion. "I never thought I'd hear you' voice again, sah! Glory be! He name's Mista Hamilton. Says he just come down on the railcars from Columbia, representin' some judge."

Abram's bloodshot eyes opened and caught Joseph's. "Entertaining angels! Send him up!"

Bette protested, "Mass' Brant says nobody comes up, not even the cats."

"Maum, send him up!" Joseph begged.

Bette looked as though to blame him for Abram's sorrows, but Joseph was thinking other things. Columbia was the state capital and the meeting place of the General Assembly. Perhaps, just perhaps, this man had something to say in regard to his freedom. He set the porcelain washing bowl aside, but before he could get the brush through Master Abram's thin hair, a large man with curly dark sideburns and an impressive suit walked in. Brusquely, without waiting for anyone to address him, he looked at Abram in bed and said, "I am Attorney Hamilton, sent by Judge O'Neall to represent the interests of the state of South Carolina."

Abram drew much of his meager strength from having Joseph with him. The visiting lawyer, young, dark-haired, and strong across the shoulders, imposed upon him like a bear.

"This is Joseph, then?" the man said after accessing that Abram was still of sound mind, though feeble bodied.

The whole language of bondage pained Abram now, almost as much as did the fatal fevers. It was difficult to speak. "I pray you come bearing his freedom papers."

"Mr. Callcott, dismiss the boy. Then we can talk."

Abram was firm, despite his spinning head. "He stays."

Mr. Hamilton frowned and narrowed his eyes toward Joseph. "I am here to gather testimony on your real condition."

Abram chuckled, though it hurt to do so. The reason for this man's long-distance travel seemed absurd. "Do you wish to see my coffin?"

The lawyer soured. "No, sir."

"Then come to the point. Can the boy be freed?"

"Yes—though unbelievable. The vote decided that he can be freed if your documentation proves valid according to what I find here."

Abram tried to see Joseph, but the African had turned his face toward the window. "Dear Joseph! God has heard our prayers!"

"The vote was not to *favor* him, sir, but to *banish* him. Once his work is finished here, then no other planter will want to have him if he can read and write."

Abram felt himself fading. "Are there papers to sign?"

The attorney seemed cautious. "Yes."

"The writing desk, Joseph. I will do it immediately." Already the room seemed beset by twilight. Abram forced himself to keep his eyes open. He could feel his heart flutter. He saw when the man laid the document on the portable desk's writing surface, and he begged Joseph, "Help me sit up! Help me with the pen!"

Joseph put the pillows behind him. Mr. Hamilton eyed everything with suspicion. "How can you write in your condition?"

Even with dimmed sight and hearing, Abram sensed Joseph's fearfulness. "I can," he said as strongly as he could.

The man then pointed to the two blank lines where he needed to put his name. Abram started weeping at the sight of the true manumission agreement, but Joseph continued to stand like an arrow.

Mr. Hamilton studied Abram's dead right limb after Joseph pulled the sheet away. "Take my hand, Joseph!" Abram said with impatience. Having done the same activity many times before when he was stronger, Abram entrusted his servant to move his stiff arm to the desk. With Joseph's fingers interlocking his, Abram held the pen. Joseph moved it. By much practice over many weeks, they had perfected this system of writing. When the pen lifted, there was a moment of glory. *Two sets of freedom papers had been signed!*

Joseph seemed frozen, and there was scorn on Hamilton's face. Abram worried that he might have let himself be tricked. Would his signature be considered valid, having been written like this?

"That pen, boy!" The visitor called for it harshly. "My signature must go beside the master's." Joseph laid the pen down on the desk, wise enough to know that he should not hand it off directly. The attorney took out his handkerchief and wiped the quill ceremoniously. "Would you care to forge mine, also?"

The moment the man finished, Abram angrily told Joseph to take the quill again. This time, however, Abram placed it between two of his left fingers, and made a disconnected X behind each of his signings. "There, sir! That is my hand. And you are my witness."

Mr. Hamilton closed the session abruptly. "Your copy of the agreement should be placed with your will for the judge of probate. The other copy I will keep and return to Judge O'Neall." Suddenly he addressed Joseph directly. "Upon your master's passing, you will be required to leave South Carolina and never return. If you are found in this state again, you will be sold back into slavery. And, boy, remember this: It was not your master's compassion that freed you, but the state's desire to rid the South of all literate, colored incorrigibles like you!"

Joseph endured the statements like a deaf man.

"Any trouble you make for yourself before the will is read can send you to slave court instead of on to freedom."

Abram could not wait until the man had departed. The instant he was gone, he gathered his strength, trying to communicate his jubilation. "It's done! Thanks be to God!"

Joseph, however, appeared forlorn.

"You are going to be free!"

"Yes, sir." His words cracked. "But first you will die. And then I will be sent away from all I love."

"Write a letter now for me. I will send you up to Nathan Gilman. You can trust him to care for you." Abram gulped a hard breath of air and looked at Joseph, feeling that he might be seeing him for the last time.

Joseph looked bleak. "Sir, I do not wish to go to Boston to be cared for. I would rather find friends of my own color and study to be a doctor. That is, if I could have a letter of recommendation from Teacher Payne."

Abram eyed the portable desk and considered whether or not he had the strength for more activity. "Get paper. We are writing you a travel pass to and from Charleston. For today, by horse."

"No, sir!" Joseph was startled. "I am not leaving you!"

"Why? I am resting in my bed."

"No, I will not go."

"I have both Bette and Jewell to help me! I want you to see Payne and get that recommendation."

"Master Abram! I cannot go now. Perhaps tomorrow, when Master Brant is here at your side again."

Abram prayed for wisdom as pain roared through his limbs. He had the premonition that tomorrow would be too late. "You are still my bondsman. I order you. Write the ticket!"

It had been years since Joseph had ridden, but he made the saddle horse fly out the long dry lane. When he slowed to turn down the road to Charleston, Brant and Teddy were just ready to make the same corner in Rensler's coach. It was not surprising that the slaveowners demanded that he stop, dismount, and explain himself directly. Joseph did so with great reluctance, knowing that Theodore, and maybe Brant, too, could thwart his lone chance at freedom. "Master Abram's sending me to town."

Teddy chortled aloud. "Then why are your hands stained with ink from writing your own pass, nigger boy?"

Joseph sought Brant's mercy. "Master Abram cannot write. You know that. Yet he insisted that I go. It was the only way."

"What does he want from town!" Brant demanded.

The truth would not help him, Joseph knew. "To obtain some papers from Daniel Payne."

"That scoundrel has been banished from the South and his school closed down!" Theodore growled.

Joseph's tongue dried in his mouth.

"What are you up to?" Brant nearly pleaded with him.

"I can explain—" he paused—"when you are alone, sir."

Brant seemed dismayed and embarrassed. "Get back to the house! In fact, hand over the reins! You will walk, remembering the promise you made to stay with Daddy while I was gone."

"I can explain—or Master will!" Joseph called, but the coach was already in motion, the riderless horse trotting alongside.

When Joseph finally arrived back at the house, Theodore Rensler was at the slave door to meet him. "Your master is dead."

Joseph thought it a cruel joke and moved to go inside. Teddy blocked his way. "You left him unattended, so we cannot know the exact moment of his passing. The maum found him on the floor, as though he were trying to crawl for help. The room is in shambles. Ink spilled. Papers scattered."

"It cannot be! I was just there! I must go up! I must—"

Teddy caught him by the collar. "You will never set foot inside this house again."

"Please, get Master Brant!"

"You want him to help you, after what you've done?"

"I was ordered to go! I had no say in my leaving!"

"You forsook him in his darkest hour!"

"No!" Behind Rensler, Joseph saw Brant. "Oh, please, sir, I can explain. Your daddy insisted that I go."

Brant waved him away. "My father is dead!"

"I did not desert him! I did not!"

"Stop your wailing! The driver has been called to come and fetch you," Teddy said, closing the door in his face.

"There was a gentleman who came from the state legislature!" Joseph called in through the crack between the door and the doorframe. "Oh, Master Callcott, please hear me! He delivered my freedom papers, and then your daddy insisted that I go to town!"

Teddy opened the door again. "You are speaking nonsense! Have you no heart? No remorse for what you've done?"

"Ohhh! If you could just get those papers, then you would understand," Joseph pleaded to his face.

"You honestly think you received manumission today?" Rensler's voice was raw with judgment. "Then it is very strange that your master should die within hours of its coming. You know, boy, that only death could validate your release. If you do have papers, I submit that you will not go free but will be charged for murdering your owner instead!"

"I did nothing wrong, sir!" Joseph cried, hoping Brant could hear him, though he could not see the man. "I put the papers in his portable desk and then set it on the floor. I left in haste because of his command. I was hoping to be gone only a few hours."

Brant did come to see him. "My daddy was on the floor with his Bible beside him. That is all I know! I am done with you being in this house."

Behind him Jospeh caught a glimpse of Eric and Mayleda sobbing into each other's arms. The sight rent his heart. Brant's tearful eyes surveyed the yard. "Billy's coming to get you now."

"I loved him! I would have hastened my own death before his!" Joseph mourned as the door slammed again. He fell back and clung to the porch rail until Billy touched him. "He died while I was not with him!" Joseph wailed his confession.

"Hush. There's nothin' to be changed 'bout that now! You need come down with the rest of us." Gently he met Joseph's mourning, eye to eye. "I got some clothes for you, an' Parris an' Rosa are waitin' for you."

At Rosa's name Joseph started weeping. On the ride out the lane he had been wondering how he would even find the strength to leave her. Now he was being sentenced to the same existence that ensnared her forever. Billy chided him softly on account of his sorrow. "Nobody but the Good Lord hisself's gwine listen to no black man cryin'. Come on. Gather you'self up an' leave you' tears behind."

Rosa saw that Joseph was like a corpse himself, dressed in loose-fitting field clothes and leaning up against one of Billy's porch posts. Moved by compassion and able to fathom some of the depths of his sorrow, she attempted no words but sat down beside him. Taking his limp hands into hers, she tried to rub some life into them. "If you have something to say, I am ready to listen," she whispered gently. "Otherwise, Kwash, I just want you to know how sorry I am."

He never stirred all through that night. She grew chilly and stiff from staying on the floor beside him. She never slept, though she knew they both would face a full day of hard work come dawn. She sang to him, prayed and recited poetry, and once or twice in the lantern light Billy had set out for them, she saw his lifeless face sparkle with tears.

At daybreak a round, bright sun pushed up over the river to lift the purple lid of sky and let out the morning fog that rose like steam from a kettle. Billy's horn sounded. Rosa tried again to rub life into Joseph's flesh. "You must stand. Billy warned that it's likely there will be other drivers here today from the patrol."

Joseph's eyes drifted, studying her blankly.

"Come with me," she said, pulling his fingers. "Joseph! You must! You know Abram Callcott is in heaven. Don't weep for him any longer! Now you must save yourself."

Still he would not rise but squeezed his eyes closed. "I failed him and all of Delora by putting my wants first and not protecting him!"

"You did not. Billy's told me everything. You did more, much more, than any other human being could have done."

The conch-shell horn blew again.

"We must go!"

Suddenly his hand became firm on hers. "*Dara!* How can you still esteem me when I let the master die?"

She felt herself longing to kiss him. "It is not your fault. We all knew this day would come. Please. Billy and Gund cannot let you sit here much longer. Come with me."

"I saw my freedom papers. And now they are gone!"

She felt amazed but believed him. "Oh, Joseph. Oh, what sorrow!"

Like a bewildered child, he met her with his eyes. "Yesterday I was plotting ways to steal you away. Or buy your freedom once I was safely North. Now I have nothing!"

"Keep plotting," she said very softly, helping him to his feet. Over at the gathering place there were other white men coming to surround Delora's workers. It terrified her.

Joseph seemed sensitive to her worry. Drawing a deep, emotion-filled breath, he studied the situation and then seemed more like himself.

"I'm endangering you!" he said, peering into the distant crowd. "Go up without me. Rensler hates me. Do not stay near me. Do not even look at me if he is there!"

His intensity made her flee, but her heart was breaking. She knew this was wisdom, though it felt like betrayal to leave him alone. When she came close to the other slaves, she heard Parris praying, "God, give the brother mercy!"

It was the only devotion allowed the slaves that morning. In just moments, overseers they did not know sent them on the flatboats to the rice fields across the river. Her only comfort was that Teddy Rensler was not to be seen among them.

————

Brant awoke to find himself dressed but shoeless and lying on his bed. There was sharp pain from the top of his head to the base of his spine, but he sat up anyway. His mouth tasted odd, as though he had been drinking, but the last thing he could remember clearly was Bette and Jewell washing his daddy's cool dead body. He covered his eyes, only making the terrible memory clearer.

"Brant, how are you?"

The whole room spun, then brought Ann's face to him. She moved to the bed and sat beside him, smelling pleasantly of lavender. He put a hand on her shoulder and kept a hand on his head, thinking of the night before. "What medicine did Teddy force upon me?"

"I don't know. But it made you sleep, as he said it would."

"Ahhh! What time is it?" he said.

"About six—in the evening!"

Feeling instantly irresponsible, he pushed past her to get out of bed. How could he manage a plantation when he had slept all day and could not even find his boots? He searched the room that would not stay still around him.

"Brant, you can't be off like this. Think what you are pushing yourself to do."

"I know what I am to do! Be with my brother! My sister! And see about the servants and the slaves!"

"Mr. Gund has everything well under control. And Daddy and Teddy and some of the parish patrol are here to help as needed."

Brant groaned. "The patrol is here without *my* requesting it?"

"Teddy says it's just a precaution because of the rumor that's spread everywhere that Joseph was expecting to be freed!"

"Ann! Where are my boots? I must find him."

"What! Do you really think Joseph killed your daddy to try to make his freedom papers valid?" Her face showed horror in light of his wild animation.

Brant squinted, for all this was confusing to him in his present state. "No! Joseph might have failed him, but he would not betray him! Have you seen these papers Joseph talked about?"

"No!" She cried while he sat on the floor to yank on his boots.

"Then ring for Maum Bette! Tell her to search Daddy's room, top to bottom! Stay with her, and if she finds anything, hide it here under my mattress." He did not delay a moment more, for already he feared he would be too late to save Joseph from Theodore.

––––––––––

Hampton was along the river when Brant rushed down to him, breathless and anxious.

"Sah! I grieve for you an' you' family," he said.

"Yes, thank you!" There was extreme abruptness in his voice. "What other overseers came today, and where are they all now?"

"Bless you, Mista Brant for comin' down here so concerned," Hampton said, nearly sighing, for the day had been a long and wicked one. "Mista Clemson, the patrol captain, an' four others wa' here. An' Mista Rensler an' the colonel, of course, though the two of them stayed out of the fields." Hampton felt he now could smile. "You should be real proud of you' De-lora folk. They all went 'bout their business peaceful-like an' put in a good hard day, even though everybody's hearts been a-breakin'."

"Where was Joseph?"

Hampton felt himself tense. "Workin' alongside the rest, sah. An' now I put him in with Billy Days for the night."

"Yes! Good! Was he hurt or threatened in any way?"

"No, sah, though I sure did fear that too." Because of young massa's clear concern for the slave, Hampton dared to press him. "Anythin' I should know, sah? The rumors sure been a'flyin'—first that he might be freed, an' then that he done kill't you' daddy, which, of course, nobody here gwine believe."

"I don't believe it either. Rest assured! As far as his manumission, there's only the slightest possibility, but you keep that to yourself. Daddy had petitioned for it, that I know, but no papers have been found."

Hampton had been thinking that Theodore Rensler might have taken the papers to destroy them, but he held his tongue on that idea. Brant pulled out a folded note but kept it in his hand. "I want you to give this to Joseph. You assure him that from now on I will be the one in charge here. If there are freedom papers, I will find them and honor them. Oth-erwise, he is to live at peace in this street."

Hampton, impressed by the young man's compassion, opened the paper. "A Certificate of Marriage, for him and Rosa? Sah! I don't know 'bout this, 'specially for the gal!"

"Let Joseph make his own choice. It was the only thing I could think of to show him that I still trust him. I don't want him going sour, Mr. Gund, just because Teddy and the patrol would like to see him dead. If my daddy did have a visitor from the capital, then I can believe that he might have sent Joseph toward town."

"Bless you, Mista Brant. The people here, they gwine be pleased to get to know you. It's gwine to put to rest every fear they have."

"I wish I could say they should not fear, but between you and me, I am worried about what Theodore Rensler may try to do. You keep my brace of pistols handy. And you know the rules still stand. Other planters may not intrude on our street."

"Yes, sah. Thank you, sah. I'll keep a-watch."

"I know it's going to hurt Delora people deeply, but I'm g
no colored folk will be allowed at the funeral, the houseserva...
Then no planter can accuse them of congregating for the purpose of causi...
a riot. However, I will set a separate private time for them all to pay their
respects by filing by the parlor window to view the casket."

Hampton nodded, agreeing that was best.

"You think you need me, Mr. Gund, you come straight to the house at
any hour. Do you hear?"

"I do." Hampton could not keep the relief from his breathing. "Thank
you, sah." He noticed his own marred reflection in the sunset-dyed river
as Brant walked away. "What a God of miracles you are!" he said, looking
at his own self but thinking on heaven. "Mista Abram would be so pleased.
Yes, indeed. So very pleased with his son."

It was barely dawn on Saturday when lighted chaises and carriages
started coming in through the fog from the far end of Delora's driveway.
The dark vehicles reminded Hampton of a line of voiceless geese moving
as one and set on reaching the same goal. He stood with Ezra, directing
the traffic on the slick, sandy road. They both shivered mightily, for there
was a nonstop drizzle much too cold for May. Waving lanterns, they directed the Negro drivers up to the front piazza and then back again, so
they could park their disgorged conveyances along the muddy ditches
draining the entrance road. As they worked, raindrops continually fell and
dried on the lanterns' metal caps, making the smell of hot tin just one more
gloomy addition to the misty day on which Abram Callcott's mortal body
would be laid to rest.

The stream of coaches stopped as the hour for the service drew near.
Because of the weather the funeral had been moved to the house, which
had better access by road than Our Savior's Chapel. Hampton dismissed
Ezra so that the elder slave could get out of the rain. True to Brant's fears,
the patrol had sent its own guard to watch over the coachmen confined to
the stables.

As wet and mud-splattered as the bondsman he had just put off duty,
Hampton decided not to venture in among the well-groomed aristocracy,
even though his wife and his daughters were there. Instead, to honor
Abram Callcott, Hampton turned to be with his people. He found the
workers standing huddled together in the gathering place. They eyed him

with surprise when they saw him coming.

Arriving up close, he heard their collective sorrow pouring out in soft wailing and moaning. Their tremulous sadness bit at Hampton's heart. They had every right to mourn and to fear their future, though he was beginning to trust Brant Callcott. Hampton saw a quiet Joseph getting rain soaked with all the rest. From time to time the slave coughed violently with a barking hack that could be heard above everything. On any other day, Hampton would have put him in the sickhouse, but today he wanted Joseph near so he could keep his own eye on him.

In the stinging downpour Billy approached Hampton. His face looked warm despite the dreary chill. "Say, now that we have a *white* man with us, you think it would be p'missible to pray?"

"Yes, pray! What could honor Mass' Abram more than prayer?"

Billy squinted toward the sky. "Wouldn't surprise me none if this cold rain wa' Mass' Abram's own tears comin' down now that he knowed his Papa-God's heart on all such earthly matters."

"For true," Hampton said, full of sympathy and feeling one with the driver whom he'd known so long. Billy met his eyes in a shared, fathomless moment of woe. Both of them had been warned by Teddy Rensler that even grieving for the old master could be taken as a sign of rebellion against their new master. Surely that's why the women and men had been so quiet up till now.

Parris came through the sheets of rain. He, too, knew the warning, yet he confessed to being moved then and there by the Holy Ghost to lead them all in prayer. "You know, Mista Gund, I ain't done nothin' like this for more'n a year. Yet t'day, I repent of my silence to do anythin' Christian 'cept what wa' required of me."

"Then lead us all." Hampton said with reverent compassion. The strong young slave nodded against the elements while the fan-shaped shell on his bare neck caught the rain and channeled it into pearly drops. Hampton looked at the grown boy's daddy to show his admiration for the youth. "If that be what's on Parris's heart, then I say we all go over to Our Savior's Chapel, since it ain't no fit day for work."

Billy seemed surprised but pleased with Hampton's decision. Parris lifted a song even as they walked, and for the first time ever Hampton joined in.

> *Let us praise God t'gether on our knees.*
> *Let us praise God t'gether on our knees.*
> *An' when I fall on my knees with my face to the risin' sun,*
> *Oh, Lord, have mercy on me!*

CHAPTER 30

ANN AND BRANT'S WEDDING came only nine days after Abram's burial. Her father and Teddy had wanted to postpone the service indefinitely because of all that had happened. But the more her family advised her, the more she became determined to stick by Brant and marry him now so they could face his trials together. She was the only adult family he had now. The sooner they could be husband and wife, the better. To persuade her family, she had only to remind them of the rumors they said already had her on the edge of disgrace.

When Ann awoke at Pine Woods on the morning of her wedding, it still was raining, a sad continuation of the weather that had filled up the week since Abram's passing. Valiant about not letting anything more dampen her spirits, she called Corinth to get her Bible, and then she subjected both herself and her slave to a good dose of prayer. Her servant was almost as happy as she for the arrival of this day. Corinth knew she was moving to Delora, and she hoped Master Brant might give her a Certificate of Marriage so that Ebo could come out of Pine Woods on Sundays to be with her.

Ann hoped that Brant might even be able to work secretly through the traders to find Corinth's baby boy and buy him back. She marveled at herself, that she now embraced all of Brant's benevolent ideas so easily and so bravely, even though her daddy and cousin continued to oppose his generosity toward blacks. The only thing standing in her way of full trust was knowing that Joseph lived down in the street. Brant had told her all the details of the boy's service to his father that he felt proved the slave had morality and integrity.

To attribute character traits like these to a Negro was a new and challenging idea to her. She found herself more focused on the prime buck's indelible literacy, his exposure to abolition, and his workhouse sentence than about how highly Brant had come to favor him. But fearing Joseph was not something she wanted to think about today.

Skipping breakfast and hardly spending a moment with her daddy and cousin, Ann kissed them lightly before leaving the house one last time as an unmarried daughter. With only Corinth in the coach and Morrison driving, she rode to Delora. Mayleda met her at the door with hugs and kisses, then led the way up to her bedroom where Corinth would work to get them readied.

"How is Brant?" Ann asked with breathless energy.

Mayleda bit her lip, but still she could smile. "Today, for the first time, he seems truly happy. We all are! Oh, now we all are going to be like *family*!"

Ann kissed her proudly, feeling both motherly and sisterly, before Corinth called them to cooperation so that she could dress them. The slave did their gowns first, sewing black ribbon to the narrow part of the leg-of-mutton sleeves, a delicate sign that their joy would be tinged by mourning in remembrance of Abram. Then she worked on their hair, twisting it and pinning it and finally painting it with beaten egg whites to keep it in place against the soggy, humid day.

A little before the clock struck three, Ann and Mayleda went into the hallway. Standing on the brink of the greatest experience she could think of, Ann had only one thing in mind. She was about to become Brant Callcott's wife! Dressed in long tails and top hat, her daddy ascended the stairs to escort her down. He looked serious, and she was sure he felt pained to lose his daughter without being certain that he was gaining a worthy son or the ability to widen his holdings through this agreement of matrimony.

She looked up once at Corinth still in the hall and enjoyed the servant's look of pleasure. Then suddenly nervousness displaced every other emotion as the clock struck three.

Leaning on her daddy's arm, she descended to the large group of teary but approving guests who filled both the hallway and the study. They crowded in behind her as she walked into the parlor where Brant and the presiding minister, Dr. Bachman, were both smiling broadly. Nothing besides having Brant in her sight mattered to her now. She forgot their guests as she focused on him.

She felt the tremble of his hand as he took hold of hers. Treasuring every word of the ceremony, she searched his bright, tender face while they pledged their love to each other. To the cadence of rain falling outside the opened windows, her heart joined his.

Now all she wanted was the benediction so that she could be his wife.

When that moment came, she gratefully found Brant in full control. The moment the ceremony ended he took her by the elbow and rushed her back through the parting audience into the dining room, closing the door behind them. There he lifted her off her feet and kissed her with such passion that she could not breathe.

"My star!" he called her. "Oh, I pray you are as happy as I am this moment."

She kissed him back, feeling rewarded now for the strict Christian principles Brant had held to from the start. Rejoicing, she would not have minded leaving their guests right then to start spending a whole lifetime alone with Brant. But soon there was knocking at the door.

"Massa Brant. You' guests are growin' mighty restless out here." It was Bette. "Why I hear'd some say you'all might have just skipped off through the back door."

"A good idea!" Brant chuckled before letting Ann go. He straightened his shirt, and she brushed back her hair. Then taking her hand he said, "I have just one small surprise for you before we return to our guests."

"What?" she asked, enjoying his expectation.

"I have tickets for a special wedding trip," he said, handing them to her.

"I know we're traveling to the coast—" she stopped, and then let out a shriek. "These are Gilman tickets! For Boston!"

"Yes, indeed. I just need to know for certain that all things are secure here, and then we can go."

"Oh! You are absolutely wonderful!"

"I had very little to do with it," he said, confessing between the small passionate kisses he was putting on her lips. "I know how disappointed you were when Felicia could not come."

"Now you can see the sights of Boston too!"

He laughed. "Yes, I did think of that! However, wherever we are, my beautiful wife, I will have eyes only for you!"

———————

Two weeks after the wedding, Mr. and Mrs. Brant Callcott sailed out of Charleston for Boston. The colonel had protested, saying it wasn't wise for them to go north with the current political unrest. Billy took their decision to go against Ann's daddy's wishes to be a good sign and a bad sign all wrapped up in one. The good part was that it showed that Mass' Brant had truly grown to develop a mind of his own, and a good one, too, based on what Billy had seen thus far. The bad part, of course, was that it left Mista Gund as the only Delora white man in charge of things. With that, there was the specter of the patrol waiting someplace nearby, like an owl in the woods that cannot be found until it starts hooting. According to slave tradition, when it hoots, death will soon come.

Thinking about the patrol, Mass' Brant had tried to leave Mista Gund with a more imposing look of importance. When he went into the fields now, it was astride a strong horse with a whip hanging from the saddle laces. To Overseer Gund's credit, he had still come right up to Billy the first morning and explained everything, as though truly wanting a Negro's approval.

Now today, on their afternoon break in the shade, Gund sat quietly on the dozing mare. Of all white folk, Billy had to say that Hampton was the best he had ever known. Right then and there he said another prayer for the man, recognizing the strain Gund was under, being the only non-colored person on the property and responsible for all the watching. After so many weeks of rain, the returning hot sun made these first June days seem unbearable. Billy was choosing to wait as long as possible before putting everybody back to work, so he kept his eye on Gund to see when the man would direct him to blow the horn. Gund did not seem eager to go back out in the heat either.

While they were apart like this, Billy saw Rosa walk up to the overseer. This was quite unusual, since she still made it her business to keep to herself, especially in regard to men. In another moment Gund rode to him.

"I want you to take Parris with you and go over to that copse of hornbeams. Rosa says Joseph's real sick, though he's not 'bout to tell nobody."

Immediately Billy went over and tapped his son, who was sleeping on his back. The two of them went to find the former houseservant, with Rosa lagging behind. The minute Joseph saw Billy, he got to his feet. "Is somethin' wrong, sah?" he asked, choosing to speak Gullah.

"I guess it is," Billy answered with seriousness. Now that he was close to Joseph, he could hear the wheeze and rattle inside the young man's chest. Joseph stood only a second more, then doubled himself with a fit of coughing. Everybody had already conjectured that the boy's lungs had been damaged by his months in the workhouse, but until now, Joseph had somehow managed to keep pace with the rest of the workers. Now he looked up with distressed eyes.

Rosa spoke for him. "You know he's been sick for most of the time he's been down here."

"Just give me a moment, Billy. I can get my breath."

Because of Gund's order, Billy was glad he did not have to accept that as the final answer. "I'm movin' you to the sickhouse, Joseph."

"Sir, I can work. You don't have to give me special treatment."

"It's not special treatment," Gund said, coming up behind them. "It's my decision, 'cause it's part of my job to keep you all fit and sound."

Billy saw that the boy had little strength. Gund saw too. "Parris, you go with him and make sure that one of the old gray-heads watching over the toddlers gets him settled right with a mat and a jar of water." Gund came down from the mare. "Here, take him on the horse."

Joseph glanced at all the others now listening and watching. "No, thankyee, sir, I can walk." The last person Joseph looked at was Rosa. Then he bowed his head.

"Come on," Parris said, helping him at the shoulder rather than using the overseer's mare.

Billy exchanged glances with Gund as they were departing. "He worries 'bout what others will think if he don't carry his full weight down here," Billy said. "He don't want nobody to think of him as no pampered houseboy."

Gund stayed off his horse and pushed back his hat to look fully into the face of every slave gathered there. "Whether you all know it or not, Joseph bein' in the big house made it easier on us all, for without his servin', Massa Abram never would of lived as long as he did. If any of you have hard feelin's again' Joseph, you'd best lay 'em down."

Billy nodded in full agreement, and Gund went on. "You all go back to work an' finish the task you wa' assigned. When you done, Billy or me will come 'round to send you on you way. Seein' how it's Saturday an' nobody's here but us, we all gwine gather at the sickhouse 'bout an hour afta sunset to pray. Mista Brant done give me a registered license to oversee worship, so I do think we all free an' clear when it comes to holdin' Christian meetin's."

After the workers dispersed, Gund spoke just to Billy. "You know, I done thought a good deal 'bout quittin' Delora an' headin' west, where I hear there's free land just for the takin'."

"Hmm" was Billy's only response. *That would be glorious, to have the freedom to think of just picking up and going.* But he said nothing harsh to Gund about it. He had come to settle it in his mind that he should not fault the man for being who he was or for looking out for his own wife and family the best he could. Still, Gund's leaving could have serious consequences for all Delora people, and to show that, Billy merely had to grimace at the whip hanging on the horse's withers. "Next overseer to come along probably won't just carry that for show, sah."

Gund agreed somberly. "That's what keeps me here."

Billy joked to hide his embarrassment about how much he liked the white man. "I'm a mite disappointed, boss. I thought you'd have to stay due to the fine company you keep here."

Oddly Gund nodded back. "Billy Days, I sure do wish you could know by now that it *is* the company I keep. *Your* company—friend."

That was just too much for Billy. Let him be allowed to judge Gund as tolerable as the best of white men, but don't make him go so far as to shoulder the burden of having to have this man as his friend.

Gund saw his distress and stepped back. "Hey! I apologize. I was just sayin' how I saw the matter. I weren't askin' you—or assumin'—that you'd ever want to say the same of me. An' you have every right to feel that way! More often than not, I am plum ashamed of persons with as little color as me." To prove he wasn't waiting for any kind of response, Gund climbed back on his horse and rode off slowly.

Billy lifted his head and watched a breeze stir the trees. His recollections included all that had gone on between them, from the flogging in the barnyard to the night when Gund had walked away so that Billy could deal with Parris, father to son. There was no doubt that the man tried to put flesh to his ideas about how they should be treating each other.

Billy felt the tug of God, strong but as invisible as spider silk, telling him that holy forgiveness was something believers were not allowed to mete out by the spoonful. In that moment of revelation, the same white man who had been kindest to him also became the hardest to bear. God was using Hampton Gund to tell Billy that judgment could not be made based on skin color, no matter how much he might wish it were that way.

He looked at Gund on his horse in the distance. For the first time ever, Billy admitted to himself and to God that he had to see a brother there.

"I'm fine now," Joseph said to Parris as one of the old women of the quarters swept a corner of the sickhouse floor with a cornhusk broom before putting down a mat.

"Yeah, you fine," Parris said, "if you s'pose to sound like a man sawin' wood with every breath."

"At least I am breathin'," Joseph managed through several barking coughs that sent jolting pains piercing across his rib cage.

"I wa' sent to help you keep on breathin', so lay you'self down."

Joseph sat down. "I can't, or I will suffocate." Coughing again, he added, "While I was caring for Master Abram, I was taking medicine for my condition, and it helped."

"But now you don't have it," Parris concluded, sitting down beside him. "Is it still up in the big house?"

"Maybe." Joseph felt less distressed here because it was cooler than it had been in the fields. "I kept it wrapped in a cloth under the dressing-room bed."

"Then I'll go up to my mama and get it for you. Mista Gund couldn't fault me for that."

"Don't risk it!" Joseph said, taking a drink from the water jar that had been given to him and then offering it to Parris. "I will be able to catch my breath if I keep still. I used to get this way in the workhouse."

"You want company?" Parris asked, drawing his knees up and wrapping his arms around them.

"Sure." Joseph smiled. He tried not to be embarrassed that each breath was as hard as a day's worth of work to a strong man.

"I can go to the house," Parris offered again, after waiting some moments and still seeing how much Joseph struggled.

"I'll . . . manage. But maybe . . . you should tell your daddy to see if he can get it from Bette. That way . . . I could save it . . . for some real emergency."

"Worser than you is now?"

Joseph nodded to save his breath.

Parris pulled off his sleeveless shirt and rolled it for a pillow. Like a guard dog at Joseph's side, he stretched out on the dirt floor, watchful. It was not a sign of laziness that Parris always napped when he could. His daddy and the overseer counted on him to shoulder tremendous amounts of the work. They all were fed a limited diet and had limited rest, so Parris, over the years, had simply learned to rest in spurts to conserve his energy.

When Joseph felt stronger, he spoke again. "When others get sick, what happens to them?"

"Mista Gund, he lets you have time off in here, long as you are sick for real."

"I mean, what do they do *for* you?"

"Missus Callcott used to be charge of all that. Afta' her passin', well, young Miss Mayleda took over, an' she done pretty good in her mama's stead. Sometimes Mass' Abram would tell Mista Gund to let Mass' Theodore come on down, since he the official parish doctor now, afta' the other doc done moved away. But nobody here ever trusted Rensler farther than a brick can be throw'd. Not even from the start."

Joseph knew that Dr. Rensler would be the last white man on earth to ever help him. He sighed, feeling hot with the fear that his lungs might never fully open up again.

"You a'right?"

Joseph broke down his guard by shaking his head. "No. Not really. I'm worried. What's going to happen if I lag behind?"

"I s'pose Mista Gund will find somethin' else for you to do. The important thing right now is to get to breathin'!"

Joseph felt his face fill with shame. "I hate being weak. I've been fighting as hard as I can. But I'm so weary. . . . I don't know . . . if I can . . . keep up much longer."

"They sent you back here to rest, not to worry. You think you can lay down now?"

Joseph answered by pulling off his shirt as Parris had done to make a pillow. Immediately he was sorry for doing this, for Parris saw the cord he had taken from his neck and knotted around the upper muscle of his left arm and the piece of paper underneath it.

"What is that?" Parris pointed.

Reluctantly Joseph pulled loose the sweat-dampened square. He let Parris unfold it.

Parris studied the words just for a moment. "It's one of Master Abram's Certificates of Marriage, ainty!"

Joseph nodded with discomfort.

"An' that's Rosa's name!" Parris said, guessing correctly.

"Yes."

"I didn't know the two of you was married!" There was hurt in his voice.

"We're not. She doesn't know this paper exists."

The other slave eyed him unbelievingly.

"Master Brant gave it . . . to Mr. Gund . . . to give to me . . . before he left. But Rosa's not ready. Maybe . . . neither am I."

"Because of your sickness?"

"Yes. She should have someone . . . strong. Besides . . . I can't see birthing children . . . into slavery. A man's moment of pleasure—a son's or daughter's lifetime of pain."

Parris's eyes brightened. "Huh! I sure won't worry 'bout you none in death, man, for you more than half a saint a'ready!"

Joseph smiled. "You think . . . you could father children . . . without regret?"

The other man considered it quietly. "I still pray for freedom in my lifetime."

Joseph hung his head.

"Brother, is it for true that Mass' Abram got ahold of special manumission papers for you 'fore he died?"

"It is. I saw them."

"No wonder you feel so low! Then you think Mass' Rensler took 'em or destroyed 'em while he wa' in the massa's room?"

"I do." It was such a relief to hear Parris so easily coming to that same conclusion. "Where else . . . would they be?"

"Umm! Then you' heart's 'bout as heavy as you' lungs, ainty. And that's some of what's ailin' you."

"I guess it is." Joseph smiled unhappily. "You know . . . you're a first-rate minister . . . and counselor."

Parris rolled to his side and casually propped up his head. "I'm gwine do better an' better the more I learn to read."

"So . . . you're not afraid to keep on studying."

"Sure I is, but I'm gwine do it anyway. For true, a man's gotta know the truth 'fore the truth can set him free."

"You are right. A man should study . . . to show himself approved of God . . . and ready to do His will."

Their eyes stayed fixed. "So you willin' too!" Parris clarified, not letting his vision go.

"I am . . . if I can get my strength."

"Then you hush up an' get well!" Parris started smiling. "For I'm not 'bout to lose the one an' only teacher I got."

"Rosa . . . could teach—"

"I won't risk her life for it!"

Joseph nodded gratefully. "Then we . . . will work . . . together."

Parris looked at the certificate again. "While you rest, I'm gwine look this over, though I sure could wish for a P-A-double-R-I-S to be put in there, 'stead of you' name."

Joseph pushed himself, though he would have welcomed silence. "There's the word *certificate* and *marriage*."

Parris, however, was not looking at the paper anymore but at the door. The boy Colt was spying on them. "You two is readin'!"

Leaping to his feet, Parris chased after him in a corner. "He showin' me his weddin' paper, you little scoundrel!"

"He ain't sick, an' neither is you! You just hidin' out!"

The huge, muscular Parris stopped just inches from the boy. "You think that, you just go ask Mista Gund or Billy!" Parris dared. "Joseph is sick, but you the one what's gwine be hurt if you don't run off, an' now!"

Joseph struggled once Colt was gone. "You think he'll tell?"

"You *wa'* showin' me the certificate." Parris stayed by the door. "But just for safety sake, I gwine down to tell Mista Gund 'xactly what done happened. Mebbe nothin' will come of it, since he knowed you got that paper. An' I gwine ask him 'bout gettin' you' medicine too."

"Thank you . . . for helping me . . . again."

The other man twisted his head, not seeming unhappy. "First I save Rosa for you. Then I save you for her. Next thin' you know, you' gwine *have* to add my name onto that paper, since the two of you can't seem to get 'long without me!"

"Neither could anybody else on Delora." Joseph leaned back.

Parris grinned. "You can pay me back, brother. My *learnin'* in exchange for you *livin'* long 'nough for love!"

"I will help you . . . so long as Colt doesn't find us . . . again."

"He won't," Parris promised, " 'cause the next time he starts in here I gwine *gently* string him up by his heels."

A deepening friendship, Joseph discovered, was almost as good as medicine. He found himself breathing easier and with a new confidence that he was not alone on the street. Mentally he put down the heavy burden of trying to hide his weakness. Concealing the paper in his shirt, he lay down.

His lungs kept burning. His eyes stung with the fear that he would stay unwell. *God's will!* he prayed. *God's will . . . be done!*

CHAPTER 31

MR. GUND KINDLY ARRANGED IT so that Rosa could be in the sickhouse alone after all the slaves were settled. "He's still struggling," the overseer reported with concern as he brought her to the door and then let her in. "Try to keep him from talkin'."

Rosa nodded tensely, for Parris had told her differently. He felt sure the brother would be on the mend by nightfall. Rushing in to see for herself, she found Joseph leaning against the framework of the room's back door, his face to the blue night air. Appalled by his wheezing, she dared to touch his arm.

"You still can't breathe!"

His wordless look to her was nearly apologetic.

"Parris says you know what the illness is. Mr. Gund's going now to look for the medicine."

Joseph closed his eyes. "I don't desire . . . illness."

"Of course you don't. Who could say you would? Everyone knows your health was broken in the workhouse."

"I don't think . . . it's . . . consumption."

She was puzzled and scared for the sufferer to be showing such an odd sense of wanting to assess what ailed him. Refraining from questions, she gingerly took his hot, swollen hand. He seemed to have too little strength to hold hers in return. His limpness increased her fear. She began to pray, though she did not think of herself as an extraordinary pray-er.

After a long silent wait, Mr. Gund returned. "The house is all changed 'round. Mista Abram's old room is where Mista Brant an' Miss Ann gwine reside onc't they come home."

Joseph emitted a gasp of resignation. Billy and Parris came in too. "Is there nothing to help him?' Rosa cried.

Mr. Gund spoke with timidity. "Well, gal, this might not be 'xactly what the Scriptures had in mind, but I brought down my Bible an' my prayer book an' a little bit of groundnut oil from my wife's kitchen. Just this evenin' Billy an' me wa' sayin' how him an' I are 'bout as close as Delora's ever gwine come to havin' believin' elders."

Rosa's eyes widened to see the Bible. She never suspected that the overseer owned books.

Opening it, Gund continued talking. "In here it says, 'Is any sick 'mong you? Let him call for the elders of the church . . . an' let 'em anoint him with oil in the name of the Lord, an' the prayer of faith shall raise him up.' " He stopped. "That's what Billy an' me come to do for you now."

The overseer held a chipped pottery bowl while Billy dipped in his fingers and painted a greasy cross above Joseph's eyes. Then Billy took the bowl so Gund could do the same. "In the name of the Lord!" the white overseer said, and then Billy repeated the words. "In the name of the Lord, and for His glory sake!" Parris followed them both.

Rosa's heart swelled even more when Parris knelt down and put a hand on each of Joseph's drooping shoulders. "Dear Papa-God, this here brother's still got a heap of work to do for Jesus' sake. Come an' strengthen him. Come an' make him well, in the name of the Father, the Son, an' the Holy Ghost."

"Amen!"

"Let it be so, Lord!"

Then Rosa knew there were other believers outside gathered around the door to watch and pray, missing their suppertimes just to be there. Joseph continued to strive for each breath, his mouth opening wider. Rosa struggled, as though breathing for him. Again she mourned the fact that he was enduring all this unjust affliction because of cruelty shown him by the masters.

Parris stayed intent on him. "Brother, I think the Lord wants to say to you, 'Do not fear.' He ain't 'xpecting you to be strong or wise 'nough to save the whole wide world or even you'self. That's *His* job an' *He* gwine a'do it. You just need to rest in Him."

Joseph nodded.

"Rest in Him," Parris said again with tender encouragement.

Joseph drew a stronger breath under the slave preacher's gaze, and this time when he breathed out, he laid his head back against the wall at the door.

"Go on out an' start leadin' the others in prayer," Parris said to the two older men, his voice suddenly filled with expectant authority. "The Holy Ghost's here."

Billy and Gund went out, and the loud praying outside soon changed to singing. There was such a tremendous sense of God's visitation that Rosa began to shiver as though she were being wrapped in the finest of garments. In the street the slaves worshiped and cried and prayed with great liberty. Despite all the exuberant noise, Joseph soon fell to sleep sitting against the wall.

Rising with thankfulness and amazement, Rosa ran to the door. "He's breathing well, and he's asleep."

A shout of victory went up in the dusk. Suddenly a small, bony African, dressed only in a dirty loincloth, pushed to the front. Rosa did not know him, for no slaves at Delora endured such paucity. "You all think you talkin' with a god you cain't neither hear nor see?" the slave asked.

"Yes, we are talkin' to him, brother! An' listenin' too," Parris admitted, coming to the older man. "Where you from?"

The man pulled his wool cap low over his beady eyes and closed his mouth. Billy joined his son as Gund stepped back into the shadows. "Say now, if you honestly here to seek the Lord, nobody's gwine do you no harm."

"I'm Ebo, from Pine Woods," the man said slowly. "I used to work with Colonel Rensler's horses, but now I's on his gang what clears new ground an' puts down pilin's."

There was a murmur in the small tight crowd. Everybody knew this was the harshest of plantation chores and the one most likely to end with disease or death by accident.

"Howsumever, I slipped off here hopin' to see my gal Corinth up in the house. All she do now is talk 'bout this Jesus-God you all seem to know!"

"You can know this God called Jesus too," Parris said, cutting to the point, for entertaining any outside visitor made the night more dangerous for everyone. "He the only God what ever was or will be. He the only one what will ever give answer to you' prayers, onc't you done ask Him to come right inside you' heart to wash you' soul clean from all you' sin an' wrongdoin's."

The man exercised faith as simply as a child. "A'right. I ask this Jesus to go on in me an' do that right now! If that be all there is to it, then I ask the Unseen One to do it."

Parris quickly explained other things to him. "Jesus came from his home in heaven to earth to find us. He wa' whupped an' killed for doin' that for you and me. But on the third day God's power lifted Him from the grave—forever. So even though you cain't see Him now, He done know all 'bout what you gwine through. An' when He comes in to save you, He gwine give you power by the Holy Ghost so's you can live a whole new life for him."

"I sure do need it!" Ebo exclaimed.

"Then know the love an' power of Jesus!" Parris touched him.

"I will see it if I can get a peek in at the man you say is being healed by this Jesus."

Rosa felt reluctant when Billy and Paris let him in to see Joseph, who was sleeping with his body turned and his face still to the wall. Ebo stared at him, then walked even closer to look at the scar showing on his bare back.

"How'd that brother get marked up?"

Billy explained with caution. "You should know, an' be careful, for there're white folk in this parish what say Jesus is only for whites, an' that's how they done tried to show it."

"You know where that brandin' iron come from, don't you!"

"No, we don't," Billy said.

Ebo turned to everyone. "Well, I sure do!" But he wouldn't say more because Gund had just come in.

"The Pine Woods brother done think he knows who owns the brandin' iron," Billy reported to the overseer.

"No, I can't say!" Ebo backed himself away.

"Tell us, Ebo," Gund urged. "You' secret will be safe."

Ebo cringed. "You can whup me! You can beat me, sah! I won't say!"

"Here now!" Billy intervened. "Mista Gund ain't gwine beat you up. Him an' me are brothers in the Lord Jesus Christ what you just done asked into you' heart. Now if you know somethin', you best say it so's our eyes can be opened an' mebbe we can better protect ourselves."

Ebo looked at Billy only. "A Pine Woods blacksmith done made up that design 'cordin' to Mass' Teddy Rensler's drawin'."

Billy looked at Gund. "What do you think of that!"

"But the men who hurt Joseph came in riding on mules," Rosa said, forgetting all caution. "And none of them was Teddy Rensler."

Ebo took interest. "I can believe that! For when I wa' still workin' 'round the stables, I done hear'd an' see'd how Mass' Rensler would sometimes give hard coin to bootleggers at night to take those brands with 'em. It never bothered me none till I seen that brother's flesh scarred just now. So that's what my owner wa' doin'. Payin' po' white moonshiners to spread the fear so's that Negroes won't come askin' 'bout you' Jesus-God, nohow."

"That makes a heap of sense," Gund said softly. "For onc't a Negro's converted, you can be assured he'll drink less an' carouse less, which is gwine cost the illegal whiskey runners in customers." He looked right at Ebo. "You'd best skedaddle. But as God be my judge, I give you my word nobody gwine hear from me that you been here."

The night was deep enough to cloak Ebo, and he was gone in moments. When the gathering closed, Rosa went back inside. Billy looked down across her shoulder at Joseph, now still as death. "He's plum wore out. Even without that cough, we should have knowed he'd come to us exhausted. For days, weeks, months, he done nothin' but care for Massa."

"He's been sick all the while," Rosa said.

Gund came in and looked to Billy while the older slave dared to say the truth. "Missy, many a black man's died after his time in the workhouse."

"He's not going to die!" Rosa said with certainty. "God's healing him. You all are witnesses to that!"

Parris was there to take her side. "An' look how God also used him. Without his sickness, there would have been no meetin'. An' without no meetin' Ebo might never have got saved."

Rosa had a strong, unbelievable urge to touch Joseph in his rest. Billy seemed to sense how much she wanted to be alone with him, and soon he found reason to have Gund and Parris join him outside. In the dim silence lighted only by a few tallow candles, Rosa did touch his face, softly.

It was still strong and serene, even after so much weakness and agony. His breathing was shallow, and she struggled to hold on to her belief in the miracle. Her prayers seemed selfish, but she said them anyway. "Let him live, oh, God. Please, let him live."

———

Joseph awoke to find himself lying in the light with one arm under his shirt under his head. Though awake, he thought he must be dreaming when he saw that Rosa was sleeping just inches from his side! He quietly sat up so as not to disturb her. He was still in the sickhouse, still near the open back door.

Looking out he could see the sun on the river. It was all as silent as a dream. His lungs were tight and his chest felt filled up and narrow, but when he coughed, it was not the desperate fighting for breath that he had had yesterday.

His struggle woke Rosa. He looked away as she sat up. Surely she had never meant to fall asleep here. Though not letting himself see her, he felt her nearness so much that his flesh tingled with the desire to simply turn to find her face in the sunlight. Yet he did not turn, even when she spoke.

"How are you?"

When she moved into his line of vision, he could not avoid the golden brightness that bathed her lovely countenance. "I can breathe. I think I can work today."

Her glorious smile was almost laughing. "It's the Sabbath."

Of course. Otherwise Billy would have sounded the horn.

"Are you hungry?" she asked.

"I'm not. Are you?"

"No." Her eyes danced, but soon tears filled them.

"What is it?"

"Last night I think you came very close to dying."

He lowered his eyes. That was true. Even in the toolshed or in the workhouse cell, he had never felt himself so close to eternity. "God touched me and brought me back."

She embraced his arm with both of hers. "I know He did! And so do many others! In fact, one slave from Pine Woods was even saved because of the miracle he saw accomplished in you."

Joseph could not believe that she was touching him. "I can't remember any of it!"

She said happily, "You slept through it all. It was wonderful."

"It still is." Then he quickly looked back at the sky, remembering her past, trying to do all in his power not to frighten her.

"Don't do that," she said, actually putting her head to his shoulder.

"Rosa! Dear Rosa!" he cried, full of dismay. "I pledged not to touch you, but now it seems you will not let go of me."

"Do you mind?"

"Do I mind! I am amazed! Have you no fear?"

"Yes, I do have fear," she said, drawing closer. "Fear that you might have died without my ever knowing your loving, caring touch."

He laughed his joy. "So! What am I to do?"

"Hold me and never stop."

"Rosa! May I?"

Her gleeful face swept his heart and stole what little breath he had. Lightly and cautiously he allowed himself to put his arms around her, watching every moment how she was responding, guarding every moment against his own desire to squeeze her against his joyful heart. Then his coughing shattered the incredible moment.

She looked at him with worry while he drew away. He felt a sense of guilt, of shame. "God did not let me die. But He did not heal me either."

"He did heal you! Otherwise you would not have even seen this day. You can breathe. That's what matters. With rest, who's to say that you won't be well? Billy and Mr. Gund know you are exhausted. They will let you have time to rest. I know they will."

"Then you are not discouraged by my sickness?"

"No! I am encouraged, for you are so much better. I want to be near you." Suddenly she turned. "Unless, of course, you realize now that you have no desire for me."

"No desire! This moment has been the subject of my prayers." His voice was weak, mostly because of dismay. "Oh, if I had my freedom papers I might dare to ask to be your husband. Oh, if I were well, I would ask you to marry me, and then I would sweep you away in a wondrous rescue."

She shocked him and scared him. "Don't wait for freedom. Ask me now."

"You cannot be serious. For all the time you've known me, I've been more sick than well. More weak than strong—"

"And more wonderful, more tender, more caring, more Christlike than any other."

"Rosa, I don't deserve that."

"Just as I don't deserve you! But I believe I could be secure with you, if you could be happy with me. When I touched you just now, I felt whole. Not frightened. I know I could not bear having any man but you holding me. And just as real, I cannot face the possibility of not holding you."

"But how are we to be slaves and spouses too? How can I promise you anything, when I have nothing? How can I make a promise, when we cannot know what the next hour holds?"

"Then marry me for just this one moment of bliss, for we do have this moment."

He longed to kiss her lips but lightly kissed her cheek instead. "If you're so certain, then I have something for you." He picked up his shirt folded on the floor. "Before Master Brant left for Boston, he gave a Certificate of Marriage to us."

She gasped a little.

"I did not ask him for it. He thought of it." The idea was both numbing and touching, for in one sense Master Brant was able to dictate their futures, but in another, the man was acknowledging that God alone should be the one to join them both together. Joseph's hands trembled. "The paper was here last night! But now it's gone."

"Hallo!" Billy called before walking through the front door. "How are you two doing?" There was a mischievous twinkle in his eye.

"Better, Billy," Joseph said, then whispered, "But somebody's stolen something precious from me."

Billy broke into smiling. "I know. A cord an' a piece of paper. Mista Gund has 'em for safekeepin'. Parris done took 'em when you weren't in no condition to be lookin' out for you'self."

Joseph's anxiety turned to sheepishness. "I would like to have the paper back. And so, I think, would Rosa."

"Well, ain't that fine! A healin'! Now a weddin'! Ain't the Lord good!"

"A wedding?" Joseph mouthed the words with question, but Rosa only smiled.

"When, sir?" Rosa asked.

"Girl! You are serious, ainty?"

"I am," she confessed. "We can't know the future. We do have today."

Billy laughed. "There's no time like the present, I s'pose."

"You're saying we could get married today?" Joseph struggled.

"If you an' Rosa want it that way. Yeh. I just need to talk with Mista Gund."

Joseph could hardly risk looking at Rosa, but when he did, she was nodding and smiling. And so was he.

———

Mr. Gund read the "solemnization of matrimony" from his prayer book that afternoon while the whole African community, Maum Bette, Corinth, and Mama Jewell included, stood down in the shade beside the river. In faith the Christian overseer even voiced the part omitted when slaveholding masters presided at slave weddings: " 'Those whom God hath joined together, let no man put asunder.' "

The words broke forth a shout of jubilation. Then at Bette's and Billy's counsel, Rosa and Joseph also followed the old tradition of jumping over a broomstick, just to seal their promises as their ancestors had done before them. Parris prayed. All the people gave their well-wishes, and Rosa stood like someone witnessing miracles bound for someone other than herself. Joseph had no more attacks to his breathing, and Maum Bette had even scrounged the ingredients and time to make the two of them a special wedding supper of chicken and sweet potatoes with a little ginger cake. After the crowd was back in the street, they ate in private under the riverside trees.

Behind them the golden sun Joseph so loved slipped toward night like a wishing coin gently edged into a well. This whole day Rosa had been eager, not wary, of their first moments together. Yet they were not completely alone until well after midnight, for the folks came back to sing and dance and finally to end the day in prayer.

As their only wedding gift, the slaves had rearranged themselves so that Joseph and Rosa could have the shanty by Hermon Creek all to themselves. When she and Joseph entered through the door of that bare house with nothing more than a glowing hearth to welcome them, Rosa felt the strangest yet most wonderful sense of being home.

CHAPTER 32

JOSEPH MARVELED AT HOW QUICKLY the miraculous could become the routine. He and Rosa had been married in June. Now it was already the beginning of October. For four months he had experienced what Billy Days said a good marriage would be—*"a contented man's little patch of heaven on earth."*

Even though his recovery in the sickhouse had been God-directed, he did not completely regain his health. The same dry, barking cough arrested him frequently, especially when he was tired or exposed to smoke or dampness. What he could remember of his readings in Teacher Payne's classroom made him believe that he had a chronic lung condition called *phthisic*, or asthma. In the master's house he had used a tincture of lobelia and capsicum, morning and evening, to help clear his lungs. Though another attack like the one in the rice field might end his life, Joseph took continual comfort in believing that phthisic was not as routinely fatal as the dreaded disease consumption.

From the start of their marriage, Rosa had prayed that the cough would bring Joseph rest, and it did. With Brant still away, Gund made the decision to put him in charge of the lawns and gardens instead of sending him back to the fields. That meant Joseph had to oversee Colt, who continued doing as little work as possible. But it also put him in touch with his mother and Bette, since he was allowed to cross the driveway.

Whenever he came up to trim the shrubbery, weed, or rake, the two special women found ample excuse to make their work meet his. Then they would embrace and laugh and talk. Most of their questions were about Rosa, and he never tired of answering them with warmth, though every day she was separated from him to go to the fields. Jewell was radiant, for it was honoring to her that her son was now a Christian husband. And Bette loved to tease him, for she, like Billy, felt marriage was the greatest source of earthly human satisfaction.

The whole summer had been filled with two endless southern vexations—humidity and mosquitoes. The plantation workers had endured them both as painful blessings, for because of them they rarely saw white folks other than Gund and his family. Being with Africans only, it was almost possible to forget that slavery was their lot. Gladly Joseph would keep to the shanty with Rosa rather than go back to the mansion.

Having had no tangible wedding gift for his wife, Joseph had made a vow to her on their wedding night. The purpose of his life, he told her, would be love for God first, then love for her, and then love for all those of Delora. To love God, he explained, meant doing what pleased God. In the same way, to love Rosa meant doing what pleased her. In this way he had prepared himself for the likelihood that because of Rosa's past there would never be complete physical union between them. He had counseled himself to consider the blessing in that—he would never find himself the father of slaves.

Yet, as he had started praying for the grace to accept what he thought must be, Rosa became more and more bold in her displays of affection. As he continued to let *her* needs govern *his* actions, he found himself overwhelmed by the rewards of her intimacy. By his making no demands on her, Rosa seemed to find it possible to little by little give her whole self to him. In return he did the same for her so that from the start, their marriage rested on a sweet, mutual desire to serve and please each other.

When he thought about it now it made him weep, for he knew God had been involved in the process of Rosa's healing just as He had touched his chest and lungs. Night by night when their work was over, their greatest joy was in coming back together, not just as one flesh but also as one in emotion, intellect, and hope. Sometimes Joseph found himself so taken by God's goodness that he would go out under the stars after they had expressed their love. It was his time to be alone with God, to thank Him for the awesome pleasure of knowing another human being so fully and so wondrously.

As long as he did not let himself mourn the loss of his manumission or his aborted studies, and as long as he did not let himself fear tomorrow, he believed he was the happiest man who ever walked the earth.

After having been the two most isolated slaves while they lived alone, Joseph and Rosa as a couple had friends everywhere. Often on workday evenings Abiel and Negozi would come down to Joseph and Rosa's little house. Negozi would teach them African words while Rosa would help Negozi war against the conjuring that had been so deeply ingrained in them both. After weeks of meeting together, the two couples could recite Christian truths in words known only on faraway shores. And often while the thickness of nighttime was closing them in, Abiel would finish off with a tale set on that distant continent.

Every Saturday night since the prayer meeting that had saved Joseph's life, Mr. Gund had unlocked Our Savior's Chapel for an evening "shout." Known to Joseph and to Parris, Ebo was now secretly bringing Pine Woods people into the dark shadows around the meetinghouse so that Rensler slaves could hear the messages being preached inside. To follow the laws exactly, Gund delivered every sermon, but once in a while, Parris, full of holy boldness, would rise spontaneously and speak. Often he would draw on Scriptures that Joseph had dared to read with him in private whenever they could peek into the pulpit Bible kept in the church.

By July Ebo told them that twenty Rensler slaves had been converted; by August, forty—and that was largely because they had heard Parris expound on the Gospel in Gullah.

Hampton Gund was always the only non-Negro in attendance, but since he had a license from the parish patrol to supervise, Joseph and Parris tried their best not to worry that almost a hundred slaves—counting those inside and out—were drawing together for all-night praise and prayer.

By September, however, the overseer himself seemed wary. The mosquitoes were disappearing and the nights were cooling down. So Gund declared that the first Saturday in October would be the last meeting because most planters would arrive back at their plantations by the end of that month. That was also when Brant and Ann Callcott were expected to come home.

From the moment work ended on that first Saturday of October, Joseph had an ugly foreboding that he did not immediately understand. He helped Billy, Parris, and Gund sort and stack tools, then walked down to meet Rosa at Negozi's house where the women were cooking their usual supper of okra, beans, and rice. They ate together, the old folks and the youngsters. Then Rosa suddenly seemed eager to be home.

Drawing Joseph by the hand, she led the way to their house by Hermon Creek. She sat down on the steps of their porch and pulled Joseph to sit beside her. Placing his hand on her waist she said, "Do you notice anything?"

"Yes, you're wearing a different dress." As slaves, they had no choice about what clothes would be handed to them.

"I swapped it for mine today." She was smiling. "Don't you feel anything? I feel it—now."

His initial puzzlement changed to apprehension. He didn't have to say a word to communicate his guessing.

"We are going to have a child."

He pulled away as though his hand were on fire. Perhaps this was the cause of his inexplicable distress.

"Kwash? Why are you behaving like this?" There was hurt in her voice.

"Another slave!" he cried. "We are bringing another slave into this world! That is something I never wanted."

"Oh no. Don't think on that! There's a blessing in this! We'll love this child and nurture him or her through every God-given moment! The moments. Remember, the moments we *do* have."

"This can't be!" Rudely he jumped to his feet. "What if my papers are ever found? Then I will have *two* purchases to save up for—yours and a *baby's*! Don't you see?"

"*Our* baby!" she said with dismay.

"Another hundred, two hundred dollars! I do not know what they would charge me! Brant Callcott could make it a thousand, knowing that it would put an end to my plan!"

She reached for his hands, but he kept them away. "Joseph. Stop it. God has provided. You know I had a girl-child who died of fever. This is God's gift to me. To again have a child!"

His hands made fists. "I don't want *my* offspring raised in slavery!"

She also got to her feet and countered his mood with one that was just as firm and dark. "So you're saying that you don't want *our* offspring at all."

Her accusation widened his awareness. They were going to have a baby, and the baby would be Callcott property. He felt his cheek twitching. He bit his lip. Now he reached for her, but she pulled away. Helpless to redeem himself from his fit of anger, he watched her go inside. She lay down on the mat he had woven for them, her body becoming a dark shape in front of the low, ever present fire in the hearth.

Sitting back down outside, Joseph never let his eyes leave her as he watched through the doorway. She could have been any of ten thousand African slave women now. Lying on her back as she was, he could see only the slightest rise in the center of her figure below her shapely breasts. It was a child—*his child*—growing and waiting to be birthed. At one time Bette had carried Parris in this same way. At one time, Jewell had carried him.

Life—even life born into slavery—must not be despised, he counseled himself, for God was the author of all life. Life must be loved and nurtured and hoped for. He chided himself, then hung his head, confessing his sin of faithlessness and hopelessness in light of this new human being, as yet unseen. Very softly he went in and sat down on the floor near Rosa's feet. In the culture of their ancestors it was a way to show humility and honor. He would wait there an hour, a night, a day, a week, unless Overseer Gund physically removed him. He would wait for Rosa's forgiveness forever, if needed. But true to his wife's love for him, only a short amount of time passed by before Rosa sat up and reached for him. Instead of kissing her lips, he kissed her belly. "Child, I welcome thee," he said in Rosa's hearing. "Child, I am your daddy. Grow and be what God already knows you are."

When his eyes slipped upward, Rosa was crying. "I'm sorry," he confessed to her. "Out on the porch my faith was too small. God's will be done with us, my *Dara*. I am proud of you, for your faith was strong from the beginning."

She kissed him on his forehead, and he felt her tears. "Ah, what will Grandma Jewell be like when she hears the news?" she whispered to him proudly. "Or Maum? Or Negozi?"

With his fingers he sealed her lips. "Rosa . . . please do this one thing for me and for our child. Do not tell anybody about this baby yet. Then, if God would will it, I could get free and be required to purchase you only if no one else knows about the life hidden within your womb."

"It would be impossible for you to buy even my freedom if you left for the North this very day."

"That's true," he said, "but God's done the impossible before."

"Joseph, I am already starting my fourth month. It will not be long before I do not have to speak for others to know."

"Then just give me what time I do have. I beg you."

She nodded sadly. "You are worried, aren't you?"

"I can't see a way not to be, for worry seems to be an inseparable part of love."

She touched her womb. "This child is yours and mine, but also God's. Even so, I, too, worry."

He embraced her, for there was incredible new depth to the intimacy they shared. Instead of avoiding the touch, he kept his hand over his baby now. Until it was time for them to walk through the night to Our Savior's Chapel, he held Rosa close, staring wordlessly at the fire, Africa's ancient symbol of life.

————

Long ago Hampton had gotten over the uneasiness of being the only white face in the crowd, whether at worship, as now, or in the fields. Dell, however, and his children were still uncomfortable with being the only non-Negro family in the chapel pews. Perhaps because of his decision to make this the last meeting, the little private church was crowded with Delora slaves, both upstairs and down. The one Negro who was obviously missing was Billy, and that both worried and puzzled Hampton, because all summer long they had been working together as secret, self-appointed elders, leading folks to the Lord and to prayer.

He was just getting to his feet to see Parris concerning his daddy's whereabouts when Colt slunk in beside him. Usually the boy skipped services to stay outside and roast sweet potatoes in a fire with several other unbelievers.

"Boss Gund!" Colt said with rare honest concern. "I don't know what this all means, but I just done hear'd a conch shell blow far off down by the creek."

Gund looked at Dell, who had also heard the boy. "You keep the girls here," he told her. "But if it even *looks* like trouble, you hightail it home by way of the old King's Road Trace."

He went outside and walked out from under the pines to listen. There was a driver's horn bleating, but it did not sound like Billy's. Even so, it could be the signal for trouble. He started running toward the sound.

After much searching Hampton saw a light—a lantern set down in the weeds. Inches from it was Billy's horn. And inches from the horn was Billy himself, robbed of his shirt and bound in ropes so that his legs and arms were useless. His left hand, however, could reach the conch shell.

"I did not blow it!" his friend panted, blood leaking from his split lower lip. "Some white man did! It's some kind of trap! Oh! Get back to the church!"

"You done been branded like Joseph!" Hampton mourned, pulling his knife to tackle the ropes. The smell of scorched flesh still hung in the air. "Who done this?"

"Po' whites, again," Billy breathed, speaking into the mud and not lifting his head. "Howsumever, I do believe I glimpsed Mass' Rensler's own dark horse! Oh, leave me! The rest gwine be in danger without you there."

Hampton cut him loose but let him lie to gain his own strength once he saw no bones were broken. The driver was right. Hell could rain down if so many slaves were found without his supervision. "You come up afta' me when you can!" he yelled over his shoulder. "If I don't see you soon, I'll send Parris back to help you."

He retraced his steps at a run. His breathing became tense. Puffing. He ran first in the dark, but then in the light—*the church was on fire!* Almost out of his mind with anguish, Hampton pushed into the smoking, twisting, dancing shadows. Those who had been worshipers only moments ago were victims now, trapped between a huge semicircle of patrolmen on horses and the burning building that cracked and roared like a lion being devoured. Crying and shrieking, even Negro women and children were being held dangerously near the scorching heat. The patrollers, who had gathered out of nowhere it seemed, had their whips and pistols poised.

Hampton rushed in among the thirty or more riders. They looked red in the flames and sat high in their saddles. "Let 'em out!" he screamed. "I am in charge here! My own wife an' girls are in there!" Being inside the line of horses now with the slaves, Hampton turned around, immediately finding Theodore Rensler's ruby face. The man dismounted as Hampton plunged at him. "What is the meanin' of this! I done had permission for this meeting!"

"For Delora niggers!" Rensler shouted. "Not Pine Woods ones."

"I only had Delora people!" Hampton screamed bewilderedly, but then he saw Ebo and others he did not know trapped with his own. Like the harsh winds caused by the conflagration, his mind shifted in all directions.

"I didn't know about the others! Where's my family? Why would you burn a church?"

"Your family's been pulled aside and sent home," Rensler said bleakly. "Now all these darkies are going to pay for their sin of meeting without proper supervision."

"There was no harm bein' done, sah! But just now somebody did blow my driver's horn! He's been attacked! You must know 'bout the trouble that pulled me from here!"

"You're nothin' but a whitewashed nigger yourself, Mista Gund!" Teddy seethed, remounting. Then pointing to Hampton he shouted at the patroller to his left, "I want this man held with the Negroes!" Some from the crowd of whites came around Hampton instantly. Like panthers they clawed his shoulders and gouged his ribs, dragging him close to the flames. When they released him, he was on the ground within the mass of trembling, crying slaves. The second he was let go, Gund got up and ran to Rensler again.

"You let these people go! Any moment that buildin's gwine topple, destroyin' us all."

Rensler coldly trained his pistol on Hampton's head. "You shut your mouth, or I'll shoot you dead now."

"To do that, you' gwine have to kill me first, sah!" It was Billy. Bleeding from his wrists and mouth, he pressed himself directly between the patrol and Hampton's face. Hampton felt the pistol in his belt that he had taken to carrying again.

"Shoot the blame nigger!" Rensler yelled to other men. "Then take Gund."

Gund fell to Billy's heels, pulling his weapon and frantically loading it. "You try to harm Mr. Callcott's *property*, I have the right by law to shoot in defense!" Hampton screamed. Having prepared his gun, he stood again, his chin nearly on Billy's shoulder.

"Kill them both at once!" Rensler cried, demonlike, though no one else on the patrol was moving.

"You try to kill our overseer an' our driver, then we'all got the right to strike 'gainst you!" This next wild threat yelled from the smoke came from Parris.

From the corner of his eye, Hampton could see slaves scrambling even closer to the flames to pick up pieces of burning lumber. The circle of patrollers suddenly backed their horses without the command of Rensler or any other leader.

"Thank the Lord A'mighty! I think we got ourselves the victory!" Billy gasped, not daring to turn to look at Hampton. "They know if they harm us all, they won't got no workers to save their harvest! Never in all my days have I seen white folk back off like they's now! Glory be!"

Hampton's head was pounding for ideas. "Rensler's not the rightful captain this year. Mr. Clemson is. You see him over there?"

Billy's head moved slightly. "Sure, I do."

"You let me on my own now to go speak with him. You help Parris to get all the others to drift off slow, startin' with the gals an' little girls."

"A'right, brother," Billy agreed. "Godspeed!"

Just then they were driven forward by what felt like a tidal wave as the black and orange skeleton of the church crashed down, spewing sparks and fiery debris like brimstone everywhere. Horses reared and whined, forcing the patrol to make the circle even wider and causing it to lose its tight control. "Now's our chance!" Billy said with glee.

But as the smoke cleared, Hampton saw the slave boy Colt scurrying straight up toward Theodore Rensler's heel in the stirrup. "What's that fool up to?" Hampton cried as Billy moved off to help those slaves who already were rushing away from the scene. No time for personal caution now, Hampton dashed within hearing range of Colt's stammering conversation.

"Sah, can I earn my freedom t'night by tellin' you all something?"

Hampton dared to grab the child. "Hush you' mouth!"

Theodore beamed down on them both with bemusement. "On the contrary, overseer, I'll be *delighted* to hear whatever he has to say."

Colt grew as stiff as a fence post, but Teddy only had to touch a loop of the cowhide lash hanging on his horse to make him speak again. "You don't need to punish everybody here, sah," Colt reasoned. "There won't be nearly this many believers here if Joseph weren't teachin' others to read from the big church Bible."

"You can't believe what he says!" Hampton cried. "You all're the ones what spread the rumors how slaves could buy their manumission with talk like this. Well, then, what kind of witness does that make him?"

Rensler only chuckled as he waved for Clemson to ride over to join him. "This boy has something to say. And Mr. Gund, it's not rumor but truth. A slave *might* buy his freedom by telling on any nigger that dares to teach another. Now, boy, you said it was Joseph. *The* Joseph who used to wait on your master in the house?"

Colt was dumb, so Theodore touched the whip again. "Did you come out here for freedom, boy, or for an extra whipping?"

"Don't speak!" Hampton commanded Colt.

"The law says whites can be whipped, too, Mr. Gund, for teaching slaves to read."

"As God is my witness, Dr. Rensler, I have taught no one."

"But Joseph has!" Colt cried as the whip came free.

"You cannot prove it!" Hampton screamed.

"No proof is needed! That reading, writing nigger's character speaks for itself!"

Hampton's heart was in his throat as he pulled Colt clear of Rensler's horse the second before the planter kicked its flanks and pushed it into the smoke and firelight. Joseph had been standing protectively near Rosa, but Billy must have known what was coming, for the driver whisked the woman away in an instant. Joseph was marched up to Theodore's mare to meet the full patrol, again in control because of Colt's betrayal.

Rensler called to everyone, "For once a nigger's spoken some sense to me. Why should we damage all the property when only one boy really ought to suffer? The law calls for fifty lashes every time one Negro tries to teach another. Now some of you patrollers know this boy. No more than four months ago he got out of the workhouse after using writing to help a city stevedore escape."

There was a murmur that told Hampton they were ready to see blood. He might have called for them to take Joseph to the slave court first, but he had already heard from Joseph's lips that men were waiting there to see him hanged. Hampton's hands and arms became like water as he prayed. Fifty lashes could kill an unwell man. Surely Joseph would not survive.

Rensler turned to him. "What do you have to say for your boy, Mr. Gund."

"Fifty lashes is the *maximum* punishment, sah. He's got real weak lungs. He could never endure. Even by the harshest letter of the law, you all have no right to kill him, for he belongs to Delora."

"Oh, we're not planning on *killing* him." Teddy smiled. "But this boy *is* going to be broken this time, as he should have been more than a year ago! And he's going to learn to live like a groveling black boy should. After that, whether he lives or dies will be entirely up to him."

"You are not patrol captain!" Hampton challenged.

"No. I am," Mr. Clemson said. "You want him taken back to the work-house until your employer comes home? I'll do it. Or the boy can be punished here and now, and then we'll be done with it."

"He should take fifty strikes for *every time* he's opened the book to someone!" Teddy cried the threat. Hampton looked at Joseph, whose head was down. The weakness in his own hands and arms now rose through his chest and shoulders.

Mounted above Hampton, Clemson, Rensler, and others consulted. Finally their verdict came. "Since Dr. Rensler is a medical physician, he will stand by to determine how many the boy can safely endure," Clemson said. "I never allow whipping to go to unconsciousness, for then the damage is done wholly to the *property*, not to the Negro's *will*."

Hampton knew he had only one hope of helping Joseph, and that was to take control of how the strikes were laid on him. "I am his overseer!" Hampton loudly mouthed the words, while feeling himself die inside. "I will do the whipping."

"Fine," Clemson decided. "Two of my men will secure him to a tree for you."

Until Joseph was stripped and tied to the pine, Billy had let Rosa watch, but then his hand came tightly over her mouth so she could not cry aloud. Knowing that flogging was certain now, he turned her around and headed her into the darkness where Parris was waiting to receive her. The moment Billy uncovered her lips, she wailed aloud, "The traitor! Gund!"

"No, missy!" Billy said, harshly reasoning with her. "That white man of ours is tryin' he very best to save Joseph's life. Any other man on the end of that whip handle won't care nothin' 'bout him. But Mista Gund do! I know it!"

"They'll kill him!" she mourned. "They'll kill my husband!" She fought him and Parris too. "I must go back! I can't desert him this time!"

"He wants you safe, girl!" Parris said. "What would kill him quickest would be to have those buckras do somethin' to you."

The first whipcrack sounded. Rosa cried and doubled herself over as she used to do in the days immediately following her abuse. Parris looked at Billy with mourning. Then Billy decided he must be the one to carry her home.

CHAPTER 33

"BOY, YOUR MISTRESS IS HERE!"

Joseph opened his eyes to a dull, musty room with light seeping in through horizontal boards. He was stomach down on a dirty wooden floor, and sure enough, Miss Mayleda Callcott was at his head, crying.

"Oh, I came as soon as I could." Then she looked somewhere out of the range of Joseph's vision and said, "Please, Mr. Clemson. Leave us alone."

"Pardon me for saying it, girl, but it's not comely for you to be here by yourself with just your Negroes."

"This is *my* half-dead slave! And *our* driver," she fought back. "Mr. Clemson, I will do as I please!"

Joseph moved his eyes to see that Billy was standing beside her as she knelt on the floor, her wide skirts making a bright, pleasantly fragrant sea of green in the otherwise terrible place. Mr. Clemson must have walked away then, for Joseph heard the door close. Mayleda cried over him.

"Mr. Gund dared to ride to the Renslers' town house to find me. I don't think Teddy would have even shown me the decency to let me know. Mr. Gund pledges that he only did what he did to try to save you."

Joseph started coughing. It pulled every wound burning on his back and waist.

"I brought you medicine. The same kind you used while in the house. Mr. Gund felt strongly that you'd need it."

Still amazed and befuddled, Joseph only listened. The girl showed him a spoon and a bottle. "It's tincture of lobelia and capsicum, just like what Maum Bette found in your room when she cleaned it out. Can it help you now?"

Joseph couldn't move. He lay dumb until Billy lightly touched his head. "I'll help you sit up, son, to take some, but you gwine have to tell Missy how much to give."

"I can do without it. For now," Joseph mumbled weakly, not wanting to be moved.

"How did you know what medicine to use on yourself?" Mayleda asked gently.

Joseph laughed harshly, letting his despair fan the agony of his flaming spine. He answered mockingly, so that she would not believe him. "I was *studying* to be a doctor!"

But Miss Mayleda did not bat an eye. "You were! That explains the papers Miss Ann found under Daddy's pillows!"

"Lord, have mercy!" Billy worried over them. "Miss Mayleda, don't you tell nobody 'bout that, for then they will finish him off, for true."

"But he did everything right, Uncle!"

"Hate can take 'way the right from *rightness*," Billy grieved.

The planter's daughter unpacked a bucket of cold wet oak leaf poultice, which Joseph soon felt laid on him from neck to waist. "I'm afraid this might be the only time I see you." The girl worked slowly but spoke quickly. "Once the Renslers find out I've been here, I know they will not let me come again. So I need to tell you everything I can now. Mr. Gund's in town looking for Mr. Wahl or any other of our Gospel Society friends who might help us secure a lawyer. Gund says he had to put thirty lashes on you." Her eyes were wet and scared like a tiny rabbit's. "By the letter of the law that should be sufficient if that is all you can endure."

But then Billy spoke the bad news. "Howsumever, Mass' Rensler an' others what were there at the fire are seekin' permission to have you whupped again—twenty more at least—onc't you heal up 'nough to take it."

Joseph groaned, for it was a workhouse practice to cut, to let heal, and to cut again, sometimes until as many as a hundred strikes were given. "Where am I?" Joseph asked, dry-mouthed.

"The ol' packin' house downriver from Delora quarters," Billy said.

Joseph knew the building, deserted years ago when rice started being hauled into town to be milled. Brant and he had played in these closed walls as children.

He bore down on his teeth. "Where's Rosa?"

"She safe, brother! You the only one they harmed."

But Joseph was reluctant to believe that. With Billy here and Gund in the city, the slaves were basically being left alone. "They can get to her!" he cried.

Billy tried to calm his fears. "Parris in charge, an' nobody but me an' Missy here know Mista Gund is in town. You been here only a night an' half day so far, but Mista Clemson an' a representative from the vigilant committee of Charleston both done already 'greed that this is where you gwine stay till Mass' Brant gets home an' matters can be sorted out."

"What does that mean?" Joseph gasped.

Mayleda's face drew taut, but Billy explained. "Onc't Mass' Brant's home, Mass' Rensler may push to have you' case hear'd in slave court." Joseph knew that would mean death, yet Billy smiled. "Son, last night you done become a hero to the people of both streets. There be rumors now how some of the brothers have done run off with drums into the swampland to sound 'em the moment there's any word that any white man has come here to harm you more or to kill you outright."

Joseph panted and coughed, then made himself be still.

"Be sure that Mista Clemson will be very careful with you now, for he don't want no slave uprisin'. For true, he's gwine bring his own Negro to tend you once a day so that the boy can give testimony to how you still alive an' well as can be."

Rolling his eyes to look at the bleak dusty space, Joseph murmured, "Can it be you, Billy, who will come to me?"

"No. But you will know him."

Mayleda tried to speak more comfort. "I hope my brother will be home in two or three weeks."

Weeks! Without Rosa! Here? "Oh, my God. Help!" Joseph pleaded out loud, too weak for shame.

Mayleda showed him a basket. "Listen! Billy's told me about that secret hiding place under the floor over by the corner. Mr. Clemson knows I brought some food, but I also sneaked in a second demijohn of water and a tin of raisins. Billy's going to hide those now, just in case they do neglect you and we can't get to you right away."

He was unbelieving that all this could be happening until he watched the driver leave them and hide the provisions for him under the floor. "There's one more thing," the girl said while Billy closed the trapdoor and dusted it over with sand and dirt to hide the place. "My daddy's Bible is wrapped in a sack under there too. The weeks will be long for you, and when I was packing and praying for you, the idea came to me to let you have his Bible."

"They'll kill me for that, missy!" Joseph mourned.

"Once a day a Negro will call on you," she repeated the arrangements. "Other than that Mr. Clemson is to keep the door secure, even against whites."

"Miss Callcott!" The call came from outside. "I urge you to hurry, for I do not want to bear responsibility for your being in there so long."

"Yes, Mr. Clemson! I am coming now!" She uncovered the basket so that Joseph could see biscuits, two apples, and a jar of water before she stood and prayed out loud. Then she bent to Joseph once more. "Please, keep your courage!"

The door scraped open. Joseph felt heavy footfalls. "Get out of there, Mayleda!" The voice belonged to Theodore Rensler. "I rode over the moment I heard you'd fled our house by the servants' door. Mr. Gund should be dismissed for coming as he did!"

"He is our employee, not yours. And according to my daddy's will, Joseph now belongs to *me*! This is *my* property that you so mistreated! And you did not even have the decency to tell me he was in here!"

"Your own overseer did that to your property, *ma'am*. Now, girl, it would be better if you just left gentlemen's work to gentlemen."

"This is outrageous cruelty!"

"No, this is the law, and you're just a child who does not want to understand how dangerous it is to let *her property* go uncontrolled."

Billy urged her quietly. "Miss Mayleda, I think you best go."

She gave Joseph one last sorrowful look, her former smiling lips now like two pink petals in a dying rose. Reluctantly she went with Teddy, and Joseph fully realized he might not survive to see her again.

Though it pained him terribly, he reached out and touched Billy's rough leather shoe. The man came down to his level for an instant while Theodore was escorting his mistress out. "Have Parris take Rosa. She's with child. I want my baby to have a Christian daddy."

Billy only stroked his head. "The Lord's done brought you this far. Don't start thinkin' He gwine desert you now."

"Get along, driver!" This time the commanding voice belonged to Mr. Clemson.

Joseph breathed through a series of desperate coughs, and when his eyes opened, Teddy Rensler was there to lord over him. Lifting off some of the thick mat of leaves that Mayleda had mercifully pressed over his wounds, the doctor eyed him sternly. "Why, Gund hardly touched you, and he put all the marks where they can heal good and fast. Boy, the patrol stills owes you. And the workhouse wants to paddle you and hang you after that."

Holding his breath so that Teddy would not have the pleasure of seeing his weakness, Joseph mulled over the things he had heard being said. If Mayleda and Billy had not dared to come to him, he would have had no news except from the patrol. And he would have received no compassionate care. Teddy lingered to mock him, and Joseph finally had to labor for air.

"You still haven't given up, have you, nigger? I can see that in your face. Well, this time I will break you and make you live broken for a time. After that, you can kill yourself—whenever you please."

Joseph closed his eyes while catching an internal vision of Teddy's awful plan. The patrol feared riots if they killed him. However, it would dishearten the slaves on both plantations if Joseph gave up, or gave in, and took his own life. Silently he cried out to God, *Lord Almighty, I have no strength! No courage to match such evil from hell!*

Surprisingly Captain Clemson returned. "Say, Rensler, even you are going to be required to leave him alone. He's got enough to think about for now."

Teddy went out but Clemson stayed. "Look at me, boy."

Joseph raised his eyes.

"You need to be obedient in every way till your master gets home. If you do, I'll try my best to save you. But if you give me problems, I won't have many choices left. Dr. Rensler's not the only one who wants to see you hanged."

He went over and emptied Mayleda's basket on the floor. "There's your dinner, your breakfast, and your supper tomorrow." He took away the water she had brought him. "Our own boy will be let in to give you drink. There's a bucket by the door to be your chamber pot. I don't want you stinking up the place and drawing barnyard flies, you hear? Oh, and yes, we decided to give you candles and flint and tinder so you can have some light by night."

The warehouse grew deadly quiet after that. Joseph would have gladly died then and there except for a slim, undying hope of being reunited with Rosa.

———

Standing on the deck of the Gilman-built steamer, Brant watched the shores of New England sink into a westward sea. He and Ann were going home weeks earlier than expected, for his worries about being Delora's new owner had grown too heavy to bear. He felt concern for the brother and sister he had left alone to mourn with only the servants. And he worried about their slaves. Over all that, after reading northern newspapers he worried that conflicts between the states were heightening at a desperate pace. They certainly could not risk being cut off from safe transportation home.

Brant had gone to Boston with the single motivation of letting Ann see Felicia, since Colonel Rensler had become so adamant about never wanting the two girls to meet again. Likely fewer and fewer southerners would be entertaining Yankees. Mr. Gilman, however, remained conciliatory to the people of the South, while at the same time taking a strong stand against the morality of holding colored individuals as slaves.

Having been in the Gilmans' home for most of the summer, Brant had heard every side of the abolitionists' philosophy. He had disciplined himself to only listen so that Gilman's acquaintances would not judge him to be a slave raper, a whipmaster, or a man-stealing villain. Ann, more than he, found it hard to endure such criticism. Though the girls tried to invest their days in concerts, literary readings, and art exhibits, Ann often came home crying, devastated at how she was judged for her southern accent or her place of birth.

Reflecting now, Brant knew he had secretly gone to New England for a reason of his own—to reach a clearer understanding of who he was as an owner of Negroes. And strangely enough, the trip had served that purpose. In the sea air today, he felt cleansed of conscience as he continued working through his difficult, sometimes even disquieting, conclusions. Those who were not southern born and southern raised had very little practical wisdom concerning slavery.

Northern patriots saw the world's need for rice, cotton, indigo, sugarcane, and molasses—as did Brant. And like Brant, they could think of no way to cultivate these products other than to have huge labor forces continually put to the unpleasant work of doing it. They could not deny that

Negroes seemed better made than others for the work. Negroes endured while white indentured servants simply bled away into the mainstream of society, and native savages merely ran off to avoid gang labor.

Most northerners he met questioned whether Negroes could be consistently moral or strongly intellectual. Like Brant, most saw nothing wrong with class divisions, since it was the worthiness of their own grandfathers and fathers who had paved the way for them. Where they differed, Brant actually felt confident now that his *southern* way of thinking could have spiritual superiority. Many of Gilman's Christian friends were in business and reliant on great numbers of poor, uneducated workers, some of whom spoke less English than did southern black slaves.

Northerners expected twelve hours of work, just as slaveholders sometimes did, but then these northern bosses dropped every obligation to care for their workers, paying them only small wages and even hiring children to do difficult and dangerous jobs. By comparison, at Delora young black bodies were left outside to fish and play until the time came when they could be worked as adults.

His thoughts about children brought him abruptly to Joseph. No northerner Brant met had ever even discoursed with a darkie, and he could find no one in all of Boston, beyond Gilman, who could say that he even particularly liked dark Africans. Brant knew he was different from that in both regards. He talked to Joseph, and in many ways, he had come to like him.

Putting his face to the wind, he thought about the most difficult problem he would face at home, that of Joseph pushing the legal boundaries set for slaves. A prohibition on colored education was certainly necessary if individuals like Joseph were to be kept in bonds forever, for without prohibition, their hearts and minds might soar. But was this God's will— to make such limitations? If the black man had been made by God only for menial labor, then it seemed to Brant that the capacity to go further should not be innate in any African. This was the dilemma his daddy had grappled with until the day he died. Now the struggle was part of the legacy handed to him.

The terrible question set him pacing. As Ann had pointed out before, why should he wrestle this issue when southern leaders older and wiser than he were settled on waging war to see slavery continue? Indeed, the institution of slavery must continue for them to survive! Why would he even dare to still entertain his doubts?

As darker, higher waves rolled the deck under him, Brant knew the answer to that question. He, like his daddy before him, had let himself be emotionally and intellectually moved by one African—*Joseph. But, God, now what do I do with him?* Hopefully, the boy had taken to quiet living in the street. Brant sighed, a sound of insignificance quickly lost to the wind. In some ways it would have been easier if he had found New England to be a true holy land, for then he might have stayed on as a refugee, leaving all his wealth behind. But he had not found Boston to be any worthier than Charleston, so he was going home to reenact the benevolent slavery his daddy had begun.

Northerners would scoff at the impossibility of it, yet Brant could settle on no clearer way. *The paternalistic heart.* He needed that to make compassionate slavery possible. As the master, he must learn to care enough and be wise enough to embrace darkies and their needs. *As the law allows*, Brant thought. He could not change society, but he could protect his own within the context of legislation. He must work right away to establish peace and prosperity in such a way as to not risk conflicting with either judges or patrols.

All this was a tremendous task for one like him, who found no inborn pleasure in management. Yet he had Ann to think of now, and if her womanly guessing was right, a child was on the way. The vastness of the sea expanded his sense of being on his own. He felt unready and uncertain, even about being a daddy. Ann came out, wrapped in her shawl against the wind. Brant considered that in just four or five days they would be able to stand on this very same deck and see the steeple of St. Michael's in Charleston.

Again he applied his thoughts to Joseph. He still could feel the hate of discovering that a Negro could read. He still could be dismayed by that African's acumen. But he could no longer feel himself loathing Joseph as a living being, for circumstances had moved him along and changed his landscape. Yet rather than bringing him closer to familiar ground as this vessel was, Brant felt that life, in general, was about to spin him off onto a wild and trackless course.

He stayed so deeply embroiled that Ann had to kiss his mouth luxuriantly before he even acknowledged her presence.

"What are you brooding about out here?" she asked.

"How things must be dealt with back home."

She looked a little nervous and squinted toward the sun. "And have you arrived at decisions?"

"Only that I must treat our slaves justly, as I said before." He drew her close, needing her strength added to his own. "I don't want to merge our families' businesses. I feel we should sacrifice the added profit and influence for the sake of continuing our independence to manage Delora as we see fit."

He searched her eyes. Surprisingly, thankfully, she smiled. "Though Daddy and Teddy will be furious, I agree."

"You do! So strongly!" That was such relief.

Her laugh was unhappy, her cheeks bright red. "I suppose because we are spouses now I should be able to discuss such matters." She stayed uncomfortable. "With you, dear Brant, I have not the slightest worry about whether or not you will be faithful to me. My daddy, however, never allowed my mother to feel that way. Nor will Teddy, I fear, if he ever marries. I'd be happier, now that I know the Gospel as I do, to continue running Delora as your daddy did, with the same moral regulations."

"Bless you, Annie!" He drew her fingers to his chest. "I do pledge fidelity, and yes, that's just the sort of issue that begs me to say *we* will manage Delora on our own."

She laughed with delight now. "I like the way you say 'we.' Other men would never consider their wives worthy of the word."

"I'm going to need your support desperately. I sense that even now. And you've already shown it to me by agreeing that we should go home early."

"I agreed to it." She smiled benignly. "But now, I will remind you that we aren't home yet. Depending on how many ports the captain chooses to visit, we still have four or five days of sea and solitude. So, as much as I can, I'm going to keep you thinking on other things." She painted the worry out of his face with loving strokes.

Brant gave in to her touch. He gave in to her warm, soft mouth. It was still their wedding trip, their moment in paradise. Soon enough they would be back to the world as it was, after Eden.

———

Joseph had been left alone for a night and a day. Within that time he had gotten to his feet. He had found his shirt crumpled beside him and put it on over his blood-spotted trousers. As a precaution, or maybe as an added discomfort and insult, he had been put into leg irons. Every time he moved, he dragged the chain between his heels. In this way he explored every inch of the abandoned warehouse. The old building had four strong walls, a high cedar roof, and a sound lock on its door.

There was no easy way of escape, and in his situation, escape was useless anyway. The only place he wanted to be was with Rosa, and for them both, that would be the ultimate source of disaster.

Joseph set himself a practice of conserving food. He would eat and drink only half of what was given to him. That way he'd have some surplus if neglect did prove to be his lot. For breakfast and supper he ate biscuits and one of the two blushing summer apples. He put the other apple under one of several sacks still there from the days of packing. He did not open the trapdoor or even explore it. He would not risk doing that unless it was truly necessary. As for the Bible, he did not feel he should hazard being caught with it.

Beside the waste bucket at the door, Joseph found the box of tallow candles, a tin holder, and flint to start a fire. It was puzzling why his captors were so intent on giving him light, and that made him cautious about using it. He decided as his second night approached to keep a candle near him, ready to be lighted. When evening descended after the long lonely day, he made a little bed of old rice straw near the door. Soon, however, he abandoned that little bit of comfort, because the dust in the straw constricted his breath almost as much the rice fields had done.

He thought about taking the medicine, but again he decided it must be kept for emergencies. Going back into the middle of the room, he lay down where he had been the night before. Taking off his shirt, he used it as his cover. He put the candle and flint at his hip where he could feel it. He had heard from workhouse slaves that bloody floggings made them thirst terribly, and now his own body proved it true. His mouth was so dry that it took his mind off his burning shoulders, stiffened by welts and bruises. He had to be thankful to Hampton Gund, who had cut him hard but had carefully saved the tender flesh around his brand mark, which was painfully sensitive to even the lightest touch.

He was suffering, yes, but much less than if the patrolmen had had their full way with him. Joseph tried to override his discomforts by reciting bits of poetry, counting cracks in the floor and the squeaks of mice running under it. It was nearly dark when the door lock finally rattled. In the thick dusk Mr. Clemson came in with Delora's slave Colt in tow.

"All right. Set the water jar down and empty the bucket outside. I'll guard the door. Be quick about it, boy."

When Colt was off, Clemson called to Joseph without coming near him. "Why haven't you lighted a candle?"

Joseph considered the answer. "I have as much to do in the dark as in the light, sir." He struggled, thinking about the water he so desperately needed. It was a mean trick to use Colt as the one to serve him. When the boy came back, Clemson found the candle holder and lit a candle from his lantern. In the light, Joseph saw Colt with downcast eyes that never looked at him. The terror of retribution showed in every quick step the young slave took. Surely he had not won his liberty by deciding to tell on Joseph.

Clemson said to the boy, "Does the nigger look sound to you?"

Colt answered a diminutive, "Yessah."

"Am I doing anything to harm him?"

"No, sah."

"Fine. Then that is what you will testify to all the others when I get you back to Delora." Clemson started to close the door after putting Colt out. "You keep that candle lighted, cuffee. That's what they were given to you for." The door was closed and locked.

Joseph did let the candle burn, but only because lonely light felt better than lonely dark.

The next two days passed pretty much the same. Once each evening Colt was let in to bring him a bowl of cold cooked rice and a jar of water. Joseph abandoned his idea of saving the provisions handed him. He was too thirsty, and the one meal a day was small and perishable.

On the second evening Colt cowered mightily under Joseph's staring. They had been warned not to talk with each other. Though it was easy for Joseph to let his anger rise toward the lad who had betrayed him, his heart went out to him that night, for he could see that the boy had received significant blows to his face, head, and back. His shirt was stained with blood, and bruises swelled his cheeks. "Are they mistreating you terribly?" Joseph risked, asking in a very low voice as Colt set a new jar of water near him.

The boy was startled. "No more'n the others."

"What does that mean?" Joseph raised his voice incautiously because of his alarm.

Colt's eyes went to the door. "I can't say. I'm so sorry I ever made this happen to you, sah."

"You know things!" Joseph cried with desperation. "What's happening outside? How's my Rosa?"

"I can't say! I won't say!" Colt mourned, hardly more than mouthing any of those words.

Joseph nearly grabbed him just as Clemson strode in.

"I told you just to look at him! Not talk to him!"

"I didn't, sah! He was talkin' to me!" Instantly the youth dropped his head and rolled his eyes to Joseph, silently showing apology for his new lack of courage.

Clemson threatened Joseph. "Boy, your mouth will be sealed whenever we are around you, or you will lose your water rations for a day."

Joseph complied by not gracing the guard with any response. Clemson was quick to make a lesson out of it. "See there, boy," he said to Colt. "It's just that kind of dumb disrespect that's gotten him where he is. Be assured that more than half the company wants him stretched out again to get the rest of his fifty blows."

"Yessah." Colt's response was laced with guilt.

When they abandoned him this time, Joseph closed his eyes, even though it was early and he had already slept away much of the day to fight boredom and the dull aching of his back and stomach. After a while he blew out the candle he had, fully knowing it would be difficult to light it again in the night. Yet right then he felt an awful need for privacy, even from the light.

In his spirit he sensed that things back on the street were frightfully wrong. He feared whatever forces had panicked and injured Colt. It was the same kind of dread that had come upon him that afternoon before the patrollers had surrounded the chapel. But this time, instead of just wondering why he felt this way, Joseph drew himself up into a kneeling position for prayer.

He may have stayed there most of the night. It was hard to judge time in the darkness. His knees and back ached when he lay down again after many hours of pouring out his sorrows and concerns.

Some time later he heard someone whisper his name outside the wall opposite the door. "Joseph?" The voice was male. Familiar. *Parris!*

He got up at once. The chain connecting his feet scraped loudly. "You're taking a terrible risk to be here!" Joseph whispered at the wall.

"For true." There was heaviness in the answer.

"What's happening? I've been so drawn to prayer!"

The silence on Parris's side was terrifying. Perhaps somebody on the outside had discovered them! For that reason Joseph did not speak again. But Parris did.

"You know you told me onc't how you done thought I was called by God to be a minister 'mong our people? Well, you can start believin' you' own words, 'cause God done sent me here to you."

"What's wrong! What's happening!"

"I don't want get my head blow'd off from talkin' so loud. So you listen an' don't you interrupt me."

Parris was so close on the other side of the ill-fitting planks that Joseph could feel the warmth of his breath.

"I'm 'bout to practice somethin' the teacher Payne done once told you. How the worthy preacher is the one what does not call attention to hisself, but to God only! Well, brother, I'm here callin' you to listen to God an' God alone!"

"Go on!"

"I'm 'bout to prick you' heart, but you must promise that it's gwine only make you listen to God more. See! I cain't just reach in there an' grab you, so you must give me you' word now that you will only follow God—not Satan's wiles—afta' hearin' what I come to say."

"I am clinging to God! There is nowhere else to go!"

Parris then recited a verse that Rosa often quoted in fighting her fears. " 'The Lord will deliver his own from every evil work an' p'serve them unto his holy kingdom.' "

"What are you saying?" Joseph tried to draw breath. Instead he coughed violently.

Parris waited until his spell was over. "Yeste'day. That Scripture was proved true."

Tears rolled down Joseph's cheeks. He gasped for air. "Rensler took her!"

"No. She crossed over to glory when the patrollers an' then the bootleggers both done made a raid on the street."

"Oh no!" Joseph wailed against the wall.

"God be my witness, brother! Nobody touched her! Abiel, my daddy, me—we all got the women an' chillun safe down 'long the water. But then in the confusion, two rafts hit hard t'gether, an' Rosa an' a child 'bout five years old both went over into the river."

"No!"

"I looked! I dove till dawn! I did, an' don't you think I didn't. Everythin' wa' done what could be done. I don't think she suffered."

"Noooo!"

"When I did find her just afta' sunrise, she had this sweet look 'pon her dead face, like she'd seen an angel."

"I can't bear it!"

"She safe, man! Safe in the arms of Jesus, no matter how many more raids or buckras we all called to endure."

Joseph pulled away from the wall and dropped to the floor. Their Creator was some kind of monster! Could He not remember there was a limit to what human flesh could bear? His tears dripped down. "WHERE IS OUR GOD!" he raged.

"You promised me, brother! You promised me that when I pricked you' heart you would still look towards Him."

"Why should I?" Joseph screamed his anger. "Why should any of us! We are nothing! Even God abandons us!"

"You repent of that!"

Even though Joseph could not see Parris, he heard him weeping too.

"You done know'd I loved her! You done know'd it was only my love for you *both* what made me happy for you' union. Yeste'day God saved her in *His own way* from any more harm. That somethin' you couldn't do. You know she 'woke in glory with you' child an' her Kulo."

"I want her back!" Joseph cried, numb from head to foot. "I cannot love God anymore. He has taken her from me!"

"You *can* love God, for He will never stop lovin' you. Onc't you have endured this long night, in the blinkin' of an eye or at you' own homegoin', that last trumpet gwine sound an' bring us all home safe!"

Joseph beat the floor.

"I preached her funeral t'night, just 'fore I come here. *You' wife an' you' child is safe in Jesus' arms.*"

He pounded harder and harder.

"Our attackers done made a bloody mess of some of we. They called out the boys 'cause of how we done saved our women an' beat us all raw."

So that explained Colt's condition! Joseph heard a chain shifting as he stopped to get his breath, and the chain was not his. "You're back in irons!"

"I am."

That again awoke Joseph to their present dangers. "You need to get away from here! You'll never escape if they find you away from the street."

"First, you promise that you ain't gwine let grievin' overtake you. Then I'll go, but not till afta' I know you ain't gwine do nothin' foolish with you' sorrow."

Joseph scrambled on hands and knees to the wall. "Go! I could never forgive myself if anything happened to you too!"

"First, you promise!"

"Yes! Yes! I promise! Now go!"

It was all like a nightmare, for instantly the other side of the wall was cold and silent. Joseph kept his face to the narrow spaces between the boards, but all he could hear was the sickening clamor of Parris hobbling away, shackled.

CHAPTER 34

JOSEPH LAID HIS HEAD against the wall. "Oh, God! Oh, God!"

Groping for candle and flint, he finally got light. Crouching over the tiny flame, he found slight comfort in its glowing. In Africa it was bad luck to let the fire go out. But he did not believe in luck. He believed in Rosa and in his love for her. And he believed what God had said in the fiery sunrise, that he was a man. But now he was a man whose wife was dead. His love was dead. And his courage was dying. All he had was a tiny candle flame.

He sat there until the light burned itself down into a small watery pool on the copper holder and only a weak blue glow survived on the wick. His will was like that—all but gone out. Yet physically he did not want to be in darkness, so he pushed himself to rise and get a new tallow stick from his diminished supply. Holding the new against the old with trembling hands, he rescued the flame. Once this was done, he sat down and drew his whole self into the tiny circle of glowing once more.

For the first time since being locked in, he thought seriously about un-covering Master Abram's Bible. The book had been with the man when he died, and it represented one of the greatest joys of Joseph's life—read-ing with Rosa. Suddenly the Bible became a tangible reminder of precious moments he did believe in. Cautiously, reverently, he moved to the corner, put his thumb and index finger into the small inconspicuous knotholes, and pulled open the trapdoor. Ignoring everything else hidden there, he took the book, closed the door, and then unwrapped it. Its feel, its smell, its weight brought forth so many memories. He hugged it like a lover and a friend.

Breathing the same prayer for inspiration he had used on Anson Street, he decided to read. The book seemed to open on its own because there were papers folded crookedly and stored between the pages. Joseph could not believe this at first, for Master Abram had great respect for the printed Word of God and never polluted his Bible with anything more than a satin ribbon. Yet now Joseph touched the folded sheets. Opening the first he found Nathan Gilman's letter. Opening the second, he found his simple service ledger, signed and dated. Opening the third and then the fourth, he found his freedom papers!

He was like a digger striking gold. They were real! They were right here in his hand! Likely Mayleda did not know what the Bible contained when she smuggled it to him, yet God had prompted her to bring it! Joseph's mind raced. Of course! Surely as death was coming so quickly to Abram, the man had valiantly grabbed the Bible Joseph had left at his bedside. Using his last measure of strength, and only one hand, Abram had wisely hidden the papers where only a believer would find them.

When Bette saw the holy book on the floor she would have moved it to its shelf, never imagining what it might hold. "Oh, God! Oh, God!" Joseph prayed again, but this time in awe. With sweating hands he put the papers back into the cloth and hid them. But he kept the Bible, disregard-ing all risks. Despite a blinding headache and the sweet disabling memories of Rosa, he continued reading by candlelight all through the night.

Before dawn he hid the book again. When he lay down he slept, for peace had come to be the companion of his sorrow.

That evening it was Theodore Rensler who came in to see him with Clemson. They called on Joseph to stand before them in the bright lantern light. Joseph felt too numbed by grief to have room for fear.

"Your young mistress frets day and night about you," Teddy reported casually. "As yet she's found no one to speak for you, since all know your real crime is the mockery of true intellectual knowing." He smiled. "I am here to verify that you are still in good health. Indeed, we are holding to our agreement to let nothing happen to you until Master Brant returns."

Joseph eyed Clemson's hand as the captain slowly pulled out his pistol and cocked it. "No foolishness now," he warned. "Or I'll tell all that I shot you in Dr. Rensler's defense."

Joseph cringed at Teddy's touch as he examined his wounds. Then he was told to sit down slowly on his hands. When this was done, Teddy listened to his breathing. Joseph could hear the rattling in his own chest, which felt tight and dry. He still had taken no medicine, yet miraculously he still had breath.

"You are ill, but not because of our doings," Rensler said, with a bored, uncaring sigh. "It sounds like the start of consumption."

"We don't want him dying!" Clemson worried.

Teddy rudely felt Joseph's face. "There's no fever yet. He'll survive."

Joseph bit his tongue, still holding to his own evaluation that he did not have consumption, since he had no discolored spittle or thick mucus filled with fibrils, as the medical literature described.

"There's one more thing I'd like to do, if you'll allow me a doctor's privilege to be alone with him."

"I know you hate him, Teddy, but I am under oath to protect him."

"Very true, sir! Don't worry! For this test I must have no other sound but his breathing and mine." The captain reluctantly put away his gun and moved as far as the door. Teddy crouched down. "I would rather end your life than save it, buck." He breathed his whispers like a demon. "However, I've decided that ending your life will be your own rude task. I will be out of the parish for the next few days. I have a comfortable new cabin opened just outside Summerville and a very beautiful Negress paramour to live with me now."

Joseph could not keep his eyes from flashing.

Teddy laughed. "Your Rosa in *my* arms! Now that gives you something to think about. Hah! Didn't I say you would be *broken*, and live that way? *My* lips kissing *her* flesh, cuffee! *My* sweet comfort every night—"

Joseph looked at the wall instead of bowing. He did not want to show his suffering in any way, yet his cheek moved uncontrollably. "You hate me too," Teddy concluded. "You would kill me if you had power, but the truth is that you have been reduced to what you are—the black scum of this earth."

Joseph's ears rang from clenching his jaw.

"Hah! I *have* crushed you, you sick cockroach. When you take your life, the darkies on both streets will know you did out of cowardly despair because I took your precious little wench."

Joseph's hard breathing made his chest rise and fall.

"You will set fire to yourself within the next three days, or I will come from the outside and do it for you. I don't need Mr. Clemson's key to arrange for your dying."

So that explained the candles! Rensler had had this plan all along. But he must not have counted on Rosa's drowning. Joseph felt tears fall—out of joy. God had saved her from a terrible fate. She was gone from his arms, but more importantly, from Teddy's too. She was with Jesus.

"You spoilt houseboy! To think tears will help you." He put a small glass jar beside him. "To show that I do know mercy, here's a drug. Drink it down before you ignite the timbers, and you'll not feel a thing."

Joseph measured his breath. "I will not kill myself. If I die, you will have to do it."

Teddy slapped him hard on the face. Clemson came running at the sound.

"Are you all right, Rensler?"

Teddy swore. "The blame nigger! He won't even cooperate when I'm trying to halt his misery."

If the mental wrenching had gone just one moment longer because of these lewd lies, Joseph might have exploded, and his life would have been ended then by the patrolman's gun. Only Brother Parris's bravery in coming to tell him the truth was saving him from insanity. Still, the experience left him trembling. And it left him thinking that in three days Rensler would burn him alive.

———

When Colt brought in his first supper after the awful encounter with his guards, Joseph ignored it, choosing rather to fast and pray.

On the next evening when Colt came back, the boy saw the rice bowl, still full, and now covered with ants. "You sick?" the boy whispered, gingerly taking the full dish in his hands.

Joseph dared an answer, as Colt had dared a question. "I need to trust you with very important information. You are my only hope for telling folks what will happen."

"Uncle!"

"You must be responsible!" Joseph said, his voice very low.

"I will be! I done give my heart to Jesus last night."

"What!"

"Yessah. The buckras done come back an' beat us all again, an' then swore that there wa' no God to watch over the Negro. Well, we all done think 'bout that! If they be workin' so hard to keep us from havin' any hope, even of heaven, then sure 'nough, there must be a Savior just like you an' Parris says—"

Clemson strode toward them. "Lay down!" Colt whispered to Joseph a moment before he came beside them.

"Sah, he ain't done et nothin'!" Colt called out loudly. "I just takin' my time to judge him sound. This be what you send me in for, ainty?"

Clemson looked at them both. "You are sick, buck!"

That kind of concern turned Joseph's stomach, for it had everything to do with saving face in the white community while being devoid of care. Again Colt shrewdly bought them time. "Let me just try to feed him, sah. I think it's his shoulders. He still so sore an' so lonesome an' discouraged." Colt proved that he could make Joseph eat, for when the boy picked out the ants and put some of the cold rice on his fingers, Joseph did take it.

"All right. But be quick. And don't you talk to him."

As soon as Clemson was back at the door, Colt began eating the rice himself. "You talk while I down this."

Joseph shook his head. The boy had truly changed. "Mass' Rensler's going to burn this building down. Then he's going to tell you all that I killed myself because I thought he had taken Rosa as his mistress—"

"But she—"

Joseph stopped him. "I know! Listen! No matter what happens, I will not take my life. You tell Billy and all the rest of them that." He hesitated, then decided to risk more. "You tell them that a *free* black Christian man will not take his own life."

Colt's eyes grew tremendous as he wiped his mouth.

"Yes! I know where my freedom papers are. So at least I will die knowing that I am free. Can I trust you to remember everything and to tell it all to Delora's people?"

"Yes, indeedy! For all the wrong I done, praise God, now I can do somethin' right! Oh, sah! I am so sorry for what I done!"

Joseph felt grateful God had rescued even Colt. "I forgive you. Live faithful and forgive yourself." He patted the boy's waist to encourage him, and when he did, he touched paper. "What's under your shirt?"

"A letter. A messenger come with it right while I was in the driveway a-waitin' on Mass' Clemson."

"Does the captain know you have it?"

"No, sah! But that's what it is. A letter." He pulled up his shirt for an instant, which was long enough for Joseph to see that the handwriting matched Brant's.

"Let me see it fully."

"Uncle!"

"It's addressed from the Planters Hotel! God of mercy! Brant must be home! You must take this straightway to Mr. Gund or Billy without Clemson's knowing! Master Brant might be able to stop Rensler. You go tell the driver or the overseer to fetch young Mass' Callcott quick, because he must be right in town!"

———

Because of the nighttime violence, Mista Gund was back in Charleston yet another time, futilely searching for Gospel Society gentlemen who might come and help him guard Delora. Miss Mayleda and Mass' Eric were still in town too, and so were Ezra and Nancee, since the children could not stay alone on Gibbes Street. That left Billy to risk going in to look for Mass' Brant at the Planters Hotel once Colt had come running with the letter and the news.

Billy had no pass or permission to go into town. The quietest, fastest way was by punt, he decided, and the river proved to be a deep, dark friend to him, carrying him all the way with safety.

When he left the boat and climbed onto dry land, Billy was close to the silent rice mills. He ran through the streets, dead with the curfew, praying that he would discover which building had Mass' Callcott in it. Being a field slave, he had not been to Charleston more than twice, but the letter in his waistband helped him. With some study under the streetlamps, Billy matched the writing on the paper with the signs for one of the city's bigger buildings, which still had servants awake and active. He decided this must be the Planters Hotel.

Going behind the establishment, he found cooks and dishwashers still hard at work. Taking the wide oyster-shell path, he went to a kitchen door and spoke to the first mature Negro male he laid eyes on. "Brother, I need to find my massa!"

The worker surveyed him glumly. "That's you' own problem. You go up to the side door there an' knock on you' own."

Billy had no choice but to go to the door. He knocked. In fact he pounded, for no one answered at first. Finally a slave in untidy livery looked out through the glass panel beside the door. "I must speak with Mista Brant Callcott! Now!" Billy shouted. "Tell him it's his driver, Billy Days."

Billy looked around then, feeling exposed and alone. The face at the window disappeared. The delay that followed was so long he feared the slovenly houseboy had simply gone back to sleep. Presently, however, another slave, older than the first, opened the door. "Come in. Go up that hall an' stand there."

Billy grabbed the hat off his head and held it for security. The place smelled of wine and sweet cigar smoke. Hallway lamps burned lazily, while his nerves kept snapping with alertness. Finally he saw Mass' Brant coming toward him in his dressing gown.

"Billy! What in heaven's name are you doing here?"

"The patrol's done got Joseph! Men been poundin' you' street. Rosa an' a child be dead, and maybe they gwine kill Joseph or make him kill hisself, 'cause he done found his freedom papers!"

"Wait! Slow down! Go back to the beginning."

"There really ain't no time, sah! Mista Gund an' you' sister an' brother be in town lookin' for some help! You need find Mass' Rensler, for we all do fear he be the one behind this all!"

"How did you know I was here?"

Billy hesitated. "Joseph seen you' handwritin' on this here letter, sah." He handed the paper over to him.

"You need to take me to the boy right away."

"Beggin' you pardon, sah, please look for Rensler! If'n you can catch him, then I think you can put a halt to eve'ythin'!" This was dangerous for Billy to say, for a black man could not accuse a white man and live. But the master let it pass. They had no time.

"I'll agree! Where's Ezra?"

"At you' Gibbes Street place!"

"Then run there and get him to bring horses, or the coach."

"I don't have no pass, sah, nor do I know the way!"

The young master nodded. "Of course! All right. Let me dress and tell my wife. We'll go together."

––––––––––

Joseph had spent more than a year trying to live as a black *man*, not a slave. Now he prayed for the strength to die as one. When the sun came up, he moved to the east wall and pressed his eyes between the boards to see the light of day. A gull cried, thrilling and saddening him.

He dusted off his pants and tucked his shirt. The best he could, he planned to die with dignity. He blew out the nighttime candle, the last that he had, and took Master Abram's Bible out of hiding. He regretted that it would be burned to ashes with him. Taking one of the old sacks, he spread it on the floor and opened the Bible to the first of several passages that were coming to his mind. To read them, he took the kneeling position of prayer.

He went through all the Scriptures in Ephesians that had encouraged him with words about the power of God. Then he read the Twenty-third Psalm about the "valley of the shadow of death." There were profound spiritual feelings that broke over him as he waited to die. He wept to be losing those who were dear to him without any chance to say good-bye. He could only trust that Colt would explain he'd been murdered, even if it looked as though he had chosen to claim his own life. When he thought about Rosa, he grew still. He wondered how heaven would be heaven if he was not allowed to be reunited with her as his wife. Then he let himself wonder at the mystery of being able to see her at all. *By tonight*, he thought, *it will be eternity for me also*. Then all his questions, all his pain, would find answers.

Suddenly and almost without sound the door opened. Still on his knees, Joseph turned to see Clemson and Teddy come in. Teddy mocked his posture, but the captain demanded to know how he had come to have a Bible. Joseph knew he should say nothing about Mayleda, and it would be useless, and worse, to accuse one white man in front of another for threatening his life. He prayed for a moment more, then quietly turned the Bible's pages. Staying on his knees he raised his eyes to the ceiling, " 'Thou shalt not kill.' "

Teddy growled. "You're going to let him do that, Clemson?"

God gave Joseph steadiness in the face of the captain's indecision. " 'Thou shalt not commit adultery.' "

Teddy raged in oaths and spit on him, but Clemson held him back.

" 'Thou shalt not steal. Thou shall not covet thy neighbor's wife . . . nor his maidservant. . . . ' "

"Get him to shut up," Rensler screamed, "or I will do it!"

Joseph felt Clemson's hands upon his shoulder. "That's enough!" Clemson told him to stand up. Joseph stood and the captain took the Bible, noting that it had belonged to Master Abram.

"You should be flayed!" Rensler hissed at him. "I was brought here because of reports that you're not eating." He turned to the patrolman. "Do you still want him treated after finding him so blatantly in violation of laws and even disgracing his dead master's Holy Book?"

Joseph lifted his eyes just enough to view the man with the Bible in his arms.

"Examine him and tell me what he needs."

Unwisely, Joseph had not emptied Teddy's drug beside him. The man took up the clear bottle now. "He was to drink this the last time I was here, and he did not. That's why the nigger's still sick and not eating."

"Boy," Clemson said with authority. "Drink it down."

Joseph took the bottle that Teddy triumphantly set at his feet. He poured it out onto the floor. Teddy was on him like a rabid dog, throwing him down and punching his face and shoulders. Joseph recoiled and covered himself but did not strike back. Clemson fought Teddy off and drew him to his feet by showing his gun. "Step back, Doctor."

For just an instant Joseph saw Teddy's raging eyes. He stayed on the floor, winded, his nose and jaws and ears all throbbing from the blows. Clemson spoke to Joseph hatefully. "Put your hands and feet against the floor. And lay on your face."

Joseph slowly moved and did so.

"Answer me. Why did you defy the doctor?"

He spoke the truth. "It was poison, sir. He threatened to kill me. Threatened to burn the building down if I did not drink the drug and light the fire myself."

Positioned as he was, Joseph had no way of knowing how Clemson received his words, but he knew that Teddy was on his feet and ranting. "Curse his nigger testimony! I can't believe you even asked him to speak!"

The young captain remained silent except for his sighing. "For your possession of the book you will go without water until I get an explanation of how you came to have it. If the whip needs to be plied again to get that truth, then know I will do it."

"If!" Teddy cried. "If! This boy has had too many chances already. Do what you want to me, Mr. Clemson, but I am destroying this cursed piece of property here and now."

Joseph heard Clemson cock his pistol, but he rightly guessed that one white man would not shoot another of his own color just to protect a Negro. Joseph thought this all out slowly as Teddy fell upon him again, driving his face to the floor, kneeling into his ribs, and giving him blows to his spine and kidneys. Through his darkened sight and tears, Joseph kept looking for two faces only—Jesus' and Rosa's.

He seemed very close to seeing them when the hitting, the screaming, and all the vibrations stopped. Straining his eyes open, he did see a face— *Master Brant's!*

Brant left his slave groaning on the floor and pulled the men outside. With Billy Days and Hampton Gund beside him, he listened to Tyson Clemson's quick explanation. "He defied Dr. Rensler's medical treatment because he feared it was poison. We found him with this." Clemson turned over his daddy's Bible.

Teddy met him face-to-face in the early morning sunlight. "You're not going to let that nigger get away another time. You can press charges against me if you want, but I'm going back inside, and I'm going to finish off that dog. It's not just you I have in mind. My cousin is living under your roof now. And she will not remain there near the company of this beast!"

He took his whip from his horse's saddle. "Mr. Clemson. Take note that I have a chivalrous duty to *Missus* Ann Fox Rensler Callcott to see this darkie to his grave!"

"Clemson!" Brant pleaded desperately. "Hold Teddy! I need time. It's possible that he's killed my slave already."

Overwhelmed and blind for direction, Brant looked at Billy and Gund. "You come with me, driver, to help me see how badly he's been hurt. And you, Mr. Gund, give me warning if these two gentlemen are about to step in on me, for any reason."

"Yessah!" Gund's firm affirmation was strong evidence that he was completely on Brant's side, and Brant felt a strange comradeship with his driver as Billy strode in mightily behind him like a big, protective guard.

Shaking, for he had so little experience with this, he knelt beside his African, abused yet another time. "Joseph—can you open your eyes to me?"

His slave did so.

"I'm going to take you home. Somehow."

"No," Joseph whispered. "Let me die. I know how to die being the person God made me to be. But I will never know how to *live* that way as a slave."

"I will be good to you, I promise, just as you have been good to my family."

"No, for I cannot be good to you. I will read. I will run. I will fight for what I now know—if they do not hang me first. Let me die. For that is my only end. And today is better than tomorrow for dying."

Brant looked at Billy, not exactly asking him what to do but feeling so bewildered. "The brother got word out that he *is* free, sah," Billy said. "Mebbe, if he is, you can find some way to let him go. Would you do that for him, Massa?"

Brant looked over his shoulder, fearing any moment that the others would be with them. "Where are your papers? How could you possibly know anything being locked up here?"

Joseph's eyes went to Billy as a sign of trust, but then he closed them. "I want to die a free man. If I tell you and you destroy them, then I will not have even that one small pleasure."

Brant could not believe how it moved him to see Joseph like this again. "Joseph, I have come back from New England with a full determination to make Delora a safe and happy place for us all."

"My wife . . . was murdered. My unborn child . . . dead. Confinement of heart, of mind, of soul . . . is violence! Give me liberty—or give me death!"

Brant touched the slave's face to keep him thinking. "Joseph, where are your papers?"

Tears starting rolling across his swollen cheeks.

"I pledge that I will risk my own life to have you freed if your papers are valid."

The slave lay silent for several moments. "They are hidden under the trapdoor in the floor."

Because of their boyhood explorations, Brant knew where that was. He looked at Billy, then rose to his feet to open the secret place by himself.

Joseph kept his face down until the documents were in Brant's hand. Brant shielded them within his open topcoat while he brought them back to the slaves and easily assessed that they were official, though the date for Joseph's leave-taking was to have been within days of his daddy's passing. "You are right, Joseph. By law you are free."

Mr. Gund called, "Sah! They comin' in!"

Brant turned from beside Joseph, hardly having time to conceal the papers fully. "I want Teddy Rensler arrested for this violence," he announced to Clemson, surprised at the strength in his own voice. "I have evidence that this is not the first time he has willfully abused my property."

Brant saw Joseph's eyes open wide.

"You have no evidence but a nigger's hearsay!" Teddy chortled.

"I do have evidence, Mr. Clemson," Brant countered as steadily as he could. "I was looking for Mr. Rensler at Pine Woods around dawn this morning, and I found something quite unusual there." He didn't have to tell Gund to go fetch it from the coach, for they all had secretly searched the Renslers' smithy before heading over here. Gund presented to Clemson a branding iron with the circle and cross on it.

"You will never prove a thing with that!" Teddy raged.

"I won't have to," Brant said, "because I will never mention it to anyone but Mr. Clemson here, as long as you tell everybody in the club and all the moonshiners and bootleggers you employ for your nighttime raids to stay away from Africans and from Christian planters everywhere! And that includes my chattel here—" He pointed to Joseph, who still watched him intently. "Gund. Billy. Carry Joseph as gently as you can to my coach."

Teddy did not say a word while Brant took the iron back. "I'll keep this as a reminder. Just in case you forget our agreement." He pointed the shaped metal mark toward the Pine Woods master.

"You still will not save the dog you have there," Teddy said spitefully, shaking the whip looped in his hand as Brant headed for the door. "I will file legal charges against him for murdering your daddy, since you will never have the courage to do so."

"File the charge!" Brant said more boldly then he felt. "But by then you'll face the challenge to find him, for I would be a fool to keep him within your reach."

CHAPTER 35

JOSEPH RESTED FOR ONE WEEK behind the closed door of Brant's old bedroom and in Brant's own bed. All in the house, Ann Rensler Callcott included, knew he was there. Jewell and Bette and Billy were allowed to visit often, and Gund met with him, too, in order to give him a piece of private news.

"I'm leavin' plantation life, an' that largely 'cause of you. My wife an' girls, they be fearful of gwine, but I's more fearful of stayin' 'gainst the pleasures of my Lord an' my God."

"But what will Billy do without you?" Joseph fretted, his physical pains all but healed. "There are no overseers in all the South like you, sir."

"There may be at least one with conscience an' with the power what comes from being a gentleman too! Mass' Brant is gwine take the place of overseer."

Joseph looked away.

"I know. It ain't 'nough. An' it never gwine be 'nough till slavery is done forever. But it's no worser than it is now, an' mebbe even better, for the patrol ain't gwine just walk over a massa without some respect for his po'sition. The most amazin' thin' to me is that his highfalutin' wife' gwine let him don work pants an' go out among his people. Mebbe he'll come to see what I seen, Joseph. Mebbe he'll come to feel what I feel, an' learn what I done learn't from Billy Days an' from you all." He extended his hand, and Joseph took it with surprise, sitting up stiffly. "I'm off to Ohio or the West to find my own piece of ground. I wish you well. Yes, I surely do."

Joseph got out of bed and stood. A man does not shake hands with another sitting down. "God bless you, too, sir!"

———————

During his last hour at Delora, Joseph spent time with his mother, hugging and kissing her and shedding tears, that being all he owned to share with her. In return she gave him a scrap of blue cloth cut from the hem of her dress.

He carried it with him as he crossed Hermon Creek into hazy, uncertain sunshine to find Rosa's grave. On his knees and bowing close to the sweet-smelling disheveled earth, he almost kissed it. He knew that only her body lay there, yet he sensed it was a patch of holy ground. What he whispered there he believed the saints in glory witnessed, so he promised her and all of them that he would keep to the straight and narrow way, no matter how long, how far, or how difficult the journey. Then someday, he, as they, would rest and rejoice eternally.

Miss Mayleda found him in the slave graveyard and spent time on her knees weeping with him, keeping her eyes closed while he spoke and cried aloud his heartfelt prayers. "I abhor this life more than ever," she told him as their moments ended. "If I could, I would flee South Carolina just as you and Mr. Gund are doing." Under the gray shadow of her straw bonnet, her sincerity paled her face and darkened her eyes. She was the only white person he knew who had affirmed his equality without wavering.

"I'll continue to pray for you, Miss Callcott."

"And I, you." She pressed a small but heavy sack into his hands. "Here are the wages you earned through your agreement with Daddy. All of us, Miss Ann included, decided it was right for you to have them. Bette has a set of travel clothes prepared for you and some provisions. Do you know where you will go?"

"Yes." Yet he did not risk telling even her.

Parris and Billy Days came next to see him. Joseph stood among the graves as they embraced him, nearly crushing his bones. "You be watchful and tend this flock," Joseph told them both. "The people surely need you."

"An' you be faithful," Parris warned. "Don't you let liberty be like wine to you' head! Live it for us all an' rightly! Oh, an' help it flow right on down here to us, if'n you can."

"I will! Maybe there will be a day!" He embraced Parris again.

"Watch you'self every moment," Billy put in. "Don't you trust no white folk just 'cause they from the North. An' be careful what kind of company you keep with you' own color too."

"I will. If it weren't for you both, I would never have lived to see this day."

———

A half hour later Joseph was dressed in that same dark travel suit he so often had put on his former master. He sat astride the deceased man's horse with his sack of supplies tied securely behind him. Maum Bette stuffed hard benne-seed candies into his hand even as he was holding to the reins.

"You take care, for I hear'd there ain't no maums in the North."

Jewell stood beside him one last time. Brant climbed into his saddle, ready to escort him down to Charleston.

Suddenly his old mill boss, Mr. Wahl, appeared from the stables riding on his mare with a rifle laid across his lap. That unnerved Joseph.

"Mr. Wahl's coming with me," Brant explained. "We've kept you safe this far, and I don't want any trouble."

Reining directly beside Joseph, Wahl handed him a sealed envelope. "Before Danny Payne left town, he brought these to the mill, boy. I'll admit there was a time when I thought of destroying them. But today I concede they are rightfully yours. That's part of the reason I answered Brant's call for help from the Gospel Society to guard you."

With disbelief Joseph took time to hide the packet in his sack. Once safely away from here, he would investigate the contents, though his heart longed to do so now. In the driveway Mayleda, looking as though her heart would break, clutched Eric's hand. The boy seemed puzzled. Likely, no one had taken the time or care to tell him what was going on.

When they finally rode out, Joseph did not look back, though his mama's mournful wails sounded like storm winds. Even if her heart was breaking, Joseph knew that she was experiencing incredible joy too. He could understand those two opposing emotions, for that is exactly how he felt as he saw his friends, his family, the rice fields, the river, and the mansion disappear from the landscape of his life forever.

———

They arrived at the wharves without incident. Dismounting, Brant paid a passing lad of color to hold their horses. The slavemasters stayed outside while Joseph went in to purchase a steamer ticket with money Brant had allotted him. He had felt that slave child's eyes burning on him, for he was about to travel away by sea, as free as a bird. Rather than feeling good about the child's awestruck wonder, it made Joseph mournful to see again how small this victory for freedom really was. Thousands of others, just like this lad, would endure harassment and confinement until their dying day.

True to Brant's word, Joseph was put to buying his ticket alone so that no one—planter or slave—could be pressured to tell the patrol or Teddy Rensler where he had gone. The clerk at the ticket desk made Joseph show his crisp freedom papers. Then he charged him a special fee because he was Negro and traveling alone. The penalty did not surprise Joseph, for his time with Daniel Payne had prepared him for the many demeaning proscriptions placed upon even *free* persons of color. He stayed content in the knowledge that by sunset he would be in the South no more.

The experience of signing his name on the passengers' roster brought him another new, exquisite moment of pleasure. He emerged from that office as Joseph *Whitsun*, ready to board the steamboat *Olympia*, making a four-day trip to Norfolk and Philadelphia.

In the presence of many onlookers, Brant's and Mr. Wahl's release of him proved to be casual and full of aloofness. Neither man extended a hand, as Gund had done, and Joseph had not dared to expect it from planters to a black man.

When Joseph left the slaveholders for the vessel, he saw them as two odd men standing alone in a society that had no conscience concerning the evil of keeping humans enslaved. At least for a moment these two had been willing to counter everything in their culture and let him walk away. Perhaps their consciences had been pricked. And if they could do it for a day, then—*God help it come!*—maybe someday they would stand against such tyranny for a season, a year, or even a lifetime.

Whatever happened, Joseph could not be responsible for them. He would be responsible for himself, however, and that meant keeping those men in mind. For now *he* was among the free and thus able to instill bondage on others as they had done to him.

With his sack settling into the dip of his shoulder, Joseph crossed the gangplank. The day grew cooler and more cloudy by the moment as he waited among passengers of all shades of color—black, brown, and white—for the lines to be thrown off, releasing them from the southern coast. Before they could move away from the docks, cold raindrops began to fall.

Joseph moved with the crowd toward the ship's enclosed sitting rooms. He was stopped by the boatswain as he neared the foremost cabin door marked *Gentlemen's Hall.* Joseph spoke politely to the sharply dressed seaman. "I hold a first-class ticket, sir."

"Well, then, the ticket man back on shore holds some extra money of yours, boy. Gentlemen don't pay out of their own good earnings to share their cabin with any nigras. Your kind's out there." The boatman pointed to the roofed portion of the deck that was getting slick with blowing rain and seawater.

"But this is a northern-owned vessel, sir, and I am going on to Philadelphia," Joseph said with nervous wonder. "I am a freedman and hope to be a student and resident of that city."

The seaman shook his head intolerantly. "Who made you think that the 'city of brotherly love' is going to welcome you any more than this city did? Now get yourself settled down with the other deck passengers and don't be the cause of any more trouble."

Joseph went out among the huddled masses of brown and black travelers struggling to take cover from the cold, ill-favored weather. An ebony face, as dark and lined as last year's walnut shell, looked up at him. It belonged to a very old man who sat on tarpaulin-covered crates, completely exposed to the rain himself. Alert and curious, the owner of this wizened countenance had swollen, knotty joints that caused him to hold his bare elbows, knees, and fingers in awkward positions.

Without a word Joseph walked past the man to crouch under the overhang from the steamer's second-story deck. There, between two rivulets of water that ran down from the deck drains overhead, he found a narrow dry section of the wall to lean on.

The ancient, ill-clad observer still had his eye upon him. "Sah, ain't nothin' but bondsmen over y'ere," the old man said finally, calling in a croaking voice through the downpour. "All the free gentlemen of color are settled on the other side."

Instantly Joseph felt self-conscious in his travel suit. It pulled at his heart to see a man so frail without even a decent cap or cloak. "Where are you heading, Uncle?" Joseph called back, shivering for the other man's sake.

"Little ways out of Norfolk. Place called Brambleton." The slave leaned forward, stiff elbows coming to his bony thighs. "Last trip out of Charleston for me, sah! Unda'neath y'ere's my Marse Jones' new fightin' cocks to take back to his farm." Tenderly he patted the covered boxes he sat upon. "For the last twenty-some years I done come down here to oversee the care an' purchase of his fowl. But now these old bones is gettin' too tired an' too slow for respectable service. Mighty glad not to be sold here!" He showed a slow, toothless smile. "Mighty glad to be gwine home to breathe my last. I soon hope for paradise! Do you, son?"

"Yes, Uncle, I certainly do."

The bondsman's peaceful reception of all things present and future had a calming effect on Joseph, though sadly he thought again of Rosa, already in the paradise this old man longed for.

The small-boned traveler eyed him sharply. "You done just lost somebody to the other side, for true."

Joseph made his face hard so he would not cry in front of this most astute, unlikely prophet. "Yes, I did. My wife and unborn child." As an excuse to look away, Joseph opened the sack. Beside his papers and wages, he had a blanket, food for four days, and Mr. Abram's Bible, a gift from Mayleda. "Come in under the roof," Joseph counseled. "I have covering to share with you."

"An' leave my Marse Jones' birds?"

He could empathize with the servant's tenacity. "I'll help you move the crates."

The bondsman showed suspicion but at the same time struggled to stand. Joseph soon had the man and his master's fancy chickens out of the weather and covered up again. The bondsman stayed quite wary as he pulled a corner of Joseph's blanket around his dripping shoulders. "What's you' interest in me, sah?"

Joseph smiled slightly. "I suppose I could ask the same of you." In the dampness he felt his chest clogging but managed to stifle his cough. There was no medicine among his travel supplies.

"You all right, young man?" the tender old uncle asked, his senses as sharp as an eagle's.

"Yes," Joseph said, coughing to clear his throat. Inwardly he prayed,

Please, Papa-God, strengthen my lungs.

As evening came on and the rain changed to a cold sea-air mist, both Joseph and the slave sat down on the deck and huddled close. Once the old man was dozing, Joseph reached into his sack and pulled out the envelope from Teacher Payne. He thrilled at the familiar handwriting. Inside he found a letter of recommendation, a sample of his compositions, and Payne's record of his progress in math, language, and science. To his disappointment the teacher had left no clue of his own destination.

The passage of state legislation banning Negro education had closed Payne's school in April. The farewell to Joseph had been penned back in May, before Payne headed north. Like Joseph, the teacher had probably been careful to conceal all clues about where he would be heading. Until it was too dark to read, Joseph went over the conclusion of Payne's letter again and again.

> *My good scholar and friend. Here is sound wisdom I received at my parting, which I now pass on to you. Pursue knowledge wherever it can be found. Perform all your duties faithfully. God is on the side of virtue. Walk humbly. The proud man would conquer others. The Christian's ambition must be to conquer himself. God has given you special armor prepared ahead of time for life's battles. Do not unbuckle it except for death's shroud. . . .*

At the full return of night Joseph folded the correspondence and slipped it back into its place of safety. The bird man continued sleeping, now resting on his shoulder. After a while Joseph felt sure he would share his supper with him. Like a father with a child, he even let the stranger fully have his blanket for a while. Pulling his coat around himself, he leaned back against the wall of the cabin they were not allowed to enter.

It was clear to him already that one of the battles he would face was that of continuing to break the bonds of servitude. But while this battle raged, he saw another going on, and this one seemed every bit as important as the first. This second battle was a struggle within himself to not so quickly put off the disciplines and constrictions he had learned as a slave.

There was much usefulness in a Christian seeing himself as the servant of his God, and he saw that there would always be that need to fully embrace servanthood under the lordship of Christ. He, and every other Christian, no matter of what race or nationality, did have a Master: *Jesus Christ.*

Equality with every other man would mark his victory against outward oppression. But equality with the nature of God could be his only sign of inward triumph.

It was not the form of a cross seared into his flesh that mattered, but the marks of inward obedience to God and God alone that he needed to carry to his grave.

Joseph looked south and west. The world he had known was already beyond the night's horizon, and in the black, uneasy ocean, he had no way of seeing ahead. By faith, he embraced this new experience God had so incredibly opened to him.

Like the old man dozing beside him, he, too, was a servant on a journey toward home.

HISTORICAL NOTES

Though *The Dark Sun Rises* is a work of fiction, some real names, settings, and events have been used to help readers place the story in light of history. The historical novel is an artistic interpretation of what was and of what may have been. For facts on literacy, Christianity, and slavery in America, I recommend the following:

Cornelius, Janet D. *When I Can Read My Title Clear: Literacy, Slavery, and Religion in the Antebellum South*. University of Southern Carolina Press, 1991.

Payne, Daniel Alexander. *Recollections of Seventy Years*. Arno Press, 1968.

Powers Jr., Bernard E. *Black Charlestonians: A Social History, 1822–1885*. Fayetteville: University of Arkansas Press, 1994.

Raboteau, Albert J. *Slave Religion: The "Invisible Institution" in the Antebellum South*. Oxford University Press, 1978.

Thousands of people still speak Gullah along America's southeastern coastline. To make for easier reading, this Creole language used in *The Dark Sun Rises* has been greatly modified. Several organizations exist to preserve and interpret Gullah history, language, and culture. The Penn Center in St. Helena, South Carolina, is one of them. Portions of the Gospel recently have been translated into Gullah by The Sea Island Translation and Literacy Team in cooperation with the Summer Institute of Linguistics and Wycliffe Bible Translators. On my desk I keep the words from Luke 1:75:

> We gwine be God own people,
> an we gwine waak scraight befor um
> all de time we libe.

Currently nineteenth-century slave-trade passages are being traced in reverse as missionaries of African-Caribbean descent take the Good News of Christ to western African nations. A portion of the profits from this novel supports their couragous and self-sacrificing work.